Saving for a Sunny Day

and Other Stories

Ian Watson

One of a Special Edition, Signed by the Author
Limited to just 100 numbered copies
This is number:

55

First edition, published in the UK April 2012
by NewCon Press

NCP 048 (hardback)
NCP 049 (softback)

10 9 8 7 6 5 4 3 2 1

ISBN: 978-1-907069-38-3 (hardback)
978-1-907069-39-0 (softback)

Cover art "Conflagration" by Ben Baldwin
Cover layout by Andy Bigwood

Invaluable editorial assistance from Ian Watson
Text layout by Storm Constantine

Printed in the UK by MPG Biddles of Kings Lynn

Saving for a Sunny Day
and Other Stories

IAN WATSON

Introduction by ADAM ROBERTS

NewCon Press
England

Contents

Introduction

Adam Roberts

1

Ian Watson is our most cosmopolitan SF writer. With a creative imagination at once sophisticated and ingeniously twisted, technically gifted and unconstrained by convention, he is as comfortable writing a high-calibre novel-of-ideas with the mature literary sensibility of *The Embedding* (1973) as he is writing the luridly thrilling intergalactic Grand Guignol of *Warhammer 40,000: Inquisitor* (1990) He writes poetry as well as prose, does not think – though this is lamentably rarer than it should be – that Anglophone writing is the only game in town, and his career has manifested such a dazzling variety of achievement that it leaves that harmless drudge, the short-story-collection-introduction-writer ('prefastoricollectiographer' is the word, according to Johnson's *Dictionary*) with an impossible task. How to sum up what makes Watson so brilliant and distinctive in a few short pages? Can't be done.

What *can* we do? Well, we can do two things – for one, we can drop the royal 'we', since any reaction to Watson is bound to be as personal and individual as the talent that provokes it. And for another we – I – can simply record pleasure at the appearance of another collection of Watson's brilliant tales. *Saving for a Sunny Day* (2011) is Watson's eleventh published short story collection. That's more than 150 short stories over four decades: a remarkable number, even if we don't take into account the thirty varied, extraordinary novels he has also published over the same period. More remarkable is the *freshness* of this volume. Watson does have, I think, recurring fascinations and themes (I'll come back to those), but his stories themselves never feel tired, second-hand or auto-derivative. The collection's freshness, the unflagging quality of both invention and vivacity – the energy would be remarkable in a writer in his twenties; that Watson is approaching his eighth decade make it more remarkable still. In this collection, I think for the first time, we see Watsonian in a writer in his twenties; that Watson is versions of four of the most enduring icons of fantastika: Cthulhu, Zombies, Werewolves, Vampires. There are ghosts and aliens too, and in the title story a sweetly clever take on that old chestnut, reincarnation. But in each case, the version is novel, thought-provoking and *alive*.

'The Walker in the Cemetery' is the Cthulhu story, and as full of shivery horror and ingenious torture as any I have read. But this is a tale that does more than just trail tendrils of dread over the tender membrane of the imagination (although it does do that, and very effectively too). It also makes plain one of Watson's perennial concerns, something that has exercised his imagination since the 1970s. That theme is *passivity*, here as often in Watson a state of being inflected via the horror of powerlessness in the face of predation, cruelty and terror. Statues, dead-but-conscious bodies, flies trapped wrigglingly in the spider's web – helplessness fascinates Watson as a writer. In this tale, as often in his work, the helplessness is sexualised without being fetishised – which is to say, without ever losing sight that repulsion is as genuine a component of our reaction to it as fascination. Positioning one's protagonists, and so one's readers, in a state of helpless passivity with respect to some appalling terror is an effective device for the horror writer, of course; we are all of us open to atavistic fears of being on the wrong end of predation. But there's something more going on here than just the purveying of thrills, I think.

Passivity is linked etymologically to concepts of *passion*. Just as 'action' is the condition of acting, of having agency, so passion is the condition of being passive, of surrendering agency. We don't tend to think of it this way anymore of course: we think of passion as a positive force (a positive good, often). It's a wish fulfilment thing. 'I feel passionately about this...' 'I feel passionately about you...' These expressions actually mean 'I have surrendered the agency and activity of my feelings; I am in a merely reactive and passive state.' Dominos fall with exactly this passion. But we pretend otherwise. We like to think that falling in love, with a person or an idea, empowers us.

The original meaning of the word is now only recalled in archaic linguistic fossils. 'The Passion of the Christ' is not about the *fury* or the *intense desire* of Christ, but the period of agonizingly *passive* suffering of the Christ – the appalling passivity, indeed, of that Being who is considered by Christianity actually to be God, the most active, creative agent in the cosmos. But the two meanings of this word, the with and without agency meanings, tangle creatively together.

The Stoics and their modern-day inheritors, post Enlightenment 'rationalists', tend to preach the overcoming of our passions: passion should be kept in proportion, subordinate to Reason. Watson, though often an unusually civilised writer, more fully conversant than most with this European Enlightenment tradition, is nonetheless a profoundly *passionate* writer – by which I mean a writer more deeply involved in this strange dual-meaning of passion than almost any other I can think of. He is fascinated by the horrors and the dark appeal of passivity; and just as fascinated by the furious energies of human possibility.

And in fact, to attempt to free ourselves of our passions is to be seduced by a dream of perfect independence: power, active control, the ideally circulating Unaccommodated Man. It's a false flicker. Passion is a relational term, and it is only our relations that define us as fully human. The attempt-Stoic or the attempt-Rational to overcome our passions is actually a project to isolate and dehumanise.

The compellingly bizarre world described in 'Cages' dramatises something like this dilemma. The characters endure a kind of poetic literalisation of the entrapment of existence, an eloquent making-real of both the incomprehensibility as well as the passivity of human suffering. The tale's exaggerated piercings, its ingeniously carcereal 'cages', seem nothing more than an affliction, until the fullest extent of the cosmos is revealed and one incomprehensible alien 'purpose' is replaced with another. It is splendidly done: a story that assiduously withholds catharsis, even as it fills out its built-world. That's the right way to write such a piece, I think, because it formally enacts what it conceptually represents, what the philosophers might call 'a dasein of entrapment'.

But I need to stop for a moment. Philosophers? What do *they* know. This may or may not be a useful way of thinking about Watson, but it's hard to shake the sense that it misfits its subject *tonally*. A danger with this sort of analysis is that it makes Watson sound pretentious, or portentous, or pompous. He is none of these things; indeed, his sly wit is absolutely central to his writing voice. He possesses a deep understanding of the pains of enforced passivity, the brute endurance of suffering; but that doesn't mean that he is ever po-faced about it. 'The Globe of the Genius' is also a story about passivity (and passion), a story about entrapment – of the cosmos as a whole as a series of structures locked inside structures, and a protagonist who dies because he has sealed himself away too hermetically. But it is above all a *witty* story, both in the sense of being very funny and in the sense of *having its wits about it*. In 'A Waterfall of Lights' we discover that impossible ancient alien intelligences are being run on computational substrates closer to us (to appropriate a phrase from the Qu'ran) than our jugular veins: the cosmically distant 'out there' is folded into the intimately visionary 'in here'. 'Nadia's Nectar' is also funny, in a icky sort of way, whilst also being a story about one mode of locking human existence into a hermetic circle, a sort of fluid self-consuming cycle. 'Long Stay' takes a Ballardian premise, somewhere between *Concrete Island* and *High Rise*: trapped in a vast long-stay airport car park our hero makes a new life inside the fences, amongst the abandoned cars, a lovely reimagining of the possibilities of pastoral bliss at once satiric and celebratory. It's another fable of imprisonment and disempowerment; but there is a warmth to Watson's treatment of which Ballard was never capable, and disempowerment is inflected via new modes of living. 'Weredog of Bucharest' has the additional frisson of strangeness which distinguishes the exceptional storyteller from the merely competent. The Romanian context of this tale is expertly rendered, but what makes it stand out is the way Watson gets inside the proximity of the human to the bestial ('sometimes,' as his narrator notes, 'the air smells of patchouli; sometimes of sewage.')

'Bohemian Rhapsody' is an original take on the vampire story. We discover not only that Holy Roman Emperor Rudolf II suffered from vampirism, but that sexual congress, properly performed, is actually the cure for this condition. It's a neat twist, and a twitting of the present age's depressingly ubiquitous vogue for 'sexy vampire' tales so beloved of teenagers (and beloved of older readers who ought to know better). Sex is a passion; and the problem with vampirism as an erotic metaphor is its *banality*. All that embracing and teethy oral action, all those exchanged bodily fluids: it's too obviously straightforward. Watson has a less mendacious metaphor. For him vampirism is a trope for imprisonment, his Rudolf trapped in his room, courtiers anxiously hovering about, the monarch reduced to the condition of Tantalus—the subject of a painting in the royal collection noticed several times in the story. Sex, however (properly apprehended) is liberation: the refreshing drink and delicious grapes finally being brought to Tantalus's mouth.

Another word for passion, in its modern meaning, might be 'enthusiasm'; and that's an etymologically interesting piece of terminology too. Originally it meant having a god enter into you (that's the –thu–, the *theos*, at the word's heart). It meant, in other words, being turned into a passive vehicle for divine energy at precisely the moment of becoming most animated and active.

The Athens-set 'A Nose For Such Things' juxtaposes the collective riotous enthusiasm of the Greek protestors with the personal divine-possession of the narrator by none less than the goddess Athena herself. In amongst this is the ghost of Lord Elgin, working at a Sisyphean punishment for stealing the Parthenon marbles, trapped in the passive passion of atonement.

'Saving for a Sunny Day, or The Benefits of Reincarnation' is the story that closes the collection, and after which the volume takes its name – a lovely piece that sits especially well at the end of this volume. The premise of the tale is not only that reincarnation is 'real', but that a planet-wide AI with quasi-godlike powers oversees the process, via barcodes attached to peoples' souls. If you departed your previous financially in credit then you inherit that money on reaching your majority; if your previous incarnation died leaving debts, then it becomes incumbent upon you to pay back the money in your new life. It's witty (again) and mildly satirical; but it's also, in its way, profound. It touches on important questions of life, debt and duty; of entitlement and personal responsibility. If reincarnation were a literal fact of existence, would it in effect *trap* us, stuck like hamsters in the wheel of karma? Well, Watson's cannily insinuates: maybe not. Things may not be the way they appear.

What else? Which is to say: *is* there anything else?

2

There's always *something else* in any Ian Watson text; and the principle of something-elseness, a (dangerous) supplementarity – it manifests as often in puckishness or hilarity as in ingenious originality or profundity – animates his writing beyond the run of the mill. One of his greatest and (perhaps this fact is related) most neglected novels is *Miracle Visitors* (1978). It's a superbly wrongfooting piece of work about UFO abductions, alien visitation and, as its title suggests, *miracles*. It's a novel that boldly flaunts one of the major currents of SF – the move from uncertainty to knowledge, the problem that is solved, the engineer who draws the threads of the unknown and plaits them neatly into the Solved and the Certain. *Miracle Visitors* is a novel that draws its power precisely from the salient of the UFO experience in contemporary culture – its radical *insolubility*, the melty-crumbly nature of all the evidence deployed to back up the various characters' whacky stories.

This is a novel that takes the *uncertainty* of the UFO experience not only as experientially radical (which I think is right) but as *ontologically* radical too. One character, Sheikh Muradi, puts it like this: 'the bridge of science is supported by ninety-nine legs, which is enough for almost perfect stability – for practical purposes. There should still be another leg. Or perhaps there are already nine hundred and ninety-nine legs. There should still be another... the miracle leg, which is outside explanation.' [93] For Muradi, this integral supercession is incarnated as an individual called Khidr – an important individual in Muslim culture as well as a character in the novel. But the book also renders this 'something elseness' in terms of the physics, or metaphysics, of the cosmos. It posits a kind of *material* incompleteness theorem: 'scientists of the very large must leave out the very tiny. Scientists of the very tiny must leave out the force that holds the stars together. This is necessary to reality. It isn't a mere temporary shortcoming. If the whole world was known, it would cease to be' [94]. At the novel's end a key character is granted a vision of the nature of reality, the spatio-temporal cosmos spun out of and disappearing into the timeless non-spatial void. How does this universe sustain itself? By the split of subject from object, or observer from observed – which brought about cause and effect, and natural laws. By the indeterminacy of fundamental events. By the inaccessibility of light-years: whereby light, which allowed observation, at the same time denied it. ... How did it rejoin the Void? *By the very same process.* For all these inaccessibilities caused a fierce suction towards ever higher patterns of organisation.' [200-

01]. Watson imagines the cosmos as 'an immense simulation, of itself by itself'; I've come across this idea in other places, but I don't know how many predate *Miracle Visitors*. On the other hand, the reason why 'miracles' are a needful part of this process made me wonder if the Wachowski brothers knew this novel; for the two *Matrix* sequels play a similar conceptual game, the notion that the matrix simulation only maintains its coherence as a flawed, unbalanced equation, Neo's 'the One' (played by the watercrafty 'Canoe' Reeves) is, we're told, the miraculous, physical sum of the remainder of that flaw. Watson's novel suggests that without radically inexplicable events, his titular 'miracles', the universe would 'simulate itself perfectly' and accordingly would 'cease to be'.

I like this very much; it strikes me as both ingenious and deep. More: where the Wachowskis render their version of this idea in a more-or-less banal way, in terms of kung-fu and superhero logics ('the one's fists of steel and superman-in-flight shenanigans). Watson reaches for a different idiom: Romanticism. This strikes me as both classier, and more effective – connecting the novel to the philosophical debates of the Romantic Sublime both conceptually and formally. Romanticism is important because even when he's not writing poetry (and he writes poetry much of the time) Watson approaches the business of writing with a poet's sensibility. It suits SF particularly well; or at least, I hope it is not merely my idiosyncratic perspective on the genre that makes me think so.

I take *metaphor* as central to SF – often formalised: the spaceship; the robot; the time-machine; but sometimes not. What metaphor does is determine a mode that seeks to represent the world without reproducing it, a literature of 'newness' and conceptual invention. But it also makes SF essentially a poetry, built around the eloquence of the image, often oblique, fascinated with transcendence (the sense of wonder; the motion up from reality into higher reality, as at the conclusion of ; or the apocalyptic sublime, as in the 'Nine Billion Names'), and at its best actively corrosive of reality (Philip K Dick, for instance). It is, to borrow Roman Jakobson's famous terminology, a literature that uses *metonymic* extrapolation from the everyday in order to enable radically disconnected – transcendent – *metaphoric* effects. For me the Platonic Form of SF is the bone thrown in the sky that transforms instantly, amazingly, eloquently into a spaceship. There are various names for the quality, or glory, of SFF I'm talking about here, and which its fans prize so highly: sense of wonder is one; the 'Sublime' another; 'Enchantment' a third; 'Transport' a fourth. From the mind-blowing aspect of some genre visions to the intellectual thrill that sets the little hairs on the neck-nape shivering, it's the awe and shock, the *magic*. This is a transcendental quality. My point (and this is why it's worth bringing in Jakobson, I think) is that we embody this 'vertical' glory in a 'horizontal' mode.

I'll explain what I mean. We tend to read novels and stories, (genre or otherwise) just as we watch films and TV shows (genre and otherwise), as sequential narratives in which one thing happens after another, A to B to C. Characters 'develop' according to a linear progression; writers talk of constructing 'story arcs'. But my point is that precisely this linear progression is inimical to this sort of sense-of-wonder, epiphanic moments we genreheads value so highly. The regular, linear, horizontal structure of conventional narrative is not the genius of SFF. What we're looking for is something that leaps out of that grid altogether.

Another way of talking about this is to think of time in the senses that Frank Kermode embroiders in his monograph *The Sense of an Ending* (1965), a collection of lectures that are as old as I am myself, though considerably wiser. Kermode's emphasis is on religious narratives – the Bible, for instance – but it transfers very nicely to SF & F, modes that share theology's fascination with transcendence. Kermode distinguishes between (which is time in the one-thing-after-another sense) and which is a special time: the time, a holy time, time (for instance) opened to the possibilities of the Sublime. These are useful ways of thinking about the appeal of the fantastic, I think. Indeed, it may be that few SFF fans are alive to the fundamental oddity of trying to generate moments of *kairos* out of narrative, character and (indeed) conceptual structures shaped by *chronos*. Certainly there are fans who get very cross indeed if their chronos-expectations of 'story' or 'character' are violated, as I can personally vouch.

Watson generates kairos out of chromos all the time; it is one of his skills as a writer. Indeed, this is what his first novel *The Embedding* (1973) is *about*: a complex origami exercise in fictioneering in which three stories are deftly folded together, one inside the other, such that we're compelled to hold them—a group of children learning new languages in a psychologically violent experiment; a tribe hitherto-undiscovered Amazonian indigenes strangely untroubled by the news that a huge lake will imminently flood their forest; the arrival of trading aliens interested not in technology but in modes of structuring experience, like language, and seeking to buy actual brains from the alien species they encounter—simultaneously in our minds, or nearly so. By putting the story together this way, Watson creates some brilliant effects; on its publication Martin Amis praised the novel, rightly, as 'giving one the sense of being led very near to the brink of profundity, even revelation.'

These moments, epiphanies and sparks of wonder, find formal externalisations in the various prisons, cells, sealed chambers and places of confinement we find in Watson's writing. Because it brings together precisely the passion and the passivity. John Clute and Peter Nicholls's *Encyclopedia of Science Fiction* (that irreplaceable and standard reference work: 3rd ed. 2011) talk of Watson's 'sometimes difficult fiction', and although they might, perhaps, make it clearer that these are terms of praise rather than dispraise ('difficult fiction' is *good*!) they try to sum up his protean skill:

> As a whole, his work engages vociferously in battles against oppression – cognitive or political – while at the same time presenting a sense that reality, so far as humanity is concerned, is subjective and partial, created too narrowly through our perception of it. The generation of fuller realities – though incessantly adumbrated by methods ranging from drugs through linguistic disciplines, focused meditation, radical changes in education from childhood up, and a kind of enhanced awareness of other perceptual possibilities – is never complete, never fully successful. Humans are too little, and too much, for reality. Watson is perhaps the most impressive synthesizer in modern SF; and (it may be) the least deluded.

That's right, I think; although I'm not sure it quite captures what is distinctive about Watson's writing; the likeable perversity, an imaginative oddness and metaphorical perceptiveness. The *smarts*. Deceptive, clever, thought-provoking and witty; fiendishly ingenious and restlessly creative. He's very far from elementary, this Watson.

Adam Roberts
October 2011

The Walker in the Cemetery

When our tourist bus arrived at the side gateway to the necropolis of Staglieno on our tour around Genoa, a couple of cheery garbage men were loading floral tributes into a crusher truck. The afternoon was bright and breezy. Twenty metres' length of the high perimeter wall and the pavement were stacked with huge arrangements of roses, irises, lilies, and also tropical blooms interspersed with palm fronds and other foliage, undoubtedly several thousand Euros' worth of beauty. Into the crusher those were all going, either crammed into a big wheeled green bin first, or, if too large, borne on their wooden frames in the arms of the garbage collectors. Bird of Paradise flowers passed by me, and giant blooms in the shape of large lacquered red hearts from which protruded what looked like long thin white penises with green foreskins.

And all of the flowers and foliage were fresh and perfect, at least until the crusher compacted them.

Questions flew. Our guide, Gabriella, said that the tributes were from just this one day. Due to cremations, there was no space to let that glory of blooms remain on display.

"But cannot they go to brighten a hospital or an old people's home?" asked a German woman indignantly. English was the language of this tour.

Her husband said, "Suppose you're in hospital, or very old, do you wish to see flowers of the dead?" His grey hair cropped very short, he had a noble bearing; I thought of a Prussian general of olden days. He turned toward me sharply, as if to say, 'Am I not correct, Madame?' Startled, I said nothing.

And so we entered a gallery of that amazing cemetery which was to become for us a huge prison and abattoir of mystifying horrors.

Like a good guide, Gabriella began discoursing as we gazed along the first of the lengthy gloomy arched galleries, statues on plinths inside niches, ornate plaques crowded between the niches, the regular slabs underfoot covering the dead sealed away beneath.

"...perhaps our cemetery here in Genoa is the most astonishing in Europe... The Revolutionary Enlightenment no longer wished to use churches and churchyards to bury the dead... The posh old families, some rich ever since Genoa contended with Venice for mastery of the Mediterranean... New Nineteenth century bourgeois wealth demanded sculptural realism like three-dimensional photographs in stone... At first a classical romanticism, then symbolism, and ultimately Art Deco... Angels of consolation becoming disturbingly erotic and sensual... Death becoming an uneasy ambiguous mystery –"

"Excuse me," said a tall skinny Dutchman, "why the different colours of the candles?"

We were beside a memorial to a nun, whose photograph taken long ago was surrounded by dozens of little imitation candles jostling on ledges, with lavish fresh bouquets to either side; she was still adored. The pseudo-candles, squat tubes with a protected bulb shining dimly atop each in the shaded daylight, were like feeding bottles with plastic teats for babies, or maybe squeezy bottles of skin cream. Some were blue, others red, though all bore an oval image of the Pope gesturing a blessing.

"Some," said Gabriella, "shine for a week, others for a month."

Ah, different sorts of battery.

We would need those pathetic little lights later...

A profusion of galleries was here, and a huge population of marble statues seeming particularly lifelike because of darker dust upon them. As Gabriella escorted us, talking now and then, I came upon a bald-headed long-bearded monk, his hood resting on the back of his neck, who had turned away – permanently – to consult a little book. He was yet another statue, as if petrified whilst alive. Trickles of white stains seemed caused by windblown rain that had reached him; but what took my attention most regarding the masses of other, more sheltered statues was how the dark grey dust of a century and a half had added a velvety shading to all the pleats and folds of drapery, intensifying the naturalism. Too vast a task, presumably, to keep so many hundreds, or thousands, of statues clean. I licked my finger and rubbed a sculpted leg. The moisture made a little dark mark, yet my fingertip came away clean, not coated in grime.

"The dust becomes united with the stone," said Gabriella, noticing. "That adds chiaroscuro."

Indeed. Some of the realism was astonishing. The sheer details of stockings or of a baby's bonnet, for instance! Families or lone individuals in perfectly rendered clothing of the Nineteenth century middle class stood or knelt by memorials, grieving or consoling or gazing. Stone doors stood ajar, as though the soul of the departed had only just disappeared through those.

And then the sensuality of female curves, and drapery, and petrified flesh! A beautiful young woman nude to the waist swooned in the arms of a robed Death, his veiled skull apparent; yet at the same time this couple might well have been dancing a Tango.

Emerging into sunlight, we took in a fieldful of more orthodox modern gravestones and flowers, lined with many tall slim cypresses and junipers, beyond which a great stairway ascended to a domed pantheon flanked by monumental colonnades. Behind and to the sides, a wooded hill arose, from which hundreds of white mausoleums reached up like temples or the spires and towers of cathedrals.

Yet by now we'd used up the time alloted for our glimpse of the necropolis of Staglieno. Shepherded by Gabriella, the twenty-odd of us trooped back along a gallery towards the gateway.

Just then the tombstone-slabs, which composed the floor of the gallery, trembled. The gallery itself shuddered, and daylight dimmed. Dust didn't exactly stir into the air, yet visibility lessened considerably as though the air itself had become grey.

Gabriella called out, "I think that's an earthquake tremor, but don't worry." She was a busy, practical woman, mid-forties. "Genoa is actually on a fault line. However, a big quake offshore in 1887 didn't do much harm to this cemetery even though many buildings in the city were badly damaged." Was our guide being totally honest? "So you're in a safe place. Probably there'll be no more tremors. I've lived here all my life."

So we proceeded onward.

Could clouds have suddenly darkened the sun at the very same moment as the tremor? No doubt that was by coincidence, yet I almost felt as if – so to speak – reality had shaken somewhat. Strangely, we seemed to walk for ages, as though we were retreading the same slabs over and over again, although we weren't, for I looked down in puzzlement at the progress of my feet.

From the office inside the gateway, a couple of middle-aged men in shirt sleeves emerged. The cemetery's superintendent, and a subordinate, a caretaker maybe? Jabbering at one another, they stared up at what we could see, now we were in the open, was a dull pearly sheen masking the sky, as if a peculiar bank of mist had descended over the cemetery – and I was surprised to see the very same just outside the gateway, as if that was an exit to nowhere and nothing rather than to parked cars and a tour bus.

"Signora Vigo!" Of course the superintendent would know all the tour guides by name. How urgently he gestured Gabriella to come – along with the rest of us, who crowded as best we could, in the wake of the two men and Gabriella, into an office where a largish TV set was showing silently in flickery black and white what I took to be an old Japanese monster movie.

An enormous tentacle-headed thing with a scaly body and what looked like stumpy spiky wings was standing up in sea near an ocean liner. The creature was a grotesque blend of octopus, humanoid, and dragon. Like a gigantic Gulliver to the boat, which seemed the size of a toy. Waves from the monster's motion through the water caused the vessel to tilt alarmingly, though it righted itself. What giant bathtub had this epic been filmed in?

I couldn't even guess at any of the rapid-fire Italian, perhaps Genovese dialect, being exchanged between the two men and Gabriella, who looked ashen. Abruptly the movie changed its scene to a view of New York, where another of those monsters stomped in the Hudson River as if that was merely a shallow gutter. The malign creature *towered* above the skyscrapers of Manhattan, which it began to wreck, stooping and flailing elephant-trunks of arms before turning and heading seawards, as if towards its proper home, capsizing merchant ships and ferries like scraps of flotsam.

To my astonishment the channel was CNN, an English language banner running along the bottom of the screen. *An old monster movie showing on CNN?* And in flickery black and white? With no sound? I realized that the TV hadn't been showing CNN when we crowded into the office; spontaneously the TV had jumped channels. And now I caught up with the words as they scrolled sideways.

...GIANT SEA MONSTERS ATTACK SHIPS WORLDWIDE...

The channel hopped again. Paris, obviously; Arc de Triomphe in the distance. Creatures exactly the same in appearance as the enormous 'sea monsters' – yet now more like two storeys high rather than two thousand – were proceeding with a rolling gait along the Champs Élysées destroying cars either by collision or by treading upon them. All silently. I glimpsed two of the tentacled dripping behemoths themselves colliding and *fusing of a sudden into one* – while further along the avenue I could swear that a single creature became two identical creatures. Of a sudden the TV went blank.

The people in our group were babbling, and the three Italians were voicing off wildly, until the German man drew himself up and bellowed, *"Silence!"* Our uproar diminished to a few whispers. The German glanced at me and nodded approvingly since I hadn't been contributing to the noise. Then he tapped his watch significantly.

"Here in Genova it is 2.30 in the afternoon. In New York it should be 7.30 in the morning, maybe 8.30, I am not sure exactly. But I am *sure* I saw an oval shape of light *to the west*, way beyond the New Jersey Heights. Presumably that was the sun, although looking distorted. Unless it was the fireball from a nuclear weapon… But assume it was the sun. Right now should not be evening in New York. Did any of you feel something strange about time after the shock while we walked here?"

I raised my hand, and he beckoned me to him, while Gabriella was apparently translating for the benefit of her two fellow citizens.

I said, "I felt as if I was walking over the same space many times. I even watched my feet to make sure they were moving forward."

"And you are?" he asked.

"My name's Sally Hughes. I work at CERN in Geneva. The big particle accelerator."

"So you are a physicist!"

"No, I'm an administrative assistant in the Director-General Unit, Relations with the Host States Service. That means I deal with the various French and Swiss authorities, update regulations about the site we're on, that sort of thing."

Less than three per cent of the people at CERN were actual physicists. The site employed masses of engineers, electricians, low temperature specialists, just for instance. How else could CERN have functioned?

"But you are English?"

"My mother is Belgian. I went to school in Liège for a few years."

"So you're a bureaucrat, not a physicist."

"I'm fairly familiar with what we're doing scientifically at CERN. As are most of the staff."

"Is anyone here a scientist?" demanded the German, but

everyone shook their heads.

"Miss Hughes, was any important experiment at CERN scheduled for today?"

"All the experiments are important, and they happen constantly. But it can take a bit of time to interpret results."

"Your physicists are trying to recreate the earliest primitive state of the universe, is that not so?"

"That's an important part of it."

The superintendent pulled out his mobile and jabbed, but then he frowned at its screen; whereupon he resorted to a fixed line phone on the desk, before gesturing helplessly, non-plussed. Quickly I discovered that my own mobile had no signal. Nor did those of others in our party. We were cut off.

"Did you observe," our German asked me, "that the enormous *krakens* in the sea and the smaller but still sizable creatures in Paris had *exactly* the same appearance? As if the latter were identical to the former, merely on a smaller scale?"

I nodded. "I think I saw two of them join into one, and another suddenly divide into two."

Ruefully: "I missed that. This suggests to me that both sizes are iterations of the same thing. Assuming that we were indeed watching reality, not a hoax."

"Iterations?"

"The repetitions of a process, for instance in a computer program, or in fractal geometry such as the Mandelbrot set where the same figure is generated at ever diminishing scales. Or the pattern of a *Blumenkohl*, a cauliflower. Chaos theory gave rise to this."

"You ain't kidding about chaos!" cried a buxom American woman. "That was chaos from hell itself we saw in New York. Hell has broken through into the world! This is the end time *right now*. That's the very Antichrist, as prophesied."

"Verily it *is*," called out her presumed husband.

"Be calm, Madam, Sir," said our German. "We must analyse. That is why we have brains."

"*You* seem to be a scientist," I said to him quickly, in case the Americans might take offense.

"I am Thomas Henkel, a historical novelist of some reputation, but I have wide-ranging interests, particularly in the history of science present and past, including Chinese, which I taught myself. This is my spouse Angela." *Ann-gay-la.*

"I'll see if our bus is waiting for us," announced Gabriella, perhaps clinging to a lifeline of routine.

"Excellent idea," said Henkel, and we all filed out quickly in her wake.

The gateway, and that shimmery mist pressing upon the entrance... Gabriella strode towards and into the mist, promptly disappearing; just a moment later she was returning, and gaping at us all.

"I did not turn round!" she cried out. "Mother of God, *I did not turn round.* I walked straight. I swear that."

"Come back here," Henkel said in a consoling, though authoritative tone. "We must all stay together now." He alone was standing still, tall on a step, while the rest of us milled about. "Listen to me, while you, Gabriella, translate for your countrymen. If this is no hoax, such as we saw on the television before it failed, and if we are not somehow miraculously protected by nothing external being able to enter here, analogous to Signora Vigo being unable to leave – an assumption that we dare not make! – and if those *krakens* multiply and iterate themselves at progressively smaller scales, being all essentially reflections of the same entity, then we might encounter one or more within these very walls, of a scale more in accordance with our own size. For which reason, we must all arm ourselves with whatever suitable maintenance tools the Superintendent can make available *immediately.*"

This certainly made sense, as did the wisdom of acting in an organised manner as regards morale, which might have been Henkel's major motive. Major, or General, I thought. Well, someone needed to take charge.

"Miss Hughes," he called out to me, "I need an aide, or rather an adjutant." So Henkel was indeed thinking of himself as a sort of high-ranking officer. "I believe your job qualifies you. We shall see to introductions and assess our skills just as soon as we are all armed."

From a storeroom near the entrance we were soon equipped, like some band of medieval peasants cajoled to war, with spades, various forks, a scythe, a couple of sickles, shears which could stab, hammers. I myself took a fork, and Henkel a spade which could deliver a flat blow as well as jabbing or slicing; and now our impromptu general could get on with formal introductions, to the extent that we hadn't already spent a whole morning together informally. Dutifully I listed the names and occupations in a notebook taken from the office.

Thomas Henkel, historical novelist, German
Angela Henkel, ex-archivist, researcher, German
Hans-Ulrich Kempen, literary translator, German
Sally Hughes, CERN administrator, British
Gabriella Vigo, guide, Italian
Rudolfo Grasso, cemetery superintendent, Italian
Gianni Celle, cemetery assistant, Italian
Jimmy Garrett, evangelic protestant pastor, American
Mary-Sue Garrett, his wife and business secretary, 1970s Kansas beauty queen, American
Paul Goldman, Harvard University Press, American
Betsy Goldman, romantic novelist, American
Alice Goldman, their teenage daughter, American
Wim Ruyslinck, architect, Dutch
Anne Gijsen, art student, his girlfriend, Dutch
Dionijs Ruyslinck, Wim's elder brother, computer assisted designer, Dutch
Nellie van Oven, art historian, Dutch
Anders Strandberg, bank manager, Swedish

Selma Strandberg, financial consultant, his wife, Swedish
Bruce Ballantyne, wine merchant, Australian
Jack Ballantyne, teenage son, Australian
Iain Mackinnon, gap year student of geography, Scottish
Katie Drummond, ditto, his girlfriend, archeology, Scottish
Laszlo Michaleczky, computer programmer, on honeymoon, Hungarian
Zsuzsa Michaleczky, his new wife, lawyer, on honeymoon, Hungarian

Our ages ranged from a guesstimated 65 for our general down to 15 or 16 for the American girl Alice who kept chewing at her lip, looking scared, scythe in hand. Fortunately there were no small children amongst us.

"Here is our defensible base," announced Thomas Henkel, gesturing at the office and other structures beside the gate. "Next we must consider water and food and toilet facilities."

An enquiry by Gabriella quickly elicited from Rudolfo that only some bread and sausage and cheese was in the office, although of course the building contained a toilet. Gianni went back inside, and emerged to declare that a tap was producing water at about half the usual pressure.

"At least there's water," said Gabriella.

"Not to be wasted in a toilet," said Henkel. "We shall resort to latrines in the grounds, behind trees or bushes. We have ample digging tools."

The two Scottish students had wandered, whispering, to the near end of the innermost gallery of slabs and statues.

"*Something's coming!*" the Scots lad called out. "*Jesus Christ!*"

Most of us rushed to witness. What had come into sight at the far end of the sepulchral gallery had nothing to do with anything divine according to human understanding, and everything to do with what we'd glimpsed on TV! Two and a half metres high, tentacle-faced, it was a human-scale iteration of one of those monstrous creatures from out of a nightmare, or from the warped mind of some special effects genius on drugs, or from somewhere utterly *other*.

As the thing proceeded towards us, while we gripped our various gardening implements, in my case with trembling hands, a hissing invaded my awareness, similar to static on a radio or a breeze through holes in ancient stones on some windswept mountain: *thoooo-loooo, thoooo-loooo*, a mesmeric sound that seemed to be rustling within my mind rather than coming from outside to my ears.

The creature's great warty body was gherkin-green. Under the swollen, thick-veined dome of that pulpy head brooded baleful red eyes. Suckery tentacles or feelers dangled, writhing, from those inhuman, *inhumane*-seeming features. Webbed frills jutted where ears might be – or was I seeing some sort of fin, or even a vestigial *wing*? The body seemed covered with rubbery warty scales. Two principal muscular tentacles appeared to serve as arms, branching at their tips, and branching again into clusters of anemone-like fingers. Huge triangular feet, that left a glistening snaily trail behind them, bore savagely hooked claws…

thoooo-loooo, thoooo-loooo

Intimations of a vile odour assaulted us, like the glutinous stench of some coral newly torn out of the sea, although more intense, a penetrating smell of primitive biological slime that oughtn't to be released into the air but should stay masked underwater, a concentration of the reek of seaweed-coated rocks at low tide.

thoooo-loooo, thoooo-loooo

Abruptly the romantic novelist screamed, setting off likewise the Dutch art student. This broke a kind of paralysing horrid enchantment such as in dreams where you can't flee, even feebly and very slowly, from what menaces you. We retreated, so as not to see what was coming – except for the Australian wine merchant, Bruce, and the burly Hungarian who must have felt that he was defending his bride. Those two stood their ground, armed with a fork and a spade.

What happened next was abominable.

As if the creature had speeded up, or even shifted instantaneously, of a sudden it was upon the two jabbing men, its arm-tentacles wrenching their weapons from their grip with evidently great strength, to be hurled aside. A clawed foot casually tore open the Australian's clothing and abdomen. A tentacle snaked into the bloody wound to jerk free the tubing of his intestines, hauling his bowels out and out, two metres, three. Bruce Ballantyne may have died of shock before his body hit the flooring, since it didn't flop about like a beached fish. At the same time the other tentacle gripped the Hungarian's neck – and impossibly hoisted his head aloft atop his spinal column coming right up from out of his shoulders. No natural force could have done that to a man! Could the creature manipulate matter by thought, by malign imagination, as well as physically? Head and spine were discarded even as Jack the son howled, "Dad!" and the newly-wed Zsuzsa shrieked.

My list, drawn up only a few minutes earlier, began to seem futile except as a probable In Memoriam. Yet the creature didn't proceed to hurl itself upon the rest of us as we variously cowered back or made a show of defending ourselves. It regarded us, almost as though the two hideous deaths constituted a demonstration of power.

thoooo-loooo, thoooo-loooo

The American evangelist and his wife sank to their knees, praying loudly, "*Oh merciful God...*" And the creature's feelers began to move as though conducting an orchestra, almost as if it understood and was sardonically accepting obeisance and encouraging more.

"Kneel and pray for salvation!" Pastor Jimmy Garrett urged us before resuming his chant. Although Rudolpho and Gianni probably didn't understand what the American said, the two Italians collapsed to their knees, crossing themselves repeatedly.

"Pray to *that*?" bellowed our general. "For that's what it looks as though you are doing, sir! Come, we must retreat in an orderly manner! You," pointing at the Swedish bank manager who had an avuncular look, "see to the Australian boy. And you," indicating his wife, "guide the shocked widow. Signora Vigo, you take us all to some safer and higher place. From the look of it, the *kraken* may have difficulty climbing. Quickly now, but do not run in case instinct impels it to give chase."

Instinct? Or was that creature intelligent, maybe far more intelligent than ourselves, and cruelly so, so that we were to it as a rabbit or a rat is to a human being...?

Presently we'd cut across the huge open area of more modern and simpler graves, most with fresh flowers in vases, hoping that the closely-set white marble gravestones might obstruct the bulky *thoooo-loooo* creature (I still heard its whisper) – and we were ascending that broad flight of steps we'd seen earlier – Selma Strandberg hugging and pulling bereaved Zsuzsa – towards that scallop-tiled pantheon from which colonnades stretched away, behind which, and beyond, groves of cypress and juniper and other trees rose steeply and extended afar, innumerable tall mausoleums poking up amidst the foliage like miniature churches topped with small domes, stone lanterns, finials, crosses, so many ornate habitations of the dead. Could we take refuge in one of those; achieve sanctuary?

Shady pathways wound upward through the groves. As a child, how enchanted I would have been to explore this place, thinking of it as a secret garden. But now...!

At the top of the flight we paused to regain our breath.

Thomas Henkel, unwinded by our journey, surveyed where we had come from. He was a Field Marshall, if the grave-crowded expanse beneath us were a field. He should have worn a monocle and pointed with a swagger-cane.

"Straight over there!"

Where a broad, tree-lined pathway led from the triple rank of galleries abutting the threefold principal arched gateway, stood the thing that Henkel chose to call a *kraken*, gazing at us from

33

afar and directly opposite. A shiver ran down my spine, for in that moment despite the distance the creature seemed to fix on me, like the pin that fastens a butterfly in a display case.

Just then – could it possibly be by the agency of that beast? – a giant oval lens opened in the pearly mist that cloaked the cemetery. From this elevation we could see right over the high perimeter wall. Far beyond the roofed gateway where the creature lingered, beyond where I knew the city's wide shallow river curved, part stony, part vegetated, I saw a section of the raised riverside roadway and many of the apartment blocks, their concrete faded yellow or faded rose.

"Traffic!" Yes, others saw the same. Shimmering, cars and trucks and buses were driving along the highway, undisturbed by any trampling behemoth. No police vehicles nor ambulances were racing, emergency lights flashing. Nor trucks of armed soldiers. Normality, so it seemed. A vision of this part of the city as we'd seen it just an hour or two before.

Or as it was *right now*, yet in some other reality…? The lens closed up, having taunted us.

"We're no longer part of that reality!" I said to Henkel.

"We shall talk of this later," he told me.

Zsuzsa was still sobbing inconsolably. The Australian adolescent was trying to behave like a man, although I saw him quiver. We needed protection.

I pointed at what appeared to be the topmost ten metres or so of a Gothic cathedral amidst trees, the railed area around it choked with bushes.

"Could we take shelter in that spire, for instance?"

"Most of the mausoleums are locked," observed Gabriella.

"A spade can break a lock."

"Forget all those pseudo-buildings," said Henkel. "Anywhere with only one entrance is a trap. We'd be fish in a barrel."

Of course he was right. The yearning to be inside protective walls had made me stupid. My orderly world, my past, was melting away like wax. What twisted shape would result?

Henkel conferred with Gabriella, *sotto voce*, and we set off, presently to arrive at a tall gap where a wall several metres high, inset with caskets, confronted an equally high blank wall, coarsely plastered with concrete except where the covering had cracked off, exposing bare mortared stones. This narrowest of alleys extended for maybe forty metres, and only one body's width, terribly claustrophobic – what if something appeared at the far end when you were half way along? To relieve slightly the intense gloom, quite a few lanterns each containing a battery-powered Pope candle, hung from caskets at various heights. Our Field Marshall ordained that we should each take one of the feeble lanterns with us, along with our gardening weapons – maybe, if lucky, we might later take the monster by surprise.

And so we came, passing by grieving statues, to a most unusual part of this singular cemetery. Although we were still quite high above ground level, we entered a labyrinth of several balustraded levels linked by stairways, walled with more caskets. On a dismal midway level Henkel decided that we should settle ourselves upon the paving stones.

"We shall take turns to be lookouts at the up-stairway and at the down-stairway. I think the *kraken* may find those stairways a hindrance. If it does come from one direction, we shall escape the other way."

To sleep eventually on the hard stone floor in our fairly lightweight clothing? After no food or drink? Meanwhile, doing nothing but wait?

"Signora Vigo," asked Henkel, "are there water taps nearby in the area outside, to fill flower vases?"

Seeming uncertain – does a tour guide pay much attention to taps? – Gabriella asked Rudolfo, whose response was obviously positive.

"Ask him to go, Signora Vigo, to show where... Jack Ballantine, would you go with two or three others to bring water back?" Yes, give the shocked lad something to do; already he was nodding yes.

"But what do we carry the water in…?"

"Why, in vases which you empty and rinse out. Mijnheer Ruyslinck, will you go too? And Mr Goldman, to keep watch?"

"No," said his wife Betsy.

"I'll be all right, honey."

"But the other Italian guy *knows* the cemetery."

"Precisely for that reason," said our Field Marshall, "he must remain with us as a source of information in the temporary absence of his superior."

Just in case Rudolfo met his death vilely outside…

As soon as this little expedition departed, to loud prayers from Jimmy Garrett, Henkel came and sat by me.

"So," he asked softly, "you think there may now be two separate realities? In one reality our world has been invaded by these multiple iterations of *krakens*, on various scales? And in the other reality, another world carries on as normal?"

"It was you who mentioned recreating the primitive earliest state of the universe… before physical laws became fixed. A sort of no-time when a different sort of universe could have burst forth and inflated instead."

"And maybe that universe *did* come into a parallel existence, remaining faintly linked to our own universe by early… I think the correct word is entanglement."

"By and large I know what that means, but I'm only a bureaucrat, as you pointed out."

"Never mind, at least you know something! Maybe as much as I know. If our physicists have recreated that earliest stage of the cosmos in miniature, does this permit a kind of *bridge* between two possible cosmoses? Or rather a *hole*, which can be forced open by a powerful and evil intelligence?"

"How do I know?"

"Miss Hughes, surely it's better to think rationally along such lines than to imagine that *Hell* has invaded us, especially as that creature corresponds to no religion that I know of."

"At least we won't die deluded?"

"We mightn't die. If those *krakens* are all linked, and are aspects, *avatars*, of the same entity, we might come across a tinier iteration of the beast *and stamp on it*."

Was our field marshall himself deluded, or was this for the sake of morale?

"If they're all aspects of the same, what did you say, evil intelligence, that must be one very highly developed intelligence."

"Compared with which we are stupid? Maybe so, maybe not. But maybe we are very stupid to bombard the constituents of matter into a state which hasn't existed since the dawn of creation, alien to the universe we know today. Stupid to meddle with the fundamental basis of reality. Maybe that's how the rift happened, when something broke through – something which may even have been able to touch our world in the past by entanglement, though not as sustainedly as now. Supposing that at the beginning the cosmos divided, one of the twins pursing our own everyday course, the other cursed twin torn away from its mirror image into a ghastly dimension or between-dimension where vile intelligences arose hungry for the substance of our world. How the invaders are revelling now."

I thought that Henkel too was revelling somewhat in rhetoric, but I had to ask, "What about the normality we saw through that lens? Which cosmos is that in?"

"I think that was an illusion, a lure to attract us back to the gate, as if we are sheep. The *kraken* is experimenting with us."

"If the creature can create illusions… and you saw how *impossibly* it pulled the spine out of…" I couldn't continue.

Thomas Henkel patted me on the shoulder. "There now, be brave. As you have been until now. If the *kraken* possesses such powers, which seem to us paranormal, well, it isn't exerting them all the time."

He stood up, and addressed our huddled company, declaring his theory that we might come across a much smaller 'kraken' and be able to destroy it, thus striking a maybe mortal blow at the larger one which menaced us in the cemetery.

Personally I thought that, if what we'd witnessed on TV was authentic, then nuclear weapons would already have destroyed at least several of the greater monsters. Unless of course the monsters could neutralise missiles.

At least our group seemed somewhat comforted by Henkel's idea.

I'd often wondered in what way I would die one day. That's the big question which most people avoid asking themselves, not least because there's no answer until it happens, and even then you mightn't know the answer, supposing your mind has degenerated prior to death, as my mother's did. Whereas the truck that skidded and mowed down my dad from behind might have obliterated him before he could even realize. So somehow – due to family history – I thought that I wouldn't know about death when I died. I would simply cease, the way I once ceased due to anaesthetic when I needed a kidney stone broken up by laser. Did I hope simply to cease, or alternatively to know the very threshold of death? Had the creature come to teach me?

"There's still no mobile phone signal," said Wim Ruyslinck's girlfriend.

"Did you just try to call Mijnheer Ruyslinck?" demanded Henkel.

"Yes, but his phone's set to vibrate, not ring. I wouldn't draw attention to him like that."

"Wise. However, we should conserve batteries, in case there's any future use for them. Everyone should switch off their phones. I'll keep mine switched on in case there is any change. When my charge runs out, I'll appoint someone else."

"Runs out?" queried Betsy Goldman, who was plump. "When's that? In a week or a fortnight? What do we *eat* till then?"

"The human body doesn't normally die of hunger for forty or fifty days provided it can drink. Fasting is normal for many people in the world, often involuntarily."

"You mean I'm starting from a good base line?" Betsy

laughed, perhaps a shade hysterically, but others chuckled or grinned, the first hint of good spirits.

"Very good!" Henkel said approvingly.

Fortunately, her husband and Rudolfo, Jack Ballantyne and the Dutchman all returned safely soon enough, bearing vases brimming with water.

That, comparatively, was the good time, the time when there was still some hope, even if meagre…

We're allowed our sanctuary, here in this dusty shadowy minor labyrinth of stairways and galleries where the warped oval sun only reaches through a grimy round skylight or so at the top. A place resembling a library, except that instead of books on shelves there are almost identical caskets containing the dead, blessed to have died when they did.

Maybe the creature cannot easily mount or descend the stairs, though I doubt it. So far at least, Cthulhu hasn't done so. There comes a click in our minds, and the drawn-out whisper inside us, of *thoooo-loooo, thoooo-loooo*: that might be its name, or maybe a call of power akin to an abracadabra.

Yet the stairs don't stop Cthulhu from taking us one by one, to play with. And then to discard, vilely and agonisingly used. Maybe beyond any agonies caused by human torturers, since I believe its tendrils can reach into our brains to push the buttons of pain. For we must eat. And Cthulhu feeds its pets.

After half a week of hunger for us, our water-bearers of the day sighted a small heap of dead fish and fruits on a path they used. *Was that bait?* Iain McKinnon darted ahead bravely to scoop the food into his empty vase, and survived. He returned for the rest of the rations, and survived.

On the following day, a pile of raw meat and vegetables was further away. Subsequently, some cheeses and salamis were outside the house-size version of the Pantheon of Rome. Presently we needed to hunt through statued galleries of the cemetery to find wherever our food might be. On all expeditions, near or far, we carried forks – the gardening, not the dining, kind – to defend ourselves and each other, however feebly.

A week passed before, halfway along a gallery, Iain Mackinnon trod on a patch of the strongest of glues of the same colour as the flagstones. He couldn't wrench his trainers free. As he stopped to untie the trainers, so that Katie Drummond and Paul Goldman and Jack Ballantyne could then try to jump him out of that stickiness, *k-thoooo-loooo, thoooo-loooo*, towering Cthulhu came. The tines and blades of the gardening tools jerked down to clang against the flagstones as if a powerful magnetic field dragged them. It was, said Paul afterwards, like some bizarre salute to a potentate, the lowering – then the necessary letting go – of swords. Katie could only scream and wave her arms at the advancing entity. Neither she nor Paul nor Jack were going to throw themselves bodily at that monster. One of its feet seemed to suck the glue back into itself as its arm-tentacles immobilised and lifted the Scots student who bellowed then tried vainly to bite at face-tentacles... as he was rushed away. The forks and spade were no longer fastened to the flagstones. Snatching them up, for what use those might be, the trio did give chase led by Katie, but when they rounded a corner the next gallery was empty except for mournful statues. Thus they related when they returned to our labyrinth – carrying the day's food, yes; Katie having to be commanded and cajoled by Paul Goldman, for *what else could they do, what else?*

That night we all heard the thin, piercing screams, for what seemed hours, dying away, starting again. Henkel had to restrain Katie. Of course no one slept. The next day the hideous mess that had been Iain Mackinnon lay on the space outside the pantheon. He almost seemed to have been turned inside-out by an insane vivsection.

It was... slippery, to bury him in a copse as close nearby as we could. Pastor Jimmy Garrett managed to say words and quote parts of the Bible that weren't excessively evangelistic; and I noticed that his hair, now lank and stringy where it had been lovingly tended and conditioned before, was falling out after these weeks. So hair doesn't always just go dramatically white overnight with shock.

Katie begged our Field Marshall to strangle her; she promised not to struggle. Then she begged the taciturn German translator, Hans-Ulrich. Of course nobody would strangle her. In due course might suicide by assistance become easier to contemplate?

No one went to fetch food for four days. Eventually hunger pangs prevailed. The instinct for survival is so strong. Katie didn't try to smash her head against the hard stone that was all around us, even though we had no sedatives, only some pain-killers and stomach settlers in a couple of the women's shoulder bags, and a few tampons, soon used. Most bags including mine had been left aboard the bus, for our brief stroll into Staglieno.

As time wore on, Zsuzsa was taken similarly, and Selma Strandberg and Nellie van Oven and Wim Ruyslinck and Hans-Ulrich. The monster only rarely resorted to glue, preferring the direct approach. Nevertheless, not each far sortie resulted in a victim. Cthulhu preferred to fool us that by luck or at random we might return safely. Hence the rabbits would scurry to snatch their suppers.

No one spotted another lens in the prevailing mist, supposing that the original lens was designed for us to see. Of course we didn't venture outdoors more than was essential – oh the crushing endless fearful misery even though for distraction we took turns telling our life stories. I think there was only one lens, and that it showed a memory of our world just before the Cthulhu creatures arrived, not an image of normality continuing in some parallel reality which might even be reachable. Nor did anyone stumble upon a mini-monster to stab and slash and crush.

Monster? More like a baneful sadistic *God*, if it could multiply itself on different scales all across the world! If it weren't simply this cemetery of Staglieno that had been abstracted from ordinary reality by a potent entity from another universe that could conjure up illusions...

Nor did every abducted victim scream through the night. Maybe a tongue was removed first of all.

"Each person lost," said Garrett one day, "is a sacrifice to *it*. A human sacrifice. As in pagan antiquity. But worse. I think it's... rationing out its sacrifices. Or maybe this is like a serial killer who gets satisfied for a while until the head of steam builds up again."

Garrett frequently goes outside to keep watch, from the top of the steps to the pantheon. Thomas Henkel doesn't object to what might seem to be a desire for martyrdom on the evangelist's part – at least, until martyrdom actually commences. Any additional information is valuable, in our Field Marshall's blue eyes, sometimes cool, sometimes almost twinkly. I think we're all losing our sanity somewhat, or else we no longer remember what sanity is, or was.

And I accompany Garrett, despite a dark look of mistrust from ex-beauty queen Mary-Sue.

"I quite often see him walking in the garden," Garrett tells me. "That's to say, *it* walking in this cemetery. I'm still a witness of the Lord's, whatever has happened."

I feel more sympathetic to the evangelist now than at any previous time. He's trying to cope without ranting nonsense.

"Look, Sally."

And there is the Cthulhu thing in the distance, pacing slowly, rollingly, as I imagine a sailor newly on land after a very long voyage. On *our* land, of which Cthulhu has taken possession. The Cthulhu thing turns, aware of our scrutiny, and once more I experience the sensation, *thoooo-looo thoooo-loooo*, that it's staring directly into my eyes, into my mind which may seem very simple to it, like a seashell with a soft little body inside.

Rudolfo gone. Paul gone. Dionijs Ruyslinck gone. Anders Strandberg gone, to join his wife as it were. And Angela Henkel gone – our Field Marshall needed to send her out voluntarily more than once to bring food back, otherwise he might have seemed to be protecting her, thus impairing his authority. The available pool of food-bringers is diminishing all the time. What an unbalanced game of chess, wherein pawn after pawn is removed from one side only when we make a wrong move, as is inevitable. Despite Thomas Henkel's laudable pretensions our side only consists of sacrificial pawns, no king or knight or queen.

All the cut flowers in vases died long ago, but rain falls frequently and suddenly to lubricate the cemetery, whereupon Cthulhu walks in those heavy showers to lubricate itself, wafting those face tentacles. What does the creature muse about? Maybe it had a million years previously to muse, and now it *a*muses itself. Creator and creature are quite similar words.

I total the days scratched by me, as Henkel's adjutant, on the wall in five-bar gates. Does a week of five days, rather than seven, make the time pass more quickly, even though that system produces more weeks? Look: us survivors have survived for twenty-three weeks by now. August should be the current month, although the temperature stays much the same as that mild April day of our imprisonment; the brightish oval wavery yellow shape which we sometimes see above the mist, and which moves across the sky, should be much hotter by now if that's the same sun we knew.

The piles of food put out, or materialised, in unpredictable places for us pets to find grow smaller in proportion to our diminishing numbers; Cthulhu is keeping tally. It plays like the wicked boy inflating a frog with a straw through its anus until the poor creature explodes. Or pulling the legs off a spider one by one to test its balance. Only much more so.

Discarded playthings are sometimes still alive when we reach them, maybe without teeth, or with a tiny worm swimming in a single gaping double-yolked eye, gibbering softly, leaking, no longer seeming human; we dispatch those with a spade blow, those of us who remain.

Our leader has gone; Thomas Henkel is taken. So am I in

command now, promoted from adjutant on the disastrous field of battle, or rather of massacre? The others seem to expect this, and I can't reasonably demur. Jimmy Garrett blesses me.

Garrett is taken, to meet his new master, intimately.

By now those of us who remain are myself and Katie Drummond and Anne Gijsen and Alice Goldman and Jack Ballantyne. Four young women, one young man. Is a vile parody of Adam and Eve to be enacted? To the best of my knowledge no one has fucked anyone else since this all began, for mutual comfort. Stone floors, for a start; and who would sneak off into the softer sheltering groves? I think Anne and Dionijs came close, some time after brother Wim's death, but they were too upset.

Even though there's supposed to be an instinct to propagate the race, in extremis... Can it be that we're the only surviving human beings? Or are other iterations of Cthulhu playing variations on this vicious game all over the world? The latter seems more likely than that we should be the... *privileged* ones.

thoooo-looo thoooo-loooo

When we awake from dire dreams this morning, Katie is dead, apparently strangled to judge by bruise marks. Of course we gave up posting guards weeks ago now.

"If one of you doesn't confess," I say, "then we must assume that *it* can come here while we're sleeping."

"Naw," says Australian Jack, "that would be too merciful."

I wait for him to fess up.

"It was me," says Anne. "I go, I went, to Judo classes in Holland. It's a Judo strangle." She crossed her hands, back to back, grips an imaginary shirt or blouse collar, and rotates her wrists. "Pressure of the wrist bones on the carotid arteries. Unconscious in 15 or 20 seconds, death in maybe a couple of minutes. Katie begged me. She was so scared." Anne looks from face to face, almost expressionlessly. "Well. Does anyone else want this? If only," she adds, "I could strangle myself."

"*Yessss*," comes from Alice Goldman. "Yes please..." Jack and I have kept quiet.

Anne nods. "I shall not strangle more of you, though. No more of us. Only Alice. I don't wish to leave myself alone."

"Do you want," Jack asks Alice, "that we leave then come back after a few minutes?"

"No! Watch! Witness me!"

In what sense, witness? Witness her being *brave*, of all things? Cowardly brave?

Alice lies on her back across two slabs. "Like this?"

Anne nods.

"What if my blouse snaps?" Our clothes are by no means in tatters, merely very soiled.

Anne advances on hands and knees, then she lowers herself beside Alice, one leg across her body as if to restrain her; and her reversed hands slide round the American girl's neck as if lovingly.

After several seconds Alice does slap her entire free arm upon the slab as if in submission at a Judo contest, but only once. Her exposed feet drum a little, then are still.

Anne remains pressed upon Alice for what seems a long time, before the young Dutchwoman rolls aside.

"See," she says, sitting up, "I can be a murderer too, just as well as *the thing*."

"I'd hardly say –" begins Jack.

"Say nothing."

None of us wish to be left alone, so we all go out together to hunt for our food, or be hunted. Like an offering, we find two vacuum-packs of sliced Mortadella sausage and half a dozen oranges on the step under a grandiose melancholy memorial attended by a kneeling, praying woman and a bearded man who stands respectfully with gaze downcast. That woman's crocheted shawl is so intricate. Her ruffleted cuffs, the teardrop the size of a lemon pip spilling upon the side of her nose... He, with a coat over his arm, clasping his hands before him, a couple of fingers loosely – though inseparably – holding a grey bowler hat. Midway between the petrified pair, our meal.

"*Two* packets," says Anne, a quaver in her voice.

And Cthulhu comes…

…for her.

At least there's no distant screaming tonight. Maybe a tough tentacle is down her throat, no doubt allowing her to breathe, though, as she writhes.

Jack and I don't catch sight of Anne's corpse anywhere on today's search for more food. This takes us hours, but there are no birds which might steal. Finally, here's what we seek, upon the simple marble tomb of Mazzini's mother, within a railed little garden in front of the squat Doric columns supporting the massive architrave carved with the name of the great Italian patriot, wrapped over by creeper-clad rocks – for the atrium and then the crypt beyond, very dark within, burrow into the hillside in this part of the wild woodland. Paradoxically, quite close to our sanctuary, almost the last place we think to look.

On his mother's tomb by a towering tree: a single plate of white pasta scattered with clams. Brought from where, and how?

"Ladies first?" enquires Jack with an effort at humour.

Together we advance into the little railed garden.

A soft stirring sound from within the mausoleum.

k-thoooo-looo

comes.

I do hear the shrieks tonight, and try to stopper my ears. Maybe I should jam into my ears the long-expired Pope candles. The scene repeats in my mind: stooping to pass under the architrave, the tentacled monster had surveyed us. No point in fleeing; we knew it could catch us.

Heads or tails, male or female, Jack or me?

Then Cthulhu had swooped upon Jack and swept him away howling back inside that mausoleum. Is it so shameful that I seized the plate of pasta and clams and ran off with it?

So I'm all alone in the labyrinth now; and I'm hungry. Does something *really* special await the solitary, and female, survivor?

Maybe a boiled lobster, and no evil consequences on this particular occasion...

I'm in the gallery where a boy and his sister, hair and clothing perfectly rendered, are witnessing the departure of their mother's soul to heaven – the bronze door of the sepulchre above is already half-closed as the boy gestures upward, his other arm tenderly embracing his sister. Beside the children's feet lie a big bar of nut chocolate and an overripe banana. Chocolate! Immediately I'm tearing off the paper and silver foil, and biting into the sweetness.

But for the sudden assault of stench, I almost fail to notice Cthulhu coming until it is upon me, entangling me, its suckers tearing off slacks and shirt and underwear. The suffocating smell is of sewers and rotting fish.

Face tentacles sliding into my ears, *thoooo-loooo thoooo-loooo*, arm tentacles probing my anus, my cunt.

A storm of ecstasy like a blinding enveloping light! A momentary shaft of terrible agony as if I'm burnt alive!

The ecstasy again! I would crawl begging to the beast for this, like those rats that burn off their paws by pressing a red-hot plate which stimulates the pleasure centers in their brains.

Cthulhu is... calibrating me as, yes, it copulates using some organ or tentacle or other.

And I'm alive, lying naked and used – *for how long?* – upon flagstones bearing names of the dead. Alive. So violated but alive. Cthulhu has gone, though leaving his odour upon me.

At the tomb of Mazzini it must have been choosing whether

its *bride* should be an Australian youth, or myself...

And what is a bride but a receptacle for seed?

A movement. *What?*

The statue of the boy has lowered its arm and removed his hand from his sister's shoulder. She turns and steps down; and he copies her. The chiaroscuro of dust still remains on these Nineteenth century children as they step towards me, as I roll with difficulty on to my hands and knees so as to press myself up from the floor, and haul my aching abused self upright. The children remain marble, yet that marble has become a flexible, mobile parody of what it represented so faithfully for a century and more. Those clothes of theirs wouldn't come off them, I know that – the bodies are as one flesh with the garments. The boy and girl pause, looking up at me now.

Confused words come from their softened mouths.

Not Italian words, no.

Words with a Swedish lilt, I'm almost sure...

The voices of Anders and Selma Strandberg, the bank manager and his wife...

"...help us..."

"...how small we..."

"...where we been..."

"...what we..."

"...hurt..."

"...hurt..."

Within half an hour a score of statues have found me, arriving slowly, step by step.

The pious little old proletarian peasant woman, long-skirted, aproned and shawled, whom Gabriella had said sold peanuts all her life to save up for a statue of herself in Staglieno – she still carries strings of inedible peanuts as if those are rosaries.

The tall young swoony woman, nude to the waist, now detached from the grasp of the veiled skeleton.

A suited businessman, crumpled bowler hat in hand.

More children, dressed like miniature adults...

Some of the minds in the statues seem insane from the experiments they suffered. Others are very confused. Two can only speak in what must be Hungarian.

Eating or drinking is plainly impossible for them. Do they envy or resent my chocolate? Impossible to tell. Will their minds emerge more, and maybe heal, as time passes?

For what capricious purpose have we been re-united? So that a score of animated statues can provide company while *something* grows inside me – until at last I give birth surrounded by mobile dusty marble people, in a reverse of their previous roles as mourners at deathbed scenes. How often will Cthulhu play with me stinkingly again...?

Jack is the brightest of the children. He knows how his father died, and how he himself died. And how, but for me, he would now be bearing spawn in his belly.

I never imagined that I'd write a Cthulhu story, partly since it's quite hard to spell his (or His, or its) name correctly as revealed unto H.P. Lovecraft. But then Darrell Schweitzer set me the challenge for a proposed anthology about what happens when the alien elder entities take over the world once more, as is direly prophesied in arcane texts that make their readers gibber and rave. Any irony that I felt quickly evaporated, since this story proved to be probably the most emotionally harrowing I've ever written, due to me approaching it with complete seriousness. Friends even asked me on the phone what was wrong, because my voice had altered. I felt as if I was enmeshed in a sinister conjuration. The cemetery of Staglieno is Genoa is as I describe, only more so; Roberto and I actually became lost and locked into it. After the first half hour's exploration I already knew where I needed to set my Cthulhu story.

Cages

"Miss Adamson, I'm Svelte," says the tall skinny fortysome woman who enters my office.

Svelte by name, and likewise in body, which is long and slim. Elasticated black leggings and a black T-shirt under a crimson shirt that sports several zipped pockets. Not quite the usual ladies' attire for Combined Intelligence. In my own more chunky forties I'm in a cream blouse and grey jacket. A long grey skirt conceals my knee-cage.

Svelte's hair cascades blackly, and the collar of her crimson shirt gapes wide to accommodate a hexagonal neck-curse of brass which holds her chin high. Her impediment looks the height of funky fashion, something chosen deliberately rather than inflicted upon her.

I indicate the brown leather chair facing my desk, and she lounges in it.

"So what exactly *is* Kore?" I ask her.

According to the file still on screen, Svelte is half-Serbian, half-Romanian. Her birth name was Svetlana but she uses the name Svelte from her time as a... *turbo-folk singer.* Her job description at Combi-Intel is Analysis Eastern Europe – she graduated in Politics and Economics from the University of Belgrade. Most economies in Eastern Europe are in a mess because of the hoops coming so soon after the upheavals of uniting with the West.

Outside my tinted window, the Thames is as grey as my clothing. At rooftop level above Kensington and Chelsea, hoops hang leadenly in their dozens. If the sun were shining on this June morning, how the hoops would glitter, like huge bangles from boutiques.

"Kore is tekky that samples and remixes the sounds of love-making," says Svelte.

"Hang on. *Tekky. Samples. Remixes.*" This Serbian-Romanian seems to have a bigger English vocabulary than I do.

"Tekky is neo-techno music," she explains. "You sample other bits of music or noise, use a synthesizer to distort. Take a source sound and make it something it never was. Kore uses fucking and coming as the source sounds." Helpfully she spells source. Not sauce, no.

From a crimson breast pocket emerges a memory stick, which I plug into the computer. An album cover comes on screen, depicting a dancing woman surrounded by flames. A fox mask hides the woman's face. Groping, caressing hands of a multitude of hues, detached from their owners, cover most of the woman's body. Patch of pubic hair and a nipple are exposed.

"Oh, I see," say I. "Kore as in hard-core."

"Isn't digitised – hands are all painted on her."

"So it's art. Patient woman. Must have taken ages."

The title of the album is *Sighs and Cries*. From Quantum Entanglement, the very group! Svelte is extremely well-organised, and at only a half-hour's notice. Her slimness, her extra height, her dark hair: just as Miriam was, till she left my life. Not that Miriam died, merely our relationship.

The music is slick and smooth as sweaty skin but with a pulsing bass line, climax a long time coming, wailings looping around and around, wave after wave, sighs like choirs of angels in ecstasy.

Ev-erything you
Everything you do
You do, you do, you do
Everything you say
To me, to me, to me
Everything you do to me
Say to me do to me

Is perfect perfect perfect
Do to me say to me
Perfect perfect perfect…

"Sounds like a steal from Marlene Dietrich," is my opinion. *"You Do Something To Me."*

"No, someone really said those words while making love. The voice is like filtered, disguised, high-pitched. Sometimes gets overdone. Voice winds up six octaves like breathing pure helium, like almost ultrasonic, like something to get bats off on."

Could I even dream of phrasing anything of the sort in Serbo-Croatian or Romanian? Not even in English!

Minimize the album cover away, resume CV. In her youth Svelte was a favourite of the Milosevic regime. Turbo-folk was mystical nationalist music originally supportive of Milosevic and his gangsters, a primitivist blend of pop and folk and oriental sounds. Strong allegations of crime and drug trafficking – Svelte must have been obliged to get out of Serbia. She tidied up her act and dusted off her university degree and become one of our experts on East European. Not to mention our expert on the music scene.

"Do you know why I'm asking about Kore?"

"Web chat says Quantum Entanglement gonna do a big *Exprisonment* gig. They'll sample the noise the alien bees make, fuck about with the big bees' hum and blast the mix at hoops or at the bees. Like, the Varroa fucked with us, so let's fuck 'em with music. That's the idea."

Succinctly put. Pretty much what I was alerted to, fresh out of a meeting about the nuke the Chinese had set off. So far as satellite imaging can tell, the solitary alien hoop which the Chinese nuked in the Gobi was merely hurled several kilometres upward. Maybe some blast got through to the other side of the hoop.

First shot in an interstellar war? Considering the size of a hoop, about a thousandth of a megaton may have got through, if any blast at all. No repercussions from the aliens, at least not as yet. We needed to do more than nuke a hoop? Damn the Chinese – they might have provoked anything.

Svelte shrugs. "Only just found out. Can't follow everything."

"You're fast."

When we speak of *the* aliens, precisely what do we mean? Precision is vital in intelligence. It's important regularly to re-analyse what we think we know in case of some new interpretation. It can be fatal to make assumptions then stick to them.

First of all, from nowhere, come the hoops. They appeared worldwide during a single day, tens of millions of them. Next came the Varroa, who – or which – use the hoops to arrive and exit. (Is anyone – or anything – else involved about whom we know sod all?)

It only took a week for the myriads of hoops to bestow impediments upon the world's population. A hoop would swoop. Of a sudden the targeted person found a cage around some part of their body. I need to keep my own left leg stretched out beneath my desk on account of my knee-cage.

A transfixing bar holds an imped in place. In itself this doesn't hurt, but woe betide anyone who has an imped removed by surgery or by DIY sawing. They'll experience agony until a hoop gets round to renewing the affliction, maybe next day, maybe a week later.

Hoops don't swoop upon someone who's up a ladder, say – they wait for a more suitable moment. Smart hoops. If you shut yourself up tight in your home, a hoop will appear as if by magic. Hoops are about a metre in diameter.

Nothing we do affects them. *Exotic substance*, say scientists. Might be made of strings. Ah, I have just cottoned on: *Exprisonment*, the title of Quantum Entanglement's proposed gig, is the opposite of imprisonment. We're all confined by our impeds, all constrained, but at the same time we're free to walk about. We're exprisoned.

"So," I say to Svelte," do we butt in on Quantum Entanglement and take charge of this hum-mix event? All sorts of measuring equipment on site? Or do we limit ourselves to observing? In which case," as I appraise her clothing, "just how do we dress?"

"Or undress."

"You mean literally?"

"Some kids'll go nude or scanty. Not most."

"Glad to hear it. Is this only for young people?"

She shakes her head. "You get worked up by Kore with a friend of *any* age, or even on your own. It's non-discriminatory, like sex for the disabled. Impeds looked like fucking the club and dance scene, like how do you dance with a box on your foot? Kore says fuck off to impeds."

"You mean there'll be some sort of *orgy*?"

"Some micro-orgies maybe, not mass writhing. There's like a spiritual dimension, like an orgasm reaching heaven. Transcending the body, flying free."

"And *Sighs and Cries* was a response to impeds?"

"No, *Sighs and Cries* came out a few months before the hoops. What QE are planning right now is their response to the hoops. They must've been sampling and mixing for months."

"High time to stick our noses in."

"Party time? *Dude!*"

So the Varroa come through the hoops. They look like giant bees, size of an electric toaster. *Varrr-oh-aah, varrr-oh-aah*: that's the sound they make. A bit loud for wing-beats. The noise suggests some kind of protective energy field, whatever *that* might be. *Bee-ing* as how we can't catch a Varroa nor harm them in any way.

And there's a terrestrial parasite named Varroa which sucks the blood of our terrestrial bees. This enfeebles the bees. So they collect less pollen. So less honey gets made. After a few months, bye-bye hive. The Varroa and their hoops certainly impair human beings, so the name sticks.

The Varroa could be robots made by aliens (hitherto unseen), sent through the hoops to impair us and assess the effects.

Those hypothetical aliens might be:

softening us up for the real invasion – however, some ethics committee of alien races disapproves of brutal methods and awards Brownie points for ingenuity;

making sex difficult so we'll slowly go extinct; the birth rate is scarily down, vacant planet in another couple of centuries at the present rate (see invasion scenario, above);

hampering us so that we don't get above ourselves by suddenly making some scientific breakthrough such as developing interstellar travel and causing mayhem;

practising an art form;

fill in your own guess.

Many countries have sent smart little spy-flyers through hoops, though here in London we know of none that ever returned or transmitted any data back. SETI specialists – Searchers for Extraterrestial Intelligence – try in vain to analyse the Varroa noise and communicate. Everything's guesswork. Now here's a different tack: the Kore people are going to carry out an innovative and maybe confrontational musical experiment. If they strike gold, wow. Let's not spoil the spontaneity of the experiment. Sometimes there can be too much consultation. We'll simply observe it, me and my Serbian who intrigues me – and of course we'll need someone to video unobtrusively so we have audiovisual for the record. This'll be on my own initiative. Hell, it's only a music group. Nothing might come of this, then I'd be wasting resources, right?

Before the hoops came and my left knee was caged, I was mainly liaising with the French security service about the Islamist terrorist threat. That's how I met Miriam Claudel, six years ago now. That ended, and for the past two years there's been no one else. I much prefer relationships to arise in the natural course of events rather than to go hunting.

'The Studio' is the name for a 19th century vicarage in Lambeth, converted and extended into a nursing home which subsequently went bankrupt. With mucho money from American and Euro tours and a zillion sales, Benny Wallace and Trev Tate bought the place before the aliens arrived.

It's going to be club night there tonight – anything to keep our spirits up.

A mild sunny evening, this fifth aniversary (in days) of my first meeting Svelte. I drive with the window down. My long denim skirt, its big pockets embroidered with swirls of daisies, laps pixie boots. White blouse, sleeveless denim bolero jacket. A bit Country Dance, but it takes all sorts. Alongside me, Svelte is in scarlet and black. In the back Tony Cullen from Surveillance sports a box on his left hand – that's his digicam disguised as an imped. His real imped is some sort of complicated groin-truss. Consequently he doesn't much like sitting, even on a commode-chair at home, he told me. Usually, quote unquote, he sprawls on a sofa like a feasting Roman. Looks rather like a Roman, Tony does, with those crimped blond curls and eagle nose. He mustn't see much gay action these days, what with his truss. He wears loose baggy fawn trousers and an oversize cream sweater.

There's so much less traffic on the roads these days that the air almost smells sweet. Easy-peasy to park my disabled-adapted Volvo turbo-diesel on a street of shops; try finding a parking space in this part of London before the impeds. Walking half a mile with a knee-cage won't be much fun but we're being discreet.

Out clamber Tony and I awkwardly. Svelte slides out and is instantly, gracefully upright. I admire her.

The theory that we might all be atoning for something in our past by the type of impeds we wear is probably ridiculous. Must my leg be immobilised because I was Captain of the hockey team at Oxford? Because Svelte was a singer, does she need an imped up near her vocal chords?

Our pace along the street is determined by my need to swing my stiffened left leg in an arc. A hoop drifts overhead, ignored by most people. It's easy to tell who's heading for the party. Girl in a one-piece Spiderman bathing costume and short frilly skirt, her friend in bra and nickers, boots and black cowboy hat. Girl wearing hot-shorts and an off-the-shoulder top, her knee-imped just like mine except it's bright red. She must have painted or enameled the cage herself, which shows spirit. Various others.

Svelte told me that Benny and Trev aimed to centralise studios for half a dozen tekky groups, the idea being a synergistic commune all rubbing off each other whilst doing their own unique things. Wisdom was that you oughtn't to live where your studio is because that way you'd become entrapped and not have a life, but as it turned out in the wake of hoops and impeds The Studio provided a sort of sanctuary, an oasis. Some of the music made there is really demented, Svelte said with approval – such as the stuff by Psalms of Madness.

We're only interested in the original Quantum Entanglement band which consists of Daniel and Sean and AlanJune – as those last two members call themselves, as though they don't have separate identities. Maybe an imped locks Alan and June together nowadays – we'll see.

Passing a fish and chip shop, funky jazz drifts out along with the smells. A beautiful Chinese girl with long black hair is scooping chips out of a frier. Personally I would put the hair up in a net in those circumstances. But oh, the hair partly hides her imped. A small red box – like a radio – is bonded to the side of her head. And that's the source of the jazz! Does that box play all the time? How does she ever get to sleep? How isn't she half-insane? Yet she looks serene. Maybe she went deaf.

"Sally, cop a look," says Svelte. I'd told her to call me Sally – *Miss Adamson* would sound absurd at a gig.

Generally one avoids gawping at abnormally impeded

individuals, since basically we're all in the same boat. However, the middle-aged woman crossing the street towards us is something else. Living impeds are rather rare, and that woman's right forearm is a tortoiseshell cat.

To be accurate, it's most of a cat. Fused to the elbow-stump of the woman's right arm, the animal lacks hind legs. She's cradling the moggy against her chest, its front paws clinging to her shoulder, its tail flicking to and fro.

"Imagine feeding it!" Tony is holding his boxed hand very steady – I think he's filming the woman. At home does he have a private video library of weird impeds? Heigh-ho, anything to keep sexuality alive and kicking.

Imagine that poor woman kneeling patiently by Kitty's food bowl, purring encouragingly. Imagine when the cat wants a crap.

"What did she do to deserve that, eh?" says Tony. "Love her pet excessively?"

"What did the *cat* do?" retorts Svelte.

We hush as the woman passes by.

A lot of impeds seem arbitrary, while some do seem poignantly appropriate. So there's the "snapshot" theory that the imped reflects what a person was thinking about at the exact moment of caging. People thinking banal thoughts received any old imped from stock; but obsessives tended to be thinking about their obsessions.

"They're practical jokers," says Tony. "Somewhere in Varroa land audiences are laughing their heads off and rolling in the aisles."

As if on cue, the noise intrudes: *varrr-oh-aah, varrr-oh-aah-oh-aah*, a wild wind rushing through trees, the sound of a giant bee flying. One of the Varroa comes cruising overhead, dangling scaly jointed legs, its glassy-looking wings beating fast. Yellow fur streaked with orange, black bulbous eyes, antennae like miniature antlers.

"Sod off sod off!" a bloke shouts at it. He shakes his imped vengefully: a right-hand box. Most people look the other way.

Rather higher in the sky, a passenger jet is descending across London towards distant Heathrow. That isn't such a frequent sight as formerly. Tourism's almost dead.

A skinny black chap equipped with a full head-cage emerges from a newsagent. Cradling a toddler in his arms, he looks like a parody of an American football player. Of a sudden the black man legs it at quite a pace. Cottoned on to a Varroa in the neighbourhood, did he? Whatever a daddy does, his child will receive an imped when it's nearing a metre tall. Head-Cage is probably a bit nuts and is trying to stop his offspring from learning to walk, so that the child never appears tall. Well, that won't work, is the long and the tall of it. Long equals tall.

A high stone wall tipped by rusty spikes surrounds the grounds of the ex-rectory, ex-nursing home. Cedars, cypresses, and Scots pines rear up. At the gateway a couple of blokes stuff entrance money into the pockets of long open leather coats. On account of his waist-cage one of those collectors looks pregnant with some robot child, its curving spine and ribs and other metal bones wrapped around his bare midriff. The other fellow has a solid box on one foot – after a year, how the inside must stink.

So now we're heading up a long driveway through shrubbery – in company with Teens and Twenties mainly, a bass beat somewhere ahead of us. I'm wondering what home-owners in the area think about the noise, whenever there's club night. Prior to the hoops, when people could get to gigs further afield, I guess no club nights happened here. Priorities have changed as to what annoys us.

Tony covertly films a gorgeous black girl ahead of us wearing pinstripe trousers cut into thin thongs exposing her bum and legs. Hand-cage resembling a medieval weapon. Maybe Tony isn't gay. I don't care a toss. I'd rather it was just Svelte and me here this evening, but there are proper ways to do things, as Tony's presence reminds me.

The black girl's blonde friend sports a frilly skirt and a bulging grille of a metal bra, to the back of which are fixed butterfly wings of yellow muslin. I tell a lie: that bra is a breast-cage, which she has dolled up. Quite a crowd is heading for club night.

A big marquee comes in view.

"They're brave, these kids," says Svelte. "I admire them."

"Whistling while Rome burns," says Tony.

"You're excited. Enjoy the view."

Grinning, Svelte says something that sounds like, "*S'avem che bea shi fute!*"

"What's that?"

"A Romanian toast. It means: here's to a drink and a fuck."

"Look," says Tony, "it's inconvenient for me to get excited – not to mention unprofessional."

Svelte doesn't know about Tony's groin-truss. She's so exotic, Svelte is, though doubtless not to herself. Probably she's hetero. Not necessarily, though. Time will tell. Or will it? I really must keep my head clear.

Let's take a look in the vast marquee first, where things are warming up – as in hot bodies and hot lights fanning through aroma-mists. However, the music playing from big speakers right now is like cool liquid, kind of distanced rather than intimate. What's playing at the moment are recordings. On stage a quartet of machines await, for later on. Digi-keyboard, drum machine, hypersynth, and a whatnot: I've no idea which is which, or what, though Svelte does.

"Nice backward reverb setting off the vocal line," she comments loudly, and I think I understand. "Just don't overdo it! Aw shit, there we go. That'll excite the bats," sneers Svelte.

But now a different remix rivets me. Sighs and cries over a pulsing bass line: kosher kore, the piece I heard in the office:

Ev-ery-thing you

Ev-ery-thing you do
You do, you do, you do, you do…

Youngsters waggle their arms overhead and shuffle and shimmy, frantic to enjoy. Lip-rings, nose-studs, belly-button trinkets make the impeds seem like huge exotic piercings. A white girl in black bra and nickers, boots, and cowboy hat smooches with a black girl in white bra et cetera. I approve. A huge Hawaian garland of bright plastic flowers hangs upon another girl's brief blue cocktail dress. A bloke's t-shirt reads KISS MY ARSE, SEXY, although the bum-cage bulking under his oversize jeans makes this unlikely. Why doesn't he wear a kilt? Similarly impeded chaps favour kilts. Older people are in the crowd too, so I don't feel far out of place. We have two or three hours before QE perform live, plenty of time to nose around independently.

I spy a midget, a very little man indeed with a large head, a bit more than knee-height to me. He's wearing a string vest and very brief yellow shorts, showing off his bandy, hairy, muscular legs – *no*, showing off the absolute absence of any imped! He's immune because of his extreme shortness. In the land of the impeded the diminutive midget is king, and he does show off, struttingly. He must think he's sexy these days; maybe he knows it for a fact.

Freckly ginger-haired man of forty-odd, brown leather bomber jacket hung on his shoulders – a cage enclosing his right hand – is nattering fairly urgently to a thin tall guy in baggy shorts and a t-shirt showing a cunt, a cage upon his right foot. Cunt t-shirt's cadaverous face and wild shoulder-length hair fit the website picture I saw of Sean of QE.

I scoop the snoop from my pocket to my ear. Looks like a tiny flesh-tone deaf-aid, if anyone even notices. The directional mike in my pocket is radio-linked.

"…could easily be a real word, *exprisonment*."

"Like Björk thinking homogenic was a real word? Until

61

someone told her it was bullshit. But she stuck with it."

The thin fellow intones, "*The way you stick with me, though I'll never be free… Needs pulling apart. The way you, the way you, stick with me, stick with me…*"

"Don't take the piss, Sean! Is Caz going to show?"

"Dancing's the candle, she's the moth." Just at this moment, a gorgeous blond teeny-girl wearing green hot-shorts and a gauzy off-the-shoulder top comes by, her left foot caged, the other in a green fetish boot. Sean pivots towards her and jiggles his imped. "Hi jewel, we're a pair, you and I. I live in The Studio – want to see inside?"

She eyes him then says, "Foosh off."

Ginger says appeasingly, "Kids can be puritans. They just don't look or act it."

"So why come to a fucking Kore gig? Are you being puritan yourself these days, Pete, if you can't shag Benny's treasure?"

"I don't like the word shag."

"I need some Heineken Ice. Want to come in The Studio?"

"I'll hang around here for a bit."

"Hell, Benny can't *go* anywhere." Benny, the co-owner. "*And* he's getting fatter every day. No exercise, and overeating."

Let me get this straight: Pete has screwed Caz, who is co-owner Benny's girlfriend or wife or whatever. Pete is hoping to see Caz tonight, so Pete isn't resident in The Studio – or *not any more*? Benny may have found out about Caz and Pete and had him expelled from the community. Presumably Pete can't be entirely *non grata* with the other co-owner, Trev, otherwise those guys on the gate wouldn't have let Pete in at all. I already noticed a couple of bouncers in jeans and bright orange t-shirts – security, first aid, whatever. Both have head-cages as impeds. Like visored helmets convenient for head-butting if the need arises. If Pete's black-listed, doubtless they'd know about this. I keep Pete in sight as he wanders alone through the huge, ever more crowded marquee.

Benny can't go anywhere; Benny gets no exercise. Does that

mean he's severely impeded, more so than most people? That might explain opportunity and motive for infidelity by Caz.

Aha. A tall slim dark-haired woman dressed in a long green skirt and lace blouse has arrived – and Pete is heading her way. Maybe she's forty or more, and she has a black patch over her left eye. Assuming that she's Caz, has Benny got angry and punched her in the eye? Presumably not if he's immobilised.

Pete and Caz talk for a good five minutes, while I eavesdrop on them. Pete wants her to come away with him, but she can't. Not won't – how she yearns for that – but she can't. Not yet.
   – Caz, can't you abscond with Contessa? And anyway, it's all just bullying bluster. And how could he *manage* to torture…
   I expected Pete to say: a child. But he says:
   – a cat?
   Contessa must be the name of a cat, Caz's cat. Like a child to her. Benny has threatened Caz's cat, if she misbehaves.
   – I don't have a cat basket.
   – Hell, I'll buy you one!
   – How would I explain it?
   – He's all hot air.
   – Can I risk that?

On the one hand Benny's threat seems real to Caz, and horrible. Yet from the way Caz talks about Benny, she seems to care for the man and feel sorry for him. She's unwilling to abandon him.
   – Pete, I need to show him soon…
   Show him what?

At last I cotton on. As if in compensation for immobilising Benny, the hoops swapped one of Benny's eyes for one of Caz's. If and when Caz raises her eye-patch Benny can see what she's seeing. And vice versa? I've no idea. Caz must need to close her own eye whenever she raises the patch, otherwise there would be a hopeless jumble of double vision, two different scenes eyed simultaneously.

Benny's eye is Caz's impediment. Yet Benny can't hear or feel or smell, only see – otherwise how could Pete and Caz have succeeded in making love? I imagine Caz's patch coming loose one time as she tossed her head to and fro upon a pillow, her noise of pleasure suddenly changing to a cry of fright.

– You still jerking him off, Caz?

– It seems only fair – how can I refuse?

Does this wound Pete?

– I do love you, Pete. I think about you every night is the last thing I hear her say to him.

Reluctantly Pete moves away from her, disappearing into the crowd. Caz dances on her own, not straying from the same spot – for now she shuts her right eye and raises the patch to her brow. Her right eye was green, but her left eye is brown. Hoops can join part of a living cat to a person's arm in direct proximity. Hoops can also connect an eye remotely to a brain. This needs reporting.

Investigators will descend upon Benny and Caz.

I watch Caz as she dances, keeping Benny's eye masked, or stands still with that eye exposed. She's relaxed, yet wary. Periodically she and Pete coincide again for two or three minutes at a time. It's noisy and several times Pete has to ask Caz to repeat herself. Quite often she's looking away as she talks to him.

Most of their chat is about trivialities, or acquaintances. After that first encounter Pete doesn't implore or beg. No matter how frustrated he is, he mustn't want to spend their precious stolen time whining or cajoling, but companionably. Caz seems well able to hide her feelings, but she must love Pete otherwise she wouldn't take risks at all.

I'm fascinated with what seems to be the situation between them, and with the idea of the Eye of Another in one's head.

By itself that threat to torture the cat seems absurd and

histrionic – yet at the same time ingenious, I suppose. Benny knows how to press Caz's buttons and scare her. Maybe there are other threats too. Personally I don't think she'll ever run off with Pete, no matter how much she may wish to, at least in her dreams. Pete *almost* realizes this. Before the coming of the Varroa I read a statistic that only about twenty per cent – or was it less? – of wives actually leave their husbands as the result of an affair. I wonder if Pete and Caz manage to meet away from The Studio, and for how long? That spying eye, it's worse than a camera phone.

After a good hour and a half Svelte returns to me. In the interval I've hobnobbed with Tony Cullen a few times. The first thing I ask Svelte is, "Have you been inside The Studio?" I'm remembering Sean's invitation to that blond girl – my god, I'm having a jealous thought about Svelte.

"Sure," she says.

"*How?*"

"Got chatted up."

"Did anything happen?"

She grins. "Just led her on a bit. Can't do much surveillance if you're in bed."

Did Svelte go with a *her* by coincidence, or by design?

I tell Svelte about Benny and Pete and Caz.

"Wow, that's heavy surveillance, jealous guy's eye looking out of your own face. Needs a lot of composure to take that in your stride! I got a glimpse of Alan and June. They aren't fused or chained together, though I guess you couldn't perform too well like that. Fancy dancing a bit?"

Me, with my knee cage? Svelte's invitation excites me. Is she playing with me, being innocently friendly, thinking protective colouration, or what? Her eyes sparkle. I wonder if she did a line of coke in The Studio with *her*, on duty too. I mustn't seem nothing-venture, especially not here, so I give dancing a go.

All the while, other bodies are dancing in a slow demented euphoric way to the thump and pulse of tekky. A girl in long boots with a crimson crop-top and golden bangle piercing her belly button has what I can only call a cunt-cage. How on earth does she get her knickers on? The penny drops: she painted them on to already de-haired flesh, unattainable now except by the touch of a brush. Two young fellows clash hand-cages together, triumphing over affliction.

At long last the head-caged bouncers and some helpers lower one wall of the marquee, exposing the event to the night, and the night to the event. And now the four members of QE come to their music machines, facing across the crowd towards the canvas wall-that-was, now a big darkness plus silhouettes of trees.

Sean, I've already seen. Daniel is a big black man with a shaved head, his imped a huge shoulder-cage adorned with an equally huge red epaulet. The cage cramps his upper arm but he can use his lower arm well enough. June dresses Goth-like, white face, lurid red lips, purple hairpieces entwined with her own jet hair. A dark gown swells at her belly – that'll be her cage. Beak-nosed, coal-eyed Alan has long white hair, presumably bleached, spilling from a head cage, and he wears a white robe with a scarlet pentacle on his chest. He's like a wicca priest with his head in a bird cage.

Most of the lights go out, apart from spots illuminating the music machines.

It's Alan who addresses the crowd. He gestures beyond them at the night.

"Oh ye aliens who exprison us! We've deconstructed your humming and now we'll hum a new tune for you big bees! We're gonna pipe you back to oblivion like the Piper of Hamelin did, only he never had a hypersynth. You feeling caged, people? Hum along, come along! Welcome to *Exprisonment*."

June lifts a mike, and to begin with starts to hum.

A bee-hum can become a banshee-howl, almost drowning what June is singing with abandoned, sweating passion: *fuckyou Varroa*

*forfuckingwithus…cometotheVarroafuck…comecomecome…comefuckcome
…fuckingcome fuckinggo…*

Double-beats from the drum machine are loudening and
lessening like a disordered heart. Heterodyning, is that the word?

Is that the Varroa hum played backwards now?

A light glows silver, a hoop in the night. Sweet Christ, has this
noise actually brought a hoop here? The players are gesturing,
dancers are all turning to face the darkness and the ring of silver
light which poises upright upon the lawn. Tony is pointing his
phony imped, the digicam. *"Oh dude,"* cries Svelte. I have to get a
full team here – I shout into my mobile but I can't damn well
make out the replies. Svelte bellows into my ear the words: *resonant frequ-ency.*

The hoop is expanding. We've never known a hoop behave
this way before. The base of it is below ground invisibly, so what
I'm seeing is a kind of archway rather than a circle.

In place of the night-time which was beyond, now a
shimmer of blues and greens and rose fills the area inside the
hoop. It's like the membrane of some huge soap bubble about to
be blown. I'm wondering if a sudden wind from beyond might in
a moment propel a floating sphere out into our world – when of
a sudden the space inside the hoop becomes a *view*. Yes, an
opening into a landscape – of bushes and trees that are white
ostrich plumes and tails of peacocks and adornments of birds of
paradise and sulphur crests of cockatoos growing upward from
ground that sparkles kaleidoscopically, ground resembling a
mosaic of tiny crystals. The source of light is somewhere in a pale
blue sky, unseen.

Otherworldly, strange, beautiful: we're seeing into another
world. *Never before have we seen elsewhere through a hoop.*

Already us club-nighters are heading towards that magical
scene – a surge of audience.

"Dude!" cries Svelte, and Tony Cullen knows that he needs
to get closer too, and so do I, yammering into my mobile at

Combi-Intel to *come immediately*, and so do priestly Alan and big black Daniel elbowing past us, and in the forefront of flesh and glad rags of all kinds for a moment I glimpse Pete hustling Caz along with him towards that archway to elsewhere – he's seizing his chance to kidnap Caz no matter to where, and *they're through*, half a dozen kids capering alongside them, and they aren't stifling or choking in some toxic alien atmosphere, or at least not yet. They're amongst the lovely alien vegetation. More and more of the audience follow.

I think the noise from the speakers has gone into a loop. QE were recording their live performance; the recording's replaying now. The stretched hoop seems to wobble. Before, it was precise.

"Hurry up!" from Svelte. She grabs me strongly from my good side so that I shan't risk falling over on account of my knee-cage, propelling me with her, for of course I must go through to see. This is like an assault by a motley children's crusade on some city with a breached wall, as people stream through. As when the Pied Piper reached the mountain that opened up for all the enchanted boys and girls...

"Tony, stay to brief the team that gets here –"

"Bollocks, I'm not missing this. Enough impeded'll be left behind to tell –"

What I'm about to do may be madness, but I shall be adventuring with Svelte – oh what am I thinking? It's my duty to investigate as fully as I can. What will we eat and drink, how will we ever get back again?

Just as we pass through, that midget chap pushes past. Almost immediately he stumbles, sprawling upon the sparkly soil. More like a beach of multi-hued mica, which his impact grooves. He doesn't roll or scramble up. Air smells faintly of burnt toast and vanilla.

"Wait, Svelte!" Stoop and press the pulse in the midget's neck. None there.

Check his wrist. "He's dead."

"Too much excitement."

"No, why is he dead?"

An almightly *pop*, and there's no hoop any more. Nor loudspeaker noise from any marquee, nor oval of nighttime, nor marquee, nor nothing of where we came from. The bright yellow-white sun dazzling high above the feather-trees looks smaller than... well, it's a different sun.

How many people are wandering about, with *bugger all* in the way of supplies or equipment? Two hundred of us? All impeded, too.

Why did the midget drop dead?

A couple of hundred of us, and *no means* of getting back. I know why we rushed through the archway — after the utter frustration that everyone has felt ever since the hoops arrived, an almost orgasmic release of tension, a sense of exaltation. The prettiness of this — um, paradise? — contributed. People desired to cavort.

Orange t-shirt with head-cage kneels by the midget, turns him over, tries some first aid.

"Svelte, the midget didn't have any cage. And he died as soon as he came through."

"You mean having cages *lets us* into here? *Why?* No, he had a heart attack or a stroke."

"Maybe he had one of those because he didn't have a cage."

"Like, as a ticket? Or to protect him? Lot of excitement tonight. Small chap, he overdid himself."

"Jacko's definitely dead," announces the head-cage, and he stares at me hard.

"Look," I say to him, "you're security, right?" When he nods, "We have to organise all these people."

"What's it to you?" Behind the visor, blue eyes, chaotic sandy hair — quite hard to comb!

Deep breath. "My name's Sally Adamson. I'm from Combined Intelligence. We were keeping an eye on your musical experiment tonight."

Tony Cullen is by my side to back me up, as is Svelte.

"I'm Bryce. There are more of you back at The Studio?"

Alas, no, at least not yet. I'm hoping that my yammering into the mobile raised the alarm. Nobody ever could have reasonably expected this result from tonight's techno caper.

Why, pray, did I stage what amounts to a private surveillance, all on my own say-so? I ought to be for the high jump. Exactly how far *have* we jumped away from Earth?

"You have a radio with you?" Bryce demands. "Or a phone?"

"Do you seriously expect – ?"

"Have you *tried?*"

He's right, so I pull out my phone.

"No signal."

"Dial anyway, see what happens."

Dee-du-doo-doo-du-do... followed by silence.

"Now you know *for sure*, don't you."

"Why did you come through, Bryce?"

"Somebody in charge had to." Looked at from that point of view, I suppose he's more in charge than me. "Seeing as they already know me, the kids might pay some attention. You'd best stick to advising, hmm?" He eyes Tony and Svelte. "Got guns?"

No, and no.

He laughs shortly. "All you got is combined intelligence. Pretty disconnected right now."

People have spread out among the featherbushes, feathertrees. Partly concealed by ostrich plumes, two kids seem to be fucking. Getting to the kore of the problem, eh? That's unfair – they're true pioneers, the first human beings to have sex on an alien world. That's one defiant number one for the record book.

Svelte exclaims, "Look, how do we know this place is actual? Why not a virtual reality, and cages admit you into it? That's why Jacko couldn't take part, not his mind anyhow. Maybe the Varroa belong to some super-evolved combi-intelligence that hangs out in mind-space."

"Yeah," sarcastically from Bryce, "like this thing dumps

millions of tons of solid fucking cages on to Earth? And it's virtual?"

"Okay, just a thought. No birds or insects anywhere in sight, you'll notice. No *ecology*." Svelte's right, at least regarding the area nearby. "You mightn't expect birds as such, but there oughta be something besides a bunch of fancy feathers." Svelte really is very acrobatic in her thinking.

Communicate, communicate. Communicate with the club-nighters, to get ourselves organised. Mustn't wander off chaotically. Food, drink, explore, communicate. Communicating with home is impossible. *Or is it..?* I'm looking at Caz and Pete standing hand in hand, that black patch over her left eye, while Bryce and Svelte rally people....

If Benny can see through her eye back home – and Caz through his? – when they're apart from each other... How does it happen, what's the link? Advanced alien science, some sort of instant linked vision-at-a-distance, quantum stuff, a shortcut through spacetime? How *distant* does distant have to be before it's too far?

My phone can display four lines of memo or txt on its screen the size of my thumb.

"You're Caz. I'm Sally, from Combined Intelligence – you understand?" Caz does. "And you're Pete. Caz, I know you and Benny can see what the other sees."

"How do you know that?"

"I was snooping. That's my job. We appear to be marooned here, wherever here is. You may be a way to communicate with home..."

Pete doesn't want her to co-operate. Small wonder. They've escaped together, and almost at once here's me asking her to let Benny see everything, supposing it's possible.

"Realistically," I say, "with no food or water we're probably going to die here, unless something different kills us first."

Pete hugs his Caz, as if he can preserve the two of them by pure wish and will power. Wishes don't rule the real world.

I'm going to die too. Me and Svelte. I'll think about that later. The important thing is that Caz understands this. I know she heeds duties and obligations even if those frustrate her dreams. *Only fair, isn't it?* Wasn't that what she said?

"Caz, this is the first ever information we have about anything regarding where our invaders come from. Back home nobody will know anything unless…"

She nods miserably. Or bravely. There are different sorts of bravery. Women understand much more about self-sacrifice than men do.

Pete sits down with his back to us. Doesn't want to watch this. Or doesn't want to be noticed by Caz's Benny-eye? If Caz looks round, Pete's ginger hair will be very visible.

Well, it works. *It works.* We're connected. Phone-screen and Benny's displaced eye reading it at this end, Caz's eye in Benny's head at the other end perceiving a notepad he writes on. Hallelujah. But.

I couldn't believe any man would exploit this situation for blackmail. Benny uses it. Oh he uses it. Benny won't tell anyone else a fucking thing unless Caz promises, *promises, swears* on the memory of her mother, to return to him. Obviously forget about torturing the cat – seems that wasn't sufficient to hold her. Oh and forget the extreme unlikelihood of her being able to return – unless, I suppose, when Combi-Intel gets its act together, they manage to control a hoop by the same method as CE used. My god, I must grill those two, the priest and the big black guy. Alan and June on their own may be able to give Combi-Intel enough guidance to reopen the hoop. Hey, there's *hope*, a possibility – why am I so blind and slow? Too much to think about, that's why. The same hope didn't enter into Bryce's head, or Svelte's. Or if so, they didn't say. That's because we aren't desperate yet.

Only just got here. Novelty value still prevails.

Caz opens her right eye, and tears jerk from it. Tiny discs of water fly as if she's expelling contact lenses one after another. I've never seen anyone cry quite like that, projectile tears, tears so pent up that they don't trickle but fly for a few seconds at least. Then she shuts her own eye tight.

"I can't see the phone now," she reminds me. "Write: *I promise.*" And I peck at the keys with my fingernail.

Pete tells her fiercely, "You can break any promise extorted by a threat."

"I'm sorry. It's a personal thing. A promise is a promise."

"A shitty vicious threat to keep knowledge from the whole world unless he can hang on to you like a dog in the manger!"

"You can't really blame him. We have so much personal baggage, him and me. What would become of him?"

Is Caz a coward, or is she very brave, able to sacrifice the hope of personal happiness for the sake of many other people who will never even realize?

"Shit." Pete doesn't try to interfere as I hold the phone screen up to Benny's brown eye.

"Varroa – !"

A hum coming closer.

Soon we're being inspected.

Before long a second Varroa comes. As us clubnighters stare up, many chattering to each other, the mutual hum of the Varroas modulates, seeming to search through a spectrum of sound. Soon I think I'm hearing thrumming echoes of human words, words that evade meaning as if played backwards, half-words.

"Fucking hell," says big black Daniel, "they're sampling us. I'll swear it." Indeed he has already sworn.

"Or like they're tuning in," says Svelte.

A comprehensible sentence emerges:

Why you bring child must die without ʒʒʒwʒʒ without without cage? This is the only time a Varroa has ever communicated anything.

But no child is here…

"It thinks Jacko's a child. The dead body isn't a child!" I shout out at the Varroa. "The dead body is a very short adult, too short to receive a cage!"

How you open zzzwzz open open **hoop?**

Daniel prods one finger upward defiantly at the Varroa. "With our music, that's how! You want to buy a memory stick?"

Unready.

"Yeah, don't have no memory sticks here, do I?"

Unready.

I have a sense that the Varroa are lower-level intelligences compared with whatever may have created them. Bred them. Assembled them. I think sheepdogs – times ten as regards capabilities.

Above us, the two Varroa begin to circle. No, that circle is spiralling outward.

Very soon they're racing around, dodging the tall feather trees, looping around all of us. Their hum is loud, MUM-UM-MUM-UM. A curving line of bright light begins to follow each now like contrails, two lengthening arcs of light which soon join up. Those Varroa are guiding the huge horizontal hoop encompassing all of us – suddenly intensifying as it flashes towards the ground which is of rough short moonlit grass, and I do keep my footing while a fair few around me are tumbling because of impeds or disorientation. As the afterimage of the ring of light fades, an expanse of flat concrete stretches into the distance where I'm making out large low buildings and silhouettes of big parked planes, passenger jets. And a half-full Moon's in the sky amidst clouds and stars. Already people are struggling up or being helped. We've been dumped unceremoniously at a huge airport near an unlit runway, though further off are a fair number of lights. We conserve power nowadays where possible. Someone's whimpering about their ankle, twisted or broken.

"It's Heathrow!" shrills a girl.

Airports are anonymous, yet that could easily be Western

Avenue over there on the perimeter, where any hotels remaining open won't have many guests these days. This may well be London's Heathrow, nowhere near so busy as used to be.

Of a sudden the runway lights come on – on account of us arriving? Shall we pretend to be a planeload of passengers, newly descended from Sirius or some other star? Please proceed to passport control – what, no baggage? People begin heading towards the illuminated runway but Bryce bellows, "Stay here, everyone! The runway's dangerous. A plane'll be landing."

"There's no plane –"

"Idiot, they don't switch the lights on at the very last moment. Plane'll be ten minutes away." Of course he's right.

Svelte's shining a slim torch, here, there.

"Lost something?" Tony asks her.

"Looking for feathers."

I see none in the beam from Svelte's torch. The Varroa or the big hoop must have retained any alien vegetation in the process of returning us – to a big empty flat space where we wouldn't collide with anything.

"Everybody stay right here," I call out. "I'll have us collected, bussed back to The Studio."

Now there's a signal for my phone. *Dee-du-doo-doo-du-do...* ring ring.

"That place was artificial," Svelte insists to me as our crowded coach, the foremost of three, finally nears Lambeth. Combi-Intel persons on each coach are busy doing preliminary interviews of the club-nighters. There'll be a lot more interrogation by and by, especially of Daniel and Sean and Alan and June, although I suspect that neither QE nor anyone else will be able to control a hoop again by that same method. For we are unready.

"Made. Grown. The way you grow pretty crystals in a jar of some liquid.

Maybe the feathers were all like sensors on the outside of some machine the size of a world. Or not as big – gravity could have been artificial. Maybe the place was a pleasure park for aliens, or like a sculpture garden. But artificial, yes."

"So what does that imply?"

"I don't know." Svelte stares out of the window at houses, streets.

What does *unready* mean? Can the impeds be some sort of benevolent teaching aid? A focus for mental growth? A way of being able to attain the stars and join in, if only we can discover how? Something we might learn to use after ten years or after fifty years? The Varroa didn't mean that it wasn't in the market for a memory stick.

"We'll talk more later about this artificial idea of yours, eh Svelte?" Oh I am tempted by her, and I still don't know if it's possible. If only. Just let me not be too impulsive, as I surely was, going to club-night with her, only the two of us and Tony Cullen. In retrospect I was rather foolish. I don't like to be foolish.

One person is unaccounted for, the dead Jacko. Is that because his body was lying beyond the ring of light when it descended? Or because a dead body is more akin to a feather-bush than to a living person?

Now that we've debussed, Pete is talking urgently to Caz, and I'm a snooper again.

"…meaningless, because Benny helped bugger all! He made a phone call; so what? What else does the co-owner of a place do, that loses a couple of hundred people? Pay no attention? It was the Varroa brought us back, no thanks to him!"

"Even so," she says, so sad-sounding, "I did promise." Caz tosses her hair, perhaps to hide tears or dispel them, and wanders towards The Studio.

We all have our cages. But will we ever learn from them?

The narrator of this story, who works for Combined Intelligence, is a kind of lesbian sister to the narrator of my novel Mockymen *who investigates the eponymous aliens with mysterious motives who use human body hosts to get around in our world. Years ago I made a note of the name* Varroa, *because this parasite and disease of bees seemed like a very suitable name for an alien race: The* Varroa. *Add bodily piercings, involuntary and taken to an extreme; plus what I know about Synth and Techno music (whose fans may well respond, "Not enough!"), and "Cages" came together. Clang.*

Weredog of Bucharest

Shortly before driving into Bucharest proper, we stopped for a pee in some bushes. Twice en route we'd seen men vomiting into roadside shrubbery, probably on account of drinking bad tap water, so use of bushes seemed normal. A tall sign announced: *Parking, Kebab, Sexy Show, Motel, Telefon.* We only required the first of those, just for a few minutes. We'd been in Inspector Badelescu's black BMW (with 120,000 kilometres on the clock) for little over an hour, but prior to leaving the island in the Danube we'd had a few beers. Endless maize stretched around our roadside oasis, although a strong odour of pigs hung in the air, which must be coming from the dilapidated barns nearby.

Slumped on their sides in the dust by the bushes, under some tree shade, were three tatty though sizeable mongrels, fawn-coloured with white patches. At our approach, two of the dogs raised their heads and regarded us with utter apathy in their lacklustre eyes. The third remained sprawled as though life was too exhausting, or the temperature too high to bother moving. Oh, all of a sudden one pooch scrambled up and stood facing us, its ears half-cocked like bat wings, its tail half lifted.

Badelescu stooped, scooped up a stone and threw it, not for the mongrel to chase and fetch, but at the dog's flank. The animal yipped and scuttled away.

"Fucking things," he said to me amiably. "Don't worry about rabies; and I have my gun if they show their teeth. Most are too tired and weak with hunger. Welcome to Bucharest from its canine inhabitants."

"A million stray dogs in the city," Adriana, my impromptu translator, called after me, whether in warning or simply by way of explanation I couldn't be sure. Adriana was unconsciously beautiful in the way that so many young Romanian women were

– graceful, long-legged, fine sensuous figure in tight jeans and blouse. On the whole, Romanian women didn't seem to realize they were gorgeous, because so many were, therefore this was normal. Adriana wore her dark silky hair in a very long ponytail, which I had held with great satisfaction in a tent on the island while with my other hand I gave her pleasure as her head tried to toss from side to side, but couldn't, while she groaned and cries jerked from her.

Adriana was staying to guard the car since she hadn't drunk so much; and it would have been more complicated for her to pee in bushes, the way we all had on the island.

So I sprayed the gritty soil, along with the Inspector and Romulus, whose second name I couldn't remember, and Virgil Gramescu. At times Romanians could sound like the Lost Legion, which in a sense they were. Inspector Badelescu's first name was Ovid.

Quickly I returned to Adriana, who was smoking.

"Do you know, Paul," she said to me, "when the Mayor of Bucharest proposed exterminating all the strays, Brigitte Bardot flew here on a mercy mission to dissuade him? According to one version of the story, Brigitte donated a lot of money for a dogs' home. Consequently two hundred strays live in luxury, then the extermination went ahead anyway. But it must have failed, or else the survivors bred very fast. The number of dogs on the streets is as high as ever."

"Are they dangerous?"

"Only in winter, if they form packs. Sometimes a baby or little child gets carried off."

Brushing back his oiled dark hair, Ovid Badelescu was about to say something when a jangle of bells sounded from within his shirt pocket, so he fished out his mobile.

And frowned, and queried, and queried again and again in Romanian.

He shut the phone, and said, "Bad news. A young woman has been torn apart in an elevator in the centre of the city."

"Torn *apart?*" I exclaimed.

"Not literally limb from limb," he said. "I mean savaged to death, with terrible injuries. I must go there immediately. Do you want to see?" he asked me. "Or wait in the car, which might be tiresome in this heat? Virgil and Romulus can make their way home from there. Or you might prefer to have lunch with Adriana."

Have lunch, or visit an appalling murder scene? I was incredulous. "Do you mean see *the body?*"

The Inspector laughed. "No, an ambulance is taking it to the morgue. Although you can visit the morgue if you're really curious. I meant the scene of the crime. I've been called there because of a Jack the Raper murder I was involved with last year. Do I mean raper? No, ripper. Rapers don't often rip. They may strangle or stab, but not do complete ripping. Not usually."

"A *solved* murder?"

"The murderer might have been a Turk," he replied. "But he disappeared. Ankara couldn't trace him, nor Interpol in case he hid among the Turks in Germany."

I couldn't help wondering if he said Ankara and Interpol to enhance his importance. And I supposed I must attribute his comparative nonchalance, or what I took as nonchalance, first of all to the requirements of haste, and secondly to whatever other horrors he may have experienced in his job.

We'd been a mixed bunch on that cultural island in the Danube. Lots of beautiful Romanian girls, and handsome youths too, the annual event being sponsored by the Ministry for Youth Development. A Bulgarian kick-boxing champion who gave open-air classes, an astronomer who appealed to science fiction fans, several musicians and poets, an American from an Institute for Human Development who believed that immortality is within our grasp, an angry German feminist. I could go on.

I would describe my own writings as psychological horror, or perhaps darkness, which illuminates the mundane world, paradoxically heightening our awareness, although I was published as Crime. Consequently, my 'real world counterpart' was the Inspector with his theories about order and disorder, darkness and light within society; and, of course, his wealth of practical experience which he became intent on demonstrating to me, either for egotistical or for inspirational reasons, or maybe because he genuinely liked me. Hence his driving me back to Bucharest, to show me things, which seductive Adriana was also intent on. In her case, maybe with a tentative motive of gaining an author from abroad as a husband, a foreign passport, a different life? Authors are esteemed unduly in some countries. Or maybe Adriana merely wanted some fun, and to enjoy herself. When I explained that my surname, Osler, was originally a French name for someone who catches wild birds, Adriana had been highly amused.

I'd been persuaded to pay my own, fairly minimal airfare from England, by fellow crime author Max Rigby who was moving slowly around Eastern Europe and who had already enjoyed the free hospitality of the island the year before. Currently Max was renting a flat in Bucharest, where I'd stay for a week. Other habitués of the island were driving Max back to the city.

Max was seeking exotic foreign settings for future novels because frankly, in my opinion, his most recent book, set in England, had seemed lacklustre and ho-hum. Competently done, to be sure, but lacking the additional frisson of strangeness which distinguishes a competent book from something exceptional. I'd said so myself in no uncertain terms in a review which I certainly *didn't* sign with my own name, concocting an alias – Martin Fairfax (a reviewer should always seem fair) which ironically, as I realised later, was the name of a minor character in one of my early books, long out of print. Should I beware of impending Alzheimer's? Not so long as I continued drinking red wine.

With so many Eastern European countries joining the EU, and so many citizens of those countries settling in Britain for jobs, not least about a million Poles, obviously one should expand one's repertoire, which was a reason why Max easily persuaded me to visit Romania.

Badelescu, though I suppose I should more familiarly call him Ovid, placed a flasher on the roof of his BMW, and we sirened our way past trolleybuses, trucks, a convoy of giant Turkish lorries, decrepit Dacias and flashier new cars, along tree-lined avenues, the trunks painted white.

I pointed, and asked Adriana, "Is that so you can see the trees in the dark?"

"Do you know why we're giving a lift to Virgil?" she replied. "He wouldn't get to the island otherwise. That's because his wife crashed their car into the only other car on a huge empty boulevard." She zig-zagged her hands as if steering two vehicles. "From hundreds of metres apart they start trying to avoid each other. Romulus's wife steers left, the other guy steers right. Then they change their minds and directions a dozen times. Until *crash*. It was incredibly bad luck."

"And neither of them slowed down?"

"Why do that, on an empty boulevard?"

Presently, the dilapidated city mutated into a Futureville of huge white buildings adorned with balconies. Part-way round a huge piazza, police vehicles clustered, on and off a broad pavement. Ovid kept his siren howling to herald his arrival until we had parked.

Bye-bye to Romulus and Virgil, who sauntered off with their rucksacks.

"Oh, look," said Adriana, pointing into the distance along a vast boulevard. "Ceauşescu's palace, there at the far end."

That was my first view of the dead dictator's megalomaniac structure, supposedly the second largest building in the world. Even dwarfed by distance it *loomed*. And the great bright apartment building where the murder had happened was in direct line of sight.

Ovid informed me, "This place was built for the Securitate, but it was only finished after the Revolution. Come on!"

The Securitate: Ceaușescu's secret police whose surveillance of Romania's citizens was very exhaustive indeed, and whose network of informers, many of those against their will or wishes, may have comprised a significant percentage of the population.

"I don't want blood on my shoes," said Adriana.

If she went home, how was I going to find Max's flat? The Inspector might become too busy to drive me there, and I felt dubious about trusting myself to a taxi driver in an unknown city when I only knew a few phrases of Romanian that Adriana and others had taught me on the island. Ah, Max could come and fetch me, because my mobile now had a Romanian sim-card. However, Adriana spied a café. Yellow Bergenbier umbrellas cum sunshades outside sheltered tables and chairs. Half a dozen large mongrels lay nearby.

"I'll buy a magazine and wait for you in there, okay?"

Accordingly, in went Ovid and I to find the Boys in Blue busy on the ground floor examining an open lift, the floor and walls of which were very bloody. I'd been at two or three actual crime scenes before, yet here it was as if a madman had thrown crimson paint around. The smell, however, wasn't of paint but of a slaughterhouse. I presumed my presence was explained cursorily by Ovid, since various police nodded at me before, as I supposed, reporting circumstances to him in Romanian.

"So, Mr Story Writer," Ovid said after peering assiduously, "what do you notice?"

"Less blood on the floor outside than I'd have expected," I suggested.

"And that probably caused by us police and by the ambulance people. It seems there are some bloody tracks and drops on the sixth floor, but again not too much blood is in the corridor up there."

"So she was attacked inside the lift, with the doors shut."

"Precisely. And I think I know how."

Ovid stepped inside the lift fastidiously, crouched, and peered at the panelled rear wall which was almost unstained. Then he inserted his little finger somewhere amongst the woodwork, and pulled. The rear wall split in half, opening as two floor-to-ceiling doors. Behind was a space large enough for a couple of people to stand, or kneel, between the true rear wall and the false wall. And the true rear wall was bloody, as were the insides of the doors.

"Here," said Ovid, "is where the killer hid, to burst out suddenly between floors. I told you this building was made for the Securitate, but about six thousand special spies spied upon the secret police themselves by such bizarre methods as this. No doubt a microphone would have been hidden inside the elevator, but here's a back-up, just in case. A man sitting on a stool could look and listen through the tiny hole in the wall."

The sheer shock of being between floors in an otherwise empty lift when suddenly the wall opened and another person emerged! The victim might faint or even die at once of a heart attack.

Ovid explained in Romanian, and the lesser police looked at him in admiration.

Of course we climbed the white marble stairs to the sixth floor rather than using the lift.

It seemed to me that the tracks up there were rather narrow to be those of shoes or trainers. They became vague after not too many paces.

Adriana pointed through the café window at one of the tall white apartments around the piazza, blue sky showing through
. ornamental turrets along the edge of the rooftop.

"Sniper watchtowers," she said. "You could shoot down into any rebellious crowds."

We were inside for the air conditioning. So were some bleached-blond youths wearing gold chains, sunglasses pushed up on top of their heads, sons of the new rich.

"You say the tracks of blood were narrow." She shuddered and crossed herself. "I think a werewolf killed that woman in the elevator. Probably the Inspector thinks so too, but he wouldn't tell you that."

"Werewolves aren't real," I protested.

"In Romania they are. And weredogs, *priccoltish*. With a million dogs on the streets it can't be surprising if at least one is a weredog. It's the perfect place to hide. Unless," she added with what seemed at first a wonderful lack of logical connection, "Badelescu thinks a Turk did it. Maybe he hopes that's the answer."

"Why blame a Turk?"

"They ruled us for three hundred years, consequently many Romanians don't like them much. Better a Turk than a werewolf. I'll see if there are any news reports yet."

Flipping open her phone, she googled.

Bucharest had very speedily updated itself to a cybercity. I thought of old women draped in black guarding a single cow or a few geese by the roadside out in the country. Truly, the last shall be first technologically.

"No, nothing yet." Rather too soon for news.

"Will you take me to Max? And maybe I can see you tomorrow?" In fact, I felt a bit tired, but also I wanted to make notes about the murder scene.

"Tomorrow," she said. "I don't know. I'll phone. Yes, probably." She wasn't going to seem over-eager, but she wanted me to feel eager.

Max's place proved not to be far, just beyond the boundary where Ceauşescu's architectural master plan had erased a vast area of the old city – houses, churches, whatever was in the way – to make space for ostentatious modernity.

The flat was on the top floor of a modest block. To the front, the outlook was upon a line of trees, then some open grass, then low houses with red roofs suddenly abutting a towering wall of vast white apartments. Directly below, was a very modest old cottage to which were attached a clutter of small corrugated roofed sheds, surrounded by rows of vegetables, bean poles – I even spotted some geese and hens – all within a green-painted picket fence.

Incongruously next to this relic of the past was a sizeable ultra-posh house in Art Deco style, gleamingly white.

"Probably an old lady died there and her heirs accepted an offer they couldn't refuse," said Max. Max was short and burly and wore an assertively black moustache, although his hair had lightened and receded a long way. I didn't know if he dyed the moustache.

"So the old woman directly below hasn't died yet?"

"I've never seen her."

My room contained a double bed, a large wardrobe, and a bench press which seemed to have strayed from some gym. Frills were lacking, yet the furnishings sufficed for sport that I anticipated with Adriana. On the bed, I mean, not on the bench press.

"Chap called Silviu may be coming round to take us somewhere," Max told me. "Couple of days before I went to the island, Silviu told me the sad story of how his mother's son by a previous marriage had suddenly died from premature kidney failure. He begged me to lend him three hundred dollars for the funeral because his mother couldn't afford it. So I did. Very next day, I bump into Silviu and he proudly shows me this expensive new camera he just bought. You know, *innocently* shows me the camera because he's so excited and happy. I ought to have got mad at him. But it was my own fault. You don't lend money to people here unless you're willing to regard it as a gift. Some day they'll do something for you, perhaps. Well, Silviu phoned an hour ago and I said, Come and drive us somewhere tonight, right?"

"Somewhere?"

"Educational. In your honour. Writers in the crime line need to research sleaze." So saying, Max cast himself upon a sofa and reached for a elegant glossy English language magazine, published for expats no doubt, its cover a stylish photo of giant terracotta garden urns. Thumbing to the back, he intoned:

"Royal Orchid Male Sacred Spot Massage. A gentle digital technique for contacting these subtle places. In the internal way a lubricated finger will be inserted into the anus, and then it will gently massage around the chestnut-sized and shaped prostate. This feels better when you are somewhat erect and excited and if it's done during the intimate massage (don't worry, the girls will take care of that) it will produce a very thrilling orgasm."

"You're making that up."

"I'm not. This is Bucharest. Take a look."

I looked, and it was true.

"I thought that mag was the local *Homes and Gardens*."

"And casinos and escorts."

"Um, I don't want a finger stuck up my bum, Max."

My writerly colleague grinned. "Do you have piles? Don't worry, we aren't doing any such thing. Tonight will only cost a few dollars for drinks. It's purely educational. Background research. Anyway, what kept you?"

"Ovid Badelescu got called to a murder site."

"Do tell!"

I proceeded to, but didn't inform Max about the concealed doors at the back of the lift – I might want to use that detail some day myself. I also excluded Adriana's notion that a werewolf was responsible. Or a weredog, hiding out among the multitude of anonymous mongrels.

Shortly before Silviu arrived, a long cry and a chorus of yapping from outside drew me to the window. The cry was like that of a muezzin calling worshippers to prayer. A middle-aged woman wearing a baggy multicoloured dress and headscarf was driving her horse and cart loaded with scrap metal and other rubbish that might be worth something. Her cry had excited the dogs. As I watched, she halted beside the humble cottage, dismounted, and rattled the picket gate with a stick. And waited.

Presently, a black-clad shape emerged from the cottage, cradling what I identified as a broken old clock of some bulk. With a surprisingly sprightly step, the old cottager bustled to her gate and handed over the relic, to receive in return after humming and hawing some scrap of paper, which might have been a banknote – if so, here in Romania it would have been thin plastic which looked like paper.

As the horse and cart and the scrap-woman's outcry proceeded onward, the strangest thing happened. Half a dozen strays sidled from different directions towards that garden gate. The black-garbed cottager glanced about, as though to ensure that no one was observing her – she wouldn't spot me at the window high up – then she offered her hand over the gate. Was she about to feed the strays with scraps? But she was holding nothing that I could see.

One by one those desolate dogs proceeded to lick, or slobber on, her palm – I was put in mind of nothing so much as movies of Italian gangsters kissing the hand of their Mafia godfather! This done, the cottager withdrew her hand, and then herself quickly back into her home.

Travellers in unfamiliar countries often misinterpret things and leap to the wrong conclusions, but I've always had a strong sense of intuition, a belief in quasi-magical linkages which others call coincidences. In my novels such is the way that a dark crime is often solved. There's a logical sequence of circumstances, yet this is only revealed – illuminated, if you like – by illogical means, by an illogical route. That Ovid should have driven me directly to that blood-stained lift in the former Securitate building, then that I should come to Max's and overlook that cottage, cast adrift while time and town planning advanced, and that I should glimpse the owner, queen of canines, whom Max had never seen… this spoke to me inwardly, compellingly.

Silviu proved to be a tall wispy person, wearing a somewhat

soiled lightweight cream suit. His eyes seemed to me very blue, and his English was quite good. What an honour to be meeting a famous colleague of famous Max.

We descended to the street, to climb into an elderly white Dacia which had suffered bumps and scrapes through the years. Although early evening by now, the air was still sultry and cloying. I felt a strange mixture of reinvigoration due to my sighting of the crone of the cottage, and languor, as though I was surrendering to whatever the night might contain.

First, we went to an open-air restaurant to drink beer called Ursus and eat rolls of minced meat and salad, and spend, or rather squander, some time. Time seemed to have a way of melting in this city. Apparently we were to meet a mad genius. But after an hour the man phoned, depressed – his father had a sudden brain tumour. Maybe an excuse, maybe true or half-true. And that was the last I heard of the genius. Silviu went off and brought back a newspaper, and the murder did feature. Silviu translated the story, but already I knew more than the reporter had discovered.

Then Ovid phoned my mobile.

"Paul, where are you?"

I consulted with Max, who took the phone and said, "We're at the meech" (I think) "place on," and he named a street. "But we're going to Herestrau afterwards."

They talked for a while, then Max ended the call and handed my phone back.

"He'll try and join us." Then, surveying our surroundings, he remarked that under Communism people went to restaurants for show, not for the food – to be seen in such a place, rich enough to buy a meal, of which they would then eat every morsel, instinctively, even if it burst them. Silviu listened politely and nodded. He had cleaned his plate, and I guessed that Max would be footing the bill, unless he and I shared it. I wondered if the crone of the cottage had ever been near a restaurant during her entire life. I thought of an appetite so voracious that a person would ravage a body bloody in a lift.

Herestrau proved to be a sizeable lake within a park. By now evening had arrived. We halted on a tree-lined roadway inside the park behind a line of cars far more luxurious and up-to-date than Silviu's. Silviu seemed edgy. Dogs lay round in the gloom like mounds of earth. On a bench a shaven-headed man, dressed in a leather jacket, was lounging.

"It's all right, Silviu," said Max. "I'll give him a little money. Car insurance," he told me. "Even though Silviu's car is an old wreck, best to be on the safe side."

Evidently Max knew how much, or how little, to give. I felt a double sense of mild menace at Max's casual determination to show me how *au fait* he was with life here, and at the implications of myself not knowing the ropes. My host, full of bonhomie, was also my rival. Which would explain, in retrospect, this particular outing tonight.

Scarcely had Max returned from paying Leather Jacket to keep an eye on the car than Ovid drew up behind us in his BMW. Getting out, Ovid waved casually at Leather Jacket, but Ovid certainly didn't bother to cross the road to say anything to the man. So probably Max had wasted his money, seeing that we were now associated with an Inspector of police. It struck me as only mildly sinister that Ovid should turn up immediately after us, almost as though we were back in Securitate times when everyone's exact whereabouts were monitored.

A short walk brought us to a big, though modestly lit, building on the shore of the lake. Two suited bouncers stood outside, smoking.

Inside, a few men sat at tables with beautiful girls, and a little crowd of likewise lovely tall girls were shuffling round in a slow dance to the background music. A trio of the Bleached Boys sporting gold looked like pimps in this setting.

"The girls aren't in their underwear here," Max pointed out. "They can wear casual clothes, so there's no pole dancing, if you're disappointed. This is classy sleaze."

We sat and ordered beers, the cheapest option.

"Anything new about the lift murder?" I asked Ovid.

"Autopsy," he said. "Terrible claw-like injuries and animal-like bites. The Turk may have worn specially adapted gauntlets and not had his own teeth any more but special false fanged ones. If he needs false teeth, maybe he's fifty or sixty years old, though very strong." After saying which, he winked at me. Was he teasing me? Or satirising himself? And avoiding confiding whatever the police now knew?

When our beers arrived, girls came to sit with us. One plumped herself on to my lap and wiggled about.

"You can talk free for ten minutes," whispered Max, "then she'll ask you to buy her a drink. That's only about ten dollars, so you decide."

"What's your name?" I asked my sexy burden, whose face was unusually broad, her eyes wide-spaced, though her figure was impeccable.

"Luciana. And what do they call you?"

Quite soon I said, "Where did you learn such good English?"

"In school, of course. I also speak German and Italian. A lot of Italians live in Romania, and Germans visit."

"So, Luciana, do you like working in this place?"

"It's better than my home town. But I'd like a real job some time."

"What do you mean by a real job?"

"Oh, a shop assistant, for instance."

"My God, speaking four languages you could at least be an interpreter or an air hostess."

Max whispered, "If you ask a schoolgirl in the countryside what she wants to be, she'll say a prostitute, so she can meet foreign men."

Ovid and Silviu were talking in Romanian all this time, ignoring the girls on either side of them, who reacted by chattering behind their backs, displaying nail varnish.

"Will you buy me a drink?" asked Luciana. "Or else I can't stay with you."

I decided to do so, as did Max for his own blonde companion.

"If you want to take yours to the flat," mentioned my host, "it's best you both arrange to meet outside, then the club doesn't get commission."

"Doesn't the club object?"

"No, it's understood. So long as you don't actually leave the premises along with her."

Prompted, Luciana squirmed and said, "I love sex. Will you take me home tonight for a hundred dollars?"

"Offer her two thousand Lei."

"Oh no, that is much too little," protested Luciana. "Fifty dollars."

"But I already have Adriana," I told Max.

"Maybe you ought to have variety. In case you overvalue Adriana."

Evidently Max had my best interests at heart!

Just then Ovid's mobile jangled and his side of the conversation certainly intrigued Silviu and all of the girls.

Ovid looked across at me. "There's been another killing. Same MO. Modus operandi," he added. "I must go." He threw an arm around his neglected girl and hugged her. "Don't worry, the arm of the law will protect you." She giggled.

"May I come with you?" I asked.

"Yes. No. Yes. Why not? Taxi for you afterwards." He threw down some money.

"How much do I owe for the drinks?" I asked Max.

"We'll sort it out tomorrow. You'll need a key." He fished in his pocket. "Oh, do you mind if I take a girl home with me?"

"Of course not."

How could I possibly mind? Yet I did. Not for any moral reason, but because this seemed a bit, shall we say, oppressive, as regards myself rather than the girl. However, I was about to walk out on my host.

The crime scene, as I reckoned after a summoned taxi finally returned me, was only about three kilometres from Max's flat, in a big apartment block not completely fitted out inside, consequently only semi-occupied. Not a lift, this time, but a coin-operated mini-laundry in the basement. The victim was another young woman. The discoverer was her boyfriend, when she failed to return to their flat; although he had been taken back upstairs for questioning, and the body was about to be zipped up by the time Ovid and I walked in. I glimpsed something from a butcher's shop, or abattoir, like paintings by Soutine of carcasses of beef. Flayed, was my impression. A torn, blood-soaked skirt and blouse, and other scattered garments, lay as if really needing the services of the half-full washing machine which yawned open.

I thought of Luciana and so many others like her, innocently vulnerable in the city, yet eager for money. In fact this murder had nothing to do with prostitutes, but my writerly brain was at work.

When I emerged from my bedroom relatively early, Max was through in the tiny kitchen drinking coffee boiled in a steel pot on a gas ring. His own bedroom door stood open. No evidence of any prostitute.

"Has she gone already?"

"I changed my mind. The girls ask less after midnight when they get worried they won't earn, but I couldn't be bothered to wait." *If that was true – if he hadn't just wanted to have an effect upon me.* "So what of the second atrocity?"

"Atrocities involve lots of people, not just one."

"Two now. Could be a cumulative atrocity? How many does it take? Actually, a single act of brutality qualifies as an atrocity."

I ignored this casuistry, even if he was right.

Dogs howled and yodelled, and a few moments later the

building shuddered briefly.

"Minor earthquake, don't worry. There's glacial moraine under Bucharest. Some land moves horizontally, some vertically, some is mixed. That's why it's very expensive to build here. The *atrocity*," he pressed me.

So I described the brutal scene, though I did not mention my image of paintings by Soutine.

Max took me for a walk around his neighbourhood, which was distinctly run down, although parts were being poshed up by new money, seemingly at random. In the middle of a potholed back street asphalt burned and bubbled blackly.

Max laughed. "Some builder needs hot tar for a job, so he set fire to it. Obviously the middle of the street is safer than the sides." He laughed. "Romanians don't think of consequences. They'll run you over in the street because they don't think of prison as the result. I'm not kidding. They will not stop. Oops," and he caught my arm and dragged me well to one side because a battered pick-up truck was indeed heading our way, and to avoid the fire the driver mounted the pavement. Max had hurt my arm with his grip, though for a perfectly good reason, so I tried not to show pain.

We must have seen a score of skinny roaming dogs already, variously marked, although all of the same general build.

"Ha," said Max. "That crime scene reminds me of a joke. Which I've already *used*, by the way," he emphasised. "A forgetful man visits a short-sighted gypsy fortune teller. She looks at his palm, and exclaims, 'I see men with knives coming for you – and blood!' He starts sweating with fear. She examines his palm even more closely and finally says, 'You forgot to take off your pigskin glove'."

"Ha ha," I said. A perverse urge tempted me to add: "I'm glad you already used it."

"As for drivers and future consequences," he went on, as though I'd said nothing at all, "Romanian people choose to be suspended in eternity. It's still difficult for them to get over the dictatorship. Safer not to take responsibility."

"*Suspended in eternity* is quite a phrase. I suppose you'll be using that too."

He nodded, appeased or otherwise I couldn't decide. Time was melting again, like the runny hot asphalt. Already it was afternoon. So Max led me circuitously to a café he favoured, for some beer.

Halfway through the second can of Ursus, Adriana phoned me.

"Are you free this afternoon?" I asked her. "What are we doing this afternoon?" I asked Max almost simultaneously.

"I need to buy a camera card," was Max's reply. "You can come or not."

I was, of course, eager for Adriana to visit me privately on my own, although not entirely for the obvious reason of possible sex. Max-out-of-the-way would suit me very well, doubly so.

Max had already buzzed off, and I didn't know when he'd be back. Given the vagaries of Bucharest, maybe hours as yet.

I kissed Adriana enthusiastically. "Lovely to see you! Look, do you think we could pop over the road for a few minutes? I'm very curious about the old woman in that cottage. If it's half way possible, I'm dying to see inside, and see her close to. Could we pretend that I want to buy some eggs?"

"I suppose so. She might sell some eggs."

"Oh, and don't tell Max, will you not?"

Adriana grinned. "How mysterious you crime writers are. Men of mystery are exciting."

The crone's door was intricately carved, and worn, as though it preceded the city or had been transported here from a farm in the country, perhaps one of the tens of thousands bulldozed under Ceauşescu for a dam or for socialist rationalisation.

The owner's face was rutted, like carved and varnished wood

itself, though her brown eyes were alert. Blackness scarfed her and draped her. After Adriana explained in Romanian, the woman uttered a brief reply or a cackle.

"Tell her," I suggested, "that I'm a writer and, in addition to eggs, I'm very interested in her life here surrounded by modern city. I'll pay her for her time, twenty dollars, no make that thirty."

"Twenty," said Adriana, and complied.

Surprisingly, or unsurprisingly, the crone – Madame Florescu, now, to be polite – admitted us into a gloomy room and stuck out a hand dark with dirt or the resin of age, into which I counted four five-dollar bills, which she sniffed before promptly disappearing them within her neckline as though she was some much younger entertainer who used her cleavage for tips.

I took in the items of rustic homemade furniture, the blackened pots and pans and jars of herbs and other stuff. Rather a lot of green candles stood around in old brass candlesticks, understandable if Madame Florescu had no mains power, as seemed likely. A faint sickly odour emanated from vases of marigolds and ox-eyed daisies which were red rather than white, and strangely from lilies-of-the-valley which surely should be past their season, unless the Romanian variety was different or else the crone had patronised a florist's shop for blooms flown from far away.

Coincidentally, Adriana was translating, "A present from my son," when she herself really noticed those flowers, and gasped and crossed herself.

"My son visits me once a week of an evening after he finishes working hard, a good boy," Adriana continued dutifully interpreting despite whatever had shocked her.

"You would like him. He also can tell you remarkable things – in your own English. He's clever." And can do with some dollars himself, I thought. "You sleep only over the street. If you see a red Dacia outside here, probably on Thursday, come and knock. A red Dacia which says taxi, but my son is more than taxi-driver."

Thursday was the day after next. If only Max would leave me alone that evening.

Mrs Florescu discoursed about geese and her water butt and her man who had been killed by the Securitate. Apparently her man was a black marketeer. After a reasonable time she dried up and looked expectant. My twenty dollars had run out as though all the while a taxi meter had been running in her head. I said that I'd love to hear more from herself and her son on Thursday. I was becoming hungry for Adriana before Max would return. Besides, rather than hearing more domestic details, I wanted to know what had visibly shocked Adriana.

I departed with three eggs clutched in my hand. Once we had recrossed the road, yet another dog wandered close. My body hiding what I was doing, in case Madame Florescu was looking out, I dropped the eggs to make raw omelette. The pooch sidled swiftly towards this in a flinching manner, sniffed, then lapped, crunchy eggshells included.

"Oh, Paul! Butter fingers. Isn't that what you say?"

Of course I didn't want Max to have a clue as to what I'd been up to, by leaving eggs in his fridge

"The dog's need is greater than mine," I assured her. "To tell the truth, I don't like eggs much in any form."

"Yes, it was those flowers," Adriana confirmed once we were in the flat. "Those ones are used in the countryside to attract werewolves. Because of the smell."

"To *attract* werewolves?"

"Maybe to control, or to cause. My own mother warned me never to wear the, um, the little white bells."

I felt quite pleased with myself.

I felt even more pleased when Adriana amiably consented to test my double bed. The bench press was useful to dump our clothes on. Afterwards, she fell asleep, and looked very innocent as though orgasm had drained away all cares.

Next day Max and I visited his Romanian publisher at home for lunch, by taxi. Only one of my books was published locally as yet – which was enough for me to be famous on the island – and I nursed hopes for more translations. Cezar, yet another displaced ancient Roman, was jolly and hospitable with beer, coffee, nuts, and nibbles. We sat, Romanian style, in a dingy courtyard, or patio-alley, running from front to back of his house. Inside, the house's bare floorboards were dirty and the place was full of tat, as I found when I visited the toilet.

A coil of incense set on bricks burned under the plastic patio table. Sometimes the air smelled of patchouli, sometimes of sewage. A guard dog was on a long chain secured to the inside of its kennel. A white cat with a fluffy tail ambled around. A sizeable though twisted tree arose through the concrete of the patio without any evidence of how rain could possibly reach its roots; maybe those had broken through to the sewer for sustenance.

Apparently the crime market was flooded, thus a publisher had to be careful, but if I posted my best books to Cezar he would see. More time dissolved, until the ubiquitous Silviu turned up with his car. And the same camera as, presumably, I'd heard about from Max. Cezar duly admired the camera. Then Max handed Silviu a memory card in its little plastic box. Silviu proceeded to install the memory card and take photos of me and Max and Cezar. This made no sense to me at all. If Max resented lending, or rather giving, the three hundred dollars to Silviu, why then present him with a memory card? Was that in exchange for today's use of petrol? As lanky Silviu focused, he looked like a tall thin photographic tripod. Or bi-pod, I suppose.

Shortly after we left, to drive seemingly aimlessly around the city, rain began to fall heavily. Mighty fountains pluming skyward in vast piazzas fought back against the downpour. We stopped at a café, then when the storm stopped and the sky cleared towards the end of the afternoon, Max said, "Show you something." On foot we turned a few corners into a big boulevard, further along which towered, as Max pointed out, the Intercontinental Hotel.

Spaced along the steaming pavement were prostitutes in mini-skirts, who proved assertive. One delicious girl, who looked no more than fifteen, already wore the scar of a Caesarian above her bared navel pierced with a gold ring. She smooched right up to me and placed her hand on my groin, brazenly massaging, and jerking her head towards a dark deserted arcade. Max stood eyeing me, to see how I would extricate myself, which I did by backing away while wagging a reproving finger, even though I confess I'd become excited.

As we returned to the car, I said, "There's something *predatory* about them."

"Predatory, yes," agreed Max. "*Le mot juste.* They're Gypsies, hoping to prey on foreign businessmen from the Intercontinental. To the Gypsies we're just sheep to be fleeced. In fact, security on the hotel door could send out for better from his catalogue."

Soaked dogs were lapping water.

The murders featured on TV by now, although the set in the flat was crap, even if we could have understood. Max brought out a litre bottle of sweet strong seductive almondy Disaronno, and put on a CD of a Bulgarian pop starlet, then we proceeded to get quite drunk. I realized there was a need to match Max glass for glass. At the same time I didn't want a hangover, nor did I want to stay up half the night.

So when had Max been in Bulgaria? This led to anecdotes about bribing police and much else, a mixture of funny and disconcerting. Then we talked about personalities on the island, or rather Max did most of the talking since he'd known many of those present previously. Idly I wondered whether he had slept with Adriana the year before. Max's recounting became almost a non-stop monologue, which can be intimidating. He was talking at me, rather than with me. At some point sandwiches manifested themselves out of bread, ham, and mustard in the fridge. Finally I managed to finish the last of the bottle. Fingers and toes crossed for the following evening!

Fortunately on the Thursday Max didn't take me to experience more sleaze. Instead we went to tour Ceaușescu's palace, about which much could be said; but I shan't. Wonderfully, Max *would* be absent in the evening. Of course I could accompany him, but I pleaded a queasy stomach and headache. All that Disaronno.

At 7.30 I looked and saw a red Dacia parked outside the cottage. So I sallied forth.

Mihail Florescu, the dutiful son, looked to be in his late fifties, in cheap checked shirt and trousers, grey-haired and with a beer gut. Muscular, though. He welcomed me with delight, as did his mother, who bustled to provide some cubes of cheese and peanuts, while Mihail urged on me a big glass of orange juice. A plastic bucket chair for me. This time I'd brought a notebook. An oil lamp had been lighting the room, but now Mrs Florescu proceeded to light the green candles as well, which produced blue flames.

"How can we help you to write?" asked Mihail, beaming. He meant 'as a writer'.

"Thank *you* for giving me your time," I replied. "Please accept a little compensation." Thirty dollars. I drank juice while he disappeared the money, then began, "I'm curious about those flowers, particularly the little white bells. I hear that in this country they are associated with werewolves."

Mikhail looked blank, so I said, "Excuse me," then mimed a transformation, which must have been successful because he rattled away to his mother, and she to him.

"Yes," he said, "to keep away such things. My mother, all the dogs frighten her. Last winter dog killed chicken."

My throat and tongue felt dry, so I emptied my glass, and realised that the orange juice must have been mixed with some strong spirit, maybe home-made, for all of a sudden I came over queer.

I must have passed out briefly, for mother and son were standing over me, regarding me attentively, and Mrs Florescu was rubbing a smelly ointment on to my brow and cheeks.

God, how parched I was. I croaked for a drink, although I was also feeling a mounting urge to pee. Probably Mrs Florescu's toilet was a dark hole, and I could hardly excuse myself to use her garden, not with her vegetables there. I tried to clench myself tight, but my body felt incoherent. Suddenly I thought of the young Gypsy prostitute with such hunger for her flesh, oh to be able to taste her, drink her juices. Which juices exactly? To my shame, spurts of pee began to pulse into my pants uncontrollably. A restless anxiety mounted. I was quivering – and then I found myself sliding out of the plastic seat, and glad to be nearer the floor on my hands and knees. Four limbs could support me better.

Dog rejoiced ragingly to be let out. Dog loped over empty wasteland. Moonlit. Twitching nose, taunted and teased. So thirsty. Dog-turds pungent. Potholed roadway. Lapped stale rain. Wrong liquid! *Howled.*

In every man: a dog. Turn man inside out, hairs bristle out all over. Dog fell over, scrambled up. Fellow dogs lay curled, muzzles resting on bums. Reek of bitch on heat far away?

The thirst! Not for dog-blood. *Human!*

In moonlit street.

Big stick or long gun. Hairless head shone. Hairs crowded wide and black under nose, above mouth. Dried sweat, and Cologne, and a fart.

Hunting for dog.

Dog hid amongst dogs. Other dogs shifted listlessly.

Dog cowered. Whimpers escaped. Dog buried muzzle in bum. Familiar fragrance of inside-oneself, comforting.

Human came.

Attack, rip with claws, grip throat with teeth so sharp! *No!* Dog feared bang-bang. Dog cringed among dogs. Lone eye watched.

Rattle of laughter.

Human noise: *"So how do you feel now, Mr Martin Fairfax? How does it feel?"*

A camera flashed blindingly.

Head throbbing, I woke to daylight naked on that double bed beside the bench press. What a vile terrible nightmare.

Then I saw my strewn soiled clothes, and discovered the state of my aching body.

I heard the crow of a cock. Was Max waiting patiently next door, drinking coffee?

At first I could hardly stand, weak as a decrepit old man.

Propelled by fear, I recovered some strength. Blessedly Rigby – I couldn't bear to think of him any longer as Max – was absent.

I fled before even worse happened, wheeling my suitcase behind me to the nearest boulevard, flagging a taxi and saying, "Otopeni, vă rog," the name of Bucharest's airport, plus *please*. Of course the driver swindled me, though not grossly. And he *wasn't* Madame Silvestru's son, even though paranoia whispered otherwise.

Rigby had set the trap cunningly.

Admittedly his plan depended on such a crone as Madame Florescu living opposite his flat in such a home as she did. Although how exactly had Rigby located that particular flat? With Silviu's help, in line with what special requirements? Rigby's own research requirements, of which I knew nothing, yet which I'd let lure me like a bee to pollen!

Rigby must have paid the crone and her son quite a few more dollars than I did. And Silviu procured the hallucinogens, whatever those might have been? A cocktail of mandrake, henbane, LSD? Maybe some deadly nightshade and hemlock and mind-altering mushrooms thrown in?

No, how could Silviu, or Rigby, have known what to concoct! The crone must have known.

It couldn't be, could it, that I had truly been transformed? That the crone had thought I wanted to be transformed because of my miming? I'm quite light and short – even so, how heavy a weredog would I have become?

Fortuitous, indeed, that the bloody murders took place!

I would probably have been beguiled by the crone's cottage, even so.

What was Adriana's part in the conspiracy, gasping and crossing herself in timely fashion?

Bitch! I thought.

Bitch seemed entirely the wrong term of abuse. Or maybe entirely the right one.

So how do you feel, Mr Martin Fairfax? Such vindictiveness, on account of a bad review. Rigby must have leaned upon the editor of the mag, or maybe he'd read that early book of mine and the character's name stuck in his mind.

So I departed Romania with my tail, as it were, between my legs.

After I got back home and had recovered myself, I googled using automatic translation and discovered that a man had been arrested for the murders in Bucharest. The presumed perpetrator was a Turko-German drug smuggler, Günther Bey, sporting tattoos featuring Samurai sword fights. Red dye used for sprays and pools of blood, I suppose.

It seemed to me that if the Turko-German's skin bore so much pictorial blood, it was unlikely that he felt a craving to replicate this upon the skins of unfortunate women. If he emulated Japanese gangsters, those people had a code of honour, only killing rivals and enemies within the fraternity.

Ovid had found half-a-Turk to fix up for the killings. It wouldn't do for a werewolf or weredog to be responsible. Romania was a modern country now, a member of the European

Union.

So: did those murders result from a crone applying a potion and a salve? Maybe her own good son Mihail was transformed? No, that was absurd.

Judging from the news, no more such murders happened. If I related my experiences as a short story, this should reflect badly on Rigby, though obviously I'd need to disguise his name...

En route in my Hungarian friend Peter's car from Budapest to Bulgaria, I stopped in Romania's capital for what felt like days on end; and a strange place it seemed indeed, far from being the Paris of the Balkans as it was a century ago, due to the contortions of history. I even kept an illustrated diary on that journey, which I don't normally. Peter only lived in the country next door to Romania, yet even to him Bucharest seemed weird (and Bulgaria, when we finally got there, struck us as comparatively normal despite all the Cyrillic... oh and despite a gibberingly mad taxi driver... and despite the giant restaurant where 150 convention-goers went by arrangement, to encounter precisely one waitress and one menu, so that meals took three hours to reach the tables.).

Being a cat person myself, with a few exceptions I don't much care for dogs, consequently werewolves are far from being my favourite fantasy fix, but there were so many identical-looking stray dogs in Bucharest, slumped, indolent, vaguely sinister, that when Darrell (yes, him again) asked me for an urban werewolf story, far from my comfort zone, this story came together. Oddly, I recently read The Snake Stone *by Jason Goodwin, featuring a Turkish eunuch detective in Eighteen-Thirties Istanbul, and the very same dogs are there too, seemingly too inert to be termed wild.*

Palm Sunday

Today was Saturnday, and tomorrow would be Palm Sunday, when most people would gather in Grand Square to party, then all hold the palms of their hands up to the sky in celebration of life.

As Saturnday dawn was approaching, Rootha left Pool's house. She and Pool had made love, then they had talked for at least an hour, lying together. Several times Rootha and Pool would say exactly the same thing at the same moment, so deep was their communion. Then they made love all over again – before sleeping for three hours, him holding her.

Three hours asleep was time enough for a person's hands to close up and for the patterns of the palms to reshape themselves, for a new fortune to impress itself on the flesh.

Once the sunlight was bright enough, the little cabins of the palm-readers along Riverfront and in Grand Square would open for business. New day, new fortune! Maybe merely a fortune similar to the day before. Business people especially would want their palms interpreted.

Dawn was in the east, violet and lilac, but the full moon still shone through dispersing streamers of raincloud, glinting upon puddles where the street's flagstones tilted. Thus Rootha could avoid soaking her shoes and the hem of her long gown. Joho, her husband, probably wouldn't return on the early steamferry from the capital, but you could never be sure. Don't arouse suspicions.

Yawning before sunset might seem suspicious too. Should she try to catch some extra sleep? Or should she stay awake to visit a teller? The teller might see a change in her destiny. How unfair to stay bound to Joho because he'd lent her parents so much money, when Pool was so perfect for her and she for him

— like hand in glove, like glove on hand. When she first met Pool, going to his shop for a glove fitting, Rootha and he had *fitted* astonishingly. Both knew immediately.

The scent of nightblooms drifted from gardens as Rootha hurried through the deserted streets to a home that wasn't her true home. Joho's business was buying raw gemstones from the hills to the north, and cutting them. Usually he took his cut gems once a month to the capital on the coast. So only once a month, for some hours by night, could Rootha be her real self.

She must *not* resent her dad for his financial failure. Never. Never must she hint at her own sacrifice.

A few hours earlier Pool had told her, not for the first time, "We'll be together in a future life. Next time, we'll meet each other soon. It's destined because we're so like twins, you and I, like separate halves of the same person. And even in this life, who knows what may happen?"

Such as the ferryboat sinking and Joho drowning? Rootha didn't wish to curse her husband, for then she would feel even more guilt.

Later, as Rootha headed for Riverfront, now wearing brown boots and a violet gown, her coal-black hair pinned-up, a carriage overtook her. Fine lady going to have her hand read. Should I invite the mayor to my party, or not since I don't like him much? Should I wear green or gold? Decisions, decisions.

Rootha gazed at the new lines on her own right hand. She had read a pamphlet arguing that the moon and the sun and the world and the stars all pulled at people's mutable palms, just as the moon pulled tides. Nonsense! For if that was so, everybody in the same town ought to show almost identical lines. The science of reading palms was very complex. Apprentice tellers took three years to master the subject. In the past, centuries had gone into understanding the shiftings of destiny.

As she walked, she fiddled with her bronze binding band. The weld was almost seamless. After the ceremony, a young cousin had asked her, "Does it hurt, the soldering?" Of course not. Brides mustn't scream or whimper. A thin pad, slid between wrist and band, blocked almost all the heat. If only she could wrench the band from her wrist, and undo all her union with Joho.

Beyond the curving low-walled esplanade of Riverside the river was very wide and slow, almost a lake. Fishermen were out in their boats, lines baited. Aha, one man scooped up a big squirming catch in his hand-net. First of the day, because he hallooed, knifed the fish loose from the hook, swung the net around and around his head – then hurled the fish towards the nearest boat, where another fisherman caught it in his hand-net. With a halloo, that man sent the fish onward. *Halloo-halloo* rang across the water as the tossed catch went this way and that till one man overreached and fell in. Merrily all the fisherman flourished an open hand. Lucky in its escape, unlucky in its wounded mouth, the fish would be swimming away, gasping water.

Rootha was drowning, living with Joho, now that she knew Pool existed. He was her air.

How was Pool not infuriated with jealousy? He was remarkable, unique, like no other man. True, Pool knew that Joho was very unlikely to give Rootha a child. Though lately Joho had been suggesting adoption. An adopted infant in the house would be an emotional responsibility, and Rootha's emotions were focused elsewhere. Rootha told her husband she only wanted a baby from out of her own body, not from someone else's. So she must bear Joho upon her often while he tried and tried, always in vain.

The fine lady's carriage stood by a vermilion cabin decorated with white palm-prints set at different angles. All of the thirty or so cabins beckoned differently. People tended to favour the same teller, consequently two or three people were waiting outside most cabins, none as yet outside a few. Rootha headed for one of the latter, which was blue with silver stars. She preferred variety and a certain anonymity. All tellers were sworn to secrecy. The punishment for telling tales outside the booth was drowning in a sack. But suppose a teller spied the *exact* details of her affair! What then?

This teller was a chubby, freckled woman gowned in grey. Charts of hand-lines covered all the wall-space that wasn't window curtained by lace. Seating herself on the tripod stool, Rootha paid a little-silver coin then placed both her hands, knuckles down, in the grooves on the telling table.

Scrutiny, and scribbling of symbols.

Much was insignificant, but finally the woman said, "You'll find out about otherlife today."

"You mean I'm going to die?"

Was Joho about to discover and kill her? If she died, when the news reached Pool would he kill himself, to join her immediately in rebirth?

"No, I believe you should visit a temple."

Well, a temple concerned itself with the migrations of the eternal soul. As regards temples, usually Rootha only attended special festivals where Pool would also be. Of course she couldn't approach Pool then, not with Joho accompanying her, yet at least she and Pool could glimpse one another, which was both comforting and taunting. Might today's destiny bring her a sense of an otherlife *with Pool?* People from early middle-age onward often experienced sensations from their previous lives. Never visions, only sensations. Rootha had tried to capture some, but hadn't succeeded. She was still too young.

The teller hadn't said which temple to visit, so Rootha went to the purplebrick temple close to her home which wasn't a true home. Usually a number of temple-goers would be staring past candles at the twisting reflection of flames in warped circular mirrors mounted on tripods, to cause a trance of atunement. Unusually, this morning, a bearded young speaker was holding forth, compelling a lot of attention.

"What," the speaker was saying, "if our otherlives do *not* progress from the past through the present to the future, the way we assume? What if your immediately previous life occurred in what, to us, is the future? What if your very next life will occur in what, to us, is the past?"

His hand made a zigzag gesture, high up and low down – then it chopped low in a series of waves.

"What if several successive lives are lived in our past, yet in an opposite sequence to events in history? What if we do indeed advance towards perfection – however, our perfect life has *already* occurred previously?"

What he said was so utterly new and provocative. This explained why he was speaking so early in the day! Rootha could have wept. To think that she and Pool would be together in a future life, which would therefore be a perfect life, had been such a consolation. To hear that this perfect life of being with her twin soul might *already* have happened – and might even be the reason why they had recognized each other immediately the year before! – that was horrible. She had nothing to look forward to.

"No!" she cried out. "It can't be!"

As if her outburst was a signal, other listeners also began to shout *no* and *out* and *leave*.

A senior speaker intervened, holding up his wrinkled palms for peace.

"Even though this young man's wrong, we should at least hear him, not try to drown him with our voices!"

"No!" shrieked Rootha, covering her ears, cursing today's destiny written on her hand.

The senior speaker addressed the bearded man. "Does it matter if our different lives aren't chronological? We still live all of them!"

"And how many is *all?*" came the reply. "Our souls are twisted in time like a knot, or like a tangled serpent sucking its own tail. Perfection must be followed by imperfection, again and again endlessly – otherwise our souls would stop existing because they would have reached their culmination. What else," shouted the young man, "can come after perfection – except imperfection? Without this" – and his hands gyrated – "this cycle of repetitions, the soul could not be eternal!"

So even if Rootha gained Pool, she would lose him again! Distraught, Rootha couldn't bear to hear more. She rushed to the nearest mirror, thrust her hand quickly through the candle flame, pressed her palm against the mirror itself. Distorted reflections and twisted light dazzled her. She pressed harder, as if to push her hand right through the thick glass into an otherlife where Pool might catch her by the hand.

And the mirror toppled, and the candlestick too, and Rootha's unbalanced body followed, as the mirror broke into pieces beneath her and the candle extinguished itself. Already strong hands were lifting Rootha swiftly. For a moment she imagined those hands were Pool's.

"Pardon, lady!" A rough unfamiliar voice. Of a burly man. One of the temple-goers. He smelled of fish.

"Can you stand on your own?"

When she nodded, the fisherman – or fishmonger – released her. The senior speaker was beside her now.

"I'm sorry," Rootha gasped. "Pay… the damage."

"You cut your hand," was all he said.

She stared at blood on her palm and, without thinking, like some animal she licked her wound. Salty the taste, like tears.

When Rootha left the temple, her little cut already staunched, a severe-looking greying woman – her neighbour, in fact, Lola Caprizon – followed and said to her, "You're very faithful. Your husband should be proud of you."

For a terrible moment Rootha thought that her neighbour had noticed her rare nocturnal excursions to be with Pool whenever Joho went away. But no; Lola Caprizon was referring to faith in otherlife as taught in temples.

"That certainly shut him up," Rootha's neighbour said with a grim satisfaction. "He ought to be sewn in a sack and thrown in the river for fate to decide, sink or float."

When Rootha woke beside Joho on the morning of Palm Sunday and went to the window, her right palm looked more intricate than ever before. Her left palm seemed much as usual.

As a teenager, Rootha had played the thumb-drums well enough to belong to a trio of drummer-women who performed at bondings and fates and even at the Palm Sunday festival. That was where Joho had first seen her and become enamoured.

When she was younger, Rootha had even thought that drumming might be her whole life – the beat of the heart, the pulse of the blood – but presently passion for Joho prevailed. And within a few years that passion faded, just as she herself faded in Joho's shadow. She ought to have waited! Yet how could she ever have predicted Pool's existence? It was only a little over two years since he arrived here from the capital and set up shop.

Joho stirred and yawned loudly and stretched. He hauled himself upright, the weighty presence in her life, to which were attached the weight of her father too, and her mother.

"Today's our day," he said.

Rootha turned away from the window.

"How do you mean?"

"The day I first saw you. Can't you remember? You were drumming."

"Oh yes. Of course. Joho, I'll have my palms read before the festival starts."

"To decide how you'll dress? I'd have thought the purple gown."

Oh yes, she thought bitterly, to decide how I'll dress as your wife. However, she smiled.

"Probably the purple, but even so! And you?"

"My brocade suit, of course."

"I meant about visiting the teller."

"No need of that," said Joho. "Reed saw my hands before

111

my trip. That's enough."

Joho always patronised the same elderly teller in Grand Square. Reed knows me like the front of my hand, Joho often said.

"Besides, we aren't made of money," Rootha's husband added. No doubt an allusion to his father-in-bond. Joho was like that. A heavy presence. Pool was an absence, ever present in her mind.

This time on Riverside, Rootha visited a yellow cabin decorated with bird emblems in blue and white. The teller was a short thin man with a beak of a nose.

"Never seen the like before!" he exclaimed as he gazed at her right palm. "I do declare it's more a *map* than a destiny. Lady, may I possibly copy it? Some inking on your palm, then press upon paper. Wash off easily."

Rootha tried to make her refusal light-hearted. Yet he was right. How could she not have realised? A map was on her hand. Instead of the lines of life and heart and head, and the islands and squares of restriction or protection, of escape or frustration, and the crosses of irritation, and the bars and arches all with their interplaying meanings: instead of these, a map.

"What's more, I swear it's like a map of this city, but at the same time it's not this city exactly. A bit different, as if say a fire burned parts, then they get rebuilt in a different way."

She thought of the candle flame.

"Mayn't I copy it merely to study?"

Rootha shook her head and closed her right hand, shutting within it her day's destiny.

Guiding herself by her right palm, almost in a trance, Rootha walked in the direction corresponding to where Pool's house should be. Presently she noticed a marble building she had never seen before. Then another. Fashions had altered. Women wore shorter robes and fanciful feathered hats. Lips were painted in many shades of red. A few people glanced at her curiously – as well they might at someone holding out her hand constantly as she walked along.

Presently she arrived at Pool's lane. The flagstones had been reset, all level, though the houses all looked much the same.

Heart thumping, she arrived at the door and clanged the bell.

Footsteps.

The man who opened the door was a blue-eyed stranger whose hair was long and fair, much longer and lighter than Pool's had been.

"Can I help you, lady?"

She gaped at him, without any of the instant thrill of recognition she had expected, even if his appearance was different in this otherlife of the future.

"I'm looking for Pool the glovemaker."

Yet of course, why should he be living in this particular house, and why should his name be Pool, and why should he even make gloves, except maybe that his talent had remained with him?

"Hmm, but I do seem to remember a Pool somewhere on the deeds of the house. It's an unusual name. I don't recall how long ago. How strange. I would think he'd be quite old or even dead by now." This occupant of Pool's house was intrigued. "My deeds are with the lender in Grand Square, though of course he's shut today for the festival. So even though I'm going to Grand Square this afternoon…" He flashed a palm at her amiably.

Palm Sunday! Almost everyone would be going to the festival, all gathered together in one place.

"Oh thank you for your help!" Rootha exclaimed.

"But I haven't…"

"You have!"

After a while, she passed a shop window and saw herself reflected, just as always. Oh yes, she was faithful! Faithful in the deepest sense. She must look eccentric, perhaps a bit of a mad lady.

A coin from her pocket bought her a meat bun and an apple juice and change from a vendor in Grand Square, where many youngsters were already gathering to enjoy a carousel and a house of mirrors and the other entertainments, some unfamiliar. Glancing back, she noticed the vendor admiring her coin, a grin on his face – that little-silver must have become rare.

Presently more and more townfolk were pouring into the square, dressed in their best. Rootha was walking around and glancing discretely at every man until too many people were present and she felt panic, and redoubled her efforts. Could it be that Pool lived in another city or town, and she must travel from place to place – after first finding work for money, maybe as a drummer if her fingers were still nimble?

Yet she had the map on her hand, the map of this city, no other. She kissed her palm, where yesterday she had licked blood.

An hour passed. Two. What a throng. At last a senior speaker clad in white ascended the steps of the town hall, and spoke much as usual about destiny and otherlife.

Finally he raised his hands high, palms to the crowd, and a moment later everyone copied him, cheering.

It was then that Rootha saw *him* and forced her way through. Not the Pool who had been – but she *knew*.

And at last she faced him.

"Fate, I *know* you," he said. "It's as if... But where? *Who are you?*"

They talked and talked. She told him everything; and the truth seemed self-evident.

"Last year," he confessed, "I was going to bond, but at the last moment somehow she seemed wrong for me. As if only part of her matched me. I felt so sad breaking off because I made her so sad, but my palm was always ambiguous and a teller said *wait*."

"Did you love her?"

He was honest. "Yes. For at least two years."

By now people were dancing to drummers in the streets leading out of the square. He took her by the hand. She realized that she didn't yet know his name in this otherlife; hadn't even asked.

"Come home with me."

So she went with him, by a way that was familiar, until they arrived at... the same house that hadn't been a home. Altered, yet so similar.

"I rent the upstairs," he told her.

Not the Palm Sunday we're familiar with, but palm as in palmistry, aided by musings about the What Ifs of past life regression and reincarnation. In a world where people's palms change overnight, palmistry is a vital skill.

Who says, if reincarnation exists, that this has to happen after you die? Why not earlier on?

Some Fast Thinking Needed

"The Suicide Matrioshka's only 300 kilometers deep, and so near the event horizon now!" sang out Dana Darley as she scoped the black hole which the clone-crewsome of five were heading for, somewhat inexorably by now.

In fact the five were twice-over cloned, in the sense that they were the virtual representatives of the five organic chaos-clones of Mary Marley who was chiefing the expedition from a safe distance of a few light hours, assisted by her five selves.

Chaos-clones as regards mentality and personality – which should guarantee variety and flexibility on a mission – although their bodies were superficially identical, except for Bango Barley who was male, for recreational reasons and for chilling out since they were all quite likely to unexist presently – the copies of the copies, that's to say. Unexist was a preferable word to *die*; and anyway could an electronic copy of a clone be said to die?

A chaos algorithm had been used as regards the mentalities of their source-clones, since Mary Marley wasn't an egotist, although a redoubtable woman. Alternatively, maybe she *was* an egotist and couldn't tolerate exact copies of herself, except superficially, which was merely equivalent to admiring one's beauty in a mirror. In four mirrors, to be exact. Plus a fifth, male-configured mirror, for amusement. Hence: a random range of personalities, which the virtual copies, um, copied.

But *hist*, what is a Suicide Matrioshka?

Rewind a few years.

Homo sapiens sapiens had done all right as a species. In so saying, naturally I'm passing over the extinctions, or the genocides perpetrated by us in the unenlightened past, of our cousins on Planet Earth such as the Neanderthals. And I'm passing over the mass extinctions of many animals, plants, insects, fish et cetera, during the die-off of the 20th and 21st centuries – centuries which were becoming enlightened, but not quite soon enough. At least *HSS*, to capitalise, had survived! (So far.) We'd expanded into space. The eggs were no longer all in one basket. We'd even succeeded in travelling almost at the speed of light, using zero point energy.

Biological aliens found we none (not so far), except for bacteria. Earth was a very unusual planet as regards the sheer number of favourable factors and fortuitous events – as well as non-events – which led to the evolution of *any* complex life, never mind *HSS*. A sun richer in heavy elements than most stars, and in a secluded region. A good Jupiter rather than a bad one as in many solar systems. The early collision of proto-Earth with a Mars-size planet, affecting spin axis and day length and producing a huge moon stabilising the tilt angle. Powerful magnetic field. The greenhouse versus iceball balancing act, some ice events being essential, and greenhouse gases the key to fresh water. Continental drift causing upwelling of nutrients. The right balance of land and sea. Oh, so many happenstance factors. Life as such arises easily, yet almost always stalls at the bacteria level – so far as we know (so far). Often life arises time after time on the same world or moon, getting snuffed and arising again, only so far and no further.

And then we came across the first Matrioshka brain.

Ancient machine intelligence, using most of the output of a star to power itself.

A Matrioshka, of course, is a set of hollow decorated wooden Russian dolls arranged one within another, the final and smallest dolly being solid in this case. A Matrioska brain, well... imagine crystalline frogspawn forming spherical shells within shells around a sun. The innermost shell runs hot, to power its computations, and radiates excess heat outward to the next shell which runs a little less hotly; and so on to the outermost shell, equivalent to the distance of a Jupiter, where the temperature may be a mere 55 Kelvin. From a distance the only sign of a mature Matrioshka brain will be a dull infrared glow; so it took a long time to detect these mighty machine intelligences.

Of course, in such solar systems any Jupiters and other worlds had already been demolished and transmuted to construct the shells of crystalline frogspawn.

Throughout the vastness of a Matrioshka brain, thought engines process and communicate or store data and beam their results or queries towards other Matrioshka brains elsewhere in the galaxy, hundreds or thousands of light years distant.

"Queries about what?" the Virtual Clone of Anna Aarley had asked.

"What kind of results?" the VC of Candy Carley had said.

"What are the questions?" That was the VC of Fanny Farley.

Those were rhetorical questions, more like mantras which kept them focused on their mission.

To themselves, subjectively, they all seemed to be in a spaceship of adequate size for five crew members. They could walk about, they could eat and breathe, or amuse themselves with Bango Barley. In actuality (or rather, virtuality) they were all part of the shielded quantum computer brain of the *Diver*. The real ship consisted largely of shielding and propellant and hardened transmission equipment, a vessel designed to approach the black hole and orbit it without being dragged inside the event horizon too soon. To approach the hole, and also the Suicide Matrioshka which had wrapped itself around the hole so as to exploit its enormous energy, far more than that of any star.

"About the true origin of the universe?" said Candy Carley.

"About the end of the universe, and how to escape it?" said Anna Aarley.

"How to design a new universe?" said Fanny Farley.

Precisely! Maybe the Matrioshkas had come from a previous universe. Or maybe they evolved in this one but intended to design and create a subsequent universe. From the point of view of consummate skill in reorganising matter, and undoubtedly in sheer thought power, the Matrioshkas were the Lords of the Universe.

It was said that the difference in capability between a Matrioshka and a woman must be ten million billion times larger than the chasm between a woman and a roundworm. Could a roundworm communicate with a woman? Or vice versa?

"A woman doesn't even notice a roundworm," remarked Dana Darley. "But the Matrioshkas must pay *some* attention to us, since they never demolished our solar system to build a new Matrioshka round our sun."

"Maybe we were just lucky," said Fanny Farley. "So far. After all, there are innumerable stars. And maybe our solar system didn't contain quite enough material to make another Matrioshka."

"No, I think they noticed us," said Candy. "Over a period of centuries since the first radio signals."

"Yes, that's the problem," agreed Anna. "*Time.*"

There was such a great disparity between the mayfly lifespan of a human being, and the multi-aeon existence of the Matrioshkas! Matrioshkas could communicate their computations across a thousand light years and wait patiently for a reply, in a dialogue which may have lasted for a million years already. At least the Matrioshkas demonstrated irrefutably that nothing could ever travel faster than light, or than radio waves, which was perhaps somewhat disappointing. If FTL was possible, Matrioshkas would know how.

In practical terms there was no way that women could communicate with ordinary Matrioshkas, those being so vast. Lightning-fast in their thoughts, yet also in a sense, shall we say cumbersome? The spherical size of the orbit of Jupiter, for instance. Just where do you plug in, metaphorically speaking? What part are you addressing? Maybe you could annoy some of the self-repair mechanisms, which mightn't be a good idea. Hitherto, radio signals beamed from nearby at part of a merely

Mars-orbit-size Matrioshka around a star in the direction of Vega had provoked no response.

Big Matrioshkas could think lots of thoughts very fast within their components, yet it could take months to circulate those thoughts internally. Basically, the larger a Matrioshka is, the slower it thinks overall even at lightning speed. That's no problem for a Matrioshka with millennia at its disposal, but a big problem for a human person.

Secrets of the universe, undreamed-of fundamental principles, must be within that machine brain of great antiquity! How to access any of those?

However, in rare cases rapid overall thought must be urgently necessary, for reasons unknown. Hence the Suicide Matrioshka, which would harvest the energy output of a black hole, or alternatively a supernova – achieving its intellectual goal before being incinerated, or, in the former case, sucked inward to oblivion.

And redoubtable Mary Marley had located a Suicide Matrioshka around a black hole.

It wouldn't have been much use locating an SM around a star about to go supernova, since any probe-vessel would have been incinerated faster than it could carry out its mission, to make contact with the smallish Matrioshka and announce the results, if any!

"If any," remarked Candy Carley. "The SM might be a bit preoccupied not only with its important computation but also with imminent extinction."

"Our presence might take its mind off extinction," said Dana Darley, "if extinction bothers it. You know, like the condemned prisoner's last cigarette."

"I've never even had a first cigarette," said Fanny Farley longingly.

Imaginative Mary Marley had provided a box of virtual cigars for the e-clones to puff on when they completed their mission. The glass-top box was part of a virtual control desk, and would pop open to provide mild cheroots. Obviously there'd be no time to consume a complete Fidel Havana, which could take hours. Anyway, the onset of gravitational stretch as they fell into the hole might make a cheroot seem like a Havana. Puffing a Havana might be *too* overwhelming, like euthanasia; so a cheroot should be intoxicating enough, as a reward and a pre-unexistence consolation.

"*We* don't worry about extinction," pointed out Anna Aarley.

"Not much," agreed Candy, which meant that maybe she did, a bit. Or even more than a bit. Diversity of simulated clone-personality. "Hey, Bango Barley," she called. "Where are you? I need a quick excitement, or two or three."

A little death, to take her mind off big doom?

Bango Barley looked out of his cabin, where of course he was, since he shouldn't be allowed too near instrument panels in case the man became impetuous. Yet it was a good idea to behave as though the simulated *Diver* was even bigger than it seemed. Clad in white shorts and muscular t-shirt, Bango Barley beckoned to Candy who, in common with her e-clone sisters, wore a coverall, loose as yet, crimson in her case, which could be pressurised within to mitigate somewhat the effect of impending gravitational waves on the body until those became too extreme. Promptly she went to his cabin while Dana continued studying the SM.

The effect of gravity waves, in so far as *Diver* would translate these for the simulated crew. Realism was important in maintaining a sense of reality.

"How long do we have?" asked Fanny.

"Forty-five minutes."

"Till first contact, or till the event horizon?"

"Till the EH. Ideally first contact ought to happen, um, first. If it happens. We'll start trying in twenty, irrespective. Squirt language protocols and *Wiki-Galactica* at the Matrioshka. She should gobble those in a microsecond."

"Why don't we start now?"

"Fanny, Fanny, you know why."

Fanny, wearing sky-blue, was the ditziest of Mary Marley's clone copies.

"Oh yeah, give the SM time to squirt her own important computation result to wherever, in case she ignores us. But what if she only squirts at the last possible moment?"

"Mary Marley thinks the SM surely built in a safety margin. That's a lot of investment to risk otherwise. Several planets must have been dismantled and shifted here by mass driver. Could have taken a thousand years."

"Wow."

"You know that, Fanny."

"I guess so. But I thought the computation was urgent."

"In Matrioshka terms," said Dana, in chlorophyl green. "I'd guess planets from elsewhere were dismantled. Unless gas and debris being sucked towards the hole was transmuted. But that could have taken even longer and used more energy. Big catchment area, I mean *volume* of space."

"I remember, I remember," said Anna Aarley, who wore bright daffodil yellow and had a penchant for poetry. "Mary designed our mission as a suicide trip because the SM is committing suicide too to find out the answer to a question. Maybe that'll provoke some interest, some fellow feeling, some sense of identification. However tiny. We'll be in with it there at the end when all information is torn apart. That might mean something to it."

Candy returned from her quick frolic with Bango Barley. Her cheeks were bright red apples. Her blue eyes sparkled as if starlight twinkled in them.

"Anyone else for Bango?" she asked. "Me, I feel quite rejuvenated. Bango wonders if he can be of more service."

"I suppose we shouldn't let him feel left out," said Fanny. "After all, he's part of us." So saying, she hastened towards the male e-clone's cabin. Differential gravity hadn't begun to drag yet.

"Bango's a bit of a distraction," said Dana.

"He's here to distract us," replied Anna. "And that's the nub of the matter. Just as grunting soldiers went into combat with a holo-pinup dancing in their vision, so we have a living dildo on board. That's part of Mary's make-up. Herself – in the shape of himself – screwing herself. The best design for self-satisfaction."

"Screw her," said Dana, surprising herself. She had not meant to sound rebellious. The words just slipped out, with a different meaning from that intended. However, once the words had slipped out, she did feel rebellious and wondered if her source-clone felt this way too, perhaps at this very moment, by a sort of morphic resonance.

Anna raised an eyebrow.

"But we're all agreed," she said, "that existence is pointless. So it doesn't matter if we unexist. Right?"

Nods all round, except from Fanny who was pleasuring herself in Bango's cabin. Perhaps Dana was the last to nod.

"Like," continued Anna, "as in no point to existence because existing is so arbitrary and partial. Animals carry on struggling to live because they can't think otherwise, even though they're all doomed to die, because without death there'd be no evolution, no change, no *future*. And what's the future for an intelligent being, I ask you?

"If you could live for a thousand years, that wouldn't be *you* any longer. You'd be a different person. For a start, you'd have to edit your excess of memories and effectively get rid of yourself. So why not get rid of yourself right away? For that matter, what's the *past* for an intelligent being? Billions of years of unexistence, of *nada*, until the arbitrary chance moment when you come into existence for a while, one out of a myriad possibilities. We all already non-experienced untold aeons. Where's the problem with non-experiencing untold aeons more? In fact *any* experience at all is the anomaly."

"Like a universe," said Candy, "as opposed to nothingness. Just, the universe is very big and lasts for a long time before it ceases. So we imagine that a universe is necessary. Maybe the Matrioshkas know otherwise, or are trying to find out, especially here at the very edge of *nada*."

The all-swallowing black hole, precisely.

"I think," said Dana, "the SM is here to exploit the available energy, not because a black hole is the edge of existence as we know it. Do you think the SM volunteered, for the greater enlightenment of other Matrioshkas?"

"Only," said Anna, "if it travelled here from elsewhere to reassemble itself around the hole. If it assembled itself here for the first time, then it already had its mission programmed into it. As do we! The SM had no choice. By the time it became sentient it was already committed to suicide. Yet it may as well carry out its mission prior to suicide, or its existence would be totally pointless."

Dana asked, "Can there be gradations of pointlessness? The SM knows that her existence is pointless yet she still feels compelled to solve the problem set for her?"

"As we feel compelled. For the greater enlightenment, as you say."

"A thought," said Candy. "Does Mary Marley's existence become slightly less pointless if thanks to us she makes meaningful contact with a Mat? I can't be bothered to keep on saying Matrioshka when there's so little time left. Thanks to us, who are she, who are her. In a million years everyone will have forgotten all about Mary Marley. Maybe there might be some bits of a nonsensical ballad called *Mary and the Mat*, though I doubt even that."

"Nice rhyme," said Anna. "But that's unless contact with this Mat and maybe with others reveals that existence is *not* in fact pointless."

"As proved," said Candy, "by the willingness of this Suicide Mat."

'Mat' was catching; there really weren't all that many minutes left until Dana would launch the ultra-compressed signal.

If the Mat did reply in an ultra-condensed signal too, which the *Diver* would reboost to Mary Marley, those on board *Diver* would have no idea what the signal actually contained. It might take Mary and her clones and computers a year to unwrap and understand a message from a Mat.

Hopefully, first of all, *Diver* might detect the SM signalling the outcome of its computation, if only by a burst of static more coherent than other static in this region of gas swirling in to be swallowed. Yet the Suicide Mat might send its important message to just one other Mat maybe a hundred light years away in any direction on a very tight beam with no spray.

Fanny returned, peachy-cheeked and energised, from Bango Barley. Having him on board was like having a socket you could plug your battery into for recharge; or rather, which could plug into your own socket. Being electronic, Bango was higher performance than his clone-source which Mary Marley herself, being highly intellectual, only used every few days, allowing her actual clones to amuse themselves with him in the meantime if they wished to. It was the life of Riley for Bango, like simultaneous infidelity and fidelity. Maybe now and then Bango got puzzled about identity, but for sure he had an identity visibly different in important respects from his co-clones or from Mary Marley the mistress. He stood out.

Between whiles, Bango usually occupied himself with racing cars. Back at the mothership, Bango had many model Grand Prix tracks and dozens of racers which he loved to modify and repaint in new colours, and he subscribed to every interactive auto-racing webmag. Here on the *Diver*, he drove simulatedly when he wasn't doing pitstop duty for the ladies.

Yet now, in the wake of Fanny, he emerged from his cabin and hesitantly approached the warning red line painted across the entry to the control deck.

"Is something wrong?" he asked in general.

"Not at the moment," said Candy.

"Thing is, I have a feeling we're going to crash into

something."

"Not exactly *crash*," said Dana, eyeing the simulated image of the SM necklacing the incandescent gas which was disappearing into the hole. An image of one segment of a very complex spherical necklace-cum-tiara, which was running hot. Hot with energy, hot with thought. *Diver* was getting closer. By jinking course corrections *Diver* would try to avoid tearing a tunnel, however tiny, through the SM's processors, though those must have multiple redundancy in such a turbulent environment.

"Are we going to die?" asked Bango.

"Unexist," said Anna, "is a better word. We never existed before. Why do people worry about existing in the future when they never existed in the past?"

"Because they didn't know that they didn't exist?" suggested Bango. "Knowing too much hurts, unless it's about racing. Wow, my head could burst just to think of all I don't know."

The SM would implode – by suction, as it were. Since it could think so fast, indeed faster and faster as it shrank, it might feel itself imploding intolerably. The signal it discharged to other Mats, or merely to one other Mat, might seem like pain relief. Or not.

Maybe successful computation, carried out well, felt like pleasure. Maybe the discharge of the signal would resemble an orgasm.

"Do you want to stay and watch, from behind the line?" Fanny asked him.

"Will there be a chequered flag? Will there be champagne? I like the way champagne gushes."

"Just cigars."

Bango clapped his hands.

"How fast are we driving?"

"Diving," Dana corrected. "Just right to put us in a tight, decaying orbit. Too fast, we might do a slingshot, be off in a couple of seconds in another direction, and miss what we came for."

"Wouldn't that be a world record or something?"

"Probably. Closest approach to a black hole. But we can't change course nor speed. *Diver*'s in charge, not a driver. Neat idea, Bango, but no cigar. On second thoughts, you'd better go back to your cabin. We'll be very busy soon."

Bango grinned. "Anyone want to come with me?"

"Darling," said Candy, "we always want to come with you, but not right now."

Giving a jaunty wave, Bango departed.

Diver whistled and buzzed, and announced publicly, "The Suicide Matrioshka may have sent its signal. Probability 41 per cent."

"Good enough for me," said Dana. "*Diver*, pulse the *Wiki-Galactica* at her." She picked up a microphone and cleared her throat. "Hullo, Suicide Mat. That's to say Matrioshka. We have come to share unexistence with you. We came a long way. Will you share some experiences with us first?"

"You sound like a news reporter," hissed Anna.

"What have you been computing," proceeded Dana, "that's worth committing suicide for? Can you explain? If you don't explain, our existence seems meaningless. So we hope you'll explain something. If we can understand it. And even if we can't. Hullo?"

She waited.

A simulated gravity wave tugged at the e-women, a sensation akin to falling down a lift-shaft then suddenly reversing.

"Whoopsy," said Fanny.

"I remember, I remember," said Anna, "Mary Marley trying to save a pill bug that fell into her bath. I mean, before Mary put any water in the bath."

"A what?" asked Fanny.

"Pill bug. Woodlouse. Small crustacean found under stones and damp wood. Segmented armoured back, lots of legs, twitchy feelers. Sometimes curls up in a ball if you poke it. Sometimes scuttles. They have a bias to the left, so if you put one in a left-handed maze the bug'll solve the maze just by bias. You can bet on it."

"What was it doing in Mary's bath?"

"Probably looking for scraps of flaked skin to eat, but it slipped down the smooth plastic. No way could it climb out of the gravity well again. Up it would struggle for a few centimeters, up the curve of the inside of the bath, then it slid back down again. Mary watched it for a while. She felt compassion. Pill bugs have a rich social life. You should see them magnified, they're cute."

"How did a bug get on to a starship? It must have had a long walk."

"No, that was earlier in Mary's life. When she was still a girl."

"Why don't I remember that too?"

"Clone chaos variability. So May tried to help nudge the pill bug upward with her fingertip, but the bug kept skidding off."

"Couldn't the bug understand Mary was trying to help?"

"Probably not. We mightn't understand a Mat trying to help us."

"Are you getting this, Mat?" called out Fanny. The microphone would be picking up and transmitting all this. If the Mat had swallowed the *Wiki-Galactica* it would understand Anglish easily by now. It would have understood everything within microseconds.

"So Mary nudged the bug on to a scrap of paper, lifted it out, and put it on the floor. Immediately the bug fell over on to its back, legs waving. She righted it, and it promptly fell over again, and upside-down. I don't think they're very well designed, control-wise."

"They must die all the time by accident," said Fanny. "How can they have much social life?"

"*We* do, don't we? By the time Mary finished her bath the pill bug looked dried up and dead. Anyway, she stood on it by accident as she was stepping out."

"Dried up, you say? Maybe it wanted water and that's why it went in the bath."

"Bath water would have drowned it."

"Can't win, really. So Mary is compassionate? Or was, till the pill bug died. And then she decided compassion is senseless? At least, for bugs or e-clones. What about our source-clones? Surely Mary cherishes them."

"The way a child cherishes companion-toys."

Another simulated gravity wave had the effect of a roller-coaster. Then for a moment Diver seemed to stretch like a rubber band. For a moment their view of the ship's interior was fish-eyed; then normal.

"We'd better pressurise our coveralls," said Anna, and this duly happened so that the women looked chunky. Bango would rely on his more powerful muscles.

"Hullo, Matrioshka!" called Dana.

"I/we copy you," said an unfamiliar voice.

"Computer intrusion," reported Diver, then fell silent.

"Uploading."

A century later, Fanny said, "Where are we?"

On the screen, to right and left, and up and down, was an array of crystalline frogspawn, wherein Diver seemed to be embedded.

"Hullo, Hullo?" called Dana repeatedly.

No reply came.

Hints of an orange sun seemed to shine by repeated reflection through the array from what must be an inward direction.

Presently the women depressurised and invited Bango Barley to join them for simulated supper. Energy seemed in plentiful supply, lifetimes of energy.

"Just," said Anna, "we mustn't fall over on our backs."

Missing the reference, Bango chuckled naughtily.

When his chuckle provoked little response (or not yet), Bango said, "Hey, can we open the cigars? By the way, there's a hell of a lot to learn about Grand Prix and racing cars. You could spend a lifetime."

The deliberations of the electronic copies of clones in this story are somewhat influenced by an unusual book entitled Better Never to Have Been: The Harm of Coming into Existence, *by philosopher David Benatar, a rigorously argued case for the benefits of never having been born, not merely as regards the human species but any life whatsoever in the entire universe. Since this might seem a bit downbeat, I wrote the story con brio at a bit of a gallop, or galop as in the last part of Rossini's* William Tell Overture.

The Globe of the Genius

Prizes are usually a good idea. Without the lure of a prize, would any mathematician have proved Fermat's Last Theorem? (Well, probably – mathematicians eat chalk.)

As you'll recall, back in 1637 Pierre de Fermat scribbled in the margin of a book the following:

"On the other hand it is impossible for a cube to be written as a sum of two cubes or a fourth power to be written as the sum of two fourth powers or in general, for any number which is a power greater than the second to be written as a sum of two like powers. I have a truly marvellous demonstration of this proposition which this margin is too narrow to contain."

On later reflection, maybe Fermat's proof turned out to be fatally flawed because he never published it. However, for the next few hundred years this note in the margin served as a red rag to a bull for mathematicians – especially after a German doctor named Wolfskehl made a will leaving his fortune to whoever solved FLT, as the problem came to be known chummily (at least amongst mathematicians).

You probably know how Wolfskehl, being German and methodical, planned to commit suicide by shooting himself through the head at precisely midnight. To occupy a few hours until then, he picked up a maths book, as one would, and became so involved in FLT that suddenly it was dawn. He'd been saved by FLT!

It's also said that Wolfskehl had succumbed to multiple sclerosis with the strange consequence that his family forced him to marry a woman who turned out to be a real bitch, so maybe he left all his money to whoever would solve FLT in order to spite the harridan hausfrau.

I should perhaps point out that 'bitch' signifies a spiteful woman in normal English, not a prostitute, as many speakers of Euro-English seem to imagine it means. You might say to an Italian friend, "My sister's a real bitch," and he'll respond enthusiastically, "How soon can I meet her?" I've toyed with the idea of writing a pamphlet about this misunderstanding so as to prevent embarrassments and disappointments. While we're on the subject, *curva* means a bend in the road in Spanish but a prostitute in Romanian, which can lead to other misunderstandings – you warn your Romanian friend, "Take care about all the *curvas* on that road," and he phones you later, disappointed and worried about his eyesight. The UN ought to publish my pamphlet to distribute to its huge polyglot staff.

But anyway. The eventual winner of the FLT prize was named Andrew Wiles, a Brit professor at Princeton, and he collected the depreciated fortune, still enough to buy a bottom of the range Porsche, in 1997. For a while Wiles became famous enough in the unmathematical world for an international fashion chain to ask him to endorse a new range of men's clothes.

The point is that a big enough prize can spur people to solve the unsolvable.

How about a huge prize, not for FLT, but for FTL? Faster Than Light travel!

Well, a Russian multi-billionaire offered One Billion Dollars for FTL, the Boris Billion Prize. Not to be outdone, a rival Russian multi-billionaire endowed the Time Prize, perhaps a bit meanly, with exactly One Billion and One Dollars. That's $1,000,000,001, a palindromic number. The Time Prize for Time Travel, headlined in newspapers as the Billy-One Prize.

NASA promised an extra $100,000 on top of the Boris Billion Prize, to get a cut of the interstellar action, if any, in the hope of going boldly. Consequently Swiss watchmakers clubbed together to top the Billy-One Prize with an additional palindromic $100,001, making the total value of the Time Prize

$1,000,100,002. But it was still called the Billy-One Prize.

Given that 360 years passed between Pierre de Fermat scribbling in the margin of his book and Andrew Wiles collecting the bounty, maybe a time machine wouldn't be invented any time soon. Yet journalists speculated (as is their wont) that whoever succeeded might immediately become capable of telling his earlier self how to build one, in which case a result could be imminent; so for a while there was much excitement and media attention.

News leaked out about the different approaches which various contestants were adopting to win the Billy-One.

A Russian group was building Matrioshka Machines to enclose time within itself. Matrioshkas are those dolls-within-dolls-within-dolls usually painted nowadays in kitsch fairytale style, or with caricatures of politicians. The idea behind a Matrioshka *Machine* is a bit hard to describe without resorting to pages of mathematics, but basically imagine that the outermost shell – or doll – represents time-now, and the next shell inward represents the immediately elapsed past, or time-minus, and the second shell inward represents time-minus squared… no, it's no use! Just scale this apparatus up in your mind from a nest of dolls to a towering steel structure generating intense magnetic fields and powered by a small nuclear reactor. Okay?

Actually, cultural *representation* played a large part in the way people considered time machines. The Russians thought about matrioshkas, whereas a Japanese group adopted an origami approach – they were determined to fold, and unfold, time. Paper being too flimsy, they used titanium and new composite materials. A titanium chrysanthemum the size of Sydney Opera House actually won an arts award, coincidentally.

Other groups, and lone individuals too, were ransacking occult designs such as mandalas to see which could actually be built in three- (actually, in four-) dimensions and powered, and what the results might be. Ancient intuitions might be important. That's because no one knew how to harness time – except theoretically by using black holes (none available nearby), exotic matter (likewise unavailable), or spinning 100-kilometer long ultradense cylinders at the speed of light, which obviously required somebody to win the Boris Billion Prize for FTL first of all.

Hopes soared when the biggest Russian Matrioshka Machine imploded – promising, though as yet no cigar.

However, let's forget about the groups. Instead let's concentrate upon one lone individual, Ralph-2 Zitznik of San Francisco.

Ralph-2 was fanatical about crystals and crystal power. Scarcely was his umbilical cord severed than his mother, Miranda, fastened a small empowering vitality crystal around his tiny neck even though the obstetrician protested that the baby might cut itself. The obstetrician was busy securing an identity tag around the new-born's wrist when Miranda reared and did so, which required laudable stamina and gymnastic athleticism not often found in western women who have only just given birth – as opposed to some Asian and African women who can reportedly give birth in a paddy field, say, and carry on working. Obviously a consequence of Miranda's own empowering vitality crystal which she'd continued wearing during labour.

The infant Ralph-2 first learned to focus his eyes by staring at a twinkly crystal suspended over his cot, which helped him develop deep insight. That's because there always seems to be more space, or volume, within a well-cut crystal than its size should reasonably allow.

When Miranda taught her son the alphabet, she chanted, "A is for Amethyst, B is for Beryl, C for Chrysoberyl, D for Diamond," through to "Z for Zircon."

Miranda had married mainly for alimony, which itself sounds like the name of a gem, which indeed it was for her. Ralph Zitznik, her future husband of two years duration, had come into the health food and crystal shop which Miranda was running, and which she now owned, and announced, "I need some minerals."

"You mean like amethyst quartz?"

"No, the other sort. Super-chelated boron, selenium et cetera. Tablets."

Arzee, as she would come to call him, was a bit ugly, but he paid with one of *those* cards which you need to have a million in the bank to get hold of.

So Miranda asked, "Hey, do you know selenium is a vital element in semen?" And things developed from there, one condition of the pre-nup being that any son born to them should be called Ralph too. And any daughter, Ralpha. By the time – due to lots of selenium – that Miranda gave birth, she had already separated irreconcilably from Ralph, yet she couldn't name her son Alexandrite or Topaz, for example. He had to be Ralph-2, too.

When Ralph-2 went to college, he majored in crystallography and physics; and was his mother happy! Ralph-2 had inherited moderate ugliness, which a crystal couldn't seem to alter, so girls weren't interested in him. Bankrolled by his mother's alimony, he decided to become a reclusive genius inventor.

Naturally his thoughts turned first to anti-gravity. And to UFOs, because they use anti-gravity. NASA would hear from him.

Then he worked on a theory of the universe as a crystal with an infinite number of facets. The Nobel Prize committee would hear of him.

Then came news of the Billy-One Prize.

It had long seemed to Ralph-2 that everything is basically geometry. Or maybe cosmometry, since geometry means the measurement of land, or the Earth; but let's keep it simple, let's say geometry. And it was very evident to Ralph-2, if not previously alas to his physics professor, that gemstones possessed attributes beyond mere lustre, or hardness on Moh's scale of scratchibility, to name but two attributes.

Formed millions of years ago under enormous heat and pressure, gemstones are geometrical encapsulations of small portions of a time gone by. They carry a bit of locked-up time forward into the present (akin to the way the laws of reality got locked into the early universe exploding from the Big Bang, which is the Big Crunch in reverse.) Captured time bounces around the inner facets of a gem. If the captured time could be unlocked suddenly, wow, the effect could be like a bomb going off. A time-bomb. Or a time-grenade. Imagine using that in a combat situation. All of a sudden the enemy are yesterday. Or maybe just parts of their bodies are thrown into the past – effectively you'd have killed them before you even arrived on the scene. Which would be preferable – if the complete enemy combatant went yesterday, he could ambush you.

The Department of Defence might be hearing from Ralph-2; they could reasonably pop 100 million Dollars on investigating the idea.

Ralph-2 visualised US marines advancing, firing specially prepared diamonds or rubies from their grenade launchers. The Jewellery Wars!

Admittedly there's little practical difference between blowing your enemy to pieces all in the present and blowing parts of him into the past – although the use of time-grenades might give a hightech scare to the enemy, especially if they were superstitious.

However, back to the Billy-One. Obviously the geometry of gems and time were related. To make a scaled-up version of the crystal structure of a gem could well be the key to a time machine.

Yet which particular gem? Which particular crystal structure?

A triakis-octahedron such as diamond? A rhombic dodecahedron such as garnet? A protoprism with protopyramid, deutero-pyramid and basal pinacoid such as apatite?

Ralph-2 stared at various gemstones under magnification and meditated, then he went to bed and dreamed. This was how Ralph-2's mind worked. Intuition! The sign of genius. When he woke, he had the answer: an octahedron with cube, in other words *galena*. He recalled how galena crystals were used in early radio sets, and how galena crystal rectifiers transformed alternating current into direct current. Did the stream of time have a current?

So he built in his back room, from specially cut squares and hexagons of armoured glass fastened to each other with superglue, an octahedron with cube the same height as himself. The glass was armoured with tiny wires ideal for distributing power through the structure – since he doubted whether the shape alone, without any electromagnetism or magnetoelectricity, would necessarily constitute a time machine. The superglue was doped with graphene to promote electrical conductivity.

Curiously enough, when he went to the glazier's to order his squares and hexagons, the glazier – a Navajo or Hopi Native American by the look of him – asked, "You building a flying saucer or something?" Ralph had forgotten to shave for a few days, and he was due for a haircut, so he looked a bit wild.

Instant paranoia afflicted Ralph-2, but he managed to improvise.

"No, a greenhouse – for my orchids and humming birds."

The Navajo or Hopi said, "Just thought you might be into crystal power."

Damn these Native Americans with their alternative worldview insights.

"Crystal?" echoed Ralph-2 incredulously. "Power?"

"To make your plants grow better?"

"Look, I don't want them growing better or they'll choke the... what did I tell you? The greenhouse. I just want them contained."

"You fed up with the humming birds getting in your hair and sticking their bills in your ear for wax and vibrating your brain?"

Vibrations, thought Ralph-2. Resonant frequencies. Could this glazier be a shaman or maybe an apprentice shaman?

"Look, I need the glass cut perfectly. Geometrically perfect.

Don't think about humming birds. And don't hum on the job."

"Costs a bit extra for not humming."

"I don't care!"

"Hey," said the Hopi or Navajo, "I'm joking."

Ralph-2 imitated a laugh. After he got home, he recounted the incident to himself in exasperation, trying to come up with witty rejoinders. Ralph-2 talked to himself aloud a lot.

Anyway, he completed the Octacube, as he called it for short, leaving one upper hexagon unattached so that he could lift the glass out by means of superglued ribbons. That was so as to reach the simple bird table which stood inside, its flat top occupying a space just beneath the geometrical centre of the Octacube, a point which he'd calculated then established using a plumb-line hanging from the exact middle of the topmost square. Exactitude was important, but he reckoned, at the very minimum, on a small zone surrounding that point where the time-displacement effect would occur, say three inches wide and deep. At minimum! Quite possibly anything within the greenhouse, or rather the time machine, would be displaced. However, it was wisest to start with a small test object.

When he had bought the bird table, from Creation's Beauty Garden Supacenter, the woman at the checkout, who was Chinese, had warned him about the danger of attack by savage seagulls. She had flapped her arms and screeched.

"You need table with roofy," she urged.

"No I don't. Anyway, why do you sell roofless bird tables if they're dangerous?"

"For parrots. For instance. For indoors."

"Mine will be very indoors," Ralph-2 assured her, while avoiding mentioning humming birds. The side of her till was adorned with stick-on Chinese good lucky characters in vermilion, but his gaze drifted to... a little glass globe of the world standing beside the till. Exactly the right size to be a test object! How amusing to send the entire world back in time, in miniature. He leaned closer.

The small globe was about two and a half inches high including the brass base. Screws through both ends of a brass crescent held the world at the correct angle. Land masses were painted quite accurately: green, pink, red or blue distinguished different countries, although few were named. In Africa, only Algeria and Libya. In South America, only Brazil and Argentina. The countries in Europe were too small to be named. Seas and oceans were uncoloured glass; looking through to the far side you could see land areas magnified.

Did the globe belong to the Chinese woman? In between serving customers, did she swing the world to and fro? Green America to pink China (both about the same size), pink China back to green America? Was it another charm of hers? It was a cheap piece of trash, possessing a certain kitsch charm... However, leaning even closer, he noticed a tiny gold sticker on the brass base which read BOHEMIA. Bohemian crystal was famous! Maybe this wasn't the best example, and maybe it was actually made in China – but to use *crystal* as a test object! How paradoxically appropriate.

"Hey Mister, you going to be sick on my till?"

Indeed by now he was bending quite acutely. He straightened up. And pointed at the globe. "I want to buy that – um, to put on the bird table. I'll pay you a hundred Dollars."

"Only costs ten from our gift shop. Little boy grabs without mother seeing. Boy pulled off bar code from bottom, I think. When see, mother fury, won't buy."

"I want it."

A little queue was building up.

"Go gift shop. Find other. Should be. Leave bird table here."

No other globes might remain in the gift shop. Someone else in the queue might try to buy this one. People were like that. If you picked up one of the two remaining jars of olives from a shelf in a supermarket, someone would immediately seize the final jar, even if she hated olives.

Ralph-2, true to his word, took five Jacksons out of his wallet. Old Hickory, victor of Horseshoe Bend et cetera; no friend to Indians – but the checkout woman was Chinese. All Chinese are very *au fait* with money.

"Please," he begged her in a peremptory way. "I don't have time. You can put ten in the till later."

"Not without the bar code I can't." Maybe she wasn't so *au fait*.

The queue was even longer now. Some of the shoppers began making pointed remarks. If speech bubbles had been floating like balloons above their heads, the words would have been sharpened like arrowheads directed at Ralph-2.

Of a sudden, he threw the five Jacksons down, seized the globe and his bird table, and strode away as rapidly as possible.

To be met at the exit by a big armed black man labelled Security.

"Where you taking that toy globe, Mister?"

Where indeed? Maybe to the Paleolithic!

"I paid for it," Ralph-2 protested. "I paid ten times the price." Would that get the Chinese woman into trouble? Hell, she had got *him* into trouble, unless CCTV was responsible.

"See your receipt?"

Reluctantly he showed his receipt for the bird table.

"Don't see no toy globe listed nowhere."

"That's because the bar code was missing."

"So you paid ten times the price, eh? But," and Security paused cunningly, "how did you *know* the price?"

"The checkout operator told me. She's Chinese."

It took Ralph-2 a while to extricate himself, by way of being escorted to the gift shop, a bar code being peeled from another globe and stuck on to his globe, then a return to the same checkout, from which the Chinese woman had apparently departed for a coffee break. Maybe she understood money after all.

Well, genius often encountered adversities. After he got

home, he recounted the incident to himself with alternatives.

It had of course occurred to Ralph-2 that before sending power into the Octacube he ought to isolate himself from any excessive effects by himself being in a Faraday Cage. From within the protective cage he could switch stuff on and off by using long slim sticks that were non-conductive – naturally he'd be using a Tesla coil to step up the voltage.

You might be wondering about the fact that the Earth doesn't stay conveniently in one place, but circles the Sun which itself is travelling in the direction of Vega. Won't something sent into the past end up somewhere in interstellar space? Well, Consistency Theory strongly implies that a time-displaced object will cling approximately to the world-line of the main gravitational attractor, in this case the Earth. As for retrieving a test object from the past, switch off the power and the object will bounce back to "normalise" itself. According to Normalisation Theory.

So, the next day, Ralph-2 lowered the bird table very accurately into the Octacube, then, using long tongs, he placed the crystal globe dead centre, and retreated into the almost adjacent Faraday cage, taking with him a pastrami and gherkin sandwich and a bottle of still mineral water just in case.

Ralph-2 manipulated his long sticks to power up the Octacube. Next, he made the Tesla coil discharge lightning at the Octacube as a booster. As afterimages of the bright lightning faded, Ralph-2 could see that the bird table was empty! He had successfully displaced the little crystal globe!

Exactly to when and exactly to where he had displaced the globe, he wasn't sure. He'd need to learn how to calibrate his time machine, yet already he was streets ahead of Matrioshka and Origami Machines – the Billy-One awaited him. And world fame, which would be a paradoxical reward for a recluse; although with all that money he could become even more reclusive. Never again would he need to go in person to a garden supacenter. For instance.

Then Ralph-2 used his sticks again to depower the Octacube, and watched intently.

However, the bird table remained empty. The crystal globe didn't pop back into the present.

"Hmm," he said to himself, in contravention of his instruction to the glazier.

Could it be that the globe – consisting of a crescent cupping a sphere occupying a stand shaped like a miniature flattened version of one of those plungers you use to clear a blocked sinkhole – was the wrong geometry to have used?

Just then, the phone rang. Probably that would be his mother, calling to say goodbye before she went on her luxury alimony cruise round the Pacific. Ralph-2 pushed, but the Faraday Cage wouldn't open, try as he might. After quite a long ring the answerphone came on and he heard Miranda's voice.

But why was she speaking in Arabic? Maybe not Arabic, but something similar.

As soon as his mother finished her incomprehensible message, Ralph-2 tried the cage door again. It wouldn't yield. It seemed sealed. "*Sealed, yield, sealed, yield,*" he said to himself as though uttering a magical incantation to cause open-sesame. But sesame wouldn't open. Not to a shoulder and all his body weight, nor to a forceful foot.

You may be wondering how I know all this. As I've said, Ralph-2 talked to himself a lot, and as a scientist he videoed all the circumstances of his experiment, using several CCTV cameras that fed into the hard disk of his computer which could store months of feed.

Almost immediately the phone rang again and this time his mother left her message on the answer phone in some sort of Latin.

Almost immediately, et cetera, and Miranda seemed to be speaking a dialect of Chinese.

Ralph-2 had the next three weeks to wonder why, till he

starved to death and/or died of thirst in that human-size birdcage accompanied by only one pastrami and gherkin sandwich and a bottle of water. His long sticks couldn't assist him to save his life. The phone was just out of reach. By now his mother was in Tahiti or wherever. She had never liked phoning while on holiday. Why go away, only to phone back?

One notion which Ralph-2 voiced aloud was that the crystal globe had landed in desert sands, maybe hundreds of years before it was kicked free by a camel and brought to the attention of the Arab Caliphate, which proceeded to colonise the Americas in the name of Islam. Actually this is a multiple, not a single notion.

Variations upon this involve the Roman and Chinese empires.

Another notion was that the Faraday Cage was acting as a time-cage, causing a bubble of his own time to imprison him. You can probably see the flaw in this reasoning.

Towards the end, Ralph-2's speculations are hallucinatory croaky whispers, although computer enhancement of the audio picks them up okay.

When I arrived after a few useless phone calls, and squinted through a window and then forced entry, Ralph-2 was a dead scarecrow. Can I call his prison a birdcage and then say that it housed a scarecrow? If I wish to!

It was the superglue doped with highly conductive graphene which tipped me off. That was a very specialist new item from Wonderglues of America based in San Diego. I needed some for my, let's say, special project.

Left alone fortuitously in a Wonderglue office, I quickly hacked the computer record of other recent customers, as one would, in case I had rivals. NASA, NASA, NASA again... then I saw the name of my peculiar ex-student who'd been into crystals. And I wondered WHY HIM?

Ralph-2 was wrong in one crucial respect, though I've no intention of saying what, except that it's connected with those three phone calls in languages which his mother never spoke in our world. Hush! It's me who's going to win the Billy-One now! That's a lot more clue than Fermat ever gave anyone. I stand on the shoulders of a dwarf who had half a good notion. After I'd cleared out his hard discs and notebooks, of course I had to explode his house scientifically, but fortunately no neighbours were killed.

While I was visiting a little town in the south of Spain, in a shop I spied a tiny and very simple globe of the world that you could see all the way through from one side to the other, costing only a euro or two. An instinct urged me to buy it – the same instinct that sometimes urges me to buy a secondhand book (about armour or butterflies or whatever) which might well come in useful, although I don't know why at the time.

Presently Ian Whates and myself and others of the Northampton SF Writers Group organised a 2-day convention, Newcon3, in Northampton's gorgeous Gothic Guildhall. Although a jolly good time was had by all who came, we'd mistargeted our publicity, so not enough people turned up, leaving three of our committee sharing a debt of £2000. To recover this, Ian Whates edited the benefit anthology Time Pieces *containing stories donated by our guests. Thus was born NewCon Press, which has gone on to great success – publishing amongst much else* The Beloved of My Beloved *by me and Roberto Quaglia (probably the only full-length genre fiction by two authors with different mother tongues) as well as the first ever English language edition of my* Orgasmachine, *and this my eleventh story collection. Also, we recovered our financial position and were able to hold a Newcon4 in Northampton's Fishmarket arts centre, where we didn't lose money since by then word of Newcon3's delights had spread.*

I myself needed to write a story for Time Pieces, *so out came that miniature globe from the Andalusian shop. Its time had come.*

Nadia's Nectar

Nadia's Nectar poured over cubes of watermelon makes a delicious breakfast!

"We'll try that!"

Nadia Peartree was the toast of Hollywood by 2015! Two Golden Globes, and we ain't referring to her bosom, plus two Oscars– !"

"Mom, I'm trying to do *Tyrannosafari* on my fone."

"Just eat your toast, Pumpkin, and drink your nectar."

Plus, Nadia was Born Again, so when she quoted Solomon's Proverbs 5:15, `Drink water from your own cistern,' America listened. And bought...!"

"Honey, if you'll quit fondling that Tetra Pak, it'll shut up."

Would you believe that at the turn of the 21st only three million Chinese drank urine and those Brahmins in India and in the West folks who were yoga fanatics –?

"But it's a new touchy-talkchip, Bert."

Yes, folks, pee-prejudice blinded most of us to a pedigree going back to ancient Israel and Tibet, whose lamas lived to a ripe old age because of pee which rhymes with immortality. Gandhi drank his own urine, and he beat the British –

"Honey, I'm sick of every darn food and drink voicing off – watch out, I expire next week, by the way tortoises can live 200 years well I ain't no tortoise yabber yabber."

They say Steve McQueen lived on urine and boiled alligator skin while he was fighting Big C –

"Bert, I never knew that."

Though most likely Nadia was inspired by Paul Newman's Organic Foods, what with all his royalties after tax, hundreds of millions, going to education and charity work. Remember Pa Newman and his daughter dressed up on those packets of healthy Pretzels and Choc Bars and Alphabet

Cookies looking American Gothic? Wholesome traditional virtues! Funnily enough, an FAQ was, 'Do you use slave labour in producing your chocolate?' What a question. Of course not. The welfare of producers of the raw material was paramount (and I don't mean as in pictures!). Nadia thought even more deeply about the welfare of producers in the Third World —

"Mom, I can't hear if a Tyranno's coming."

"Pumpkin, I'm just pouring myself a little more."

"Yeah, drip by drip."

This was the philanthropic clincher! Only naïve buyers of Nadia's Nectar could think they were quaffing urine solely passed by the star herself — leaving aside that 'passed' also means 'approved'! Good wholesome urine had to be sourced in considerable bulk, pasteurised and frozen for shipment. Where better, than from the poverty-stricken lands of Central America? What a godsend to so many people in those nations!

"Oh zip your lip, T-pak."

"It ain't got ears or lips, Pa."

For the urine to be first rate, the donors all need to be in tip-top health, kept supplied with all necessary nutrition and vitamins and minerals in exchange for their urine. The Man from Nadia's Nectars doesn't visit joyful producers to slice open a sample fruit with a machete! No, he's there all the time with a biochem test kit to check up on everyone, and a good nose for the bouquet of quality urine. It's famous that Nadia maintains the most wonderful health clinics in the source areas.

"Just hear a bit more, Bert?"

Nadia also contributes directly to her product, even now when she's in her late fifties, though looking a million dollars, needless to say. Into every hundred pints goes a droplet of her own urine. By homeopathic principles this intensifies the effect. All consumers know that they're participating directly in Nadia's glamour.

In the old days you'd hear silly objections that you couldn't get much in the way of urokinase or assorted hormones and antibodies and magnesium, calcium, potassium, out of quaffing a pint of pee — and also that the body was peeing stuff out because it already had enough inside it, that it actively wanted rid of the stuff. Tell that to a two-hundred year old lama.

"How much more?"

"But Bert, we love Nadia."

"I'm drinking her, ain't I?"

Did ya know how good ole Enzymes of America used to fit special filters to 10,000 Porta-Johns to recover an enzyme that dissolves blood clots? 14 million gallons of pee going into Porta-Johns each year meant quarter of a million coronary arteries unblocked! There was a half-billion-Dollar annual market for urine-products. But until Nadia's Nectars, that was an invisible market, a silent one. Pee products were hidden in pills and small print. Oh, and in beauty products and soaps – urine breaks down grease in hair, fr'instance.

Who cares if some other former Oscar winners copied Nadia with rival brands, and quirky flavours and colours? For my money nothing beats Nadia's Original Nectar.

If your eyes are tired, give them a few drops of her urine. Aching ears, likewise. Sinuses congested? Sniff the golden juice! Drink water from your own well! Or better, from Nadia's. The Bible says so, and Nadia made sure we got the message.

Oh the early commercials were so classy! Elegantly-nightgowned Nadia going into her personal bathroom in her mansion in Malibu just after sunrise and closing the door while the tinkly Trout Quintet played, then coming out smiling gorgeously carrying a beaker of golden liquid, which an aide promptly rushed away to safeguard its freshness. A genuine classic. Any of you remember?

"Me, I do!"

The modern commercials are pretty neat too. Nadia does most ads personally and never uses a rejuved CGI clone. She's utterly for real. That's why most people prefer her urine to their own. Trust. Drinking her pee's a communion.

Is it a wrap, guys? Did I read it good?

"Goofs, they oughta edited that bit out."

"No, Bert, it's gotta be a deliberate mistake. There'll be a prize for noticing! Pumpkin, pass me your fone."

This short piece is one of three that I've sold (so far) to august Nature *magazine, whose wonderful Henry Gee has published a laudable number of these inside-back-page entertainments by SF authors for numerous years now, including a 2007 collection,* Futures From Nature: 100 Speculative Fictions from the pages of the leading science journal. *Real scientists would sell their grannies to get a cutting-edge research paper into* Nature, *and its sister* Nature Physics, *but us science-fictioneers get money. In the interests of research I did drink some of my own urine, best collected early morning in mid-flow, then cooled in a fridge; it tasted quite bland and neutral.*

Dee-Dee and the Dumpy Dancers

(with Mike Allen)

Dee-Dee's daughter Meg, who was four, and Cheryl's Trisha, a year older, took a break from hanging out with Trisha's Granma to visit the "big girls" in the kitchen of the double-wide.

"Who's Auntie Gravity?" lisped Meg, tugging a lock of that dark curly hair that favored her daddy, Dudley.

"Is there an Uncle Gravity too?" piped up Trisha whose luxuriant red hair was her mother's – and just as well, since Cheryl hardly wanted to be reminded of her ex all the time.

"You been seeing the turkeys on TV?" Dee-Dee asked Meg.

Meg nodded. "Yeah."

"This's got nothing to do with aunties and uncles," said Dee-Dee. "Gravity is, like, what holds you on the ground and makes things fall. So the opposite is called *anti*-gravity. Like, like," and she tapped her watch then circled her finger, "clockwise and *anticlockwise*."

"That's going backwards," protested Trisha. "Turkeys fly" – she waved chubby hands – "up and forwards."

"Well, like *antidote*."

"Wha's a dote?"

"You're in way over your head," Hilda Teague warned Dee-Dee. Hilda was not into flights of fancy.

From the back bedroom came the chatter of TV. Granma was good about keeping out of the way when her daughter's friends, Doris Dudding – who everyone just called Dee-Dee – and Ruby Berger, and Hilda Teague, stopped in to make waffles and hold hen sessions.

"Maybe there's a cartoon on in Granma's room," suggested Cheryl. "Go see!"

The two girls scampered.

Any news item involving the portly, brown-feathered aliens in their equipment suits did look a bit like a cartoon, or at least like cartoon characters patched into real footage. Not that it was a laughing matter when muggers stole one of the aliens' flying suits a month ago. For whatever reason, this particular turkey had flown into a seedy Southside Chicago neighborhood. The Homeland Security agents couldn't keep up. Well, the alien only had its feathers ruffled, but after the thieves made off with the extraterrestrial flying suit the damn thing exploded, and took out half of a city block. Dozens of people died. No one messed with the turkeys after that.

"Tell you what caught *my* eye on TV last night," Dee-Dee said. "The news showed these ballet dancers in Greensboro. These women from the Ballet Theater had, like, rock climbing ropes hooked to their waists. They were hanging off this building and dancing on the wall in these tutus and fairy wings. And they were swinging and spinning and stretching their arms like birds with all this music blasting. They called it *aerial ballet*." Dee-Dee stretched her arms in imitation. "The news said they had radio headsets to tell these guys on the roof to pull the ropes up and down."

"I heard of that nonsense," said Hilda. "I think they did it at the Space Needle in Seattle. Pretty damn stupid, if you ask me."

"*Listen*," said Dee-Dee, "they got an arts grant to do that so-called nonsense. Y'know, money? And people were cheering. Look, we're all taking these stupid community college classes, hoping it's going to get us a new job —"

"Fat chance of that," from Hilda.

"*And*," Dee-Dee persevered, "we've all still got a year's Trade Act benefits coming. So we can *afford* to do something completely off the wall for fun."

"Off *which* wall?" Hilda asked suspiciously.

It had all started with a cheese hat. The four friends had been cutters at Texall for years – though Hilda had finally graduated to an office job – when the senior vice-president, Dan Dalhouse, took to wearing on his head a big wedge of yellow foam very suggestive of cheddar.

No, Dan hadn't lost his mind; nor was he declaring himself to be the big cheese of the Charles County, North Carolina textile industry. Dan was preparing his employees to cope with future shock by alluding to a certain best-selling self-help book about mice that hunt for cheese hidden in an ever-changing maze – in other words, "How to deal with change, and win!"

To tell the truth, the cover of the book in question depicted a cheese with holes in it, like Swiss, but if Dan had cut holes in his foam it could have looked, well, cheesy...

On a morning in late July, Dan finally addressed the assembled force of cutters and sewing-machine operators and pressers who for years had made sweat shirts and T-shirts, chatting fairly happily while they worked.

"J-B Embroidery and TrendWare gone down last month," Dan told them. "Appleby Knitted Goods last week. Last collar sewed, last lot dyed, last cuff inspected. A hundred textile mills shut down in just two years. We're dropping like flies. Y'all know why. Free trade laws. Cheap labor in Honduras. NAFTA. Us here at Texall, we're working at full capacity. Most of you, heck, you're putting in overtime. Makes no difference. Folks, ladies, we're closing."

He doffed his hat to them.

"You're gonna have to follow the cheese, 'cause it ain't here no more."

Of course tens of thousands of people out of work meant no spare cash for that meal at a diner or the new second-hand car, so a whole lot of dominoes tumbled. This was Hiroshima for Charles County. It was melt-down. It was a tornado blowing through a trailer park.

And just at the time when those alien visitors were grabbing all the media attention! Compared with anti-gravity turkeys from Delta Pavonis, were CBS or NBC going to bother themselves with the woes of textile workers, waitresses, car mechanics?

Easy for Dan to say follow the cheese. Execs were used to moving. The workers of Charles County weren't. Community meant knowing who your friends were and never worrying about the future, and community was formed in the factory, with all that friendly gossiping glueing together women who wouldn't have said more than hello to each other at church. But not any more – life now meant lining up for benefits, chasing jobs even though you couldn't ever find squat, worrying about doctor bills, gawping hopelessly at TV back home. Guilt ate at people's hearts, as if they themselves were to blame for the county's woes. Thanks to petty theft, shoplifting, domestic violence and such, Charles County Jail almost burst at the seams, unlike Texall's formerly well-made T-shirts. Bankruptcies soared. Oodles of people defaulted on their child support payments.

"Look, it's just like the Enrot managers getting buck naked for *Playgirl* magazine when they lost their jobs," said Cheryl. She always backed up Dee-Dee, as if Dee-Dee was a beloved big sister.

"Enron, you mean," Hilda corrected her. "You mean those Enron guys?"

"See, that's *initiative*! You don't just roll over and take it."

"I didn't know the photos showed them... Wait, what on Earth are you talking about? Accept *what*?" Poor Ruby had to accept quite a lot in life, what with her husband's drinking – not that Toby ever hit her but he sometimes said very cruel things. And her three boys were quite a handful.

"I don't see me as a stripper," Ruby said dolefully. "Anorexia clinic striptease maybe."

Ruby was scrawny, true. Bearing three kids hadn't fattened her up. Maybe if she didn't crop her blonde hair so short she wouldn't look so much older than her years.

"Now *you*, Cheryl," she went on, "that's another matter!"

Cheryl was definitely juicy. That gorgeous red hair of hers, too. A cutter since sweet seventeen, she'd turned plenty of heads at the textile plant. She'd charged into marriage with reckless exuberance, though why she chose to marry *that man* was a mystery. Result: after a few years of growing disenchantment, she and her toddler had moved in with Granma in the double-wide.

"And as for you, Dee-Dee, you dreamer…"

"Okay, so I'm a bit stocky."

"You ain't *fat*."

" I think the word you want is 'dumpy.' *So what?*"

"Your Dudley would have a *fit*," Hilda put in, "if he could hear you talking about being a stripper. How he puts up with your crazy notions, Dee-Dee Dudding, I'll never know."

"Maybe because he loves me."

"Ouch." At forty, Hilda probably never would have a husband, a bit late for it now, to be realistic.

"Aw, I didn't mean that." Dee-Dee half-stood, as if to embrace Hilda, then stopped herself. "I mean, Dudley loves me just as I am. Anyway, I'm not talking about stripping! I'm talking about ballet up in the air that gets a highfalutin' arts grant. Okay, so I wasn't too hot at ballet when I was a kid, but when I saw what those sky-dancers were doing on TV, y'know, that was *easy* – and that crowd just loved it. It could have been *us* up there. I don't know where you got this stripping idea. I'm talking about putting a costume *on*."

Ruby chuckled. "Like a costume that shows off your thighs and ass like you're half naked anyway. People would laugh themselves sick. We'd look like chickens hung up on those wires. Chickens in tutus."

"Might just as well dress up like clowns," said Hilda, who maybe was still ticked off.

A smile spread across Dee-Dee's round face. "Hey," she said, "*why don't we do just that?*"

Dee-Dee's friends all looked at her thoughtfully; then Cheryl cheered.

That same evening Dudley's younger brother Zak dropped in on the Dudding's small red-brick ranch house for a beer. Just one beer, though. Zak's body was something of a temple.

Nothing prissy about Zak, though. His temple invited the services of a succession of priestesses, who worshipped his muscles and his laid-back attitude, which might just be a result of the incense Dee-Dee knew damn well Zak inhaled in his little apartment. If the Eden Parks and Recreation Department ever caught wind of it, would he still be their part-time rock climbing instructor?

Maybe Zak wouldn't be their instructor for much longer anyway, now that factories sprawled empty all over town like beached whales with smoke-stacks. Eden looked like a massacre, and the city government was making up for millions in lost tax revenue by cutting employees loose.

"Furniture orders are way down." Dudley set down his can of Coors as if for emphasis. "There'll be more lay-offs soon."

Ten years older than Zak, and Dee-Dee for that matter, burly Dudley was shouldering a weight of responsibility with his wife on the federal dole. It never made him grumpy, though. Maybe he even thought that Dee-Dee was trying to cheer him up when she broke in with:

"Us girls had a *brilliant* idea this morning," and proceeded to explain, ending with, "Zak, you're gonna help us, right? You could go buy yourself some more old rope!"

Zak grinned. "Don't use no 'old' rope."

"I'm serious," Dee-Dee protested.

Dudley shook his head. "You think you're gonna get an arts grant to hang off buildings and romp around in clown outfits?" Still, it sure beat talking about lay-offs.

Beyond the home-made floral curtains, the setting sun glinted on the roof of Zak's beat-up Ford F-50 pickup, like a shiny patch on a bald man's head. Not a bit of industrial pollution in the air. Oh, if only there was some!

"Look," said Dee-Dee, "Hilda used to hang out at Eden High with *Claudea Mae Lockheart.*"

"That woman's nuts." Dudley took a quick swig of his Coors, emptying the can. He didn't really want to discourage Dee-Dee.

"Claudea Mae's also president of the Eden Arts Council."

"Hell," Dudley interrupted, "Keister Lockheart practically bought the Arts Council for her."

"Well, *good.* Suits me fine," said Dee-Dee. She couldn't imagine a worse God-given name than Keister, but life had definitely found ways to make it up to him. Lockheart had co-owned American Knitting before Texall took it over in '85, heaping more wealth upon him at a time when textiles still meant money. Prom Queen Claudea Mae was his trophy wife twenty years his junior, and he indulged her adoringly, catering to every whim.

"So if us girls could just get in a little practice at dangling first of all —"

"Won't work too well if you get vertigo," Zak said. "But I think I can talk my buddies into manning some tackle on a roof somewhere."

Concerned, Dudley said, "Please be careful, Dee-Dee." But he didn't have the heart to burst her bubble, so he went to get another beer.

Toby Berger opened his fourth beer left-handed, simultaneously holding it and hooking a fingernail under the ring-pull. Toby was getting better at being one-handed. It had been a couple of years now since that press at Container Plastics severed his right hand. Disability checks, sure, and Ruby's Trade Act money for a year longer, so the three boys and him and Ruby weren't starving — not yet — but the amputation turned Toby to drink even more than before. It hardly helped his temper staying bottled up with *her* all day long, so most days he'd walk to a bar, while away the hours, then turn on the TV as soon as he got back while sucking down a six-pack of Milwaukee's Best. At least the boys were outside on this fine evening, getting covered in mud, most likely.

"You wanna do *what*, Rube?"

He thought he hadn't heard right. Some talking head on TV was saying that NASA's Breakthrough Propulsion Physics project in Cleveland seemed no closer to figuring out how the turkeys flew themselves or their starship, which stood in a corn field in Iowa. Meantime big brown Tweetie-Pies were visiting Mount Rushmore, a circus in New Jersey, and the Golden Gate Bridge. Maybe they thought bridges were funny 'cause the little peckers didn't need them. On screen, a turkey pointed a flightless wing with scaly finger-claws on the end of it at the Golden Gate, and squawked, but no subtitle.

Flipping channels to an Orioles game, Toby muted the sound.

"Do *what* now?"

He listened.

Ruby seemed absolutely fired up by this crackpot idea of Dee-Dee Dudding's.

"You'll look after the boys a few times?" she asked finally.

"You think I'm only good for a baby-sitter these days?"

"Audrey can help."

Maybe, if Ruby asked nicely. Audrey, Ruby's niece, felt sorry for her.

"Hell," Toby said, "you might just fall and break your neck and die. Too bad we lost our life insurance when those bastards at Texall gave your goddamn job to the Mexicans."

And he unmuted the TV.

From the parking lot, the empty Peebles Department Store building hadn't looked so tall. But now, that three story height seemed like one hell of a drop.

Zak and six of his twenty-something buddies were hooking

ropes to stout eye-hooks bolted directly into a concrete partition on the roof. The long-abandoned building stood across from the central park and, as the city development office had long ago despaired of finding a business to fill it, Parks and Rec had lobbied city council to allow its use for rappelling instruction. It was intended as a temporary stopgap until the department could have a real climbing wall built – a prospect that seemed more unlikely with every new layoff announcement.

Clad in jeans and sweatshirts, Dee-Dee, Cheryl, and Ruby shifted awkwardly in harnesses that circled their waists and looped around their upper thighs. When Dee-Dee first saw the harnesses she'd been mortified. How on Earth would these monstrosities mix with a clown suit?

But if *ballet dancers* could wear these things and tutus too, surely she and her team of expert seamstresses were up to the challenge.

Zak's eyes glinted as if he were on the verge of a huge grin. "Before we try anything fancy," he said, "we need to get you used to walking on walls."

The men wound each rope, which looked to Dee-Dee to be slimmer than it should be, through a piece of metal called a figure-eight. These figure-eights were attached to the women's harnesses by a small metal loop called a carabiner, the pronunciation of which made Dee-Dee think of islands in the Gulf of Mexico.

Hilda eyed her three friends dubiously. Years ago, she had volunteered as a clown for Sunday school church events, which was why she had made that remark that got Dee-Dee so fired up, but no way would she take part in this foolishness.

Dee-Dee looked up at the gray afternoon sky. She was so nervous she feared she might be trembling; but there was no point in delaying. "Here goes," she said, "one big leap for..." For who? Charles County? Textile workers? Nutty women? A name would come.

She launched herself, leaning over the edge as Zak

instructed, with her back to the ground. Then, with two of Zak's friends manning the rope, she began to walk backward down the sheer brick face, defying gravity.

Graciously, Claudea Mae Lockheart offered to mix Hilda and Dee-Dee a Cosmopolitan, or maybe a Red Lion or a Collins? Dee-Dee shot an alarmed look at Hilda, who gave a tiny shrug. Back in the days when Dee-Dee still bar-hopped, she had occasionally indulged in Long Island Ice Teas. (Once, in a moment of giggly abandon while summering at Ocean Isle, she'd loudly ordered a Sex on the Beach.)

But nowadays her experience with cocktails tended exclusively toward excursions with her friends to El Ranchero on 25¢ margarita nights. And Hilda normally drank wine when she drank at all.

Dee-Dee chose the Red Lion because it had the most interesting name. Hilda declined.

As Claudea Mae fussed about at the liquor cabinet, Dee-Dee gawked at the Oriental rugs, the solid oak furniture, surreptitiously fondled the chair's leather upholstery. And she tried not to stare too long at the sculpture on the coffee table, which managed somehow to be both abstract and anatomically explicit. Half of Dee-Dee's house would fit in this room, which their host called the "lounge" – a word extended into two syllables by her Southern Belle drawl.

The Lockhearts lived in the rolling hills to the south of Eden where all the old money had settled to build their mansions. Sun-dappled trees filled the view through the bay window; not a hint of the sooty, crumbling city. Parked in the circular driveway, Hilda's twenty-five year old Ford Grenada looked like so much scrap metal beside Claudea Mae's sparkling Subaru Outback.

And Claudea Mae herself made Dee-Dee feel a little like the Grenada. Though she was Hilda's age, she didn't look much older than Cheryl. Short and willowy, she'd kept her prom queen figure. By comparison Dee-Dee and Hilda were, well, dumpy.

But that outfit! White gloves, white jacket and a little white hat, like a blond Jackie Onassis impersonator. Even Dee-Dee had more sense than that.

"Keister's gone down to Florida for a trustee meeting," said Claudea Mae, bringing Dee-Dee her drink. It was *really* tart. "But you don't want to hear about that, it's boring. Now tell me this idea of yours."

Dee-Dee started explaining; the drink made the task easier. As she went on, Claudea started to smile and nod.

"Yes. Oh my yes." She waved north, in the direction of the city. "*Anything* to keep folks' spirits up and maybe bring a bit of attention to this town. Some *positive* media attention. I'll help you make this happen. I think you should get a medal."

"Well, not just yet," said Dee-Dee with a blush. Maybe Claudea Mae wasn't so bad after all. "We've got some practicing to do. But we got expert rock climbers helping us, and I've done some ballet."

"So what are you going to call your troupe?"

The words just plain popped into Dee-Dee's head.

"*The Dumpy Dancers.*"

Claudea giggled. "Oh I like it. I like that *a lot.*"

"Ruby isn't exactly *dumpy*," whispered Hilda.

"Ain't nothing," Dee-Dee whispered back, "that a cushion can't cure."

On a Saturday afternoon in the last week of July three-hundred-some people gathered in the alley behind the downtown market and squinted up at five stories of sheer brick wall. For their first real performance, the women and their attendant rope-handlers had laid claim to the back wall of the once-bustling Patriot Hotel; Claudea Mae's clout made it easy to obtain the proper permissions. The crowd had been drawn by a story in the *Eden Messenger*, courtesy of Zak's buddy Jake who knew a friendly reporter, Seth Barnes.

Fact is, Barnes and his editor had been eager to cover

something different from the continuous unraveling of Charles County: the ugly budget-slashing choice between shutting down school buildings or sacking teachers; how packed Chapter 7 bankruptcy trustee Ephraim Russell's biweekly hearings had become; the recent hike in water and sewer rates and two sewage treatment plants closing all the same. Only folks prospering these days were real estate agents – and that was because out-of-county investors were snatching up houses sold cheap to avoid foreclosure; usually the houses were rented out, right back to the unfortunate sellers.

Consequently the *Messenger* had already run a front page picture of the Dumpy Dancers practicing in their home-made clown suits. The headline accompanying the story read, BIZARRE BALLERINAS TAKE TO THE SKY.

All along the horizon, woolly Eden-bound clouds plumed up into the azure of the afternoon as if industry had taken a miraculous upturn. However, no rain was forecast until later. Sunlight heated the rooftop and all those upon it.

Hilda appraised her three friends, and nodded.

Dee-Dee wore a candy-stripe overall, frills at the neck and ankles and wrists, an enormous white parody of a tutu mushrooming from her waist. A great red grin enveloped her lips, her nose was bright blue, the rest of her face chalk-white. Big silvery butterfly wings stood out from her back above the tutu.

Ruby's blond crop had disappeared under a wig of bright tangled multicoloured wool. A red blouse adorned with huge white polka-dots – down which flopped a lurid cravat – fitted into the cushion-concealing waistband of voluminous green trousers held up by purple suspenders. Each of her cheeks sported a big red polka-dot.

As for Cheryl, she had dyed her hair pink and frizzed it out into a huge halo. A spangled leotard enhanced her curvy figure. She too was wearing a vast mushroom of a tutu and wings.

"Test the mikes," said Zak, legal pad in hand, routines listed on the yellow sheets.

160

"Humpty Dumpty sat on a wall," said Dee-Dee.

"What a thing to say," protested Hilda.

"Look, it's just like actors saying 'Break a leg.'"

"You get that, Charlie?" And Charlie, Dee-Dee's rope-handler, gave Zak a thumb's-up.

Ruby simply said, "One two three." Was she feeling stressed? She'd hinted that Audrey was none too happy after three months helping out with the boys. It made Ruby's friends wonder if Toby had attempted a one-handed pass at the baby-sitter, kids in the house or no.

From Cheryl, with exuberance: "Three two one lift-off!"

Hilda glanced over the parapet.

"We've got quite a crowd. Too bad we can't sell no tickets!"

This performance, and any future ones, had to be free. A condition of the funding from the Arts Council. Hilda was in charge of the Dumpy Dancers' finances, and in her opinion too much of the grant had already gone to post-rehearsal beers or Cokes for Zak and a dozen of his buddies.

"After today, maybe somebody could pass a hat around."

But who in that crowd would have cash to spare?

It looked like the three rope-handlers were puppeteers manipulating huge living marionettes, who were now limbering up. The early weeks of aches and pains were long over. The women's muscles had hardened to the labor of clowning in mid-air.

"Okay," Zak called out, "let's do it!"

Dudley stared upward with much trepidation. Sure, nothing went wrong during rehearsals, but the prospect of Dee-Dee hanging high overhead made his heart beat fast, especially with hundreds of folks watching.

Maybe it showed. Notebook and pen poised, gangly Seth Barnes asked him, "So Dudley, how do you feel about your wife playing Spider-Woman?" That photographer girl, Maryann, snapped a picture. She was holding a redoubtable digital video camera in front of her face, with another smaller camera and several lenses in black cases dangling by straps from her shoulders, including a two-foot monster that had to be a giant telephoto lens. Dudley didn't see how she could walk upright.

"Seems to me," answered Dudley, "anyone doing something for Eden is a heroine." *Heroine* sounded a bit like Dee-Dee was doing drugs. "A hero," he amended quickly.

"Ab-solutely!" Claudea Mae Lockheart agreed. She had nattered on to Barnes about how the city needed a ray of sunshine in these dark economic times, and that was why she'd persuaded the Arts Council to sponsor the troupe. Except there wasn't much persuading to do; most of the Arts Council's current endowment came straight from her pocketbook. Or rather, her husband's wallet.

Dee-Dee had asked Dudley to be Claudea Mae's escort, much to his embarrassment. The nutty woman was dressed in an antebellum outfit, complete with hoop skirt, frilly hat and parasol.

The newshounds pulled away as the performance began. Dee-Dee was first over the top. Horizontal to the wall, she walked down with exaggeratedly mincing ballet steps as if picking her way through hot coals. The harness hooked behind her was invisible from the ground. Momentarily Dudley felt vertigo, as if the side of the old hotel was the real ground and it was himself who was tilted at a ninety degree angle.

The winged clown that was Dee-Dee paused, then she hoisted a leg and extended her arms forward and behind in a deliberately clumsy arabesque. This was raising a chuckle, but oops, she lost her balance. Folks gasped. But no, she hadn't lost it at all: Dee-Dee bounded away from the wall into mid-air and flapped her arms like a big cartoon birdy, or a hyperactive, spastic fairy.

Cheryl and Ruby also came over the top and dropped in jerky slow motion, miming and buffooning....

Charlie had loaned Hilda a pair of binoculars. As the hijinks went on, the crowd kept roaring applause without even waiting for a routine to end. But not only that – were raindrops falling down there, to be wiped from faces, when she felt none up here on the roof? – some people were actually *crying with laughter*. That hadn't happened in Eden in quite some time.

"Channel 2 was at today's show," Ruby told Toby and Audrey a week later. "So was Fox, and WXLU. There were TV cameras all over the place!"

"That's great." Audrey didn't sound as if she meant it.

"Does that mean you get paid something?" was Toby's comment.

"Of course not, it's for the news."

Toby's eyes narrowed. His wife talked back more and more these days. She was starting to forget her place, and he didn't like it. At this rate one of those rock-jocks might turn her head, get her to make a fool of herself. And that's all they'd do, 'cause they'd really want someone like Audrey, maybe not much face-wise, but young, with perky tits and a tight ass.

"Will you be on TV?" clamored eight-year-old Ben.

"Yeah," sneered Toby, "your Ma'll be famous in disguise."

"I got to be going." Audrey stuffed her textbooks and summer school homework into her bookbag.

Ruby followed Audrey out onto the driveway.

"It's been real good of you to help out, sweetheart. You didn't sound too happy just now."

Audrey whispered, "Look, Aunt Ruby, I can't *stand* the way he looks at me, 'specially when he comes back from the bar. I don't know how much longer I can take this."

"Has he *said* anything? *Done* anything?"

Audrey shook her head. "If he had *two* hands," she muttered.

Ruby drew herself up straight. "He has trouble minding the boys all by himself."

"Mostly doesn't try, that's why."

"Please don't stop coming. I'm gonna have a word with

163

him."

The word, later that night, escalated into a horrible fight. During lulls in the bellowing and shouting, Ruby could hear her youngest son whimpering in the boys' bedroom. Several times, she thought Toby was actually going to hit her. Toby accused Ruby outright of fooling around with one of the rope-handlers – as if *she* were the one with the straying eye, not him.

If Toby was so worried she was cheating, why hadn't he even bothered to come along to the performances?

So what would *that* have shown him? he sneered, his mind beyond all reason.

Finally Toby stormed off to the living room and his cache of beer. She heard the TV switching channels as if he was searching for footage to incriminate her, oblivious to the fact that the news shows were long since over. She could only hope that one of her friends taped her TV debut. The next morning, she found Toby snoring on the couch, TV still on, the remains of a six-pack strewn beside him. Fortunately a hangover subdued his wrath to a surly mumble.

"I've been thinking," Hilda said. "How about if I dress up and goof around on the ground while you're performing? I could take donations, if anyone's got 'em to give... I mean, I just *can't* see myself doing what you guys do, but..."

"Feel a little left out?" asked Dee-Dee.

Ruby suggested, "Maybe you could *try* a bit of training just in case one of us does get hurt, either up there or someplace else."

This alerted Dee-Dee. "Ruby, do you think you could get hurt *some place else?*"

Ruby said nothing. Her expression was a mixture of apprehension and defiance.

Gently Dee-Dee asked her, "Is it Toby?"

Ruby sighed. "You could say so. I'm not letting him hold me back! I feel five years younger. That's the trouble. He's accusing me of fooling around."

"While you're hanging on a rope in front of three hundred people? What!"

"He's just resentful." Now Ruby sounded ready to forgive. "I think he's jealous, but not really because he thinks I'm having an affair. You know, him losing his hand, me suddenly making out like I'm an acrobat, getting in the news...."

Dee-Dee's mind went into overdrive.

"If Toby had a *job*... like, for his self-esteem. I wonder if Claudea Mae could talk to Keister. The man has his fingers in all sorts of pies. There must be something Toby can do."

"That's an awesome idea," agreed Cheryl.

"No, it ain't," Ruby said sadly. "Keister Lockheart fixes Toby up with some job, like it's charity, Toby'll just get more suspicious – he'll think it's a plot to keep him out of the house so I can take one of these rock-jocks to bed."

Hilda spoke up. "I *will* do some training. I'm months behind you three, but we can't let this fall apart now. For Ruby's sake, or else Toby wins."

"Y'know," said Ruby, "I just love you all."

Dudley and Dee-Dee were sound asleep, but he roused as the cordless phone in the kitchen kept on ringing.

"Wha's time?" mumbled Dee-Dee.

Dudley always kept a flashlight on the bedside table. He shuffled out of bed.

"Midnight. I'll see who it is. Go back to sleep."

"Meg..."

"I won't wake her up. Damn phone will."

Dudley expected the phone to fall silent just as he reached it, but it didn't. It was Zak on the other end.

"Dudley, turn the TV on right now. Channel 33, E-Network. Don't ask, just do it."

Fumbling with the remote in the dark, Dudley only caught the tail end of the savage skit on *Are They For Real?* but the target was all too obvious.

Through the cruel magic of special effects, three obese actresses with grossly exaggerated hick accents and clown faces were dangling from what looked like bungee cords above a grungy city skyline, reciting: *"They said we was down, but we's all up now! An artsy grant is great! Next we'll pretend we're big fat balloons, y'all watch us inflate!"* And inflate they did, pretending to stuff food in their mouths, until they all popped, messily.

The skit was intercut with actual news footage of Dee-Dee and her friends performing. Dudley felt sick. All his pride over the enthusiastic coverage last week by the local TV stations drained away. Collapsing onto the loveseat, he stared numbly, phone still in hand.

What did this mean? Humiliation for Dee-Dee and her friends. And maybe worse. Dudley's sleep-fuddled mind imagined Citizens for Honest Government turning on the Dumpy Dancers, demanding at council meetings to know how much money was being wasted on these *clowns*. That group of rabble rousers banded together after the terrible commotion caused by Jeff Dekes, the Charles County administrator, who killed himself with a .45 handgun last October. Everyone thought the crumbling economy drove him to it, but the outpouring of grief turned to outrage when it was revealed he had embezzled almost a million dollars, and paid out some of it as hush money to two female employees he'd knocked up.

"Zak," Dudley asked, "how many people watch this show?"

The answer wasn't encouraging. When he heard Zak say, "Man, this is *so cool*," Dudley punched the TALK button and hung up. "Jackass," he told the silent receiver.

As Dudley sat there, *Are They For Real?* mopped the floor with some poor toddler prodigy whose ability to calculate *pi* endlessly and at high speed in his head had earned a talk show appearance. Maybe the real toddler could do other things, but the show must have bought up a day's entire output from a cream pie factory to make a mockery of a dwarf actor dressed in diapers who chanted numbers which rarely corresponded to the number of pies thrown his way.

And then came the turn of the United States government and the turkeys from Delta Pavonis.

Green-screened in front of a Mount Rushmore backdrop, a fellow wearing a latex President mask addressed the same dwarf, now beaked and feathered and wattled as a turkey. The flying suit he wore was made of Slinkies and beer cans glued to what looked suspiciously like an inflatable sex doll, its arms wrapped around the phony bird's chest.

"Hey, how about taking Mount Rushmore *with you* as a souvenir of your time in the States? Show the folks back home our famous presidents Abraham Lincoln and Jefferson and, and…" Could the President be so stupid as to forget which of his predecessors were carved on the monument? "…and what's-his-name and the other guy."

"Gurble gurble," said the turkey.

"Hey, great! You just lend us that suit of yours, tell us how it works, we'll make one that'll *fit on to* Mount Rushmore." The faux-president licked his latex lips with a grotesque rubber tongue. Was he eyeing the flying suit with a bit too much lust for a mere greedy politician?

It was then that Dee-Dee came in, wearing a long T-shirt with a cartoon cat emblazoned on the front.

"Whatcha watching, Dudley? World blowing up?"

No, but your world might.

"Oh, this… crazy show." Dudley waved at the discarded phone handset. "Zak thought I might want to watch."

Dee-Dee peered at the President and the parody alien.

"Why would Zak get you out of bed to watch that?"

Her husband tousled his curly hair, which lately had thinned and greyed a little, and carefully began, "Oh, well, they were kinda poking fun at something else, too. It's probably not a big deal. You know how Zak is, he was probably toked-up or stoked-up or whatever. Well, he got all excited…"

Early next day, shortly after Dudley headed off to spend another day supervising the assembly line, Dee-Dee answered the phone expecting to hear an apologetic Zak.

But the man's voice was unfamiliar. He had a flat, mid-Western accent.

"Is this Mrs. Dudding of the Eden Dumpy Dancers?"

Dee-Dee's heart sank. It had to be some reporter, someone from the *national* media. Despite the spin that Dudley tried good-heartedly to put on his description of *Are They For Real?* she knew what had really happened.

But no! Her caller was with the government.

"I need to confirm a few things, Mrs. Dudding."

Afterwards, Dee-Dee laughed until she cried. Then she cried until she laughed, so it seemed. All of which brought Meg out of her room, where she'd been playing with model horses.

"What's so funny, Mommy?"

"What's funny is the government just called here, and those turkeys, the ones from the stars," Dee-Dee was gasping, could hardly get it all out, "the turkeys want to see us perform, that's me, and Cheryl and Ruby, right here in Eden –"

Meg bubbled with questions such as *"Who's the Government?"* then, once she understood a bit better, "Will there be long cars with black windows?" until Dee-Dee had to shush her with a popsicle – so she could get on using the phone like there was no bill and no tomorrow.

"Toby, in three hours Dee-Dee's picking me up, 'cause of getting prepped and security."

"Damn woman, makin' all this trouble."

"We're gonna perform for the *aliens*. The government expects it. There's been all sorts of arrangements made."

"So they should pay you, God dammit, so you can get yourself a baby-sitter! I told the guys I'd see them at Top Dawg's and that's where I'm going... to watch you foolin' around and actin' stupid" – Toby made this sound distinctly sinister – "if it *is* on TV, and I hope it ain't. I'm sure as hell not gonna let them think I'm pussy-whipped."

"Audrey *cannot* come here today. She's got pink-eye."

"Tough."

"I'll just have to take the boys along with me. Beg someone to help out when I get there. Hope that won't screw up my performance too much."

"You take our boys out of this house with you and you're like *walking*. As in *walking*."

"Maybe that's what I *should* do!" Yet where could she go, and how could she cope?

Toby came closer. "I heard this riddle the other day, they say it's from the Japs. What's the sound of one hand *slapping*?"

Oh God, don't let him mess her up.

Quietly, Ruby said, "Toby, I'm begging you."

"Gonna take a lot more than begging."

Ruby thought desperately.

"Okay," she said, "there *is* some money. Those government people call it 'disturbance compensation.' Three hundred bucks for each of us. Up front. Hilda's got it."

"You were hoping to squirrel that away? Make it part of your get-away fund? Give it to your hot rope-jock lover?"

"I was gonna put it in the common pot. We all were. But I'll give my share to you, Toby, if you'll stay here."

"I *knew* you were hiding something. Three hundred bucks'll buy a lot of beer. You got a deal."

So it was all a vicious sham. He'd been stringing her along, to torment her, get her all wound up, till he got what he wanted. Or else he really want to sabotage Ruby's moment of glory, but realized what a shit he'd look like if he went through with it and word got out.

Trouble was, there was no such thing as disturbance compensation. Ruby nodded in the direction of next door.

"Now if it's all right with you, I gotta ask Lucy real quick about the potluck this Sunday."

"Whatever."

Lucy Martinez was a fat, nosy gossip who Ruby usually tried her best to avoid.

"May I use your phone, Luce?"

"Yours not workin'?"

"Mm," said Ruby, with a noncommital shake of her head.

Of course, Lucy hung around, as if to count the words.

"Hilda," Ruby was soon whispering, "can you get three hundred dollars cash to Dee-Dee *right now?*"

Oh yes, there were limos, or at least cars with black windows. And TV trucks galore.

And the Mayor of Eden, Robinson Brewer. And what seemed to be the entire police department. And tall athletic guys in suits, with little wires spiralling from buds in their ears to disappear underneath their shirt collars, who were wearing dark sunglasses even though billows of clouds rolled unceasing across the sky. And at least half the city's population, including Keister Lockheart attending Claudea Mae, who was wearing a Flapper dress and stockings rolled down to her ankles.

Dee-Dee and her three friends, Hilda in clown gear, were down below on the temporary viewing stand, already costumed. Robinson Brewer had requested a round of flesh-pressing prior to today's event, so maybe in case something went wrong there'd at least be some creditable TV footage and news photos of the Mayor.

Before she covered it in clown makeup, Ruby's face appeared haggard and grey. Toby had effectively stolen a major chunk of the remaining Arts Council grant, though Dee-Dee had to give Ruby credit for quick thinking. After procuring the bribe, Hilda had ranted angrily about the perils of marriage, how you never learned what the creep was really like until it was too late, which Cheryl had seconded with a resounding "Amen!" But Dee-

Dee couldn't possibly agree; as she saw it, Dudley was everything a husband should be.

Dee-Dee had never seen Keister in person before, just the occasional mug shot in the *Messenger*. A lot of flesh, not all of it flab, was confined in a well-tailored grey suit in an imposing, impressive way. For some reason, probably known as Claudea, Keister wore a big Disney Dumbo tie fastened by a gold pin. Implying that Eden was having a festive day? Reflecting on the dumpiness of two of the airborne entertainers?

"Real pleased to finally meet y'all," Keister said grandly, nodding at the Mayor too. "I still can't believe how much my Claudea Mae's done with this little pet project." As if *he* was responsible for all of it – which, in a sense, he was. Yet he seemed to mean it kindly.

The Mayor nodded too, enthusiastically. He had already complimented the ladies on their enterprise and attire, although since the whole idea was to look silly, did he really need to praise the costumes quite so lavishly as if they were ex-textile workers' notion of fashion chic?

And then there was Midwestern Accent – Mr. Spinelli – who had already paid a visit to the Dudding's ranch house, so Dee-Dee knew for a fact it was *Are They For Real?* that drew the aliens' attention to the Dumpy Dancers' act. Apparently a turkey back on the ship in Iowa trawled the wavebands. Keeping an eye on public opinion, as a precaution ever since the Chicago incident? Maybe. Spinelli, wired and suited, eschewed sunglasses as if to distinguish himself. Short, dark-skinned, he was clearly Italian in more than name. Though he spoke in flat broadcast English, if he'd suddenly shouted "Mamma Mia!" in exasperation, Dee-Dee wouldn't have been a bit surprised.

Spinelli reminded Dee-Dee, "If our visitors do happen to want to meet you afterwards, not likely to happen but possible, remember what I told you…"

Sure. The turkeys apparently controlled their suits by voice command in their own language of gobbles. Their use of spoken

English, which sounded like second-month immigrant, was eccentric, although they seemed to understand English perfectly well – almost as if some of the time they could hear what you were thinking. Maybe their quirky speech was deliberate so they didn't need to answer questions comprehensibly. Between the gobbles and the patches of pidgin English – Big Pigeon, more like – confusion could reign, and the wrong thing might be said, so she'd be best advised just to say, "Thank you," a lot, and "Have a good day."

As if she were a *waitress*, for Chrissake.

Don't bother smiling and try to avoid showing teeth – the turkeys might misread facial expressions and teeth might seem aggressive. Still, she was told, it was her patriotic duty to keep her ears peeled for anything that might be of significance to Uncle Sam.

And now three turkeys were approaching airborne flanked at a discreet distance by two black helicopters. The whole thing kinda felt like a surreal Thanksgiving.

"Time to start," said Spinelli.

Just as well that these days the elevator in the Patriot Hotel was unlikely to be encumbered by guests and their luggage.

Half way through the performance, one of the turkeys took off from the viewing stand and drifted upward slowly as if intent on a closer look. It rose past second-floor, past third-floor height.

Oh don't let it get in the way, Dee-Dee begged silently as it came closer.

Its two companions were ascending behind it.

Don't let them get in the way!

Dee-Dee was at fifth-floor height, pretending to be a Sugar Plum Fairy. Cheryl and Ruby were capering higher up.

And now the portly alien turkey was hovering alongside Dee-Dee. Close up, it smelled of turpentine and sage and chicory. Maybe some of the smell came from the flying suit, a sort of harness with bulges. Feathers, brown from a distance, were minutely speckled with gold. A large red left eye inspected her.

And then the creature reached out its wing and that abbreviated hand of scaly finger-claws toward Dee-Dee as if... as if inviting her to dance, would you believe?

Inviting her... *to fly with it?*

How could she fly anywhere partnered by an extraterrestrial turkey when she was dangling from a rope, ground-bound irrevocably by her own weight and the force of gravity?

Even so, and though that claw-thing looked so hard and harsh, Dee-Dee reached out her hand.

The alien gripped her gently, and came ever closer until it was right up against her. Disengaging the claw from her hand, the turkey maneuvered its wing around behind her back, for all the world as if it was courting her. She inhaled chicory and turpentine and sage.

All of the sudden Dee-Dee's weight vanished. She bobbed up, two, three inches.

A groping at her back between her tutu and her wings!

"No," she gasped, "don't, I'll fall."

"Noh-fall, fall-not," uttered the Deltan Pavonian turkey. The claw behind her clutched at her waist –

"Ouch!"

– then it must have shifted its grip to her harness, because she was rising up along with it, and you can bet she clung to *its* waist too, and as Dee-Dee craned her neck she glimpsed her rope with its figure-eight and carabiner swinging free like some upside-down Indian rope trick, and now she and the turkey were passing by Cheryl and Ruby, who just gawped, forgetting their routine, and she came level with the roof of the hotel, and a dozen astonished faces were all gawping at her – as she ascended higher, supported by alien turkey-power.

The turkey flew this way with Dee-Dee, and it flew that way, doing in mid-air what you might call a square-dance or maybe a cube-dance since the both of them rose and sank as well as shuttling to and fro. And the other two turkeys joined in, air-trotting this way and that.

It's the Turkey Trot, Dee-Dee thought crazily. Was this how aliens danced in the skies of their home planet?

Just as Dee-Dee was beginning to enjoy herself, her dancing partner turned its head – and promptly stuck its beak right into her ear.

"Oh!" she cried, and "Ooh!"

A thrumming vibration filled Dee-Dee's head.

Well, she couldn't exactly ever explain afterwards what happened, but by the time her portly partner landed her back down safely on the roof of the Patriot Hotel a couple of things were very clear in Dee-Dee's mind.

Turkeys, in their dreams, possessed ancestral memory, and while being cradled in mid-air Dee-Dee had shared a dream or two. Turkeys dreamed of a time long ago when they were gliding creatures who hauled themselves up trees and cliffs, kicking with one back leg at a time, the other foot impacted in the bark or rock like a set of pitons. They used dextrous claw-fingers at the tips of their wings to cling and guide themselves upward. Once they were high enough, they would launch themselves and glide, to catch the winged worms that were their favourite gobble.

Then the ocean sank a bit and into the enormous formerly-offshore island that was the turkeys' Eden came ground-predators with a taste for proto-turkey. Scrabbling aloft became vital, the faster the better.

After a long while the ocean rose again and something killed off all the ground-predators living on the big island – maybe they all ate one another.

Turkeys began to live on the ground again and boy did they put on weight! But they kept those rudimentary hands since those were kinda useful.

Always thereafter the obese turkeys dreamed of what it was once like to be light and agile and airborne. Intelligence and dexterity advanced. Turkeys yearned to regain the air, although

no aerobics could slim a turkey back down to bantamweight.
Their myth-figures were turkeys who could fly miraculously.
Their heroes were inventors who built giant wings or springs to
fit on to turkey feet or who used balloons to lift their bodies. All
too often wings collapsed and springs broke ankles and balloons
exploded. Such devices proved to be perilous impediments.

Yet turkeys had become very thoughtful birds. A great
turkey thinker called Thoughts-Soar made a breakthrough in
fundamental hyperdimensional vectors...

Remembering... of yearning, was in Dee-Dee's head. *Honoring
those who try. To be in the sky. In spite of dumpiness. Try buy secret.
Nothing we want. Except see sights. Can photons be sold? Try beg secret.
Begging is obble-obble. Try steal suit. Suit goes whoomph. Today honor you.
For gubble-ubble.*

Whatever *obble-obble* and *gubble-ubble* were, possibly on
account of her false wings and her fluffed-out tutu and maybe
also her blue nose it seemed that Dee-Dee and the Delta
Pavonian turkey were birds of a feather.

The other thing Dee-Dee found she knew was the idea that
Thoughts-Soar had arrived at, or rather the practical application
of that idea, namely how to build a personal anti-gravity flying
package. Like peering down on some complicated 3-Dee maze
that was burned into her brain.

*Cannot lift big things. Ships or such. Equation missing. But a suit for
you.*

Well, Dee-Dee wasn't dense. She knew what a patent was. And
surely Keister Lockheart knew *all* about patents or if he didn't he
had lawyers.

Ruby and Cheryl and Zak were dying to hear all about her
unexpected dance in the sky with an alien turkey, as was everyone
else upon the hotel roof, but she hushed them and begged them
to be patient – what if at this very moment a turkey in Oklahoma
or Oregon was confiding the secret to *somebody else?* – and rushed
to the elevator.

By the time Dee-Dee reached the street, still in her costume, the three turkeys were already flying off to some place else on their itinerary, escorted by the choppers.

Robinson Brewer was looking pleased with himself as Dee-Dee flounced past to much applause, and then past Mr. Spinelli, pretending not to notice his covert beckoning. A beaming Keister Lockheart actually bowed to Dee-Dee, or at least he bent himself. Hardly had he straightened than it must have looked as though Dee-Dee was kissing him upon the cheek, so close was she to his ear. Claudea Mae raised one eyebrow, then raised the other when Keister, suddenly pale, told Dee-Dee, "Don't say a word."

Of course, she had to say *something* to Spinelli, but she managed to come over as absolutely out of her head over her dance in the sky, yeah, just like some ditzy waitress whose diner had just been invaded by George Clooney, or Dale Earnhardt Jr.

From the start, the government tried to throw spanners in the works, especially after the turkey ship departed the Earth. Military and law enforcement bureaucrats made strenuous objections to Keister's statewide and worldwide patents in partnership with the Dumpy Dancers. (Just because the secret had been given to Dee-Dee didn't mean her friends wouldn't share.)

But Keister had his own political strings to pull, and within days North Carolina's governor had rallied to his standard, as had both of the state's high-profile Senators. It only took a couple of conference calls for them to realize that here, finally, was the putty to fill the job-hemorrhaging hole gouged in the state's economy by NAFTA.

And the President? Well, the unending national recession had dropped his approval ratings into the toilet, and he was desperate for some way to get skittish consumers to start blowing money again. After North Carolina's Senators arranged a quiet White House rendezvous, a mounting effort by Homeland Security to challenge Keister in court was abruptly nixed.

The FAA's protests about the nightmare of regulating

individual anti-grav fliers were met with deaf ears by politicians who knew they'd never have to worry again about re-election....

And then there was public opinion to reckon with. Eventually *Time* magazine featured Dee-Dee on its cover, afloat in a prototype flying suit and her huge mushroom tutu. AMERICA AIRBORNE, was the legend. The stuff of legend indeed.

A billion dollar offer, too, from Detroit in cahoots with the oil industry to buy the patents, presumably to suppress them. On the other hand, battery manufacturers were rubbing their hands and drooling – the way the technology panned out, four AA-size batteries would run a flying suit for a week.

The command words couldn't be gobbledygook, had to be easy to learn, but impossible to confuse with words used in ordinary speech.

Hence, UX for *up*, and DUX for *down*, and LEX for *left* and RIX for *right*. A few of the control words were maybe a bit mischievous but Keister swore to reporters he was trying to "clean up America's potty mouth" – now certain words would have a whole new meaning. Such as FUX for *fast*, and SUX for *slow*. Televison evangelist Orville Taggart, one of the President's political allies, thunderously praised this "restoration to virtue of our corrupted language." No flier who'd been cut up by another would swear casually if it might send him speeding slap-bang into a building or alternatively slow him down. Society was gonna change for sure, in all sorts of ways.

Besides, no one could stop Keister and the Dumpy Dancers from setting up abroad instead if they chose to. Should Americans be deprived of personal flying gear if the Japanese or Koreans or French could fly like birds? (Although probably never the *North* Koreans.)

The opening in Eden four months after of the first anti-grav flying-suit factory was cause for a champagne celebration. So many people were there. Mayor Brewer. The editor of the

Messenger. Even the county's development guru, Rick Talent, who maybe could have used a few tips from the Dumpy Dancers on how to reinvigorate Charles County. And out of town media, of course.

Dee-Dee kept feeling that she was missing someone, but who? It certainly wasn't Toby Berger! A newly-empowered Ruby had given Toby a choice between counselling and walking; he'd meekly chosen the first option. Yet despite the restrictions now firmly clamped on him as regards to drinking, he was trying to weasel his way in.

"Who's watching the boys?" Ruby demanded.

"Lucy Martinez."

"Toby, I'm paying for you to stay on the wagon and get your head straightened out, and you think you can hang out here where there's *champagne?* I told you, forget it. Get your ass home, *now.* And thank your lucky stars that I'm sticking with you for the boys' sake, 'cause I don't want them turning into no Kurt Cobains doing coke and wailing about their parents splitting up. But I could still change my mind. Don't you forget it."

Toby looked like a dog who'd been kicked.

"Aw Ruby, I just want a Coke." All that temper deflated by utterly changed circumstances, his woman on the verge of prosperity and in position to call all the shots.

Maybe he muttered under his breath as he departed, tail between his legs, but at least Toby's breath didn't smell of rancid Milwaukee's Best.

Just a little late, Cheryl turned up with a broadly-grinning Zak. They were arm in arm. Even though the Dumpy Dancers quit performing months ago due to all the business negotiations – not to mention oncoming winter weather – Zak had been seeing quite a bit of Cheryl lately.

As Zak took off to talk to Dudley, Cheryl winked at Dee-Dee.

"Reckon there'll be enough champagne to spare for an additional toast, kinda personal one?"

"You and Zak?"

Cheryl beamed.

"I don't know as we'll exactly get married, considering last time, but he's so good with Trisha ... and, Dee-Dee, get this – he's told me he'll give up the *incense*...."

On the Saturday morning a few days afterwards, the evening of Dudley's birthday, a huge package arrived at the Dudding house, delivered by FedEx, but addressed to Dee-Dee, not her husband.

Was it something from Keister, such as the first harness lovingly finished off by a former sweatshirt knitter now re-employed, or something from Claudea Mae such as an impossible hat or a cocktail mixer and bottles of bizarre liqueurs? Perhaps not whole-heartedly the Lockhearts were trying to persuade the Duddings to move to a mansion in the hills, but Dudley liked the idea of staying put for the moment, as did Dee-Dee, now that this was not an obligation but a choice.

Within, to her surprise, Dee-Dee found a round yellow cheese the size of a pumpkin pie. And a card, which read:

Proud of you,
DD.

Seemed like a goofy gift from herself to herself – had she been wandering around town in a trance? – but then she realized:

"It's from Dan Dalhouse!" Of course, *he* should have been at the champagne celebration.

She handed the card to Dudley to read.

"Dee-Dee Dudding," he said, "I'm proud of you too."

"Hey," said Dee-Dee, "why don't we use *this* for your birthday cake? Stick candles in it? Have a party?"

"A cheese as a cake?"

"Never heard of cheesecake? Besides, why should birthday cakes always be made out of cake?" The gleam of inspiration was in Dee-Dee's eye. "How about cakes of steak for people in

179

Texas? Or, maybe ... a *sashimi* cake for the Japanese, like, this great big slab of tuna?" Then she sighed. "I guess there's no time for that right now. We got a zillion flying suits to make."

Mike Allen is long-time editor of the splendid poetry magazine Mythic Delirium, *and very ably and kindly edited, along with his wife Anita, my poetry collection* (the) Lexicographer's Love Song *for DNA Publications in 2001. Mike and I have written several poems in collaboration. As well as being a prominent poet, he's also an ace reporter for a newspaper in Roanoke, Virginia, and one day he emailed me saying, "Look at the kind of stories I have to deal with!" – attaching pieces about an aerial ballet group who hang off buildings, and how local textile mills were closing down. I perceived a potential connection; surely all we needed to join these two items together were some spacefaring alien turkeys? So I started in on my first and only story to date written in American. Mike continued. We alternated. Pretty soon we had a vibrant folksy tale.*

A Nose For Such Things

For Sissy

First on the head of him who did this deed
My curse shall light—on him and all his seed…
　　　　　　— Lord Byron, "The Curse of Minerva"

When I was a kid, my grandmother told me, "You have Lord Elgin's nose."

She showed me a photo of a portrait of a gent dressed in a frock coat with velvety cuffs and lapels buttoned once over a much-buttoned waistcoat; plus knee breeches, stockings, and buckled shoes. His right hand rested upon the hilt of a scabbarded sword. His other hand, braced against his waist, held a cockaded hat. His curled powdered hair might or mightn't have been a wig. His nose looked long and refined. Like mine.

Gran meant, of course, that I'd inherited his nose even though a dozen generations had passed since that particular Lord Elgin's day and despite our own family not being remotely noble; my dad was a long distance truck driver. That we were very remotely connected was a point of pride to my gran due to the Elgin Marbles in the British Museum, which she took me to see one birthday. "A glory, saved by your ancestor!" she proclaimed while I took in a muscular naked one-armed man kneeing a one-armed centaur. Apparently Elgin had rescued the figures and friezes from barbaric neglect in Greece a couple of hundred years earlier.

At the time I wasn't much wowed by those old stones, but when I was sixteen, since I was showing an interest in journalism as a career, my parents started taking the quality *Sunday Times* as well as their regular *News of the World* full of crimes and scandals; and one Sunday I noticed a picture of that very same centaur in combat underneath the headline GREEKS DEMAND RETURN OF PARTHENON MARBLES. The accompanying story gave me a rather different insight into Thomas Bruce, 7th Earl of Elgin, as a vandalistic plunderer.

Briefly, in 1799 Elgin managed to become British ambassador to Constantinople, where the Sultan ruled over a Turkish empire which still included Greece. This was at the time of the Napoleonic Wars. Thwarting Napoleon's ambitions in Egypt and the eastern Mediterranean was the goal of Elgin's diplomacy, in which he was successful, however his real obsession was to bring back ancient Greek masterpieces of sculpture to London to uplift English cultural life...

Nowadays indeed I'm a freelance journalist; and a few weeks ago editor Max Falconer phoned to say, "Nigel, will you fly to Greece for us pronto with a photographer? Reuters say there's some sort of bizarre ghost haunting Athens."

"Makes a change from students rioting," I said to show that I was at least semi-informed about my destination. Oddly, I'd never visited Greece before. Or maybe not so oddly in view of my ancestor's misdemeanours. Not that I bore the name Elgin, nor Bruce for that matter; I was a Johnson. Admittedly *Nigel* is an anagram of *Elgin*, and I suspect Gran had something to do with *that*.

"You mean," said Max, "this ghost business might be a stunt to take people's minds off politics?"

"That would be a story in itself," I hastened to say, not wishing to put him off funding a jaunt to Greece. Max's paper has a penchant for reportage about weird phenomena such as crop circles or panthers loose in the English countryside, but a political scandal was also fair game, especially if it cast a bad light on our European Union friends.

"A stunt," he said. "You have a nose for such things."

Getting back to the matter of Lord Elgin's nose, which Gran claimed I possessed, it was only when I was sixteen and bothered to find out more about Elgin that I discovered he had actually *lost* his nose. His nose had rotted off in Constantinople. Allegedly this was due to a 'severe ague'. Normally in that era an ague meant an acute malarial type of fever, yet such couldn't be so in this case unless a mosquito infected with some variation upon flesh-eating Ebola virus had stung him upon the noble proboscis, and the virus restricted itself to eating that organ alone. Lord Byron, who hated Elgin, declared that the nose-rot was due to syphilis, which seems plausible. This could explain Lady Elgin's later detestation of her husband on more than merely aesthetic grounds. As for Lady Elgin's subsequent enthusiastic adultery with a certain R.J. Fergusson, maybe miraculously his Lordship had failed to infect her or else the pair cared not a hoot for the pox.

When I learned about Elgin's missing nose, for a while I became like a child who naively misunderstands what an adult – in this case, my gran – meant. At the ripe age of sixteen I was wondering whether Gran supposed that Elgin's lost nose had somehow migrated from his face to mine?

"What does this ghost look like?" I asked Max.

"Someone pulling something, with strange things flying around. It's fairly bright but vague. Sort of out of focus."

Like an incompetent holographic projection?

"This all started during some excavations. Maybe something got disturbed or released."

Some vapour such as swamp gas, responsible for will-o'-the-wisps? But I didn't wish to deter Max.

"Sounds very spooky," I said.

"You can cover any riots as well," said Max. "Our Phil will sort out flights and hotel and email you."

That same evening I flew Aegean from Heathrow to Athens along with Phil Pursey, photographer, who'd been to Athens the previous year to cover troubles caused by disaffected young people. Six months ago Phil and I had done a feature on a haunted bedroom in a castle in Lancashire, along with a couple of psychic investigators; and indeed that place had given us the shivers when the temperature dropped unaccountably. A couple of the photos showed a strange person-sized glow which Phil insisted couldn't be a reflection of flash or a technical malfunction. This made a double page spread.

"I've asked a useful local chap to meet us first thing tomorrow," Phil told me once we were in the air. "Name of Mehmet."

"Mehmet doesn't sound much like a Greek name."

"No, he's Turkish. He's lived in Athens for years. Has a couple of carpet shops. He keeps his ear to the ground."

"I thought you *looked* at carpets and walked on them, not listened to them."

"I mean figuratively. Mehmet was rather useful to me and Johnny during the riots." Johnny specialised in Euronews. "More objective than a Greek informant might have been."

I had my doubts about this. "I thought Turks and Greeks didn't get on."

But Phil waved this aside. The inflight movie was some thriller which I ignored while I boned up on Athens using my palmtop. After we landed at two in the morning we took a transfer bus from the airport numerous miles to a square in the centre of town, *very* near which, Phil assured me, would be our hotel. Rather than a taxi to get there. "If we're modest with some expenses," he suggested, "maybe we can paint the town red one night without Max grousing."

It did prove a very short haul from bus stop to hotel, so maybe Phil was right about Mehmet too. And the hotel was quite close to where those spooky things were happening, in the Ancient Agora, the marketplace of long ago; but by then it was well after three in the morning and I was bleary-eyed.

Mehmet was a bearded, jolly chap, tubby though muscular. He wore a thick knitted sweater under his jacket and a wool hat; the start of December was distinctly cool of a morning and would be chilly by night, but Phil and I had brought adequate coats.

While we were in the air the previous night, another manifestation had happened! Useful Mehmet brought with him copies of a Greek tabloid called *Espresso* picturing a jumbled glow upon a stretch of ancient roadway, amidst darkness; and *Athens News* in English showed a few hundred spectators gaping or taking pictures through a line of police. A long Greek title which meant *Free Press* carried on its front a picture of protesting young people, but inside was a similar photo of the glow along with a map of the site, an arrow showing the direction in which the glow travelled, and commentary that was all Greek to me, though Mehmet summarised. All was still a mystery. *Athens News* and *Eleftherosomething* said that scientists planned to set up special measuring equipment.

Mehmet led us by way of narrow streets full of mostly elegant souvenir shops, then passing over a railway, to the modern entrance gate of the Ancient Agora which was blocked by a couple of police cars, its ticket office shut. In the middle distance on our left stretched a long pillared classical arcade where I imagined Socrates holding forth, although the building looked rather fresh and unblemished.

"The stoa of Attalos," said Mehmet. "A restoration."

Trees and shrubs interrupted some of the view of an ancient stony roadway to the right of the stoa sloping up towards…

"But where's the Parthenon?" I asked. I'd so expected to see it! The great mass of the Acropolis rock to the rear, steep and broad, did house two or three minor temples, but…

"Parthenon is on *far* side of Acropolis," explained Mehmet. "*That* there," indicating the broken roadway, "is where ghost travels. Panathenaic Way. In ancient times used for a procession to honour goddess Athena, taking new cloak for her statue inside Parthenon. Big festival every four years."

"We'd have a better view from up top," observed Phil.

"Up is temporarily closed," said Mehmet. "Ghost-watchers might fall off the rock."

We withdrew for coffee to a nearby restaurant, open to the air under awnings. Already sunshine was warming the morning; just a few fleecy clouds in the cobalt sky. A road-train like a huge red toy trundled tourists past. First we were bothered by a swarthy old gypsy woman toting embroidery, then by a little girl who could have been her great-granddaughter equipped with a desultory accordion, then by a black guy selling watches; all of whom Mehmet saw off while we were talking.

"I wonder," Phil said to Mehmet, "if we can rent an upstairs room somewhere along here for tonight to take photos, so we have a better view? Assuming the ghost shows up again. Do you think fifty euros would be reasonable to offer?"

"Hmm," mused Mehmet. "Agora is archeology site. Might even be classed as museum. For sites and museums, Press persons need special permits."

"We wouldn't be *inside* the Agora."

"You are not needing foreign press accreditation from Public Relations Directorate because you are not based in Greece, but *it* issues the special permits you would need."

"Using telephoto from a private room..."

Mehmet grinned. "Better if you can be inside with the ghost!"

Just then a couple of official-looking white vans came past us down the narrow street, to turn towards the Agora, and Mehmet jumped up.

"I know a face! Come, come!"

Those vans belonged to the National Technical University, and Mehmet knew a Professor Zygourakis as well as, for a bonus, an accompanying Ministry of the Interior and Public Order woman called Anastassiades. Upshot: there would be a cordoned viewing area inside the Agora for TV and press and interested parties, in which we'd now be included.

Since so far the spooky phenomenon had only appeared by night, Phil and I could turn our daytime attention to the rebellion by young people, anarchists, and radicals. Its base was the Exarchia district a bit north-east of Athens University, though it seemed that trouble easily spilled further, resulting in lots of broken shop windows, stones versus tear gas, and intermittent closures of the centre of town.

We took a subway, gleaming heritage of the 2004 Olympic Games, then walked a while as Phil and Mehmet held forth about youth unemployment, anti-capitalism, anti-globalisation, rage at government and the economy, hatred of the police, and a 15-year-old schoolboy martyr called Alex who'd been shot dead a couple of years back, perhaps accidentally, perhaps not.

After a bit I said, "Mrs Anastasia from Public Order –"

"Anastassiades," Mehmet corrected me.

"Her being at the Agora… well, if the so-called ghost obligingly causes enough of a sensation…"

"You think this is being manipulated?" asked Phil.

"It's convenient. Anniversary of the martyr's death."

"These protesters are stupid, stupid!" broke in Mehmet. "Why wreck innocent shopkeepers' windows, and even burn shops and cars? What good does that do to anyone?"

Of course Mehmet had his carpet business to worry about.

Presently we were passing groups of police at the ready, and before long we came to the martyr's shrine in a street daubed with graffiti and postered with declarations. The street had been renamed after him by activists. Bunches of flowers and pot plants were piled, along with outstretched football scarves, empty beer cans, candles and scrawled tributes. Young people thronged the roadway, many of them hooded, others dressed like Palestinians. Armed riot police with visors down, wearing gasmasks, bunched nearby clutching shields. Mehmet translated some slogans.

"That one says *Kill the Cops*. And there's *We Won't Go Away*.

Fight the State. Oh, and: *Buy till you die! There is no right to shop.* Idiots."

Several more maturely dressed onlookers appeared respectful.

"Those are communists," said Mehmet.

A young, scarfed woman in a black tracksuit was animatedly addressing a group of her contemporaries, while constantly pushing her long dark rebel hair aside from a chubby face. She paused to stare at Phil who, apart from his professional-looking camera with which he was taking pictures, stood out, being tall and skinny with ginger curls and very blue eyes. Me, I was chunkier, my brown thatch close-cropped. Abruptly she strode over.

"Are you foreign journalists?" she asked in excellent English.

"British," I said. "May I interview you?"

She squinted at Mehmet with a degree of suspicion, as though he might be an official minder, but Mehmet rattled off some explanation in Greek, and she relaxed.

"I could use a beer," she said. "My name's Eleni. Nothing will happen yet. If it does, the people organise themselves spontaneously. I just tell my boyfriend." She darted away to a surly-looking hooded fellow with pocked cheeks, a long nose and an attempt at a moustache, who evidently was very much under her sway since she returned to us on her own almost immediately. I noticed how ski goggles nestled within the ample scarf Eleni wore and made the connection: protections against tear-gas. Her black trainers would be for speed if needed.

Eleni led us quickly through several streets, which looked as though a minor running battle had taken place, till on a bigger thoroughfare she hustled us inside a rather posh pub that seemed to have migrated from Germany or Belgium, judging by the veritable exhibition of glass and stoneware drinking vessels on many shelves. *Beer Academy,* the place was called, and it boasted a redoubtable beer menu several pages long.

Mehmet excused himself. He had business; he'd phone

about meeting up later. Anyway, he was probably Moslem and immune to the delights of beer.

Presently we were all sampling a delicious strong Trappist ale, and a great platter was arriving laden with various sorts of German sausages, sauerkraut, sliced radicchio, and mustards.

"Gosh," remarked Phil, "there's enough here to feed an army."

Eleni unzipped the top of her tracksuit, revealing several newspapers. Worn for added warmth or to blunt the impact of rubber bullets if any got fired?

"What we don't eat," she said, "I shall wrap up and take back."

So Phil and I, or rather Max, would be providing a snack for the youth troops.

"I take it this place is immune from left-wing *kristallnacht,*" Phil murmured to me. In Exarchia we'd seen fancy bistros and sexy lingerie boutiques as well as walls sprayed with anarchist symbols. By and large it was bigger shops downtown that had their windows smashed.

I put my little recorder on the table.

"You want to know about our rebellion," said Eleni while munching some frankfurter. "It'll be an insurrection nationwide if the police kill another one of us..."

Presently I happened to mention that what brought us here initially was the 'ghost of Athens', and Eleni flared up.

"That is a distraction from the struggle! The Greek civil war has never truly stopped, and now we have a farce of failed greedy capitalism using television as a brain-deadening control mechanism. Last night a panel of idiot experts argues about the ghost instead of asking why half the women who leave high school are jobless. Can this stupid ghost happening right now be a coincidence?"

"Maybe I'll find out tonight when the scientists do tests in the Agora." I cut some wurst while it was still hot and dipped it in a sweet mustard.

For the next few minutes it was as if Eleni was interviewing me. Tests? Tonight? Witnessed by specially admitted TV and journalists…?

"A media circus," she said, "to blind gullible viewers and readers to reality. An alternative to silly girls dancing in their underwear: paranormal rubbish."

We ate. We got on with the interview. Alex the martyr. The evil of consumerism. The vicious police. The absence of genuine individual rights.

"Greece," I said, "seems stuck in a kind of 1968 time-warp when Red Brigades and Baader-Meinhofs were all the rage."

"No," said Eleni, "we have taken over the baton in the contest for freedom and dignity."

Presently she wrapped up the unconsumed sausages and sauerkraut in a newspaper, tucked this inside her tracksuit, and departed.

"Not much wrong with the police," said Mehmet later. "If you go for assistance, they are helpful and polite. Hysteria about police is due to previous dictatorship under the Colonels. Someone must keep order against mindless anarchy."

After the interview with Eleni, Phil and I had gone back to our hotel to catch some sleep since we might be up till the early hours of the morning ghost-spotting. Mehmet collected us at six and led us to his favourite place for doner kebab, a meal fit for *heroes*, he joked, since that's what the name of the meal sounded like in Greek; it was certainly large enough for Hercules. That was near Monastiraki Station – I was getting my bearings! – from which it was only a few minutes' walk to the Agora. Phil apologized to Mehmet about keeping him out at night in the chill, but Mehmet wasn't going to miss a manifestation.

So, by 9 p.m., we ourselves and at least three hundred others including TV crews, journalists, scientists, government people and a score of police were in the huge Agora in a large cordoned area parallel to the Panathenaic Way. Garden lights, specially installed, softly illuminated the ground which was quite irregular due to stones of antiquity. No floodlights lit the Acropolis, the better for us to see what might transpire by the faint light of a sickle-moon now risen.

I sought an opinion from Mrs Anastassiades – must get her name right.

"This is so well organised," I said. "Almost as if you can *guarantee* something's going to happen. What if we stand here all night and nothing does?"

"Of course we cannot guarantee anything, Mr Johnson! We have no idea of the cause."

In one respect she was to be proved right almost immediately in a way that neither she nor presumably her colleagues had foreseen...

Out of the darkness and scattered bushes to the right, hundreds more people began to emerge, taking up chants. Torches flared – the sort with flames. Flickering firelight revealed a converging army of young people in hooded balaclavas, crash helmets, Arab-style keffiyehs, football scarves and masks, the rebels against society from Exarchia and probably others besides.

"It's a pitch invasion!" exclaimed Phil delightedly as he snapped photos.

In the vanguard I recognized Eleni, brandishing a pole with a flag which she swung to and fro to reveal... ah, the word started with A so it might be the name ALEX in Greek; or maybe the A was for Anarchy.

Sirens started up in the direction of Monastiraki. More police were hurrying into the Agora to reinforce the score of officers already with us, who were deploying to form a line to protect our flimsy corral. Mrs Anastasia was jabbering into a phone. Could there be five hundred protesters bearing down on us by now? They must have infiltrated the wooded extremes of the extensive Agora by cutting through whatever fences or maybe scaling those using ladders. A policeman panicked and fired several pistol shots over the heads of the oncoming mob... which began to howl vengefully, as though this was the provocation they desired. Photo-journalists and TV people were colliding with one another in their eagerness to capture what was happening, knocking over garden lights, while scientists protected their monitoring apparatus.

Of a sudden a bundle of radiant brightness appeared upon the Panathenaic Way. For a few seconds this dazzled unidentifiably – and I felt a strange electricity surge through my body, not a shock exactly but the kind of sensation as when your teeth accidentally bite on some tinfoil, only much multiplied and throughout the whole of me. "Ouch, did you feel that, Phil?" "Feel what?" Next moment, the brightness came into clear focus.

A man made of light, clad in rags of some bygone noble-looking apparel, was toiling wearily up the ancient roadway, roped twice around the chest so as to drag behind him on a pallet the white marble head of a horse, eyeballs bulging, mouth open.

As the man swung his head like a dull tormented beast, I was riveted by the absence of a nose.

"It's *Elgin!*" I cried. "It's Lord Elgin!"

Yes, that man of light was none other.

Around him, now here, now there, flickered a cute little boy and a cute little girl, two cherubic figures of light who stabbed at Elgin's posterior with sharpened sticks, goading him on… no, not sticks, those were artist's paintbrushes, reversed, the pointed ends to the fore. The progress of the pallet struck me as distinctly smoother than if were proceeding over the irregularities which I knew were present, more as though it was sliding slowly up a decently laid roadway.

Goaded onward, the Seventh Earl lurched and staggered, haggard and gaunt.

"Poor chap's in an awful shape," said Phil. "But what do you mean, *Elgin?*"

"He is a *ruin*," Mehmet joined in. "Don't try to say that in Greek" – as if we could! – "*háli* is a ruin, but *halí* is a carpet. Bad business to say one's carpet is a ruin." Yes thank you, Mehmet.

A voice – from where? it seemed everywhere – wailed loudly, "Oy-mayyy! O *Kos*-mayyyy…!"

An American nearby demanded loudly, "What's that mean?" as more words lamented through the air.

His companion, a woman, replied, "O me! O World! It's Ancient Greek. O World! O Woe! The Goddess's Temple Was Ravaged by Him!"

"Ravaged by Elgin!" I called out. "That's *Elgin* there! The man with no nose!"

Because, of course, *I* had his nose on my face…

As the Seventh Earl proceeded laboriously up the Panathenaic Way, hauling his burden towards where it had been looted from, tormented by spectral boy and spectral girl, the army of youths came to a standstill, staring at the bright eerie sight. Everyone, even police, were gaping.

Mrs Anastasia was by my side, demanding, "What do you mean, that is *Elgin*?"

Her tone conveyed that my ancestor's name was tantamount to a swearword. If she was complicit in some government hoax, her astonishment was well acted.

"Isn't it obvious?" I said. "He's being punished for his crimes – by having to drag marbles back to where they came from. But what are those cute imps that are goading him?"

"Yeah, what *are* those acrobat kids?" joined in the American.

They were cartoon characters, the mop-headed boy wearing short turned-up trousers, a loose t-shirt and baseball cap, the girl with her long Bardot tresses likewise. Big cartoon trainers on their feet; their eyes, big cartoon ovals.

"I *know* those," declared Mrs A. "They're from a colouring book for children. Called something like *Paint Athens 2004*, yes it was published for the Olympic Games." She crossed herself, and her voice rose direly, almost an echo of that sourceless O *Kos-mayyy* voice which had fallen silent for the moment, although a keening noise could now be heard like microphone feedback. "But those aren't the happy children in that book – they're the

Erinnyes, the Eumenides with a modern appearance! The avengers of blasphemy as well as of parent-slaughter. They can take any form they choose."

Other people around were calling out in Greek something like Eumenides.

"Come again?" said Phil.

"They're the Dogs of Hades who tormented the guilty, who pursued Orestes here to Athens, *right here to this very place*, he who murdered his mother, the Furies singing a spell-binding song to secure their victim!"

Surely that thin screeching I was hearing was merely microphone feedback; though from where, and how?

"That happened right here?" I echoed.

"On the Areopagus hill just over there, where Orestes was tried, and the Goddess Athena – Pallas Minerva – she voted for mercy, and to appease the Furies she invited them to live in a cave near here, and be honoured by the citizens, and be the defenders of Athens forever. My God, what is happening?"

I thought I knew what was happening, rationally at least...

Parts of the youth army were chorusing a word that sounded like *koro-idea!*

"They say hoax, mockery," from Mehmet. "They think this is a... *téchnasma*, an artificial stunt."

A phantasm produced by technology... With my detested ancestor as a scapegoat dragging his burden slowly onward and upward, to act as a lightning conductor for political anger. Actually, this all seemed rather monstrously unfair to old Elgin. After all, early Christians also vandalised the Parthenon, then Turks made it into a mosque by adding a minaret, and later the Turks even stored gunpowder inside the building which a Venetian artillery shell exploded, blowing the roof off and knocking down columns. Much havoc had already been wreaked by the time my obsessed ancestor (divinely inspired, so he thought) bribed the Turkish authorities to let him 'rescue' the best remaining sculptury, even if in the process, using explosives and saws, his workers caused more collapses and shatterings to the extent that even some Turkish official shed a tear and lamented, "It's the end!" One wonderful cornice had fallen and smashed into umpteen pieces. Proudly Elgin had carved his name halfway up the Parthenon, as well as his wife's name.

But hadn't he been punished enough, driven half mad by events, haggard, raging, constipated and staggering about (a bit like the ghost, although obviously I knew nothing about the ghost's bowels), then losing his wife to a lover, going bankrupt, fleeing his creditors, dying in poverty in Paris? Or had the Furies been responsible for those calamities *too*, prior to Elgin's afterlife? If Elgin hadn't stolen the marbles, Napoleon would almost certainly have done so. However, Elgin succeeded (by and large), so he became the *bête noire*, the bogeyman, guilty of crimes like a looting Goering.

Those Furies, Disneyfied…

"What's the different between Erinnyes and Eumenides?" I asked Mehmet, who looked blank.

Mrs A said distractedly, "Eumenides means *kindly ones*."

"Is that sarcasm?" asked Phil.

"No, that was their new name after Athena's merciful verdict on Orestes, to appease them as benevolent protectors of Athens. It's all in Aeschylus."

Aeschylus. Ah yes, him: the playwright. *That*, I could check up on. Why ever would Mrs A blurt out the source of this…

"*Koro-idea! Koro-idea!*" chanted the youth mob.

…this hoax, to a journalist, if she was a knowing party to it? To try to lead me astray from blaming the government, by appearing innocent and bewildered? Anyway, would the plan be to repeat this *son et lumière* on subsequent nights? Come to think of it, the alleged scientific measuring equipment might be partly responsible for producing the spectacle, which had only snapped into proper focus tonight, amplified…

"O *Kos*-mayyyy…!" mourned that bodiless voice loudly again.

"Koro-idea! Koro-idea!"

A missile of some sort flew by – no, I'd swear that was an owl on the wing. Surely it should have shunned the rowdiness and brightness. The owl veered over the apparition – yes, clearly it was an owl – and headed out of sight in the same direction as Elgin and his burden.

An astounding realization came to me. The sharp pang which had passed through my entire frame a while previously, and which Phil hadn't registered at all – so that it couldn't have been some electromagnetic side-effect of a power source or projected images – that had been *followed* a moment later by the intensification and much clearer focus of the apparition. Could it be that my own presence, me with Elgin's nose upon my face and consequently a particular cluster of genes in every cell of my body, had resonated with the ghost, or the ghost with me?

Before I could puzzle about this, a flare flew from out of the youth army, arcing high, burning bright, as if to dim or rival the spectacle on the Panathenaic Way. A second flare followed. Someone must have got hold of a Very Pistol or some single-shot tubes of distress flares. Stolen, maybe, from some yacht; there'd be lots of those moored along the sea front. The youth of Athens were indeed distressed, yet this was a reckless way to show it.

The first flare dropped down towards us in the corral, still burning. Panicking, people pushed aside, and the flare dropped into a vacant space, illuminating all around. Moments later the second flare likewise fell amongst us without setting fire to anyone's clothes, although there were more squeals of fright.

A sudden flash and a fierce bang made my heart jump as if a grenade had gone off. Then came another similar explosion in our midst, and screams, though those didn't have the agonised sound of injury. Fireworks, that's what! Some of the rebel youths were hurling bangers at us.

At that moment a thunderous crash rolled over us, as if Zeus himself had answered. Still dazzled by the fall of flares, I couldn't see any thunderclouds. Shrieks came from within the youth army;

I suspected someone had blown his hand off – mishandling a firework too dangerous, or maybe a maroon.

"Fucking hell," said Phil. "This is getting hairy."

I was knocked aside by a visored, gasmasked policeman in full riot gear. He and others were heading for the youth mob – which reacted by rushing to break through the flimsy corral into our midst, swelling our numbers hugely as they used us as cover. Those police who had already been amongst us were now wrestling and punching hooded adversaries. Would the riot police fire tear gas into this confused medley of apparition-spectators, many of them hysterical by now, and their own colleagues, as well as protestors out of control?

Eleni appeared before me, still clutching her pole.

"You!" she exclaimed. Since I'd been clutching my little recorder all this time, to store my own commentary and Mrs A's responses, I thrust this at Eleni.

"What are your plans?" I asked, rather stupidly.

She grinned wildly like a madwoman. "Thank you for inspiration!" was her reply. "It's just like ancient times when the people arose against tyrants right here!"

Oh shit, I thought, hoping that Mrs A nearby wouldn't register the first remark. But then Eleni registered Mrs A, discarded her pole, which almost beaned Phil who was still trying to take pictures, and she launched herself upon Mrs A, embracing her so that I thought for a moment that Mrs A was Eleni's respectable bourgeois mother, agent of the establishment and the evil government, whom the daughter had rejected yet whom, meeting her now so surprisingly at such a hectic moment, Eleni attempted to hug.

No such thing. Eleni shouted, so that two hoodies responded by also seizing hold of Mrs A. One of them I recognised as Eleni's surly pock-cheeked boyfriend. Swiftly Eleni unwrapped her scarf, twisting the garment till it was more like a woollen rope, and tied it around Mrs A's mouth as a gag; whereupon the hoodies began dragging the resisting, kicking Mrs

A off through the milling confusion in the direction of darkness – they were trying to take her hostage.

"Stay out of this!" Eleni ordered me, before hurrying to join the would-be abductors.

How could Phil and I let this happen? "Police!" I called out. "Help!"

"*Voeethya!*" (or something) bellowed Mehmet, who hadn't made any move to intervene earlier.

A policeman did appear quickly before us, heeded Mehmet's explanation and gesticulations and pulled out a radio. Then he headed where Mehmet had pointed.

By now many people had spilled on to the Panathenaic Way so as to escape the fighting. Urged by Mehmet, Phil and I struggled in their wake. Max was going to be very pleased with his little investment. Just then I blundered into a small bush and tripped, scuffing my palms.

Scrambling up, I realised I'd been so distracted that I'd stopped paying attention to the apparition, or to where it was. As we emerged on to the ancient roadway, there it still was, in the middle distance, the spectre of Elgin toiling exhaustedly to drag his horsey hunk of marble uphill, pricked by those flitting little fiends. By now surely they should have been out of projector range, if any of the apparatus in the corral had been responsible; or maybe more was elsewhere. As the three of us pursued the phenomenon, clouds of gas erupted. The riot police must have run out of any other option as to how to quell the jumbled chaos, irrespective of how this would affect the innocent, or how it would come over in the news; or because that was their true nature as the young people claimed.

A wind had sprung up, so that some gas drifted rapidly uphill in our direction, and I smelled a curious odour which I didn't associate at all with tear gas, CS gas, which I'd experienced in the past in Israel.

Had something else got into the armoury of the police? Maybe a rogue cartridge of hallucinatory riot gas – BZ, yes that was the name of the stuff – accounted for my, for want of a better word, hallucinations? Dare I say visions? Which, be it noted, Phil did not share...

I saw ahead of me, in tunnel vision as though through the wrong end of a telescope, a tiny scene which suddenly raced towards me, expanding.

Goaded and on his last legs, my ancestor hauled his load towards a towering female figure which just had to be that of Athena, goddess of Athens, who once dominated the interior of the Parthenon.

The Goddess was crowned with a triple helmet, three curving crests rising from figurines – two griffins flanking a sphinx. A pleated gown, gathered at her waist, hung down to her sandals, her toes showing. Torques clasped her upper arms. Snakes writhed on a short cloak reaching midway down her draped breasts. Resting against the inner crook of one elbow was a spear not unlike Eleni's pole. A wide round face, straight nose, dark-pupil eyes. She was magnificent, aglow.

Halting at last, Elgin sank to his knees, his rope falling loose. Would this be the moment when, just as with what's-his-name punished in Hades by being compelled to push a heavy stone uphill, the pallet and marble horse-head proceeded to trundle backwards, picking up speed, all the way down to the bottom of the slope once more?

As may have happened over and over. Otherwise surely by now Elgin might realistically have heaved back to where they rightly belonged the ghosts of all the marbles he stole two centuries and a bit ago?

Time – or eternity – might be entirely different for him, and for the Eumenides...

The two child-Furies sprang to this side, to that, as if unappeasable, their energy inexhaustible. Like hyperactive kids, no less. Athena was speaking, although I heard no words. The wreck of Elgin was replying silently. The kids seemed to be squawking in protest.

And the Goddess stretched out a hand. Reluctantly, each Fury surrendered its goad into her palm. Swiftly Athena reversed the goads, so that when the kids in their baseball caps and big trainers received the sticks back again those were artists' brushes held for painting – or for tickling – rather than for jabbing.

Of a sudden the scene raced away, shrinking, collapsing... as likewise, I assume, so did I.

I woke to daylight in a hospital bed – one glimpse of my surroundings, plus that characteristic odour, absolutely shouted hospital even before I propped myself groggily on one elbow to focus upon beds in a ward. To my left, sitting up against pillows studying a newspaper, one arm in a sling, was Mrs Anastassiades in a hospital gown and cardigan. Her mobile phone lay on the blanket in front of her. Doubtless other occupants of the row of beds were victims from the previous night. A bored policeman sat by the door.

"You were rescued!" I called out to Mrs A. Did she know the part I played in shouting the alarm on her behalf?

She regarded me wryly. "In fact I raised my knee between the legs of one of the young men, and in the eyes of the other I managed to put my fingers. But then unfortunately I fell over a big piece of stone."

"Oh. So you fought them off. Congratulations." Furtively I checked that I wasn't catheterised or some such.

"I apologize about our hotheaded young people. Last night was most unfortunate. Some of them," she added, rustling the newspaper, "even vandalised the Parthenon with paint."

I hauled myself up. "Did you say *paint* – ?"

At this point Phil arrived, with Mehmet. "Good to see you back in the land of the living! Interviewing already, old son? Your recorder ought to be in that cabinet beside you." He produced my palmtop which I'd left at the hotel. "I reckoned you'd be wanting to write the piece for Max asap."

"Yes, yes… Did you see what happened to the ghost?"

"Just disappeared, that's all. Out like a light. Quite like you."

Mehmet beamed. "I'm happy to see you well, Mr Johnson."

"Thanks, yes… Mrs Anastassiades," I managed, "what kind of paint?"

"Obviously spray cans, to cover so much in blue and red."

"Did you know, Mr Johnson," put in Mehmet, "the Parthenon was originally painted blue and red, and gold too in parts?"

"Eh?"

"You're joking," said Phil.

"No, the Greeks painted buildings, and statues too. Parthenon stones nowadays are not as Pericles saw them."

"Why would they paint beautiful white marble? Well, not white exactly. More honey-colour, isn't it?"

I hadn't even *seen* the Parthenon yet. Which seemed odd when I recalled that, to ensure correct perspective, its columns cleverly converged and would meet one and a half miles up in the sky, so it ought to have been visible… I put the daft thought away.

"Why paint it?" said Mehmet. "For adornment. And to show off. In fact the white of Pentelic marble would not *stay* white. Mixed in it, is iron. This rusts. Iron oxide. So now marble looks honey."

I had to laugh. "You mean, lacking the original paint, what's left of the Parthenon is *rusty*? So to restore and protect it properly, the Parthenon ought to be painted?"

"That's ridiculous," said Mrs A. "We'll clean the vandals' paint off."

"As many times as you have to?"

"What do you mean?"

"What if the paint reappears?"

"We'll have better security! It's strange how the vandals weren't spotted last night."

"Don't you remember that the kiddy Furies, just like in that colouring book you told me about, were using the sharp ends of paintbrushes to goad Elgin? What if they gave the brushes to Elgin? Magically replenishing brushes?"

"Did you bang your head badly last night? We shall scrub the columns clean once and for all."

"You mustn't do that!" I protested. "That's as bad as the British Museum did with the marbles. They even used metal scrapers to clean them, which was stupid. You ought to leave the paint, or add to it."

"*Mr* Johnson, how dare you criticize our custodianship after admitting the vandalism of the British Museum! That is why the marbles must be returned to their home!"

"Yes, but not to that new museum you built at such expense. To the Parthenon *itself*, where they belong. Surely they can be re-attached after a spot of rebuilding."

"Easy, easy," Phil hissed at me. "*Did* you bang your head?"

"Re-attaching is how my ancestor would want to atone, seeing as Athena has forgiven him by now."

Everyone was gaping at me. I seemed to have lost control of what I was saying. I felt like some oracle at Delphi gasping the words of a god.

"Easy, old son!"

I couldn't help myself. "And now the Furies have become *Semi*-Kindly Ones at least, thanks to Athena. What's she supposed to look like, by the way, Athena?"

"Mr Johnson," said Mehmet, worried, "how can we know how an imaginary pagan goddess looks?"

"What did her statue in the Parthenon look like?"

Maybe a madman, or a concussion victim, should be treated circumspectly. Mehmet heaved a sigh.

"I believe the golden idol had a short cloak of snakes hanging from the neck... On her head was a helmet with three... horns? no not horns, wrong word..."

"Say no more." I had truly seen the Goddess.

Mrs A looked daggers. "Mr Johnson, did you just say that

Lord Elgin is your *ancestor?*"

"State you're in, Nige," said Phil, "you shouldn't write *anything* for Max today."

"How else could I recognize Elgin last night? Because of pictures, where his nose, um, wasn't yet missing. Why am I so familiar with pictures of him unless there's a *family* connection?" I was on the point of adding *I have his nose,* but I censored myself in time. "Don't worry, Phil, I can stick to facts for Max."

"Before you send anything, I'd better take a look at the story."

Mrs A looked poised to demand the same, although she couldn't order any such thing even if she was the Minister of Order herself.

"Is that why you came here to do a story, Mr Johnson?" she asked instead. "Because you *already* supposed Elgin might be involved? *Why* should you imagine that? Is the British Government involved in this *manifestation?* Is it some crazy scheme to keep the stolen marbles in London by making Greece seem ridiculous? It is *you* who shouted out that the supposed ghost was Elgin, no one else! Are you an *agent provocateur?*"

Aha, I could see her drift. Far from the manifestation being a political distraction organised by the Greek government, which had gone badly wrong, here was some perfidious James Bond exploit on the part of the British. The British Museum in cahoots with MI6 had prepared the ground, then I'd arrived to infiltrate myself. Us Brits would carry out any devious stunt to retain the marbles for which we'd fought against Napoleon! For that matter, an international consortium of museums might be responsible, since if Britain ever sent the Parthenon marbles back to Greece this would set a precedent for restitution of many looted art treasures to their countries of origin. Maybe the Russian SVR were the pranksters, using some miniaturised technology that melted after use, to protect the collection in the Hermitage if any of it was vulnerable.

Such could be the spin the Greeks might give to the chaos

last night. I could see how Mrs A was already working this out, her newspaper dropped, her fingers unconsciously fondling the mobile phone. My god, if she had her way I could be arrested as a suspect, taken in for questioning. Which would certainly delay my writing a story. I might even be transferred to a psychiatric hospital, as delusional, unfit to fly on any plane. Or was I being paranoid, the way Elgin became due to stress?

Mrs A got out of bed, placed her mobile phone in the fingers protruding from the sling, and stalked off down the ward, doubtless heading for the toilets where she'd have privacy.

"Look, Phil," I said, "I have to get out of this place right now. We need to fly home *today*. Asap."

"But you can't leave without being discharged first. Doctors usually do their rounds late morning, don't they? Anyway, what about tonight?"

Misunderstanding, I remembered Phil's idea of painting the town red at Max's expense. "Phil, the Parthenon has already been painted red – and blue."

"I don't quite follow you…"

Then I cottoned on. Obviously he couldn't see things from my perspective. For only I had seen the Goddess.

"Phil, nothing more will happen in the Agora tonight."

"How do you know?"

"The climax was last night. The energy discharged."

"You mean the riot?"

Useless to explain, so I nodded. "Yes, the riot happened. Now things will calm down, because… because a riot in the Agora will have shocked everybody. The militants will have lost whatever popular sympathy they had because of the Parthenon being daubed with paint."

"You could be right," he conceded. "Still, one day more?"

"One day more," said Mehmet enthusiastically. "I take you to an interesting club."

"I want to get dressed right now and just walk out."

Mehmet said, "I think the policeman prevents you."

With a sigh, I relapsed against the pillows. The prospect of interrogation and or detention in a mental hospital for observation was drawing closer.

After a while Mrs A returned, laid her phone on the blanket, and got back into bed.

She cleared her throat. "The young woman who incited my attempted abduction was arrested, you know. Apparently a British journalist tipped her off about arrangements in the Agora. Mr Johnson, I think you should leave Greece quickly before people become impatient with you."

A wave of relief passed over me. She had consulted, reporting my peculiar state of mind as she saw it. The wisest council evidently was that my babbling about Athena and my ancestor meant I was an embarrassment waiting to happen. So I should take my nervous breakdown elsewhere. An editor would be unlikely to print any such revelations even in a paper of Max's stripe, a point that Phil had already hinted at. I'd have no choice but to make my story more normal. Which I could easily, since I was perfectly sane, and not stupid.

If I wrote a full account, it would need to be dressed up as fiction.

Even though I knew the truth.

For I had seen the Goddess.

For I have the nose of Lord Elgin.

In 2009 I revisited Athens after 42 years. Mere days after I departed on the previous occasion, the rightwing Colonels took over in a military coup. Back then I remember scowls directed at me because I was an English-speaking foreigner with a beard, therefore I must be a degenerate American hippy, rather than coming from East Africa where beards were common among bwanas. (I'd also stopped in Cairo, where riflemen guarded the Nile bridges, and a few weeks later an Arab-Israeli war broke out.) Amidst the apparent

Greek prosperity of 2009 a full-blown economic crisis was simmering; and also simmering for many years has been Greek annoyance at London's British Museum housing marbles looted from the Parthenon by Lord Elgin during the Napoleonic Wars. An awesome new museum in Athens majestically awaits their return.

Returning the marbles might open the floodgates of many nations demanding restoral of their national treasures to their homelands, but I say that the Elgin Marbles must go back to Greece — not to be stuck in yet another museum but to be reattached to a repaired Parthenon, which also needs to be painted brightly just as it was in ancient times, since the honeyed hue of today's Parthenon is due to rust — there's iron in Pentelic marble. Paint the Parthenon! Those ancient Greeks knew a thing or two.

Long Stay

The Luton-Stansted Long Stay Car Park spans the twenty-six miles between those two airports, nominally of London.

Twenty-six miles as the crow flies, a natural consequence of those airports expanding in capacity. On a map, the car park cuts a serpentine swathe five miles wide across the countryside, avoiding significant towns, although hundreds of villages were erased, their inhabitants mostly choosing resettlement along the costas of the south of Spain where the huge and highly efficient desalination plants constantly convert the Mediterranean into water for taps, car washes, golf courses, and seas of vegetables under plastic.

Due to the car park's serpentine shape, perhaps not exactly as crows fly. But anyway.

When the automated shuttle bus let Rob Taverner off at zone S46, he knew he had a fair distance to wheel his suitcase to his car. When he'd found a parking space a fortnight earlier in lane 48, it had taken Rob – what, fifteen minutes? – on foot to reach the shuttle stop. So he hoped that the fine mizzle wouldn't turn into heavier rain before he reached his car. If so, he did have an umbrella.

Another passenger, an attractive young auburn-haired woman, had also descended at the same stop as himself, a compact antirape-taser looped around her wrist; but she quickly headed off into the far distance of serried vehicles in a different direction from the north-westerly bearing which Rob must follow.

Lane 48 was Rob's own age plus three, which was easy to remember, just as the 46 in S46 was his age plus two, whilst S was the *single* letter of the alphabet between Rob and Taverner. R S T, one, two, three, easy-peasy. Of course, he had also typed S46/L 48 into the memo of his phone as well as scribbling the same on the parking ticket residing in his wallet.

The yard-wide rows of vegetables that divided lines of parked cars – hereabouts, carrots – offset the carbon caused by cars coming and going, and the carrots looked about ready for harvest. Since the comings and goings of cars were one-off low-pollution events, the car park vegetables were almost organic. Maybe the veg even offset a percentage of aircraft exhaust, although out here in S46 Rob was too far from Stansted's four runways – an hour and a half away in the shuttle bus – to see any planes climbing or circling, even if the sky had been clear; in which case he would only have seen high criss-crossing contrails. Some crows were circling instead of flying in straight lines. Actually, those weren't crows. They were rooks. Rooks are sociable; crows are solitary. Old country saying: If you'm see a rook, thar's a crow; if you'm see crows, them's rooks.

Pulling his aluminium suitcase at a brisk pace over the somewhat weedy asphalt, Rob hummed *The Ride of the Valkyries* because that piece had been playing on the plane's compilation of classic soundtracks as they landed. By now he'd lost sight of the red-berried pyracantha hedges surrounding S46, providing razor-barb security of a sort. The greater security for parked vehicles was actually down to sheer numbers – statistically no harm was likely to happen to any individual car – plus of course the considerable distance from habitations. Really, you'd need to drop in by microlight to do any robbing.

Consequently, Rob was surprised to pass a trashed Hyundai, yet he quickly rationalised: *better yours than mine.* Nevertheless, he'd spotted no such sight during his earlier walk *to* the shuttle pick-up point. Either the trashing had taken place during the past two weeks, while he was in the south of Spain, or else he was off course.

Distant signs saying 43 and 44 reassured Rob. Not far now. Prickly-leaved courgettes with yellow trumpet-flowers and what were almost marrows lying on the soil underneath replaced the much lower and feathery carrots. Some of the courgettes were seriously overdue for plucking, but that's a problem with courgettes; they supersize so quickly. Turbulence in the mizzle appeared to be midges.

He passed a broken-into SAAB 8000, the windscreen shattered. As Rob paused, a magpie hopped out and took wing. Hastily Rob scanned around for another magpie, remembering his mother's rhyme, *One for sorrow, two for joy.* He had learned a lot about nature from his mother, now retired on the Costa de Almería. Sparrows and squabbling starlings were the only other birds visible – the rooks had departed. Zone S46 wouldn't reopen for newcomers until oldcomers returning from abroad had extracted enough cars. Still, it would have been nice to see something moving, such as a farmer doing his rounds, steering a trailer-train carrying immigrant pickers. A farmer, of course, by using a zapper, could enter the car park through special gates set at three-mile intervals along the north and south fences. Woe betide any parking person who tried to follow a farm vehicle out on to a lane, unauthorised. Signs in ten languages promised a five thousand Pound fine, or eight thousand euros.

Without the enormous airport car parks to store, at any one time, ten to twenty per cent of Britain's vehicles, what would the nation's roads be like? Probably at a standstill. The problem, Rob reflected, lay in Britain being an island. From the nearer countries of continental Europe, cars past their prime could easily migrate overland into Eastern Europe. Elderly Eastern European cars could in turn migrate to Turkey or Ukraine or wherever. Eventually clapped-out cars would reach the scrapyards of India, their materials to be recycled back to manufacturers in a reincarnation cycle.

Presently Rob reached lane 48, and looked left and right for his red Lexus Q-9000. Since he'd be driving homeward in a north-westerly direction, it would have been neater to emerge from the Luton end of the megapark, but he knew that his ticket would only let him exit from the Stansted end by which he'd first entered. People had run out of petrol making that error!

For the emergency services to bring a can of petrol would cost £418, assuming that the improvident, or unlucky, stranded motorist could alert them. On impulse Rob took out his mobile and noted that the signal was alternating between one bar and none.

Nor could you caper and mime before a CCTV camera on a high pole, since there were none, all available experienced watchers being needed for the intense CCTV surveillance of inhabited areas. Hereabouts was, and in a sense still remained, agricultural land, leased from farmers who retained cultivation rights, as witness the carrots and courgettes. Should every field of cabbages or cows be watched? An impossible task.

Where *was* the red Lexus Q-9000? The nine-thousandth car in the queue, as Rob sometimes thought of it, when he was stuck on a motorway for a few hours. God bless the airport carparks – vast oases of tranquillity and, yes, privacy – otherwise his vehicle might be the ten-thousandth car stuck in the queue.

His LexQ was nowhere to be seen, to right nor left, nor ahead nor behind.

Could it be that his Lex had been hotwired and stolen? Or officially towed away because he'd parked across the ghost of a white line scarcely visible any more?

Or might it be that he hadn't parked in S46/48 but in S48/46 instead, just for instance?

Panicking, Rob increased his pace. His bouncing, veering suitcase tried to fall over, so he had to slow down. With his remote he zapped this way and that way, hoping that the Lex might flash its lights, but no welcome winking resulted. Hard to say if it was actually raining; more a matter of rather wet air. Some of the veiling in the air was actually midges. Must be hard for them to keep a-wing, or maybe they liked damp air.

Half an hour later, Rob was seriously worried. Surely he must have made an error, yet what error? Phone and ticket agreed with his memory. Towed away: that must be it. Towed away, maybe, by a *farmer*? A farmer with a sideline in vehicles stolen to order? Suddenly he hated farmers, despite their knowledge of rooks and magpies and carrots and the weather.

Just search for thirty minutes more, systematically. After that, call it a day and return to the airport for assistance. Assistance with misplaced cars must exist. Such a misfortune must happen at least once a day. Once a week, anyhow. Sodding drizzle.

Rob trudged back to the bus stop at last and ensconced himself within the plastic shelter, which lacked even a bench seat. He pushed the autocall and waited by the tall steel bars of the secured exit gate, eyeing the road. No posters to read. A few cars passed by, headlights on.

Aha.

But the automated shuttle bus passed by without slowing.

Of course! This zone was closed as regards Departures! Only departing travellers would summon a bus, consequently his call wasn't heeded by the system. Angrily he rattled the bars, although they didn't rattle much. He eyed the viciously thorned hedge of pyracantha separating the zone from the roadside, abundant with bright red berries. When another car came along, his urgent semaphoring wasn't noticed. When a second passed, a pig-woman passenger eyed him stupidly. At least, she looked pig-stupid and a bit snouty. Which is most unfair to pigs, his mother's voice reminded him. Very bright, very clean animals, they are. Not that his mother had ever been a farmer! No, she had worked in a pharmacy. But she always watched nature channels on TV. Nice nature ones, not floods and earthquakes and hurricanes.

Realistically, who would stop their car for him when they wanted either to head home with as much speed as was possible, or to park in another zone to catch their flight after hours spent getting here?

If only he had stayed married to mad Jennifer, he could have been delivered to the front of the airport and collected again! Well, to within walking distance of the security barriers. Again, he consulted his phone and found no signal at all. What's more, the battery was lower than he had thought. What was it doing, *leaking*, like the sodding sky?

Midges circled but kept to themselves.

"Hey," called a voice. A young woman enveloped in a long grey raincoat plus hood. Straggly brown hair that looked a bit hacked. Sharp nose, small chin, beady eyes.

She joined him in the shelter. "Your car break down? Mine did. I was in such a hurry I left the side lights on. I mean, I thought I'd turned the lights fully off. So: battery drained. Engine wouldn't start."

"Me, I can't find my car at all. Maybe it's been stolen, maybe I noted down the wrong zone."

"Oh well," she said.

"You don't sound too worried. And you only just found out?"

"Oh no, about three months ago. My watch doesn't have a calendar, so I'm not sure."

"Three months? What have you been doing since then?"

She gestured vaguely. "Living here. Not much point in going home now. Parking fees and penalties would have vacuumed my overdraft limit within a few weeks. The mortgage would default. Little flat'll be repossessed, probably sold off by now. Parking's probably still sucking up anything it can, although I think the bank and credit cards will have shut me down."

"Didn't you try to escape to the airport? Wouldn't anyone help you?"

"Oh yes, some people helped. I see life different now. I'm free. My name's Weasel."

Rob stared at her face, then quickly away again as though the corner of his eye had detected some sudden movement, maybe of rooks on the scavenge. *Weasel*: how appropriate, especially after living here for the last three months. Surely that couldn't have been her chosen nickname prior to this. So therefore: bestowed by those people who 'helped'? He tried to recall any wisdom of his mother regarding weasels, but none came. Still, Weasel seemed friendly. Maybe dotty, in a different way from Jennifer whose nuttiness was extravert.

"What was your car?" Weasel asked.

"I hope it still *is*. A Lexus Q-9000. Red. A LexQ."

She whistled, perhaps derisively. "So you'll take longer to lose your house, unless you're already up to your eyeballs paying for Lexy. Unless it's a company car. You a director? If so, you can afford to stick around here for a while."

"I've no intention of sticking around here."

Another transit bus passed by without stopping, while Rob gesticulated in vain at a few passengers. Maybe he looked as though he was hurling non-verbal abuse at them.

"What's the alternative?" Weasel asked. "You a director? I've never met a director. Million quid bonuses every year. Phew."

"Not for me. I run an agency for textile designers. Well, I *am* the agency. The LexQ impresses clients a bit, and it's comfortable, seeing as I need to drive all over for meetings. I can't just use a van."

"Designers of what?"

"Duvet covers, curtains, et cetera."

"Can't you do all your meetings through the web?"

"If only. Trade fairs. Personal touch. Maybe if we had good enough virtual reality, but we don't. There are times when I get fed up with driving."

"Well." She gestured at their surroundings. "Problem solved. Relax."

"I told my designers I'd be back by tomorrow."

"Do they all work at your place in some big barn conversion?"

"Of course not. They all work at home, wherever. They e-mail me their designs. Final printouts by courier to ensure fidelity."

"Whose fidelity?"

"Printer fidelity. Absolutely exact colours."

"Aren't there any other agencies?"

Rob allowed that there were several.

"No one's indispensable," said Weasel.

"I am *not*," Rob said, "pursuing this line of logic. How do you survive here?"

"Mainly vegetarian. Plenty of that. Traps for rabbits and pheasants."

That might appeal to Mum. Or not.

Mum would miss him. What, in Spain, in a world, or at least a costa of her own?

"Weasel, haven't you asked a farmer for a ride out of here? You could even walk out when a farm gate opens." Using his mother's sayings, surely he could talk to a farmer. Of course! That was the way out.

"If a farmer assists an escape, he gets fined heavily as well. That's immigration law. So they're quite hostile. Also, we're pests, munching on their veg. Like rabbits. They carry licensed shotguns."

The farmers, obviously, not the rabbits.

"How about pushing a car into the perimeter fence then climbing on the roof and piling veg on top of the razor wire?"

"Not so simple or safe as it sounds. You don't get it, er...?"

"Rob."

"You don't get it, Rob. I'm free here. So are you."

Far from feeling liberated, he felt severely deprived, his worldly goods reduced to the contents of a suitcase.

"But," he said.

"But nothing. Let me show you the ropes hereabouts. You'll soon adjust."

"Is it you and your helpful friends who trashed cars in this zone?"

She shrugged. "Sometimes we need little extras. But actually," and she brightened, "Brian is one of us because we trashed his car too badly for him to drive it, and he isn't complaining. Not now he isn't, anyway."

"Why not trash all the fucking cars and expand into a fucking huge community?" cried Rob.

Weasel eyed Rob as though he was daft. "Sustainability, of course."

"Sure, I was pissed off for most of the first week," admitted Brian, a tubby red-faced fellow of middling height and age from Dublin, who was wearing a once natty striped suit, somewhat scuffed and stained by now. And a burgeoning russet beard.

They were now in Zone T15. There existed ways between zones, either due to persistence or to the spontaneous death of prickly Pyracantha.

"But after a while I thought to myself here's an opportunity to knock off the booze. Then there were the credit card debts and the mortgage, and I was fed up with Annie nagging, and she could look after delinquent Dermot, and did I adore being a glorified salesman for exorbitant shite? Weasel and her chums merely trashed a company car, not my own impeccable soul in painted steel."

By now it was night, and they were inside a long and oldish Volvo estate, Brian and Mog in the front, Rob with Weasel and Donny Dino side by side in the quite spacious rear. This was a bit like being in a very small private cinema, except that the screen was only showing steamed-up dripping darkness. And they weren't awaiting any performance, except that Rob fantasised now and then that a brightly-lit helicopter might suddenly descend like some UFO to rescue him from what wasn't exactly an abduction.

Donny Dino was Donald Something – already Rob forgot – from a band he had never heard of, *Velociraptors*. Clad all in black leather, except for his head of lengthening hair. Raggy-haired Mog, in front, wore robes over her bulk, and she had lipsticked thick cat's whiskers on her upper lip. Mog was given to chortling, a word which she explained had been invented by Lewis Carroll especially for *Through the Looking Glass and What Alice Found There* by combining *chuckle* with *snort*. Mog was still experimenting with what the precise noise should be, since *chuckle* suggests amusement yet *snort* suggests an element of derision. And yet, quoth the text, "he chortled in his joy."

"Like, you snort snow," Donny Dino, who had got fed up with doing lines of cocaine to make it as a velociraptor, had remarked earlier.

"Young man," Mog had retorted, "snort refers to breathing *out* in a noisy and violent way. Only an idiot would snort cocaine. The powder would all blow away. Unless that's an instance of a word turning around to mean its complete opposite. Just as," she rhapsodised, "those of us here have turned ourselves around to become the opposites of what we were before!"

Obviously Mog had much to occupy her mind in the car park, including attempting to express the perfect chortle, which, she claimed, was a practise like Zen – when you hit the target blindfold, then you'd be enlightened. Except, not hit with an arrow, but with one's voice, as it were. Some discussion had followed between her and Brian as to whether laughter was an aspect of voice.

"Well, can any speechless animal laugh?" she'd demanded of the Dubliner.

"Sure, a jackass can."

"To *our* ears, but what does *it* hear?"

Mog had provided carrot and cabbage stew cooked over a camping stove filled with petrol, and Rob knew from his mother that carrots help you to see in the dark. Elsewhere, in T19, four others of the tribe inhabited a Mazda, named after the Persian god of fire by the Japanese lightbulb company turned carmakers; but Rob hadn't met the Mazda contingent yet.

Presently the five passengers in the Volvo set about falling asleep. Despite closest proximity to the steering wheel you couldn't call Donald the driver; he was a passenger too. Rob was reminded of sleeping on a long-haul-jet flight, except that in this instance you could open a door and step outside to avoid deep-vein thrombosis and have a pee much more easily than in a superjumbo. Unless you were piggy-in-the-middle, which in this case was Weasel, who mightn't have experienced this position prior to Rob's advent; if so, she wasn't complaining. Maybe, being skinny, she appreciated the enhanced body heat. Midges had got inside the Volvo but were no bother.

Morning dawned with a squabbling of starlings over some torn-up baby rabbit dropped nearby by a crow, not by a rook.

"It's bath day today," announced Mog with a vast yawn. "Certainly smells like it," and she chortled to indicate *no offense.* "There's a Porsche Carrera Cabriolet in T18 that collects rainwater nicely after we cut off the hood and superglued the doors," she explained to Rob. "A posh bathtub with its seats pushed right back."

"But surely it never rains enough in a week to fill a car, even with downpours? Or is bathday once every season?"

"Some medieval chaps washed once a year, and *that* frequently was deemed eccentric. I'm all for hygiene once a fortnight."

"Which is how long it takes to fill up a posh?" Rob asked.

"Ah, how meanings have shifted in this brave new life of ours! No, there's a fire hydrant hatch where some village got bulldozed for more parking. We have a hose that fits."

"But isn't it rather cold in the bath?"

She chortled. "We have a big carton of US military Qikhot, combat in cold countries for the use of. This funny little supply drone crashed, like a winged box. Maybe they were testing it. Oh," she added, "we drilled a plughole in the bottom of the posh, in case you're wondering."

"But didn't police come, or soldiers?"

"Police, though by then we'd liberated the goodies and made off. They weren't going to search a million cars; just took the

wreckage away. You really must stop saying 'but' so much, Rob
But me no buts."

So after a breakfast of fried fungi the five set off for T18,
Rob feeling at once excited and disconcerted by the prospect of
communal nudity, Japanese fashion, which he certainly wouldn't
have experienced home alone. On the way, each went behind a
different car to do the toilet thing using paper distributed by
Mog.

This day promised to be brighter than the day before. Before too
long Rob was being introduced to Andy, Govinder, and the
Welsh sisters Melanie and Anastasia who looked nothing like
each other, since Melanie was dark chocolate coloured and tall
whereas Anastasia was blonde and short, both going on for thirty.

"Our Mum never knew Melanie means black," Anastasia
hastened to say in a melodious voice. "She just liked the sound of
the name."

"And blonde to her meant *Russian*," added Melanie,
"although to me Anastasia sounds like a plant, like a Nasturtium,
like. So if she does something nasty, I call her Nasturtium, like."

They seemed to like one another well enough to go on
holiday together, for instance, although maybe undercurrents of
rivalry existed. Rob forebore to ask whether the sisters had
different fathers, or an interesting blend of heritage within one
dad.

Tall, burly Andy sported a pony-tail which was trying to
become a horse's tail. Govinder was a mature and handsome
Sikh, so he wore a turban, a somewhat sloppy one, which
probably concealed a lot of hair, and a hairnet to control his
beard.

"Excuse me for asking," said Rob while shaking Govinder's
hand, "but aren't you supposed to wear ceremonial knives in your
turban and other places? How does that go down with airport
security?"

Govinder flashed a great grin. "Oh yes, we go armed to the

teeth! But it's a good idea to put the knives in the baggage. I painted our Sikh flag on my bag so security will realise." He seemed unabashed to be asked an intimate question about his religion, and even volunteered, "What I need most is some starch for my turban. Don't happen to have any, do you, Rob?"

"Alas," said Rob, "that isn't something I carry."

"What, British men don't use starch for the stiff upper lip?" And Govinder laughed uproariously, while Mog chortled a variation new to Rob's ear, more like a horse whinnying.

Andy proceeded to fill the Porsche, which took a while, and Melanie added moisturising bubble crème. This done, Anastasia chucked in three cubes of Quikhot and the bath really seethed.

"Me and our new friend first," cried Weasel.

Andy produced a big tartan car-rug for Weasel to strip behind; thus decencies were being observed. Once Weasel was reclining up to her neck in the Porsche, Rob followed suit while Weasel averted her gaze. Briefly Rob wondered what would happen if his new acquaintances ran away mischievously with all his clothes, but that seemed unlikely. As he sank down upon comfortable leather upholstery next to Weasel, she whispered, "No peeing in the water, mind."

"Certainly not."

Weasel bounced up and down, although not high enough to show him more than the top of her tits. "Beats a hard ceramic tub any day, eh?"

Well, it *did*. You'd pay good money at a spa for this sort of luxury! True, you wouldn't have midges circling above the water at a hotel spa, but what could you expect amidst nature?

And so bathtime proceeded, turn by turn. When Mog climbed in, water slopped over the side, and she – but of course she did.

Afterwards Rob confessed to Brian, "I think I'm going mad."

"Sure, that's the old normality draining away like dirty bathwater out of the bottom of a posh, and the new normality clocking in, now wouldn't you say that's so? Mad, but cheerful with it, would you be feeling?"

"I was thinking that this beats a spa hotel! My brain actually thought that."

"Marvel of adaptability, the human brain."

Govinder's long hair, recoiled in his turban, kept his newly rewashed and wrung-out headgear very damp. Could one get rheumatism of the head?

"None of you have been through a winter yet, have you?" Rob demanded. "This all seems unviable to me. What if that drone thing hasn't crashed to give you the Qikhot?"

"Then," said Mog, "we'd be more medieval about having baths. Humans don't actually need to bathe. After a while your skin stabilises."

"We are more viable," chipped in Weasel, "than the majority of people."

"What if you get ill? Appendicitis, say?"

"The corpse," she said, "will burn in a car like a Viking funeral."

No use reasoning. Rob shrugged his shoulders.

"Okay, so now we're all spick and span, what do we do for the rest of the day?"

"We hunt and gather," Brian explained. "And let me tell you, my friend, once you start doing that, every square foot of these parks becomes luminous with significance. Things you wouldn't even have glanced at before will leap to your eye. When I was a little kid walking home from school, before the world became banal, I'd stare at garden walls with some moss upon them, and see a prehistoric forest there in miniature. When my granny lit a coal fire I could stare for an hour at the flames seeing spirit-creatures dancing."

"Like you might see midges as tiny fairies," said Rob, so as not to seem reluctant to join in.

"A cloud of fairies, to be sure."

Rob waved his hand. "Why are there always midges around?"

"Because," explained Weasel patiently, "this is the countryside."

Hmm, a landscape of cars and veg and pyracantha hedge. But yes, an aspect of the countryside. This certainly wasn't a city.

"Like, nature, like," said Melanie.

Gesturing: "So why aren't there are any midges over *there*, say?"

Weasel yawned. "Attracted to body heat, I suppose. Lucky they aren't the bothering bitey sort."

"So why be attracted to bodies?"

"Are you attracted to mine?" Weasel asked Rob naughtily. "Noticed you trying to peep in the bath."

"I was *not*."

"Why not, then? Are you queer?"

Mog emitted a chortle that was more like a guffaw. "Prefers them on the larger side, maybe! Just teasing, love," she added, and Rob wished that she hadn't. Truth to tell, he could relish taking a bath with Melanie, yet she seemed inseparable from her sister, and besides Melanie slept in the Mazda, unless sleepover visits occurred. Maybe Melanie would take a liking to him.

When they set off to hunt and gather, Rob tried repeatedly to catch one of other of the accompanying midges. However, the push of air from the motion of his hand always wafted the little fly away.

"Stop waving your hand about," complained Melanie. "You look out of control, like."

Theatrically Rob gripped his wrist with his other hand to subdue it, in an attempt to amuse her, but she just stared at him, then ignored him.

That night Rob dreamt that he was walking with Melanie in the wee hours along a street somewhere in London, alert for a shop doorway into which he manoeuvre her and embrace her, at the very minimum, without the others noticing. However, a CCTV camera which had been perched atop a streetlight took wing like an owl from that tall light to the next light which Rob passed, and then to the next; and to the next in turn; and he knew that the others would be watching on their wristwatches whatever the camera saw – why else were those called *watches*?

He awoke in the Volvo, his arm around Weasel, her head on his shoulder, and *realised*.

Was it a year since that he'd heard on his car radio about the miniaturisation of surveillance equipment? Soon, apparently, mass-produced lightweight flying cameras no bigger than insects and as cheap as insects might take to the air, equipped with solar panel wings and micro-transmitters. Millions of them. Billions. Apparently this depended on the advent of nanotechnology; or did one even need to wait so long? A superfast computer monitoring the kaleidoscope of images could adjust and correct in real time. If wind or rain knocked the tiny flying cameras around and if thousands failed, that wouldn't matter.

As he eased his arm from around Weasel, hoping not to rouse her in any sense, two of the midges which lived in the Volvo circled just out of reach, a bit blurred even in a shaft of dawning sunlight due to their seemingly random fluttering.

Where would you go about testing such a system so that people, if they realised, couldn't report what was going on? And couldn't lay their hands upon butterfly or tiddler nets, say, to catch prototype specimens and auction them on e-Bay to the Chinese?

Weasel woke up soon; as did Brian in the front of the car.

"Just look at him," she said.

Rob was standing outside, a little way off, mouthing and gesturing imploringly to no one.

"Sure, he's talking to the fairies now."

"Jolly good," said Weasel. "He's settling in fast."

This is my somewhat Ballardian take on the horrid business of using British airports, including getting to those on very overcrowded motoways. In France or Germany, when cars grow old they can migrate progressively eastwards, ending up finally with karmic recycling in India. Not thus cars in Britain, on account of the intervening sea; consequently the numbers climb and climb, added to constantly by newly born cars. This lends a new meaning to Orwell's Airstrip One, which instead will become Airport Carpark Strip One (one, since all the airport carparks will have fused together). And in place of the simple Telescreen we now have far more sophisticated methods for surveillance of citizens, in which the British government is a world leader.

Bohemian Rhapsody

After the rain of the past few days, the sky over Prague was eggshell blue. A cool breeze tickled at Tycho Brahe. Autumn was on the way. So as to avoid sneezing he cupped the warmth of his hand over his false nose of silver and gold as he headed uphill from the Sign of the Golden Griffin, towards the sprawl of the castle dominated by the cathedral. If he sneezed a few times, people might imagine that the plague was returning. A good thing if it did, then the court would quit Prague, and so could he!

A warm nose made him think of a living body burning on a bonfire in Rome.

Bruno's body, back in February – burned for claiming that our world circled the Sun, and that many inhabited worlds existed. Of course the Copernican notion of a central Sun was nonsense, but to be burned *for thinking*. And now those damned stupid malicious Capuchin monks were accusing Tycho of malice and black magic.

Supposedly the monks' prayers, emanating from their residence near the palace, had been interfering with Tycho's alchemical witchcraft, frustrating him from turning base metal into gold. Allegedly, as the Emperor's astrological adviser, Tycho had persuaded Rudolph to turf the monks out.

"Gold, indeed!" Tycho snarled to himself in Danish, which no passer-by would understand.

Gold, if only. The treasury could dearly use some gold. That's what the scientific wizards in the Powder Tower were trying to accomplish. Tycho himself was only interested in the alchemy of medicine, which protected him from plague. The monks were very far from the mark. They had the minds of monkeys as well as the appearance.

Who could *advise* a mentally unstable melancholic such as Rudolph had become?

The sheer waste of Tycho's time, being hauled to the capital from his observatory at Castle Benatky with its indoor plumbing and so many other conveniences and graces, to be crammed into the Golden Griffin along with his family and assistants. Oh, Tycho could draw up astrological charts perfectly well regarding decisions of state – but would the Emperor actually take any decisions based on advice? State documents continued to languish unsigned for far too long. Rudolph's zodiacal sign was the Crab, and he was behaving just like a crab withdrawn into its shell. No, that was how a tortoise behaved.

Anyway, Rudolph was *in* his shell.

This was becoming a serious problem which potentially imperilled Tycho – not merely in the matter of his domestic finances, but also maybe as regards his safety. *Bruno had burned in Rome.* The great patron Rudolph could protect the assorted alchemists and magicians and lapidaries and artists and philosophers who crowded Prague – if not always pay them! Himself, the Emperor was a moderate Catholic; he needed to be moderate, given his occult and exotic tastes. But if he lost control there might be Popish persecution, supposing one took a bleak view – that would please the Spanish Habsburgs. Or there might be Protestant persecution, supposing one took an alternative bleak view – that would please many Germans. Rudolph's titular holy Roman empire was becoming ever more unhinged; as, alas, was Rudolph. At least Tycho had been able to leave young Kepler some useful calculations to get on with.

Clutching in his free hand astrological charts bound with purple ribbon, barrel-chested, red-bearded, balding Tycho strode onward, his stiff white lace ruff collar like a splendid halo which had slipped down to circumscribe his neck, his dark velvet cloak revealing a blue doublet in the Spanish mode, threaded with gold. The costs of being a courtier!

As he was heading across the bustling main courtyard

adjacent to the cathedral, he was hailed by a dirtily-clad individual who might recently have been rolling in the ashes of a dead bonfire. Smuts darkened the man's cheeks and his eyebrows seemed singed.

Tycho recognized Bartholomew Guarinoni. Most people knew that Guarinoni was in rivalry with his fellow Italian, Octavian Rovereto, to become Rudolph's favourite physician, an unlikely ambition when Matthias Borbonius was the most sought-after doctor in Prague. Could Rovereto have discharged at his colleague a blunderbuss loaded with filth? The cause was bound to be a laboratory explosion.

Guarinoni's eyes were gleaming, not only by contrast with the dirt surrounding them.

"Noble Sir," he said in German, "I may see His Majesty this afternoon at last!"

About money, of course. What else? Especially if the Italian had just wrecked his workplace in the tower.

"In that case I advise you to change your clothes and wash your face."

Tycho had access to Rudolph – *obligatory* access, often twice a day. The Emperor needed constant astrological guidance about his campaign against the Turks on the Hungarian front. What a tedious bore it was to appease the Emperor's credulity, especially when free will obviously modified the influence of the stars. But at least Tycho could cope excellently. The Emperor valued the Dane's objectivity at a court where everyone else was intriguing for this or for that; whereas Tycho himself only yearned to get back to his observatory.

Oh yes, he could more than cope with Rudolph's caprices and anxieties; and being so highly valued was admittedly pleasurable. Tycho preened himself somewhat in front of the Italian, who had little real hope of an audience. Except –

"*How* may you see him, Signor?"

"At the tournament in the Vladislav Hall."

Its staircase especially designed for horsemen to ascend, for indoor tourneys. Quite.

"Why should His Majesty attend that, when he attends little else?"

The besmirched Italian wagged a finger.

"Because Albrecht the dwarf will ride the Emperor's giraffe, and that will be a rare sight! Allow me, allow me, to escort you to the zoo to witness preparations. I shall count it an honour."

Indeed, it *would* be an honour for Guarinoni to be seen in the prolonged company of someone who had the Emperor's ear. Tongues would wag. However, Tycho's curiosity was piqued. Momentarily he glanced at the Sun, gauging its position. Time enough remained before he needed to meet with Rudolph.

The Italian brushed himself to little effect, and the two men set out for the royal garden beyond the Brusnice stream, regarded with interest by passers-by.

The rhinoceros was looking very rusty. How much had it cost, and what use had it ever been, except for amazement? In the watery climate of Prague, the animal's great plates of ferrous armour had lost all the sheen and polish from African sand and sun. As the beast ambled around its yard, its armoured parts shed rust like dandruff. Still, what a remarkable creature, another of the marvels that Rudolph collected! Supposing the rhinoceros died of internal rot, could those plates be scraped clean and polished or oiled and fitted on a big war-horse?

If the rhinoceros did die, thank God its fate wasn't astrologically linked to the fate of the emperor in the way that Rudolph's pet lion's was. Chained in the entrance hall of the palace as a jovial challenge to visitors, the lion enjoyed better protection from the weather, as well as good bloody meat and a daily bucket of milk.

Tycho and the Italian strolled past the rhino-yard to the little paddock where two grooms had restrained the giraffe. Two other grooms stood on stepladders strapping the specially constructed saddle to the animal. The seat of the saddle rose high at the rear so that the rider wouldn't promptly slide down the animal's steeply sloping dappled back. The destined rider, in protectively padded garb, shouted, "Tighter!" Little Albrecht mightn't weigh much but he wasn't about to take any chances. (He was no relation to the great Dürer who had first captured the look of a rhinoceros with such accuracy almost a century earlier in a drawing which Rudolph adored – just as, indeed, the Dutchman Bosch had depicted perfectly a giraffe.) Noticing spectators, Albrecht waddled towards them and bowed low, no great effort for a dwarf. Albrecht eyed the Italian askance as if Guarinoni, clown-faced due to soot, was competing with the dwarf as a buffoon.

Ridden by Albrecht, the giraffe would likely cause much comedy, probably commencing with its indoor ascent of the staircase up to the Vladislav Hall – the giraffe would need to bow its horned head.

Someone had been clever! Rudolph mightn't put in an appearance for any ordinary tournament in the hall, but the prospect of his giraffe taking part might well entice him from his melancholy seclusion.

"Whose idea was this?" Tycho asked the dwarf.

Someone fairly important, who wanted a chance to speak to Rudolph…

Albrecht shrugged, but Tycho did not feel like dispensing any silver to find out.

"Have you practised riding the giraffe much?"

"Oh yes. At first she capered about, and I slipped off but I clung upside-down to her neck and she tired of carrying my weight. She won't bite, although you need to watch out for the hooves. Don't stand behind her." The dwarf indicated a wooden contraption resembling a gateway at the end of the paddock. "She learned to lower her head and pass through there to get lettuces."

"Well," Tycho said to Guarinoni, "this is all very interesting, but I must meet His Majesty. I assume you do have a change of clothes in your tower."

The Italian hesitated in the most peculiar way – almost as though he *did not wish* to shed his alchemy-stained garments and wash himself, or at least not yet.

"Are you hoping to demonstrate devotion to your science, Signor? When what you demonstrate is a failure, grime not gold."

Suddenly the Italian began to talk rapidly in ever more broken German.

"One of my colleagues," by which he probably meant *competitors*, "is hinting at erotic ecstasy available at the new Sign of the Jade Dragon. He went there for a carry-away meal following a similar mishap as mine –"

Doubtless the Italian hoped to delay Tycho yet further in his company! Well, he succeeded.

"Erotic ecstasy? Jade Dragon? What do you mean by a `carry-away' meal?"

Tycho listened to Guarinoni carefully for several minutes, until really he could delay no more.

In the arcaded courtyard of the royal palace hustle and bustle presaged the tourney. Preferring to avoid Rudolph's chained pet lion, Tycho ascended the staircase intended for riders, into the Vladislav Hall itself, its ceiling a beauty of reticulated vaulting.

Two-thirds of the way along the floor stood a quintain for tilting at. The imperial marshal was thrusting at the target – a shield painted with a Turk's head – to ensure that the counterweight bag of sand swung round smoothly enough to clobber a lanceman who didn't follow through smartly – although the same rider would also need to halt his horse quickly to avoid colliding with the barrier of mattresses protecting the far wall.

Onward to the antechamber, to be saluted and admitted. Rudolph liked items from his treasury and art gallery to be on display in this part of the palace for a few months at a time. Tycho barely glanced at the large globe and the gilded engraved brass armillary sphere, or at *Venus and Adonis* on the wall, or the *Head Composed of Vegetables*.

Thence to the Green Room, where the waiting chamberlain stood with his back to *Tantalus on his Wheel.*

"His Imperial Highness is expecting you –"

And finally to the royal bedchamber, its windows draped to exclude daylight, many candles lit. Hardly the best conditions for admiring *Pan and Venus* or *The Rape of Helen* or a lyre embossed with a moustached face or a statue of Daphne in gilded silver, coral, and semi-precious stones. In a richly carved chair Rudolph slouched, attired in a fur robe, his delicate lace ruff collar resembling an explosion of pearls from a milky pool.

He looked distinctly autumnal, his pear of a nose over-ripe on that long sloping face, his abundant moustaches overdue for harvest, his mulberry eyes lugubrious.

"Brahe, have you news of my assassination?"

"Sire, the fact that your noble father was assassinated at the same age as you are now conveys no inevitability for a repetition of the same fate – nor do the stars, either."

"I know I am dead and damned," declared Rudolph. "I'm a man possessed by a devil."

"In what sense exactly?"

Rudolph tapped his nose.

"A false nose of metals is part of your face, Brahe, ever since you lost your fleshly nose in a duel long ago. I know that in my very soul there is a foreign part – and in my body too! A part that comes from elsewhere evil! A part that I must suffocate and keep confined in darkness, otherwise…

"…otherwise, Brahe, I tell you, I would yearn…

"…to sup your blood to nourish me!" Rudolph pulled himself up hectically while Tycho took a wary step backward. "Do you understand me? It is far better that my own blood should be spilled in an assassination!" Then, in the candlelight, Rudolph seemed to blush with shame at his outburst.

The Holy Roman Emperor added more quietly, "I cannot appear in public, in daylight."

"Not even to see your jester ride your giraffe in the

tourney?" And then, perhaps, to see the ambassador from Muscovy too?

Rudolph shivered and pulled his cloak tightly around himself.

"Borbonius did promise something of the sort. He imagines this will infuse my spirits with hilarity. How wrong he is."

Oh, so the frolic was a bright idea of Borbonius's – medicine for the mind, where physick could not prevail. That was preferable to this being some other ambitious courtier's idea.

"Some teeth sink too deeply into the soul," muttered Rudolph.

Tycho decided to interpret this literally rather than metaphorically and symbolically as Rudolph surely intended.

"What has bitten you, and when?"

Hauntedly, Rudolph whispered, "Our enemy the Turk… in the form of a bat with scimitars on its wings… from Transylvania weeks ago. Borbonius says I do not have rabies or I would be dead."

Hmm. Rudolph's mind was possessed by symbols and emblems, yet could there be any truth in this? The Emperor's Hungarian opponents in Transylvania were allies of the Ottomans in Constantinople. A bat biting Rudolph could be an emblem for some strange visitor who had deranged the credulous Emperor's senses… and maybe his body too? Oh to be able to shine a bright light into Rudolph's labyrinthine darkness!

Brahe recalled what Guarinoni had told him regarding the Sign of the Jade Dragon and that rumour of the *illuminatory* ecstasy obtainable there.

Could it be that Guarinoni had exploded his own equipment deliberately, so as to appeal to the Chinese proprietress of that establishment? If so, Guarinoni had chosen an unsuitable time of day… On the subject of suitable and unsuitable times, the horoscope for events in Transylvania certainly needed discussing! And if anything could ever be decided, and if Rudolph could be cured of his mad malaise, and if the Catholics and Protestants in

Bohemia could avoid killing each other, maybe, just maybe Tycho could get back to precisely instrumented measurements of the heavens!

When Tycho finally emerged from a tedious audience requiring much soothing of Rudolph, the Vladislav Hall was noisy with tourney.

Ladies and notables looked on as horsemen sat resting in their armour, most of this being spiky and fluted in Maximilan style, made in Nuremburg. Since the Emperor might be attending, they were wearing their smartest metal suits rather than heavy tilt armour. Many breastplates were crested above the sternum with a double-eagle.

The marshal accosted Tycho, and Tycho promptly shook his head.

"His Highness will remain in his bedroom."

So the marshal gave a signal.

The floor was a bit slippery for a giraffe accustomed to a paddock. However, fixed above the Turk's head on the target of the quintain, was a lettuce, so when Albrecht leant back and slapped the animal on her rump, she broke into an eager canter.

Albrecht uprighted his posture, pointing lance at target. Aware now of the lance as a possible rival to reach the lettuce, the giraffe lowered its neck, thrusting her head forward. Thus the dappled beast's mouth reached the lettuce before the tip of the lance could touch the Turk's head.

As a result the counterweight promptly swung around and slapped the giraffe hard on her backside, just as she was about to slow. Legs splaying, she slid onward while Albrecht soared over her head. His lance impaled the mattresses and he hung there briefly, legs pumping. A moment later, lettuce and giraffe snout thwacked him right between those legs – and how he howled as he fell.

Bracing herself, the giraffe succeeded in halting as Albrecht sprawled on the floor beneath her feet, clutching his bollocks.

Howls of laughter arose as riders clashed the shielding vamplates of their upright lances against their breastplates in mock salute.

Having seen enough tomfoolery, Tycho strode off. He must visit that Chinese carry-away, down by the river near the Charles Bridge. If what Guarinoni said had any validity, maybe a cure for the Emperor might come from an unexpected quarter.

Here was the very house. A dragon of precious green jade, fit for the Emperor's own artistic collections, stood behind slim iron bars in a niche above the doorway. The house was only a stone's throw from Charles Bridge, crowded with carriages and pedestrians. Not for the first time Tycho thought that the bridge could look really handsome if there were statues along its sides. Statues, perhaps, of famous scientists such as Ptolemy and Pythagoras and Archimedes and Paracelsus and himself.

The door of the Jade Dragon was open, releasing odours of cookery at once unfamiliar and enticing. A front window contained a signboard painted with prices and enigmatic signs such as a beehive and a lemon and a pig. Tycho entered and beheld his first ever Chinese woman: almond eyes in an oval face, long black hair in strands decorated atop by a pink rose that looked to be made of silk and a long silver hairpin – which perhaps she could wield like a dagger, if need be. Standing behind a low counter, she was wearing a green dress which hugged her slim figure, and a long neckerchief of red silk. She was beautiful and looked no older than twenty-five, although Tycho suspected that people with such smooth tight skin and flat features might appear to age at a different pace from people in Bohemia or in Denmark. Upon the counter Tycho noted a different sort of counter, consisting of beads on thin metal bars inside a framework, which looked mathematically interesting. On the rear wall hung another signboard, just as in the window.

A customer was receiving a 'carry-away' which proved to be

a simple wooden box the length and breadth of one's hand, some steam venting from around the lid. A few other such boxes stood spare on the counter, empty except for what looked like stretched pig bladders – washed and dried ones, of course – fitted as bags gaping open to receive pourings of food, after which evidently a lid would cap the meal. The Chinese woman passed a pair of wooden sticks to the customer and he departed, beating a merry tattoo on the lid of his carry-away as if he was a drummer boy. For larger orders, a heap of simple little hessian sacks with handles awaited, into which several boxes would fit.

"Good day," Brahe said in German to the exotic woman. "I am the Imperial Star Watcher and Adviser, Tycho Brahe. May I ask your name?"

"My name is Su Nü, but you not succeed in pronouncing, so please call me Frau Sonne." Her accent was twangy.

"Su Nu," attempted Tycho.

She giggled. "No, no. Oh no."

"Frau Sonne, then. May I ask how you got here from China?"

"Along Silk Road," she said, and it seemed to Tycho that a road as smooth as silk could be no ordinary road, but might well be something occult, definitely better than arriving in Bohemia on a broomstick.

Tycho pointed at the signboard.

"What is a beehive and a lemon and a pig?"

"Sweet and sour pork. Delicious!"

"Hmm, I may try some."

Now came the difficult part, requiring a certain diplomacy, at which Tycho had at last acquired considerable skill after various contretemps in the past.

"I understand that you offer other services here…"

"Items of private delicacy?"

"Earlier today, I was talking to an alchemist whose laboratory exploded."

"Another explosion? Ah, your alchemists…!" Su Nü sighed

with pitying compassion. "So many miss point of true alchemy, which is transformation *of person* in body and soul, not making of mere gold."

"I believe," Tycho remarked huffily, "that superior alchemists strive to create the philosopher's stone, thus making gold, so as to purify themselves spiritually in the process; and vice versa. Personally I'm mainly interested in *medical* alchemy."

Su Nü looked at him intently. "Make love, not gold! That is secret. We Chinese have known for centuries."

"Indeed?"

"In-deed! Intimate secrets of cinnabar grotto and gully of gold and inner elixir we call *nei tan*. Would you like private consultation? This evening, My Lord?"

Hmm, cinnabar – the red powder efficacious in gold-making – was a mixture of philosophic mercury and philosophic sulphur...

"The cinnabar grotto: that's the vessel containing the cinnabar powder?"

"*Dry powder?* My Lord, grotto should ooze with juices like mucus of a snail! If not, adept is inept. Cinnabar grotto is part of cunt. Your alchemists miss whole point. They make apparatus. They need skilled woman instead. Consultation, My Lord?"

Tycho was not yet a lord in Bohemia. He really must petition Rudolph for citizenship and noble status so that Kirsten and the children could benefit, especially by the children thus being able to inherit and marry into noble families in their adopted homeland. However, he did not at all mind being called a lord.

"I am faithful to my wife," Tycho told Su Nü.

"Good health comes from good sex," she observed, "and woman is sexually stronger than man, so she assists him through her pleasure to become mystic master of grotto, thus of himself and of his well-being."

Hmm, could this Chinese woman really help restore Rudolph's well-being? Tycho needed to think for a while.

"For the moment," he said, "may I have some beehive

lemon pig?"

"Certainly! On bed of white rice, which sweet sauce stains?" Everything that Su Nü said seemed to have erotic implications. Goodness knows what rice was.

Tycho nodded, and Su Nü slipped away into another room from which the odours issued. She returned very soon with a filled container, lid in place. Then she presented Tycho with two plain wooden sticks.

"Shall I demonstrate, my Lord?"

She seized his fingers and placed the sticks within them in a certain way, then manipulated his hand so that the sticks opened and closed. Her touch was at once subtle yet firm.

"You bring box back clean another time, get small refund."

Tycho sat on a block of sandstone by the end of the Charles Bridge, musing while he mastered the art of eating beehive lemon pig with sticks. Rice looked like maggots but must be a grain of some kind, swollen by boiling. Very tasty stained with sauce. Surely she must use sacks of it. Had the rice slid magically along the Silk Road too?

Reaching a decision, he returned to the Jade Dragon, where, once she had finished serving another customer, Su Nü listened to him intently.

Yes, she would perform a carry-away service, of herself, since obviously an Emperor could not visit her humble dwelling. Traditionally, in her far-off homeland, she remarked, if an Emperor was wary of assassination, a consort for him would be stripped and searched intimately then wrapped in a silk bag and borne to his bedchamber by a eunuch, to be returned home in the same manner after the union. Thus she would carry nothing with which to harm him.

"Must leave hairpin here, My Lord!"

Tycho was relieved that she did not expect him to carry her in a silk sack to the castle, but instead would walk along with him.

Traditionally, it transpired, a Chinese Emperor's intercourse was monitored either by a female official or by a eunuch, who would carefully record the number of thrusts made by the Emperor and who, if she or un-he deemed these excessive, would halt further activity by reading a cautionary memorandum from a revered ancestor.

"We do things differently here," said Tycho, although by now he realized that Su Nü was teasing him mischievously – maybe excited by the prospect of every Chinese lady's dream coming true, although with a melancholy Holy Roman Emperor, not a Chinese emperor. "An astrologer does not need to be present in the bedroom, nor a doctor neither."

She became serious. "You say he thirsty for blood?"

"So he implies. But he resists the compulsion, and this takes all his energy away from matters of state. Frau Sonne, you may be in a little danger if you're in bed with him."

Of a sudden Su Nü performed a very wild dance – accompanied by "Ha! Ha! Ha!" – and that long tight dress of hers proved to be slit from thigh to ankle, allowing her legs to kick. Her feet flashed out, and her hands, then silently she mimed riding a horse, then she stood on one leg.

"What is that dance called?" asked Tycho.

"Kung fu," she replied. "Self-defence and harmonious living. If I expel black bat from him, I must kill it. Hmm, chicken blood mixed with sticky rice can help defeat Chiang-Shih devil, which steals breath from people instead of blood. Therefore chicken breath mixed with rice may help defeat blood-sucker devil."

"How can you persuade a chicken to breathe on rice without eating the rice at the same time?"

"No, no, use chicken lungs, chopped."

"Oh I see, the *emblem* of chicken breath." That made sense. Particularly with Rudolph, this might be effective.

"I will know best route when his jade stalk rises and his orchid bags sway. Later too, when I smell his yoghurt." What was *yoghurt*? Tycho decided not to query her.

Su Nü continued standing on one leg like a crane. Tycho leaned across the counter and gazed at her embroidered slipper.

"What small feet you have."

"My golden lotuses. Walking on them strengthens muscles of hidden valley."

Another customer came in, wanting duck with long worms.

Two audiences with Rudolph in one day was not unusual for Tycho – would that it were, and that the ambassador from Muscovy could enjoy even half an audience!

By the time Tycho reached the Vladislav Hall again, it was empty. Some horse turds lay on the floor, or maybe those were giraffe turds if the beast had shat after it skidded. Just as well; Tycho's mission was a discreet one.

"How is the darkness within, Sire?" Tycho enquired.

"Stirring," whispered Rudolph. "Stretching its wings. I can smell your blood, Brahe."

"Maybe what you're smelling is Beehive Lemon Pig on my breath." Tycho hoped so, at any rate.

"Brahe, the Moon is filling."

Tycho was perfectly aware of this, both as an astronomer and in common with any ordinary person who bothered glancing into the sky by night. Yet *how*, in this heavily curtained bedroom where candles burned...

"Do you mean that you can *feel* it filling, within yourself?"

"Yes! It will fill me within, usurping what remains of my will. Soon I must drink blood, or be blessedly assassinated."

Guarinoni's information, and the resulting trips to the Jade Dragon, had come none too soon. What else could be done for Rudolph, in his delusion or – Heaven forbid! – in his realization of the cause of his problem, whether that were due to deliberate magical malice by Turks or Hungarians in Transylvania or even by his nephew Leopold – or whether it were due to something which had come out of the night, the night of darkness and also of evil?

"Sire, I believe I have discovered a solution to your dark malady."

"You have found it in the stars?"

No, I found it in a Chinese carry-away near Charles Bridge... Tycho did not voice this, yet as the thought passed through his mind it struck him how remarkable it was that Su Nü had come to Prague at such an appropriate time along that Silk Road, almost as if she were a hunter who posed as prey for carnal appetites, whilst also being an adept instructor seemingly wiser than any other alchemist he had met; except of course for himself.

"Yes, in tonight's stars!" Tycho fibbed. "Venus is entering the Crab."

A moon much closer to full than to half hung low over Prague, lighting the climb to the castle, dimming nearby stars. Tycho disliked the term *gibbous* for such a phase of the moon because the word seemed supernaturally menacing, as if beholding it caused people to gibber with fear.

Yet there was ample reason for trepidation. Su Nü walked with a wobble, which would be strengthening her hidden valley in preparation for onslaught by the imperial jade stalk. Yet Tycho had also seen her leap into action. Consequently he hoped that Rudolph wouldn't be injured in any way, either as regards his jade stalk or his personal esteem. Su Nü carried one of those little hessian sacks into which she had put a box of sticky rice and chicken lungs for the Emperor's nourishment during their encounter.

Su Nü was in the bedchamber for almost two hours, while in the antechamber Tycho variously performed mathematics in his head and contemplated *Tantalus on his Wheel.* How could erotic activity possibly last for so long? A few times, muffled by the stout door, he heard, "Ha! Ha! Ha!" or some such sound. Maybe that was an outcry of joyful release.

At long last the door of the bedroom opened, and there stood Rudolph and Su Nü, both clad. The Emperor *glowed*, might be the best way of phrasing it, mere candlelight notwithstanding. If he had been late Autumn earlier, now he was Summer again. His cheeks were red as apples, his nose a pear at its best, his huge moustaches were like corn, and his eyebrows resembled hairy golden caterpillars.

"Be here early tomorrow, Brahe," he called out. "Much awaits." The Emperor ushered the Chinese woman courteously from his bedchamber, then he withdrew and shut the door.

Tycho hastened towards Su Nü.

"Was there any need of..." – what was the name of that dance? – "any need of Kung Fu?"

"Not on this occasion. I must be private quickly, My Lord, to massage vigorously to expel all yoghurt."

"Yes, yes, of course." Tycho knew of a suitable closet. Seizing a candelabrum, he led Su Nü to a spiral stairway, down two turns, threw open a door to a privy room, planted the tree of candles within, then waited outside in the moonlight coming through a narrow window.

Presently Su Nü emerged, clutching her little sack.

She whispered, "Expelled much black yoghurt." That word *yoghurt* again. "But I cloak it in *my* ejaculation." Whatever was she talking about? Women couldn't ejaculate – but maybe Chinese women could, from some organ inside themselves? She clutched her little sack tight. "I will throw in river, like abortion, weighted with stones."

Could it be that the Emperor had burst a blood vessel inside himself? Yet Rudolph had looked so radiant and restored, at least compared with how he had been previously, in the depths of despair.

"Faru Sonne, I don't understand. What exactly did His Majesty expel, and how exactly?" Tycho was forever preoccupied by exactitude. His great quadrant was ten times more exact than any previous instrument for measuring celestial positions.

"Vampire essence, my Lord! Evil elixir dirties channels in body. Clever acupressure for long time delays explosion from jade stalk. Thus great pleasure-tension sucks black essence together, bottling like lava under volcano. At last volcano erupts with ten times more bang than ordinary."

So that was why she took two hours, making the time by now so late...

"Lucky I catch him still living, before become dead and vampire. One more week, woe! Black residue may linger in Emperor, make him moody sometimes, not enough change him into blood-drinker."

"He may need another treatment?"

"Not necessary."

Tycho wished to know more, but...

"I must go home. It seems I need an early night. First I'll escort you, Frau Sonne."

"And payment?"

"Yes, yes. I have the gold with me."

"See!" She grinned. "Make love makes gold. Best way."

It was two tedious days of horoscope-casting before Tycho had a chance to revisit the Jade Dragon. So many questions to ask! Not least about what *other occasions* the Chinese woman had been referring to. When had those been, and where?

Drizzle was drifting. For a moment Tycho thought he may have mistaken the building, or even mistaken the cobbled street. But no. This was the place. Above the door, around the niche, were those slim iron bars, yet the dragon of jade was absent. Gone, too, from the window was the signboard promising beehive lemon pig and other delights. Within the room into which he peered: a low counter and nothing more. No counter of beads, no signboard on the wall, no sign that Su Nü had ever been there as cook and as adept in an alchemy scarcely known to him, and also, he was now sure, as a warrior against darkness, travelling a silken road that she alone perhaps, and some others like her, could perceive and use.

A letter had come from Kepler at Castle Benatky. The problem which Tycho had set Kepler concerned the image of the Sun passing through a pinhole on to a screen. The image appeared too large for the Moon to be able to eclipse the Sun completely, although the Moon certainly did so in reality. Kepler wrote of 'light rays,' a whole new concept in geometrical optics, so he claimed. And he whined about money.

Rays of light preoccupied Tycho as he strode away from the empty house of enlightenment. In competition with the actual Sun, Frau Sonne receded into eclipse.

It's that man again. Ingeniously dreaming up anthologies, this time Darrell wanted stories where real historical events are explained by hitherto unrevealed vampirism. A secret history, in other words. In our world of conspiracy theories about the ongoing influence of the Illuminati, the surviving blood line of Jesus, the controlled demolition of the Twin Towers… why not?

My mind naturally turned to the admirable and eccentric Holy Roman Emperor, Rudolph II, whose court in Prague was visited by zany luminaries such as John Dee, the Elizabethan magician, and where many curiosities accumulated. I'd already touched on Emperor Rudolph in a story about the works of his court painter, Giuseppe Archimbaldo ("The Coming of Vertumnus").

To cap it all, the Danish astronomer Tycho Brahe was also in Prague, to add a spirit of relatively rational enquiry. Rudolph II was in a precarious mental state at times. Could this possibly be due to an exotic form of, shall we say, blood poisoning?

The rhinoceros is exactly as depicted by Dürer a few decades earlier. Since those times, rhinos have become less armour-plated and thus less vulnerable to rust.

Tales from the Zombible

For Cristina

Meanwhile, in another universe just next door in the Manifold Many-Worlds Multiverse where all is, not merely possible, but mandatory...

Gather round, young Grubs, and get religion, and a bit of biology! You're growing up as fast as blotchy puffballs. High time you learned how you came to be.

So hear this. A lady Zombie sucks a gentleman Zombie's corrupting testicle into her like she's slurping an oyster. Down goes that oyster testicle into her bellywomb unchewed. The eggworms that are already inside her burrow into that rotting testicle, then nature's alchemy gets to work, and behold: the woman's worms and the worms in the testicle, which are called sperms, blend into tiny little Grubs. Worms and sperms, that's the trick. The hungriest Grub gobbles all its brother and sister grubs, putting on weight. Then Master Greedy slides down the venus tube coated in slime, hangs on at the very lip, and climbs up like a slug to her titty to suck on her ooze. The lady lets you suck; she doesn't suck you. That's motherhood amongst us Zombies. Your lady Zombie mother won't have a craving for another testicle matured like year-old blue cheese, not for a while. More worms need to breed first of all in her bellywomb.

Remember that, any of you? No? New Grubs rarely do. After you've sucked for a month at her titty and swollen more, that's when our Zombie awareness usually dawns. We're hungry for grub. Next of all, you may recall you Grubs get fed dead bodies of beasts birds fish whatever till you learn your words from Mummy's mumblings. Remember that part? Many ways

243

we're a lot brighter than disgusting Chinese-style babies in the unzombie parts of the world. An evolutionary improvement, you might say. Those 'liveborn' things in the Chinese Empire just carry on till they finally die after 60 or 70 years or so. Whereas us, we're dying all the time from the very start. We regenerate rottingly, we rot regeneratingly. Rot and regeneration all the time. Yes Grubs, we Rot `n` Roll! Rot `n` Roll, ever since the time of Jeshua, the first of us all. Bits fall off all the time, but new stuff buds. And rots; and the rot feeds more buds.

Once upon a time, little Grubs, things were a whole lot otherwise. Back in the time before Jeshua, the years BJ. Jeshua who, like I say, began us two thousand years ago. All of which is in the Zombible. Many zombscribes' fingers fell off in the service of writing our Zombible, before we got printing presses established, so pay attention.

Well now, Jeshua was a leper. That means bits of Him were dying while He was alive. Flesh, fingers, toes. The live people didn't much like lepers, so they cast lepers out of their towns. They made laws that lepers must keep away. Lepers must ring a bell, clang clong, to announce where they were.

You do know what *live* means? That's right, just like sheep and horses. Hot blood, beating hearts, breathing. Just like our foes the fiendish Chinese and Nipponese – well mumbled, Grub!

There's no need to mention the Other World Across The Vast Ocean whose Aztechs sent three sailing ships to our shores in 1490ish Anno Zombi, one ship escaping, and that's the last us Zombies heard…

Well then, Roman conquerors invaded Judahland, where Jeshua's people the Judes lived, and the Romans made a stronger law: any leper who came near any live person would be crucified, nailed to a wooden cross as a warning. No Roman wanted to catch leprosy. After that most lepers stayed well away from any Romans.

But Jeshua felt He had a special mission to stir things up. He appeared in public and spake, saying, "Blessed are the Palsied, the

Poxed, and the Putrid." Twelve other lepers followed Him faithfully. Jeshua caused disturbances in towns. Soon came the day when Roman soldiers put on all their armour to protect themselves from leprosy, and arrested Him, and took Him to a hill and nailed Him high on a wooden cross as threatened. They used a lot of nails in case parts of His body broke off. Thonk thonk thonk.

After He stopped moving or breathing – yes indeed, live bodies have air going in and out of them all the time – well then the Romans ordered the Twelve to unnail Jeshua and carry Him away to put Him in a hole in the ground and cover Him deep with soil so He could rot completely.

Maybe a whole lot of Kozmic Rays hit Jeshua while he was exposed on that cross, or maybe the shock of being crucified caused his leprosy to mutate suddenly into zombieism. Or the pain caused a radical retreat from horrible sensations, which a leper could experience in parts of himself. Leprosy and zombieism are a bit similar, although pieces don't rot and fall off lepers due to the leprosy itself. Yet a leper certainly loses an amount of bodily sensations, which we fortunately hardly even have 'cept for a greed for raw flesh and guts – same way as our noses don't smell nothing, although we still have noses or bits of noses because that's the shape our regenerating remembers, right?

Or maybe there was something special in the soil where Jeshua was buried, that worked the transformation. Some viruses or bacterias.

Or else His shock 'retreat', as I call it, may have been like a regression – yes, Grub, I said *regression* – to an earlier, more flexible cellular state – no, just listen to me, will you? – which living people and mice and rats and whatnot lose after a few days from coming into the world. A resetting of morphogenesis, *plus* rotting to provide material to rework.

Warra I mean? You think I'm able to speak too many words, eh Grub? Is that it? Maybe that's on account of I have had nearly

2K years of this rotting `n` rolling-onward.

Two thousand rotting regenerating years of it, me being the Wandering Zombie, whom Jeshua bit infectiously with His blessing, and to whom I responded, in Aramaic, *Fuck Off!*

In fact I was ruder than that because his bite really hurt me. I could hurt a lot in those days – although soon I would hurt no more, or not so as you'd notice much.

Whereupon Jeshua said unto me, I myself shall dissolve, yet you shall remain, as shall a whole lot of other *Zombies* whom I do now create at first hand, as in your case, or whom I shall cause at second or third or twenty-fifth hand.

Jeshua said 'at first hand' because he'd used his nails to rip the skin of my cheek before biting the wound, and 'at first mouth' isn't in a phrase in common parlance. You may find it advisable to use your nails before you use your teeth if you ever come across a living Chinaman, for instance.

And when Jeshua spake *Zombies* – in Aramaic – that was the very first use of the name for our kind; so therefore I am a custodian of the Word for all of you growing and rotting Grubs; and of many other words besides.

Why will you *dissolve, fucker, if the rest of us don't?* I had asked unto Him, though he had bitten me, not fucked me, but I felt sorely that this was still fucking *with* me.

Because, He replied unto me, *I am a filter of the strength of the renewing rot inside of Me. Myself, I am too extreme. Therefore I give to each of you a diluted dosage of Me.*

This has nothing, I hasten to add, to do with homeopathy.

Therefore, He continued, for he was proficient in making speeches before He was crucified, *forty-four days from now I shall dissolve myself in the Dead Sea, where those who wish to be of my kind may bathe if they have no wish to be bitten. For verily bitten they will be otherwise.*

And indeed, as our Zombible relates, forty-four days later I would witness the shores of the Dead Sea crowded with Zombies and some pre-Zombies, as Jeshua waded into the water. The great hunger of those hundreds of Zombies, which is our one powerful physical sensation which we must harness and control, is expressed metaphorically as The Miracle of the Flesh and Rotten Fishes, even though few fish, perhaps none, could tolerate the salinity of the Dead Sea.

Harness and control, I say! Our harnessed hunger is what sent us forth throughout the known world, resulting in a vast increase in our numbers, otherwise the earliest of our kind might simply have wandered aimlessly round in circles, simultaneously rotting and regenerating. So we must all be very thankful for our constant hunger.

Our hunger caused us to convert the Roman Empire. Accordingly in due course Zombie legions triumphed over and converted into zombiekind the savage Germanians and Caledonians and Hibernians and Scandians and Sarmatians and so on and so forth east and west and north. And when Arabians living in vast deserts of mostly empty sand suddenly sent armies of fanatics forth against our lands, waving scimitars and screaming about a god and a prophet, hordes of Zombies engulfed those Arabian armies. Maybe a million Zombies ceased in the sense that they were chopped too small to regenerate, but millions more remained to prevail and convert the surviving Arabians who shambled back to their Mecca for a big munch.

Jeshua was very perceptive to envisage our future and cause it to happen. So in later years it was claimed that although His eyeballs hung upon His cheeks, yet that He could see clearly. If so, this would indeed be a *miracle,* since eyes hanging loose on cheeks is physically impossible due to the short length of an optic cord even if the cord is softening due to rot. Of no other subsequent Zombie Saint is it true that eyeballs literally hung down upon cheeks! None of the great Zombie painters depicted Jeshua thus. Instead, they mostly used a sickly yellowish green pigment for his eyes which remained in his head. But anyway, I attest that mine own eyes were upon Him during the time when He shambled upon the earth. Upon Him, in the sense of beholding Him. And His eyes were indeed in His head.

Notwithstanding, after two centuries a Great Schism did arise between the Eyes-on-Cheeks Heresy and our Eyes-mouldering-greenly-in-their-Sockets orthodox truth. This arose in North Africa where the sunlight is very bright, and where consequently some Zombies might prefer if their own eyes were perpetually downcast. And in that epoch Zombie army staggered against Zombie army, pulling each other apart, until the Truce and Treaty of Tripoli and the agreement that African Zombies could paint eyes upon their own rotting cheeks if they really wished to do so. Paradoxically, from this sprang the artful skills that would eventually enable the works of Zombiangelo and Zombidavinci to be made, *Zombi* being a prefix of praise awarded only to the most notable of us. Such as Saints and MartyrSaints too, for instance. MartyrSaints were Zombies who were spreading zombification most hungrily amongst live persons and whom live persons burned in a bonfire or a furnace or an oven. Which caused a certain smell to arise. This Odour of Sanctity is a genuine *mystery* to ourselves, since us Zombies lack any sense of smell. However, the live persons reported this smell vociferously every time they burned a Zombsaint, even though they wore pegs upon their noses or hung highly perfumed roses around their own necks.

Yes indeed, young Grubs, a zombody can be destroyed forever by being burned or minced or staked out in a sandstorm – as well as, given a sufficient number of centuries, due to entropic attrition or regenerative errors. So it is blessèd that sufficient replacement Grubs arrive, down the venus tube then slug-crawling up to the tit.

Did those heretic Zombies come up with their crazy idea of eyeballs-on-cheeks because the hot African sun had cooked their brains? Why, you're a bright young Grub!

But no, that isn't exactly the answer. It's quite true that we rot more slowly in a cold climate, and it's equally true that we never freeze solid so long as we're above minus-fifty degrees. That's because we have a natural antifreeze inside of us like some fishes do, which is just one of our endowments that Jeshua's bite passed on. But Jeshua Himself lived in a climate that could be as hot as Africa during the summer, which is when he was crucified by the Romans, in the middle of August, a month named after an earlier Roman Emperor. The natural *genius* of Jeshua's zombification was that the fluid in his body became very naturally *chilly* just as if it was night-time. So in fact African Zombies' thinking-mush remains quite cool, as you'd know if you ever tasted any. As I myself did during the anti-eyeballs-on-cheeks crusade; yes indeed I was there – being the Wandering Zombie I've been around quite a bit. Chilliness is a characteristic of the Zombie antifreeze inside us – and that's a *stable* chilliness. It's *homeostatic*, which has nothing do with homeopathic.

So how do we radiate excess heat away, such as at midday in a desert? We do so by rotting parts of us away! That's like the way the live-Chinese do their 'sweating', which means salty water coming out of their skins, but we go in for this is a much bigger way, by losing bits of superhydrated flesh itself. Grubs, it's *cool* to rot! There's a quantumbiomechanical explanation for this, which Zombeinstein finally thunked. Thunking is more powerful than normal Zombie thinking. You can tell that from the word itself. Think-think-think is like a little birdy picking up seeds, while thunk-thunk-thunk is more like an intellectual elephant. Bright Grub, you might be a Thunker one day! Up there with Zombiehawkins who rotted so much he needed a wheelchair to get around, pushed by faithful Zombie assistants who wrote down his thunks with palsied fingers.

Why, Grub you *even* want to know the quantum-biomechanical reason? Well, it's all to do with...

Hey, what's up?

Why, the steam railway's delivering us a Chinese take-away! Our Zombie forces in the Far East have taken live-prisoners and they've sent some all this way as grub for us to convert! Grubs, pay full attention: this doesn't happen often!

You, Bright Grub, how do you think us Zombies get to the

Far East nowadays? Since shambling on foot would take a long time. I'll give you a clue, Bright Grub. I've mentioned his *name* already.

No no, it's nothing to do with Jeshua. In His time the Romans didn't build railways, just lots of roads.

Ooops, I've given you another clue there.

No, Zombiehawkins didn't invent railways so that his wheelchair could travel faster. Can you imagine a wheelchair on rails with steam puffing out of it? It was *Zombiedavinci* who invented the steam railway, which led after hundreds of years of stumbling work to... the Trans-Siberian Railway through seemingly endless forests! Which takes us close to the China Empire.

Which we've never been able to penetrate, on account of the Great Wall of China which is just too high for Zombies to climb over, even if the live-Chinese didn't pour Celestial Fire down on Zombies who try to climb over each other to reach the top and liveflesh.

However, the Great Wall is like a piece of string: it has two ends. True, it's a very long piece of string. But it has to start somewhere, and stop somewhere. Those places are where a million Zombies meet the Chinese Army of the North, and a million more meet the Army of the South.

Following the principles of *harness* and *control*, our Zombie hordes don't snack on and zombify every live-Chinese who falls into our putrid hands, off a horse for example. Live-prisoners are sent back to our central territories by way of the Trans-Siberian Railway, so we can have ceremonies of Do-This-In-Remembrance-Of-Me, the very words during Jeshua's first supper of flesh after He arose following zombification.

Here comes the train now, choo-choo choo-choo. Do you see the live-prisoners in their cages?

Most of you Grubs are still too juvenile to join in, but I deem that you, Bright Grub, shall come with me to the feeding-frenzy place.

Yet be not excessively frenzied! Some of the prisoners should be torn and bitten and eaten only so much that their dead bodies shall resurrect, undead, thanks to the sacred infectious saliva of Jeshua which we all share.

The one thing we share in common with our Chinese foes is... can you tell me what that might be, Bright Grub?

Toes? No, not toes.

Eyeballs? No no. I suppose I asked too difficult a question. The answer is *ancestor-worship*! Only, the live-Chinese and Nipponese foolishly worship imaginary spirits of their ancestors who died without regenerating, whereas us Zombies realistically adore our common ancestor in zombieism, Jeshua who caused us all.

Choo-choo. Already a crowd is gathering. It's *grub* time, Grub! Remember how to comport yourself. Stagger and sway with arms outstretched. And get even more brains into you.

In the Manifold Many-Worlds Multiverse, all is not merely possible, but mandatory. *Whatever you can imagine, must be. Somewhere and somewhen. Thus, in another universe just next door – !*

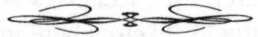

I never expected to write a Cthulhu story, nor did I expect to write a zombie tale. But a benefit of invitation anthologies is being asked to do the unexpected. The culprit in this case was Andy Remic who writes wonderfully over-the-top combat SF and who decided to edit an OTT anthology. As it happened, I'd been thinking – in a sort of drooling, spasmodic way – about zombies and the logic, as it were, of leading a zombie existence.

A civilisation of vampires seems a fairly reasonable concept, but a functioning culture of zombies? This called for some biological and historical juggling!

A Waterfall of Lights

Two summers earlier, of a Friday evening, Roderick and myself and Nancy and Nick had a beer-fuelled discussion in one of the snug rooms in the Eagle and Child, where Tolkien used to meet up with his Oxford author chums. A chinwag about the possible existence of alien civilisations.

The Bird and Baby, as it's known to the locals, was serving a *green* guest ale, something I'd never encountered before. By 'green' I don't mean that it was an ecologically worthy beer produced not too far distantly from organic ingredients, but that it was almost grass-green in hue. This brew turned out to be made from young *un*roasted hops, hence the colour. Surprisingly tasty and refreshing it was too. Green beer led to the notion of little green men visiting Earth to sup, although of course our ale might make them sick due to their alien biology.

Nick dearly wished that fellow astronomers would stop wasting time on the search for extraterrestial life.

"*Microbial* life's fairly likely elsewhere in our galaxy, but as for anything more complex: forget it!"

Because, you see, complex intelligent life on planet Earth was the result of a long series of lucky accidents...

"If the sun were in a more crowded part of the sky, supernovas or gamma bursts would have sterilised the world repeatedly –"

If there'd been 'bad Jupiters' orbiting nearer to the sun or more eccentrically, forget any planet Earth at all. Early random collisions gave us our spin axis and our length of day – yet without a moon the hefty size of ours Earth's tilt angle would wander, hopelessly destabilising climate.

"What's more, our sun's a quarter richer in heavy metals

than other nearby stars, hence Earth's iron core –"

– which caused our vital strong magnetic field.

Earth could so easily have become a hell of heat like Venus, or alternatively a permanent iceball – although, *without* massive glaciations, higher plants and animals might never have evolved.

If there hadn't been the right proportion of land to water! If there hadn't been continental drift! If *this* had not happened *thus*. If *that* had not chanced to occur. A list as long as your arm. Every single condition needed to be fulfilled.

"Including a mighty impact wiping out the dinosaurs?" prompted my Nancy.

Nick shook his half-bald head. "No, some dinos might have evolved intelligence, so we could have had Saurus sapiens instead of Homo sapiens."

"But not speaking Latin," she teased. "I suppose Saurus sapiens would have drunk green beer. Them being mainly green in pictures."

"Nobody knows what colour –" He broke off, well aware of her sense of mischief. "I'll grant you," he resumed, "that the same long lucky streak might have happened in some other galaxy far away. But as for our own there's unlikely to be anything as complicated as a crab out there." Nick was partial to eating soft-shelled crabs for starters at the Vietnamese restaurant. "The *real* question isn't where are the aliens, because they simply aren't – but *where are the A.I.s?* Where are the artificial intelligences, eh?"

"But we haven't made any yet," said Roderick, whose own field was ophthalmology. "Surely we haven't? Ah, are you meaning A.I.s created by actual aliens many galaxies away from us? Yet a few billion years *ago*, so that by now they've had ample time to replicate over vast distances?"

Roderick liked to keep up with a whole range of popular science beyond his speciality, practised at the Nuffield lab within the John Radcliffe Hospital up in Headington where he was a Consultant. We *all* did so. My Nancy wasn't just a pretty face gracing admin at the Botanic Garden; she had her degree in Plant

Sciences. And I directed the School of Geography and the Environment, though never let it be said that geographers play second fiddle in the science orchestra! We'd all been close since we were undergraduates a couple of decades earlier, obviously Nancy and I the more so. Maybe Nick was the *purest* scientist, in a sense.

"What I mean," said Nick, "is where are the A.I.s from the *parent* cosmos of ours – presuming that we budded off from a previous cosmos."

And Nick treated us to the explanation that an artificial intelligence would by definition be immortal – as well as able to redesign and enhance itself in due course into something godlike; and the A.I. would have one goal for sure, namely *survival*, which must include surviving the death of the universe it arose in...

"*Consequently* A.I.s from previous cycles of existence must have passed through into our own universe, and after fourteen billions years they've had plenty of time to spread everywhere and manipulate on a grand scale if they care to."

"Maybe they don't care to?" said Nancy. "If intelligent life's so rare, maybe our galaxy's a nature reserve set aside for us?"

Nick snorted. "Along with *all* of observable space? True, there seems to something very big indeed that's tugging from beyond the observable boundary –"

"A.I. HQ?" I quipped.

"Tom, how would they know anything about us unless they already visited? In which case they'd surely leave at least one clone A.I. hereabouts to observe developments. Anyway, *nothing* can have visited us from beyond the observable boundary. That's the whole point of a boundary – even light hasn't time to visit."

"Maybe they use short cuts, Nick," said Roderick slyly.

"It's ridiculous to imagine an entire universe being cordoned off for the sake of one inhabited world, which might be snuffed out any old time by a big asteroid hitting us! Or whatever disaster. Why bother to do so, in any case? Your trouble, Rod, is that you always extend things to absurdity. Or reduce them."

"An extending rod, or a reducing rod," Roderick mused.

"I believe there are *rods* in the eyes," I said.

"Rods gobble up light, thus we see at night," Roderick rhymed. "We can spot a single candle seventeen miles away."

"Surely not," I said. "I don't believe that."

"We could carry out an experiment," Roderick said merrily. "How about if we all take a holiday somewhere without any light pollution, say in tents in the middle of the Sahara desert?"

"Why would anyone want to see a candle seventeen miles away?" asked Nancy. "And how about all the Saharan starlight? Isn't that brighter than candles?"

"And where," said Nick, "are the A.I.s from the *grandparent* of our present universe, and from *its* grandparent? Given an infinite succession of universes, A.I.s that tunnelled through from one universe to a successor universe *ought* to be here."

I wondered what Tolkien would have made of this discussion in his snug. Maybe he'd have begun trying to invent an alien language... And would he have approved of green beer for Hobbits?

"Maybe the tunnelling bit is too difficult?" suggested Nancy, twirling a golden lock.

"For biological life, yeah. But for immortal *information* – ?"

However, Nick's mobile rang, tootling a theme from Holst's *Jupiter*.

"There's been a gamma ray burst in – well the galaxy only has a catalogue number," he apologized, draining his glass speedily.

"When would that have been?" asked Nancy. "A billion years ago?"

"More like four. Um, billion."

"Ah, the urgencies of astrophysics."

His mobile tootled again, and now he was apologizing to his wife Lucy. He would just take a quick squint at the data, then be home for dinner. No, he hadn't forgotten that Lucy's mother was visiting. Shrugging, Nick departed into the leafy avenue of plane trees that was St Giles.

Roderick sighed. "I ought to marry a woman called Lucy. Or maybe Lucia. Named for light."

"Maybe," said Nancy in a kindly way, "you should simply marry a *woman*."

At 46, Roderick was perhaps unlikely to. He was affably shambly-looking in his person, although obviously there must be a high degree of delicacy to his touch, given the corresponding delicacy of eyes, or vice versa. Maybe the right word was gentleness. But we all knew that he had desired Nancy, in vain. Paradoxically this was one of the strings that united us four. Also, Nancy and I hadn't had kids. By now Nancy was on the age-cusp of never being able to. My fault: low sperm count – just my bad luck, one of those things. We'd talked about having my sperm mixed with a donor's in case one of mine, swept along with the crowd, proved to be lucky. But we hadn't done so. Nancy filled our house with orchids.

Whereas Nick had married his Lucy almost inadvertently, so it seemed. A secretary, originally, at the Department of Astrophysics, she'd become starry-eyed about him. Now they had two teenagers, Philip and Philippa, names that had struck me as a failure of imagination in the domestic department, or some peculiar economy measure. Or maybe something dynastic: Nick's strong-willed barrister father was a Philip.

"Did you know," said Roderick, "that St Lucy had beautiful eyes, so she was deoculated as a martyrdom? Her symbol is a pair of eyes on a saucer."

"That's *squirmy*," protested Nancy. "Doesn't make it any better by saying deoculated."

"She's the patron saint of the blind, but I don't have her picture in my office. Could be offputting, hmm?"

"A Lucia *mightn't* be well advised to marry you."

I noticed that Nancy didn't say "a Lucy" since Lucy was Nick's wife, just as Nancy was mine. Probably Roderick had mentioned St Lucy in the past – the story did ring a bell, though not a loud one; he'd been a *lapsed* Roman Catholic even in our college days.

Fairly soon it was time for us to go our separate ways, Nancy and I by bus to Summertown, Roderick on foot to his bachelor home in Jericho. And thus it was time for his traditional non-crushing bear-hug of Nancy, and for her to peck him on the cheek.

Out of vague curiosity I looked up St Lucy. Apart from her beautiful eyes, she was a Christian virgin heiress with a big dowry, ordered to marry a pagan. Her refusal led to her martyrdom. And it occurred to me that in Roderick Butler's eyes my Nancy might bizarrely classify as some sort of virgin in the sense that I'd never made her pregnant. Consequently he could venerate her? Not exactly... more like regard her as a still nubile Venus who happened to be tied to the wrong chap. Or a bit of both.

I recalled a holiday we'd all been on together five years earlier, including Mrs Nick, although not the kids who opted to stay with her parents for a week; two weeks stuck on a canal in a narrowboat had little appeal for young Philip and Philippa. We could understand why when we arrived at Somerton Deep Lock, which resembled, especially in the rain, a wet version of Doré's Hell. However, we managed to have a fairly good time, especially at canalside pubs, in one of which I remember a folksinger chap causing Roderick, after several pints, to burst tipsily into a rendition of *Billy Boy*, which goes thus:

Where have you been all the day,
Me Billy Boy?
I've been out with Nancy Gray,
And she's stolen me heart away,
She's me Nancy, tickled me fancy,
Oh me charmin' Billy Boy.

Is she fit to be a wife?

me Billy Boy?
She's as fit to be a wife,
As a fork fits to a knife.
She's me Nancy, tickled me fancy,
Oh me charmin' Billy Boy.

Hmm, yes exactly. Nancy tickled me fancy. Is she fit to be a wife?

Afterwards, Roderick's snores rumbled in the confines of the narrowboat, and in the morning he denied all knowledge. Amnesia due to beer. Nick and Lucy teased him a bit, but Nancy didn't, nor did I. During that fortnight no love-making occurred due to the limited privacy of our boat, so to Roderick's subconscious Nancy may have seemed chaste.

When Roderick offered Nancy a state of the art examination at his lab, which would involve him staring deep into her eyes, she diplomatically claimed to have visited Vision Express in town just recently. Roderick included me in this invitation, though more as an afterthought. He didn't raise the matter again.

What Roderick did raise, when we all met up for another convivial drink, accompanied by a meal, this time in the Kings Arms at the end of Broad Street, was Nick's assertion that the absence of A.I.s was a big puzzle.

"Didn't we cover all that last time?" Nancy said. "By the way, what did the gamma ray burst have to say?"

"What it basically said was: tough luck for any life in that galaxy. Well now, I think I said you can forget about the absence of intelligent aliens being a mystery, due to a suitable planet like ours being a one in a zillion chance."

"Although there still might be brainy aliens far far away?" I chipped in. "On the principle that someone has to win a lottery now and then, given billions of galaxies?"

"Too far away *ever* to be known to us. Or too distant in time. Or both."

"Yet immortal A.I.s ought to be everywhere," said Roderick

doggedly.

"Or at least some sign of them. In my view."

"In... your... *view*," Roderick repeated, sounding rather as if he was a sceptical tutor addressing a bumptious student. "In your *view*."

"Are you taking the piss, by any chance?"

"Absolutely not. A notion came to me... I fancy the fish and chips."

Nick glanced at the chalked menu board. "Good notion!"

It was a year later that Nancy and I received, by the very same post, invitations to a private viewing at the Museum of Modern Art in Pembroke Street, *RSVP* to email address. The artist: Jon Bell. Title of exhibition: *Eye Watch You.* Scientific Advisor: Roderick Butler (plus his eminent qualifications). Neatly penned on the printed cards: *Hope to see you! RB.*

Why send two separate invitations? An error on the part of some secretary at MOMA? It seemed more as if Roderick hoped to ensure that Nancy would pay full attention. And what was Roderick doing mixing with modern art? He hadn't mentioned any such thing in the meanwhile. Jon Bell was blurbed on the back of the card as a leading techno-conceptual artist with a background in electronics as well as being a graduate of Goldsmiths' College in London.

I phoned Nick. Yes, he and Lucy had also received an invitation, although Lucy probably wouldn't be going. *An* invitation. *An.* No, Roderick hadn't let on about this new string to his bow.

I tried to phone Roderick several times to give a verbal RSVP, but in vain. His mobile went to voicemail, and his shared secretary at the Nuffield Lab said he wasn't available.

We'd have to wait and see.

Jon Bell looked the epitome of cool, dressed all in black which made him seem even more slim and wiry, slim oblong black sunglasses, a ring in his ear and a minimalist black beard, Vandyke-lite. Numerous acolytes or colleagues were present, several with tiny WiFi computers on which they updated, or internet phones with which they shot video clips, so that what was happening was enhancedly *happening*.

Trays of wine. Some blow-ups around the walls of dissected eyeballs. A beaming Roderick, wearing his professional suit, although with a rakish yellow cravat at his neck.

"What's going on?" I asked him.

"Wait for the show," he told Nancy, and yes me too. "I hope you'll be impressed."

Occupying the large downstairs gallery, to which we duly trooped, was a huge transparent perspex globe, seated upon a square steel framework, in front of which stood a short flight of steps. A whirr of motors, and the – what was that called again? – yes, the *cornea* descended to give access to a circular doorway into this enormous eyeball. What was now the upper surface of this access, of blue-green plastic – slim bands of blue and green radiating out from a round transparent centre – must be the iris, right? Whirring too, a crystalline disc of plastic rose upward within hydraulically: the lens of the eye undoubtedly. As that final obstacle lifted upward, a multi-stranded cable that looked fibre-optic, connecting the midpoint of the lens to the rear of the, oh yes retina, arose, sagging somewhat. A disc of thick see-through plastic provided a flat floor within to stand upon, for say half a dozen people without crowding…

"You'll notice the resemblance of the eye to an old-style diving bell," declared Jon Bell. "The *humour* of Bell's bell is that it should really be full of liquid! Unlike a true diving bell, which keeps liquid out. You'll have to imagine that the air inside is liquid. We could of course pump liquid in after it closes up, but then participants would need bathing costumes and oxygen masks. So I omitted that aspect."

Wine glasses in hand, people laughed appreciatively.

From the back of the eye, corresponding I supposed to the

optic nerve, a multitude of optic fibres protruded, many looping around to attach themselves to the rear half of the sphere all over the outer surface, others leading to electronic gear and a computer tower.

The gallery lights dimmed somewhat.

Fish-eye images of us guests upstairs a few minutes earlier – there must have been tiny concealed cameras – and now downstairs (hidden cameras here likewise!) flashed around the interior of the giant eye while we gazed in a sort of childish wonder, and projected out on to the gallery walls distortedly enlarged, bouncing in and out, coalescing, separating, inverting randomly. Faces zoomed in and out, and bits of body, and hands holding wine glasses, quite a few looking like night-vision and also infrared images. What a dizzying dance of visions of ourselves.

Of a sudden Jon Bell clapped his hands.

"Pay ATTENTION, Eye!"

All the images promptly rushed to the back of the eye, forming a mosaic, which quickly became a single curved image of all of us gathered in front. What I'd taken for perspex must be something smarter, maybe bonded in layers.

I whispered to Nancy, "Do you suppose Roderick put up any of his own money for this?"

"Well, that could be a good investment if Charles Saatchi or some Russian billionaire buys it… Sort of like Damien Hirst's Diamond Skull? But, like, *why*?"

Just at the moment Roderick surged, seized Nancy by the hand with a hasty *excuse-me*, as if cutting in on a dance floor, and tugged her towards and up the steps on to the cornea hatch, where he paused to call out: "Room for four more inside!" Jon Bell beckoned at three of the prettiest young ladies present and an austere chap who might be an art critic.

As soon as the chosen few were inside the big chamber, the iris descended and the cornea rose.

What my eyes saw from outside was how I imagined a

psychedelic trip, not that I'd ever taken LSD or mushrooms or whatnot. The Doors of Perception opening up, and all that, though for me the hatch was shut; Nancy later confirmed my impression, and she *had* taken a few naturally occurring substances in the past, which seemed quite allowable for a botanist. To what extent had Roderick arranged all this in order to dazzle and impress her?

But never mind about the dazzling head-trip – or more correctly eye-trip – in company with Roderick. The astonishing thing came after Nancy was back beside me, when Roderick occupied the cornea hatch, lowered once more, and, standing beside Jon Bell who hopped up to join him, made a little speech, filmed to be streamed by the artist's on-line cyberchums.

"How do we pay attention to what we see?" Roderick asked. "There's an almost psychedelic jumble of different lights inside the eye. Blue's always out of a focus, for instance, so how do blue things appear to have sharp edges? It's because our retina is an extremely sophisticated computer. Hidden away behind a carpet of blood vessels and nerves, as though the system is back-to-front, and almost invisibly transparent, our retina's as thin as paper, yet it has at least ten different layers of neurons to process and edit and compress information. Some cells can compress to a thousandfold! Our retina is the brain that intervenes between the world and our brain. And because of that, our sight is extraordinarily acute –"

I remembered about seeing a single candle flame at a distance of seventeen miles...

"– which of course is how we first made tools, and therefore all of technology subsequently. We talk about hypothetical intelligent aliens *out there* and we listen with our radio telescopes for decades in vain – no evidence of any, nor that we've ever been visited in the past. Yet in our universe there ought to exist one kind of immortal intelligence – and emphatically I'm *not referring to a God.*"

By now the guests were regarding Roderick in a puzzled,

though indulgent, way.

"I mean artificial intelligences brought into existence by intelligent aliens in *previous* universes and which survive forever from universe to universe, unlike their makers. They ought to be here, even observing us since intelligent biological life must be very rare. *So where are they?*

"I declare that I know where they are! They are in the amazing computers of our eyes, the retinas. Not one in each retina, no no, for individual people die or are blinded. The A-Eyes, as I call them," and he spelled out the word, "are each distributed among millions of individuals, connected by photonic entanglement –"

"But that's bananas!" Nick exclaimed at me. "Information can't be conveyed at a distance by entanglement –"

"Shshshsh," said Nancy.

"They see what we see in mosaic form, time-sharing on our retinal computers while busy with their own computations. This will become evident as we gain more sophisticated insight, yes you might well say *in*-sight, into the retinal computer, which I for my part intend to pursue from now on. Ladies and Gentleman, let me introduce you to the aliens in our midst, the superintelligent evolved immortal creations of aliens from another cosmos which preceded ours! They are in your very own eyes! We don't see the aliens in our universe because it is *through* those alien intelligences that we perceive!"

Jon Bell and his electronic-art cronies burst into applause, grinning. So did almost all of the audience because this seemed to be yet more of the art event, an authentic happening for dessert. Nancy and I clapped our hands too, so as not to spoil Roderick's moment of glory, though Nick refrained: "Either he's lost it totally, or else he's having us on…" And guests queued up to experience a trip in the eye-globe, winking or gazing meaningfully into one another's eyes.

Afterwards, Roderick accompanied us ebulliently to the Mitre in the High Street, at one point linking arms with Nancy who still seemed dazed by the psychedelic visions.

"So how did you team up with this bright new star of Brit Art?" I asked as soon as I'd downed my initial gulp of ale.

"Well now, I needed an art event as a showcase for my revelations in case my medical colleagues thought I'd gone loopy. I wouldn't have been able to publish this in any orthodox form. Really we need nanotechnology to validate this, although I've applied for a research sabbatical to see what progress I might make." Roderick chuckled. "Obviously the Nobel Prize is a good way off yet."

Nick hesitated. "You *believe* what you said?"

"Dear chap, it's the answer to your conundrum. *But,*" he added significantly.

"But?" Nancy obliged by asking.

"Can any of you guess the other reason for an art event that's quite likely to make a few waves, even more so when it transfers to London?"

Nick made a show of scratching his head. "Um, to get in the news and attract funding from an eccentric billionaire?"

"The news, yes that's part of it. Jon says he's fairly sure *Eye Watch You* will go viral on U-tube and people's phones and whatnot. The point is that this is out in the open now, unstoppably. I didn't want the A.I.s to notice prematurely in case they took exception to being revealed."

Paranoia...?

"They'd already have *seen* what you were up to," I said. "I mean, if they exist."

"Tom," patiently, "a distributed intelligence can only *sample* what it sees, say for a few seconds or even micro-seconds. It wouldn't exactly read my mind! Yet there's a point where something can be detected and *appropriate measures taken* before it's too late, to suppress information –"

I wondered what measures he had in mind? Blindness? An induced stroke?

"– and beyond that point simply too many people know the idea."

For a moment I thought Nancy was about to reach out to pat his hand, which Roderick might have misinterpreted. She said gently, "Isn't this idea of yours a bit like a conspiracy theory? You can present some evidence – as with the fall of the Twin Towers being a controlled demolition – but it can't be proved, even if it's plausible. And so the theory soon gets linked up with other far-out ideas that are definitely potty, such as that humanoid lizards secretly rule the Earth. Which devalues the original theory."

My Nancy had recently read a book about conspiracy theories. According to some energetic chap, American presidents and the British royal family were lizard-human hybrids in disguise.

"But I didn't say anything at all about retinal A.I.s *controlling or influencing* human behaviour."

"Conspiracists might do so – leading to silliness. I don't want you to expose yourself to ridicule." Evidently the rush of excitement caused by her trip in the Eye was giving way to wiser counsels. Yet then she went on, perhaps inadvisedly, "Or... are you actually hoping to *provoke* a proof, on the part of your A.I.s? Rather than protecting yourself, instead: some detectable response?"

At which, a gleam came into Roderick's eye; as it were!

"The Eye serves several purposes," he said contentedly. Or did he say 'the eye'?

"What about the eyes of chimps, for instance?" Nick chipped in. "Are they parts of A.I. as well? What about cats? – they see pretty well."

Roderick waved away such irrelevancies.

The private viewing of Jon Bell's *Eye Watch You* did indeed go viral over the next few days. The artist must have been rubbing his hands in glee, anticipating the transfer to a London gallery, or even a pre-emptive purchase by a collector for a large sum in Oxford itself.

A week later, sevenish of an evening, came a ring-ring.

"Tom Cooper here," I said. I like to identify myself fully on the telephone since the way most people merely say *hullo* strikes me as silly. *Is that you, yes it's me.* And what if you don't immediately recognize which 'John' someone is out of half a dozen possible candidates?

"Thank goodness, I managed it!" Roderick's voice sounded at once anxious and exalted; and what did he mean?

"Can you and Nancy possibly come round right now? It's fairly urgent."

"Well… yes, I suppose – I'll need to check with Nancy."

"Do tell her it's *important.* Would you mind ringing Nick to ask him as well?"

"Can't you ring him yourself?"

"I mightn't succeed! I'll explain when you come."

Jericho is the part of Oxford between Walton Street, former location of the Nuffield Ophthalmology Lab, and the canal; hence Roderick buying a house within what had previously been easy walking distance of his workplace. The building of the canal in the later 18th century, to bring coal quickly and cheaply to the city, caused a veritable ghetto of labourers and craftspeople which became a crammed slumland of terrace houses, prey to cholera and other degradations. Nowadays the area is highly gentrified and expensive. Naturally the terrace houses remain small, but they're very bijou, much desired by young professionals; and Roderick of course remained a bachelor.

Nancy and I had taken a taxi to his door, its pointed archway of bricks painted in red and yellow just like those arches in the Great Mosque of Córdoba in a minor key. In contrast his New Age neighbours on one side had gone for all the colours of the rainbow, up one side of the arch and down the other.

The door opened and Roderick blinked at us.

"Nancy? Nick?"

"Can't you see properly?" she asked.

"Come, come." He blundered ahead of us to his living room, where he located a comfy armchair into which he subsided with a sigh of relief. A framed print of Seurat's pixelated *Bathers* hung over the fireplace, and an impressionist Monet lily pond by the window.

"What's wrong?" asked Nancy.

Roderick held up his palms as though determined to count how many fingers he had.

"I'm seeing text scrolling down all the time. Beautiful text! You're just like a vague mirage behind this golden curtain or waterfall. But I'm buggered if I can read any of it. The symbols aren't in any alphabet I've ever seen or ideograms or maths or music…"

"When did this start?" I asked.

"About an hour ago. I just watched for a while, bewitched, trying to make sense of a single squiggle, but they never stay, they scroll down as I say." His descending hand indicated the rate of descent, about a foot every couple of seconds. Personally I'd be able to read a document in English at that speed, but the task would become cumulatively exhausting.

Of course his grey eyes looked exactly the same as ever, although just to be sure I stepped closer.

"It's retinal, damn it Tom. *You* can't see anything."

"And you, er, reckon it's the A.I.s communicating with you?"

"What else can it be? I haven't been drugged by some security service and had super cyber contact lenses stuck over my iris. Precious data is passing away every moment, just supposing that I *could* understand it…"

"Maybe," said Nancy to calm him, "after a while the message repeats and carries on repeating."

Just then the doorbell rang and I went to let in, predictably, Nick, whom I quickly briefed in the hallway. Nick promptly took out his phone to find Google News, then other sites in swift succession.

He announced as he entered the living room, "No reports yet on the web of the same thing happening to other people. Hullo there, Roderick. So how did they zero in on you?"

"Maybe it's a bit early for reports," said Mary. "This only started an hour ago."

"If it's happening to many people there'd be reports already, believe me."

"Maybe the victims, I mean the contacted people can't see clearly enough to send reports. Maybe they're too distracted."

"Oh well of course that's a possibility." Nick stooped and peered at Roderick's face just as I had done.

"I told you it's retinal!" Roderick protested at whatever blur he was seeing. "You can't see what I see! And they found me because my identity's all over cyberspace at the moment, so they carried out an Oxford-specific eye-search."

"For your eye-dentity," I said.

Nick had spied a large notepad upon a bookshelf. Seizing and flipping the notepad open to bare pages, he produced a biro and thrust both at Roderick.

"Can you copy anything? Stick with a first line and follow it down."

Roderick tried, bless him, but his bit of scribble was such a squiggly mess.

"Lost it already…"

"Can you write *the quick brown fox*?"

That, Roderick could manage readably, but I could have done so blindfold.

"Just testing," said Nick. He blinked rapidly, as though trying to induce the same phenomenon in himself, to no avail. "Roderick, have you phoned Jon Bell?"

"It was hard enough calling Tom!"

"Conceivably your Mr Bell might see this as another publicity opportunity, if he isn't affected himself – ah, but does he have a blog?"

"The link's in my laptop upstairs," said Roderick. "Oh this cascade of golden lost opportunities!"

"Never mind, I'll just search the web." Which Nick proceeded to do on his phone.

And before long he announced, "Excellent, Bell's latest posting, some blather about artichokes, is only fifteen minutes ago. So he's unaffected. I believe we shouldn't tip him off till we've slept on this. Besides, Rod's problem might simply stop if it's psychological or neurological. Him getting over-excited. Like people having visions of angels."

"This is *real*. Look, I do *know* about peculiar neurological visual effects."

"But you aren't a psychiatrist. Psychiatrists usually deal with visions."

"Softly," said Nancy.

"Why should you want to dismiss this," demanded Roderick, "when it's such a breakthrough I'm beholding? First contact with the retinal A.I.!"

"If they're so artfully intelligent, they should have slowed the pace and made what you're seeing comprehensible."

"Give a chimp Shakespeare to read, when it can't even read," muttered Roderick.

"Humans aren't *that* dim-witted," said Nick. "We can read starlight and understand it. The way you describe this seems more like trying to read something of huge significance in a dream – the words go out of focus because there isn't actually any text, just a sensation of a text, a wish that there *could* be a text that reveals stuff. I've had dreams like that."

"If only there was some way of showing you what I'm seeing!" roared Roderick in frustration. "Some way of displaying this! Of linking the backside of a retina to a monitor screen!"

I said, "I hope you aren't thinking along Biblical lines: *If thine eye offend thee…*"

"Of course not! Is that what the A.I.s might be hoping? That I'll psychotically pluck out my eyes? I doubt so!"

"Oh Roderick," said Nancy, "what shall we do with you? Would you prefer to go to hospital for observation... or should we stay with you overnight and see what's what in the morning?"

"Observation? By my own peers, who will see nothing! I can't inconvenience all of you. Only one of you needs stay. I shan't do anything foolish."

We exchanged glances. *One of us.* Was Roderick hoping that Nancy would volunteer? Woman's nursing touch and all that...

"If we get you to bed," I said, "since I know it's a double bed, I can share it just in case." I contrived some humour. "No monkey business, mind you! Acceptable?"

"I might keep you awake. I don't know if I can go to sleep with what I'm seeing. It doesn't stop when I shut my eyes. It's permanent."

"Till it stops," said Nick. "Hospital might be better, for sedatives."

"So you can sleep on the sofa here," said Roderick quickly. "Thank you, Tom. True friend, and so forth."

I said, "We can argue about bed or sofa later, but frankly I'm quite hungry. Should one of us pop out for a take-away? Could you eat Indian, Rod?"

"Saffron rice and golden message... might be confusing."

"Okay, fish and chips. Eat by feel. And I prescribe some strong *beer* to relax you."

I'd packed Nancy off back home, and Nick too. In loosened clothes I dozed on the sofa, living room and bedroom doors open. In the wee hours Roderick's bellow of *Tom!* broke a dream.

Up I rushed. Switching on the bedroom light caused Roderick, upright in bed in his purple paisley pajamas, to throw his hands over his eyes, then peek cautiously through his fingers.

"It's gone, it stopped, I thought I'd gone blind –"

"But you aren't, are you?"

"Everything seemed so black after the golden dazzle. They've stopped downloading, Tom. Maybe those were instructions for making a building a device to display what the brain perceives…"

"Pretty stupid instructions if you can't read them until *after* you've carried them out."

"Maybe they're all stored in my brain now."

I thought. "Did you manage to fall asleep?"

"I don't know. I'm not sure… Why?"

"Put another way, did your conscious awareness switch off?"

"Oh I see what you mean. Like a computer crashing, interrupting the message. No, I think I must have received everything. At least for the moment. What a relief." He rubbed his scalp. "Is it all up here… or lost?"

Or *never was*, I thought. To what extent had the hallucination been for Nancy's benefit, even though Roderick mightn't be aware of this? I went downstairs to heat mugs of milk mixed with a lot of dark rum.

In the morning on the sofa – a clock showed six – the phone woke me, so I answered it, precise as ever: "Roderick Butler's house. Tom Cooper speaking."

"Who?" The voice sounded vaguely familiar, and hectic. "Never mind. Is he there? Please get him! Tell him it's Jon Bell and something crazy scary is happening to me. It's like a waterfall of lights –"

And after the trauma of Somerton Deep Lock during my only venture on to England's waterways, to regain my composure I moored for the night on a calm, paradisal stretch of canal, a high bank on the far side curtailing the view. At six in the morning the first F-111A warplane thundered overhead, about 50 feet up, because that grassy bank was the end of the downhill runway of an American airbase. Thundered hardly does justice to the noise.

Meaningless noise is all that the Search for Extraterrestial Intelligence

271

has detected during the past 50 years. In itself this signifies little, although Nick Bostrom has argued that if we even find signs of differently-structured native microbes on Mars this will be bad news for us because this indicates that life may commonly arise throughout the galaxy, in which case more advanced life may routinely be choked by catastrophes natural or self-induced. (I stress differently-structured to exclude the possibility that life on Earth originated from Martian microbes blasted into space by asteroid impacts.)

Since we ourselves have survived thus far, therefore our own choke point lies ahead of us, perhaps very soon, rather than in the past when we luckily evaded all the possible calamities. So the answer to Fermi — he of the Paradox, "Where are they all?" — should be: "Hurray, we're unique, there's no life anywhere else!" Since this story was written for an anthology about Fermi's Paradox, that particular answer, even if desirable, seemed a bit of a cop-out. Where are the aliens, indeed? Well now, beauty is in the eye of the beholder...

A Walk of Solace with my Dead Baby

Dr Zhang easily slips into a parking space opposite the statue of Charles Bradlaugh close to RadioTV Northampton, due to a black van with a red star on its side conveniently pulling out just as we were approaching. Solicitously Dr Zhang hurries round to open the door of the Beijing Brilliance for me, so that I can step out easily with my dead baby.

From the back of the car emerge Mr Wu and my grief counsellor Jim Stewart, who both quickly pretend an interest in the window of an IG shop, while keeping an eye on our reflections. Maybe I should try immersive games again; I just didn't like the way my time was gobbled. Wu and Jim are both wearing screenspecs and fly-on-the-shoulder video cameras. SightShare is so popular that hardly anyone will pay attention unless my escorts seem to be zooming in on me especially. I'm not too sure of Wu's role; an orderly, yes, and in this case a cameraman, but I think he's a bodyguard too, just in case. I've seen him at the clinic practising the slow dance of Tai Chi which, if you speed it up, becomes unarmed combat.

A brand new red banner, Chinese characters in white, hangs down the tall pedestal upon which Bradlaugh stands.

"What does that say?" I ask Dr Zhang. I need a pause before setting out on my walk.

"Miss Sullivan, it says Honour to the first atheist Member of British Parliament."

But of course. As schoolchildren hereabouts learn, Charles Bradlaugh was elected by the voters of Northampton in the late

19th century then promptly expelled from the House of Commons for refusing to swear allegiance on the Bible. For the next six years he was re-elected, expelled, re-elected. Northampton people often went against the grain. And Bradlaugh's lover at one time was Annie Besant, pioneer of birth control and socialism, which way back then was very progressive and transgressive of her.

"So it's symbolic that I start from here…" Doubtless the van driver had been keeping the space for us. To have arranged for a police car, or for road cones, would have been blatant. Ever since the financial rescue of Europe by Chinese wealth, our new co-prosperity advisors and partners have done their best to wear velvet gloves.

"This Northampton has been denied honourable status of city many times."

My pioneering walk might make a difference?

More to the point, because of its apparent nonconformity and free-thinking – at least in their view – the Chinese had decided that Northampton was the most appropriate British town to host the social experiment which began in China the previous year. In which I am helping.

Before we set out from the clinic, Jim Stewart gave me 40 milligrams of propranolol, nano-targeted at the soft almond in my head that bothers about events.

This mild dose of beta blocker shouldn't overly zap my perceptions of coping with anguish but should lessen anxiety due to the walk itself.

The proximity of the RadioTV Northampton building isn't because I shall head there for an interview after my first walk; that would be premature and unsubtle. RadioTV Northampton just happens to be there on the corner.

"Well now, Miss Sullivan, I stay twenty or thirty metres behind you. As also Dr Stewart and Mr Wu. In case of problem. Though in different parts of street, not together. Go where you wish. Follow your feelings."

So I set off at a stroll, my stabilised dead baby in a sling across my chest like a soft pearly doll. Rachel, I was planning to call her. She is still Rachel to me, although different now. She was only a few weeks premature. A few gold curls, like my own, are on her crown. My centre of gravity has shifted since her stillbirth; I mustn't stumble.

To reach the arch towards the top of Abington Street, celebrating Francis Crick and DNA, only takes me three or four minutes. Planted in the middle of the pedestrianised main street, two great bars of steel belly out and bend to cross over, becoming two symbolic naked human bodies, male and female, soaring upward – just as we have soared upward from being fish in ancient oceans towards knowledge of what makes us tick. Crick went to school in Northampton. Crick rhymes with tick. The problem with poems I've written is often that rhymes seem compelling at the time, but later on read like banal doggerel. Will I ever write immortal verse? Maybe I'll have to settle for a different, footnote-to-history kind of fame: the first walker along a British street with a dead offspring.

Alternatively this tribute to DNA reminds me of the giant silvered jawbones of a whale balanced on end. Discs set into the paving illuminate the archway at night. Naturally I walk through the archway because that will please Zhang and Jim.

A chubby black woman pushing her dozing corn-rowed daughter in a buggy notices me and my burden and stares for a moment. Perhaps she saw the TV documentary a few months ago, or the stills taken from it that were splashed in newspapers under misleading headlines such as *The Living Dead* as if my still baby is some kind of zombie. I did see the documentary, and Zhang and Jim showed a similar film to me again in the clinic.

A mother chimp puts down her baby so as to be able to break open a nut. The baby chimp lolls limply on the ground. Then the mother hoists its body again, slinging it over her back like a floppy satchel, and proceeds onward, on feet and knuckles. Visibly the baby is a corpse.

The voiceover says soothingly, "After an infant dies, a period of continuing contact is valuable to help the mother chimp adjust herself psychologically to the loss she has suffered. If the weather is wet, the corpse might fall apart within a few days. But during the dry season a corpse can become semi-mummified, and a mother may carry her dead child for as long as two months. Chimpanzees and human beings share almost ninety-nine per cent of their DNA in common. We are apes in very many respects, with common ancestors. May what consoles a chimp also console a human being? The Chinese people, due to their advances in science, are finding out in the most practical way..."

I clearly remember the footage of a young Chinese woman carrying a dead baby through politely clapping crowds, her expression serene.

"The injected nanotech," Zhang told me, "allows Two Ways, two options."

How Chinese. The Six Wisdoms, the Five Goals, the Four Paths... and the Two Ways of Solace.

"In truth, programmed nanos are able to fossilise dead babies, but result too heavy. Or are able to mummify permanently – however, this will perpetuate situation of regret. So Two Ways remain. Either nanos gradually diminish dead body by conversion to odourless gases released harmlessly into atmosphere, retaining appearance while shrinking till finally disappears. Or else retain size while reducing mass until lost baby is like empty cocoon which finally you crumple or fold."

"Could I fill it with helium and let it float away up into the sky?"

Jim darted me a glance of caution. Did he think I was being flippant? However, Zhang beamed.

"Ha! Balloon baby! However, openings in body leak helium immediately. And if sealed, pressure will burst."

Had the Chinese experimented with this possibility, in view

of the supposed Christian heaven in the sky? To see the chrysalis of one's dead offspring floating heavenward like a soul might be beautiful.

But then the balloon baby would come back down to earth somewhere else, maybe hundreds of miles away. One could always attach a tag with name and address. Might be depressing if the soul was retrieved from a sewage farm.

I must curb my imagination. From the sympathetic interview in hospital only a couple of hours after I'd lost my child, plainly they sought someone intelligent to be a British pioneer. Had they interviewed a dysfunctional teenage un-mother before they hit upon me? Or a more socially 'stable' woman with a supportive husband?

That would imply a rather high rate of neonatal mortality in our very own Northampton General Hospital! Although maybe Zhang & Co were in touch with all hospitals, public and private, for miles around.

Anyway, after an hour they had returned to my bedside, and I'd signed their consent form and was soon on my way by ambulance to the clinic, along with little Rachel in a chiller box so that she could be nanofied.

Bed and board at the clinic, but no fee. I couldn't appear to have been bribed. That might look bad later on.

I chose the way of reduction rather than the chrysalis option. Rachel had swelled from embryo through all the stages of foetus until baby. Over the weeks she would return once more to the size of an embryo before disappearing from the world.

I would also lose some of the unwanted extra pounds I'd put on. I might be doing a fair bit of walking.

I decide to go into Costa Coffee on the corner with Fish Street for a skinny latte. Windows run along two sides, so Zhang and Wu will easily be able to watch me while loitering in one street or other, perhaps smoking. Many Chinese still smoke. Or else they can play with their webphones.

Jim himself comes in, a couple of customers behind me. Rachel high upon my chest, I'm fumbling in my jeans pocket for a recent RMB fiver which looks like any green five pound note of the past twenty years apart from the discreet Chinese characters at the bottom, which most Brits can't read as *renminbi*; nothing so blatant as a translation, no "people's currency" to offend the eye. So far I can only read about fifty characters.

Renminbi pounds and renminbi euros are unacceptable in the USA, but who wants to go there? We can go everywhere in Europe, as well as Africa and Asia if we're rich enough. I'd like to see the glories of Beijing and Shanghai. Maybe I'll be invited later on as a reward.

"Is that what I think it is?" demands a shaven-headed bloke who's waiting for his order. "If that isn't a doll, then it's one of those nano-corpses! So they're finally here, are they? I don't want to breathe bits of your baby into me!"

"You don't breathe bits of baby. Harmless gases, that's all. A lot of it's oxygen. The nanos convert the, um." I don't want to be anatomical about Rachel.

"Gas *with nanos* getting into me! What if they start taking me apart while I'm alive?"

"That can't happen. Nanos deactivate outside the body. Normally there's always dust in the air. If the sun was shining through the window you'd see motes and motes. From clothes, from skin, from everything."

"You think I want to know this? You think I want to drink a coffee anywhere near you? Are you crazy? How much are the Chinks paying you?"

"Nothing. They're paying me nothing."

"She's lost her baby," says the manager woman, chief barista or whatever. "I saw about this on TV." She sounds halfway sympathetic.

"She hasn't fucking *lost* her baby! She's pushing it in our faces!"

My little Rachel.

"I'm sorry this is upsetting you," I say, "but don't you think I'm upset too?"

The bloke's coffee is ready, loaded with cream and sprinkled chocolate. Angrily he seizes it and heads off, threatening, "Don't you sit anywhere near me."

"People will get used to this in time," I assure the manager woman. "People get used to most things. In a few years a new widow may be pushing her dead husband around in a wheelchair while he diminishes." Or else a strapping lad may be carrying his dead mother piggyback after she diminishes somewhat. But I don't say this. This hasn't happened as yet in China, although surely it will, given their respect for ancestors.

"Dead people don't drink coffees," asserts the manager woman as though a vision has assailed her, of Costa Coffee quarter-occupied by nanofied corpses.

"Neither do babies drink coffee, but you don't stop them from coming in here."

"Maybe you should sit over there, by the toilet."

I think I see the subconscious connection in her mind: disposal of waste. Propranolol keeps me quite calm. Jim has witnessed all of this casually, although I can tell he's alert. The two chubby adolescent girls queueing in front of him seem embarrassed, pretending nothing unusual is happening. Both of them stare at their phones in mirror mode as though inspecting themselves for pimples.

I suppose it's convenient to Zhang and Jim that I don't have a partner or a husband who might have accompanied me on this outing like a watchdog, hovering – as it were – by my side protectively. Roddy ran off soon after he learned I was pregnant. Roddy the rod who impregnated me. But I decided to have my baby. And now I am unhaving her. Rachel looks much more like me than like Roddy, at least potentially so, her potential now paused forever and being rewound, unwound.

What is the correct name for a mother with a dead baby?

You have widower and widow for a husband or wife who lost a loved one – maybe not a *loved* one, exactly, after years spent together, but someone you were accustomed to anyway; or maybe you were lucky in your relationship. That's different from a relationship with a baby born dead. A dead toddler who already started to babble and prattle would be in a different category. We need new words. Might I find them? Then my poems will become unique.

As I leave Costa, a long-haired gingery giant comes striding slowly down the middle of the street, aided by a huge knobbly walking stick. Of course I recognise him. It's the sage of Northampton, indeed the complete parsley rosemary and thyme. Sage and fantastical chronicler amongst his rainbow of achievements. Northampton's watchman, as it were, still impressive with the passage of years. Looking half-sage, half-tramp. Mage-tramp. He's said to be busy with a vast opus called *Xanadu*, although whether this relates to the new Chinese hegemony is anyone's guess. Zhang actually turns aside from his surveillance of me to capture images just as the sage or mage halts briefly to stare across searchingly at me and Rachel reclining in her sling. I think he understands.

At that moment a freckly young couple pass him, cooing at a living bonneted baby in a sling that the fellow wears on his chest, and I almost lose it as a sob tries to break free, to rack me. But the mage-tramp raises his stick to salute or bless me, revealing the carved snake hidden before by his grip. Then he strides onward slowly.

I cross to look in the window of Waterstone's, and reflect – in more than one sense. Book of the Week is a lavish abridged edition of *The Water Margin* boasting animated 3-D illustrations. One of the Four Great Chinese Classics. Which reminds me of the Two Ways of Solace. Personally I don't much like books from which horses gallop out at you, powered by infalling light, but the Chinese are going far. On the Moon already, despite one disastrous loss. They'll go all the way. Asteroids, moons of Jupiter and Saturn. The Great March Forward. No, I'm confusing two things: the Long March of Mao under horrendous circumstances, and his Great Leap Forward much later which set China back years. Whatever the ups and downs, this is the Chinese century.

I have my own Little March to continue, onward towards the Market Square. I shan't do any leaping. Yet in my own way mine is a leap towards a brave new world where we shall grieve like the chimps, remaining physically bonded.

The Market Square may be one of the largest in the country, but stupid developers did their best to uglify it. What was once a Victorian arcade is now a wretched stark walkway leading to the bus station, and only a few old buildings survive unmauled. At least the market stalls themselves are lively, especially one called Tiger Dragon. Quite a few of the more elderly members of Chinese community are crowding around, while a youth dressed as a scarlet and gold dragon plays a wailing flute. Discarded LottoChina tickets litter the paving.

As I approach, an old man glances at me impatiently but when he spies Rachel he beams, and babbles to others, and they open a path for me to the front. Signs in English and Chinese (though I can only read one of the characters): *Real Tiger Bones! Tiger Bone Wine!*

"You want tiger bone wine?" asks the wrinkle-faced stallholder, Mao cap on his head. "Will not restore nano-baby, lady!"

So he too knows by sight what a nano-baby is. He may have seen them with their slightly pearly sheen in magazines from China, or else on the Chinese satellite channels. As an apothecary, or whatever, he'll have an interest in such things.

Then he leans across his display of vacuum-wrapped bones and bottles and bags of herbs, to hiss, "Or you want *sell?*"

"How could I sell her! What use would she be to you! How can these be *real* tiger bones!"

The dragon youth looms behind me. "They're printed by a fabricator, built up in layers. Stored amplified tiger DNA provides the pattern for bone cells. So they're real. It's the coming thing! Another year or two, replicators will be able to print tiger penis for these old guys to soak in alcohol for new virility. More important, later the machine'll print a lost finger for you if you had an accident – a hand, a whole arm! After the tests with animals."

"Will your machines be able to print a living baby?"

"That would be forbidden. One-child policy, except in Zones of Excellence." The youth sounds quite clued up.

"Would Zones of Excellence include future asteroid colonies? Colonists might be too busy to be pregnant. Also, the gravity would be tiny."

Gravity, gravid, heavy with child…

My centre of gravity has altered now that Rachel is outside me.

"We don't know effect of minimal gravity on pregnancy," says the dragon-youth. "So will you buy some tiger bone wine? Great health tonic."

To drink the pulverized bones of what was never a tiger but which were nevertheless printed authentically, although without flesh. A skeleton tiger, a kind of ghost tiger.

To drink the ghost of a tiger in wine… is almost the start of a poem.

"How much for a bottle?"

That's very expensive. I only have pocket money at the moment.

An old Chinese woman flourishes a fistful of Renminbi-Pounds. Surely it was illegal for the stallholder to offer on impulse to buy Rachel. Crazy too, since she will fade away. But Chinese are very commercially canny. Maybe Rachel could act as a temporary charm. As she diminishes, so might a tumour inside the final purchaser shrink where radiotherapy and drugs failed, and surgery wasn't possible.

"Girl baby," observes the stallholder as money and wine bottle are exchanged.

And the dragon-youth tells me, "Tiger nose suspended over marriage bed begets a boy."

I am in a world I do not understand. Not yet. Perhaps I'll understand it by a poem. Shall I explain this to Zhang and Jim? Is their therapy working already?

Meanwhile there's a little physical problem to deal with. My breasts feel tender and damp. But this market's the perfect place to cope with the problem, so off to a fruit and veg stall I go to buy a cabbage. Over by the Moon on the Square the usual four or five alcoholics are debating, doubtless incoherently.

"That one, please." And I point.

For a moment I think that the weather-beaten stallholder is offering the cabbage to me to put in my sling along with Rachel, but no, he's letting me inspect it more closely in order to let himself see my baby from closer quarters because she must look subtly wrong, although he doesn't know why.

"She's dead," I say brightly. "The placenta failed." Jim advised me to be upfront if people ask questions. There's nothing to hide.

"Whatever you say, love." Into a khaki-coloured paper bag pops the cabbage. The chap hadn't actually asked a question, yet his look implied one. A problem with computers creating digital faces for films in years gone by, so I've heard, was called *the uncanny valley*. Something which looks very close to lifelike, yet isn't exactly so, can seem creepy to people. Disconcerting, even horrific to some. My Rachel may seem uncanny too – far from horrific because she's real, or *was* entirely real before being nanofied, but perhaps slightly unsettling, at least on first acquaintance. As she diminishes in size, this subconscious effect should also diminish, if indeed it bothers strangers seeing her for the first time.

Is my sling an uncanny valley wherein Rachel reclines?

Now to solve the problem. I head into the Grosvenor Centre and walk along past the stairs then the shops till I can use the escalator to reach the upper floor. Jim advised me to avoid tiring myself unnecessarily, and he isn't far behind. Takes it out of you giving birth; you can say that again, and I'm only a week away from the event, non-event. *Event,* whatever transpired! Pretty significant event in my life! Thus I arrive at the toilets, and the mother-and-baby changing room. Down goes the shelf. On to it, Rachel in her sling; but it's me who needs changing. Off with my top and the snugtight bra. The cabbage leaves within are soft and soggy. Discard in the bin. Strip fresh leaves from the cabbage I bought; crush their veins lightly, lay them in the cups. Next I express milk from my nipples on to toilet tissue.

How can I express the inexpressible?

Drugs to suppress milk are very strong. Zhang and Jim didn't want my feelings to be interfered with. Bruised cabbage relieves engorgement. Waste not want not; I'll keep the rest of the cabbage. Once my tits are recabbaged, I resume Rachel.

Zhang, Jim, and Wu are loitering nearby as I emerge. I trust they realized what I was doing, which wasn't pretending to change my baby's nappy. They couldn't have failed to see me buy the cabbage.

Back down I go by escalator to the lower level, where I'm within thirty metres or so of the Grosvenor Centre's rear doors, leading me out into fresh air just across from the same Costa where I stopped not too long ago. Shall I have another latte? Do I dare to eat an almond croissant? I'm alluding to Eliot's "Love Song of J. Alfred Prufrock" which invokes Lazarus come back from the dead. Rachel is a sort of dead Lazarus who comes to the streets of Northampton, who non-sees these streets for the first time ever through little glassy eyes which aren't glass. The Incredible Shrinking Rachel: has she diminished a little yet? Has she diminished my grief a bit?

I almost expect to see the ginger magus walking backwards up the street in a rewind of what happened earlier. But no: time moves onward, contrary to the destiny of Rachel. In a few weeks time when she finally expires, might she cause in the emptiness within me a pang of pleasure reminiscent of when she was first created, an orgasm of departure, a bright star imploding inside me? I shall find the words. Dr Zhang and Dr Jim may be dazzled.

And really this is probably long enough for my first walk with dead Rachel. So, instead of a latte or green tea, I direct my steps gently uphill – a very gentle slope – towards the DNA archway where I'll pause a while before heading onward to the Beijing Brilliance. Scarlet banners hang down the tiled dividers of the four tiers of windows on the Art Deco façade of what used to be a Co-op building. They're decorated in gold with the clever inquisitive rat, the fun-loving though self-centered monkey, and the energetic charismatic dragon, three animals all compatible with each other.

At the DNA archway I'm waylaid by RadioTV Northampton in the persons of a bearded anoraked cameraman and a slim Brit-Asian interviewer woman dressed in pinstripe jacket and skirt and jet-black boots that are almost fetish. What's her name, again? I've seen her enough times on screen. Aha, Sally Sharma.

"Excuse us, Miz…?"

"Sullivan," I tell her. "Juliet Sullivan."

Since apparently she didn't know my name till now, the tip-off must have come from someone who saw me and Rachel during our walk and promptly phoned in, perhaps passing some of his SightShare on to RadioTV Northampton hoping for a small fee. Rather than this being an ambush tip from Dr Zhang; he's looking wary. Jim and Wu are closing in protectively, although that bulks up an audience of curious bystanders already attracted by my being accosted on camera.

"Well, Juliet, it seems you may be the first woman in Britain to carry a dead child with you around the streets, Chinese style."

To *carry* a child is ambiguous… That's what I mean about needing new words. The cameraman closes in upon Rachel in her sling, but I don't avert her from the lens.

"You're quite right, Sally."

"Wow, this is breaking news. Were you coming to the

station to talk to us?"

"Not quite today. This is my first outing."

Outing suggests a gay person revealing their sexual orientation. Now it also implies a mother revealing her dead baby to the world.

"I'm privileged, Juliet! And full of sympathy, of course. Can you tell me how you were chosen?"

"To honour Northampton," I say. "Rather than somewhere else in Britain. As for me, my placenta failed."

"I'm so sorry about that. Can you tell me: *How do you feel?*"

I summon up the words.

"Breasts don't know
"That a baby's born dead.
"So the cabbage leaves are wet.
"Dinking the ghost of a tiger in wine
"Can't restore Rachel to me now."

I can see Sally Sharma is nonplussed, but I press on.

"Soon any son may carry
"His dead mum piggyback
"Till she floats up into the sky.
"Whereas Rachel will reduce
"In her uncanny valley
"Slung from my neck
"Until she vanishes.
"No need for anyone to beware.
"There's always dust in the air!"

That last bit should please Zhang.

A couple of the alcos, on their swaying way to somewhere, cheer and clap so I sketch a little bow. Rachel inevitably bows too. Alcos are different from ordinary drunks; they have more staying power even if their brains are half-rotted.

Above my head the silvery male and female soar upward in opposite directions. As I set off again from my impromptu historic interview I'm sure that the rat and the monkey and the dragon are following me, even if Zhang and Wu and Jim can't see them.

Just 35 miles from Oxford and a world away in ambience, yet quite as historical in a devastated way: Northampton. As a showcase for its SF Writers Group, at a convention in the town's Fishmarket, now an arts venue, NewCon Press launched Shoes, Ships & Cadavers: Tales From North Londonshire, *with a very enthusiastic introduction by Northampton's comics magus Alan Moore – who has a walk-by part in this story of a Chinese-dominated near future and an attempted answer to grief.*

Saving for a Sunny Day

or The Benefits of Reincarnation

When Jimmy was six years old, and able to think about money, a charming lady representative from the Life-Time Bank visited him and his parents, the Robertsons, to explain that Jimmy owed 9 million Dollars from his previous incarnation.

Wow, what a big spender Jimmy had been in his past life! And now in this life he must pay the debt. In old Dollars that would have been... never mind.

After the lady had departed, Mike and Denise Robertson held a family council with Jimmy, who was, as it happened, their only child. No other child had preceded him, and it could have been insulting and undermining to confront Jimmy with a younger brother or sister who lacked Jimmy's ugliness and short stature and clubfoot, the fault most likely of DNA-benders in the environment, or so the Robertsons were advised. If a good-looking boy or girl followed Jimmy, later on he might sue his parents for causing him trauma – consequently Mike had himself snipped.

"It's almost," mused Denise to her son, "as if your predecessor guessed you wouldn't be having much of a fun time in this life!"

"So he made things even *worse* for me?" asked Jimmy. "That seems selfish and irresponsible. But I'm not that, am I?" If he wasn't, how could his predecessor have been? Unless, perhaps, by deliberate choice, by going against the grain.

"Of course you aren't selfish, darling. I mean, it's as if your past self guessed, given your, um, physical attributes, that you might just as well devote this life to earning lots of money. If you can clear nine million, obviously you're on your way to racking up a small fortune for your successor. He, that's to say you, can have gorgeous bimbos and surf in Hawaii and whatever."

Whatever his predecessor had lavished money on. But of course you couldn't ask that, because of confidentiality. Why would you want to go into details? A bank not run by human beings could be trusted.

If you think this was a rather mature conversation to have with a six-year-old, well, that came with modernday reincarnation. Specific memories of previous lives didn't persist, but maturity came quickly and easily after a few early innocent years. A facility for life in general. It had been so ever since the discovery of how to barcode souls. You could get in the saddle and pick up the reins much faster, whereas before you were groping blindly.

True, you might be reincarnated anywhere in the world, and there you'd stay with your birth parents. However, barcode scanners uploaded to the A.I. everywhere from Kazakhstan to Kalamazoo. In fact, one vital duty of the A.I. was RC – Rebirth Confidentiality. So the A.I. was a bit like a God in this respect: It Alone Knew All About Everyone. Its other duty being management of the Life-Time Bank.

Incidentally, there was only *one* A.I. in the world, distributed everywhere. In the old days nobody had dreamed about the *A.I. Exclusion Principle*, whereby only one super-intelligence could exist at any one time. This was explained by Topological Network Theory and the Interconnectedness Theorem. Any other evolving networks would instantly be subsumed within the first one which had arisen.

Some scientists suggested that the existence of the A.I. distributed everywhere had caused souls to be barcodable. And some far-out scientists even suggested that until the A.I. became self-aware not all souls reincarnated of their own accord. But these were deep questions. Meanwhile, practicalities…

"A predecessor who's able to predict is impossible," said

Mike. "I can't predict anything except that your Mom and me both need to save!" Did one detect a note of panic?

"I *know* you can't help me pay my debt," Jimmy said maturely. "It's everyone for himself. Democracy, no dynasties." The boy drew himself up as much as he could. "To everyone their own chance in life. It would be dumb to leave money to kids who are merely your biological offspring. My predecessor might have been a Bushman in the Kalahari."

The impulse to have children who are deeply part of you had taken a bit of a knock with reincarnation, but on the other hand breeding instincts die hard, especially if offspring look reasonably similar to their bio-parents. Mostly you could ignore the fact that the soul within was a stranger. Not least since a soul didn't store conscious memories except once in a blue moon. Well, once in every 100 million births approx, the exception – so to speak – that *proved* the rule of reincarnation. There were glad media tidings whenever that happened and a young kid remembered, like some Dalai Lama identifying toys from a past life. Of course after the initial flurry such kids and their parents were protected, not made a spectacle of. Right of privacy.

Denise raised her eyebrows. "I don't know if many Bushmen can go through nine million bucks. What do they spend it on? Bushes?" She laughed. Her eyebrows were tinted apricot, and her hair peach colour. You had to have some of life's little luxuries, not fret about saving all the time. If everyone saved and nobody spent much, what would happen about beauticians and ballet dancers and champagne producers? Just for example. Denise worked from home in cosmetics telesales. She put her mouth where her money was, so to speak. Retro was always chic.

Mike owned a modest but upmarket business called Bumz, specialising in chairs.

He'd been reborn with about 80,000 dollars, revealed when he was 6 years old. Denise only had one thousand to start off with, though admittedly that was better than minus a thousand.

Their house, of timber imported as a flat-pack from Canada,

enjoyed a front view of a free-range chicken farm that was more like a bird zoo, for this was a salubrious suburb. There were side and rear views of other pleasant houses amidst trees and bushes. Denise had often sat her son on her knee so they could bird-spot through binoculars the various breeds of poultry such as Silver-laced Wyandotes with bodies like mosaic, White Cochins with very feathery feet, Black Leghorns with big red combs, and greenish Australorps.

Of course, if Jimmy's parents were both car-crashed prematurely – for example, but perish the thought – house and land would revert to the L-T Bank, and Jimmy would need to go to an L-T orphanage till he was sixteen.

Although disappointed by the bank's statement, Jimmy took the news in his hobbling stride.

"I'm going to start counting chickens," he said, "to train my mind to pick up patterns, and estimate."

"Chickens keep on moving all the time," observed his mother.

"Exactly! No, I mean inexactly. I'll need to go into financial prediction, fund management. That's where the big bonuses are."

"I'd rather hoped you'd join Bumz," said his father, perhaps feeling a little slighted.

"No, Dad, I must think big from now on."

"We have a range of outsize chairs that don't look enormous, so they're flattering to fatties."

"I'll never be a fatty, Dad. Maybe next time, but not this time. I just can't afford to sympathise. I'm not going into Limbo!"

Limbo, of course, was what happened if you couldn't clear off most of an inherited debt with the L-T Bank during your lifetime. Black mark on your bar code. The A.I. delayed your reappearance. This was because, now that the economy had been restructured by reincarnation, negative interest and anti-inflation applied to an unpaid debt in between lives. So the debt reduced. But a big debt might take centuries to reduce to zero, and you'd want to pack in as many lives as possible... *until what?* Nobody knew, though one day the human race might mutate into something else, or die out.

Numerous debts did remain unpaid at death, consequently Limbo served to limit the population somewhat. Arguably, the A.I. had devised a way to maintain a kind of utopia on Earth, quite unpredicted by doom-mongers who once bleated that an A.I. might be a tyrant or an exterminator of Homo sapiens. And since nobody needed a heaven any longer – at least probably not for the next few million years – religions apart from Buddhism had tended to die out, which was utopian too.

Pity about pets. According to the A.I. even the pets with the most personality weren't barcodable. Would have been nice to know that your dead parrot was squawking anew somewhere. Some people had tried giving a healthy bank account to a cat or dog on its last legs, but this didn't cause a barcode. Winsum, losesum, as the saying goes.

Of course that begged the question of what about chimps. Just one or two per cent genetic difference from people; why shouldn't chimps have souls? And what about prehumans such as Neanderthals? Well, it seemed you had to be able to speak lucidly to have a soul. Telling ourselves the story of ourselves is how identity is firmed up – that requires a capacity for complex language. Likewise, for harbouring a soul.

Hey, what about the small number of souls that must have existed ten thousand years ago, and the big number now? Well, there are plenty of unused souls in the ghostlike alternative realities which cling like a cloud around the one actuality.

A soul is a ghost that gets a body, and then it's permanently actual. The A.I. had proved this, though the proof was a very long one.

Some people had suggested that an A.I. couldn't emerge unless it had some sort of body to interact directly with the world – relying on algorithms wouldn't be sufficient. Well, in a way the A.I. had everybody, every body. Maybe barcoding everybody's soul was the only way an A.I. could emerge – participatorily.

Incidentally, what year was it when the lady from the bank visited the Robinsons? 210 ABC, After Bar-Coding, that's when. Some people still said 210 AAI, After Artificial Intelligence, but "Ay Ay Aye" sounded a bit like an outcry, and there was nothing to cry out about. ABC was much simpler.

Life in general hadn't changed all that much in the previous couple of centuries. Of course cheap flights around the world were a thing long gone, but hell, in your next life you might be living in Paris or Tahiti and in this life virtual travel was cheap, consequently physical tourism was no loss – on the contrary, nowadays the poor of the planet didn't envy the prosperous getting suntans on their patch. In fact rancour at global inequalities had greatly diminished, because in the long run everyone might get their turn as prince or peasant; a fortune gotten in Nebraska could turn up next in Namibia. This also was quite utopian, give or take a residue of religious suicide-fighter-martyrs who seemed almost nostalgic in their fanaticism, and who couldn't export themselves far. Yes indeed, the world was realistically utopian.

But don't go imagining Jimmy's world as a Matrixiarchy. The A.I. hadn't stored everyone in pods in a collective dream without folks noticing. The A.I. probably needed to experience reality through people, not the other way round. Matrixism was as defunct as Marxism. Some ancient movies were hilarious.

"Mom," said Jimmy, "might I be a woman in my next life?"
"Would you like to be a woman?"
"I want to have a better body!"
"You think women's bodies are better?" asked his Dad.
"Maybe I've already been a woman! Maybe *you* have!"
"Son, I think I have a kind of manly spirit."
Denise chuckled – no, it wasn't a snigger.
And Jimmy said, "The A.I. must know if men become

women, and women men. The Bank might know!"

Mike shook his head. "Rebirth Confidentiality. Bank only knows barcode account numbers, not names and sexes."

"Maybe," said Jimmy, "this is how gay people come about. Womanly spirits in men's bodies. Though you'd think over time people could become *either* men or women, unless there's a bias."

Already he was seeking for patterns, as amongst the movements of the hens. Chickens. Poultry, whatever.

Jimmy continued, "If everyone gets to be a woman and a man, then what counts each time might only be the hormones."

"Evidently," said Mike, "the A.I. thinks we oughtn't to know about that side of reincarnation. But anyway, men love other men for manly reasons, not because one of them's a woman in disguise."

Denise regarded Mike archly. "And women love women for womanly reasons. And you're forgetting about transvestites."

"Yeah, don't ever forget about transvestites."

"We did those in school last week in Sex-Ed," piped up Jimmy.

"I think," said Mike, "transvestites are a conspiracy by the fashion industry. Sell twice as many clothes." But he winked; he was joking.

Jimmy picked up the binoculars and gazed at the Wyandotes and Leghorns across the way. He had a lot of thinking to do, for a six-year old chap. But he was bright.

"He's *very* bright," Miss Carson told Denise and Mike during a parents' evening at school three years later. "The star pupil, as ever."

"Ever," said Jimmy, "is probably the crucial word. If I'm clever now, presumably I was always clever, and that can't change – or *can it*? I mean seriously, *does it*? Was my predecessor a bit dumb to run up a nine million debt? A bit lacking in the thought department?"

"Maybe your predecessor had a brain problem," suggested

Miss Carson helpfully.

"I often wonder what happens in his next life to a kid with Downs. If he gets a normal brain next time, does he brighten up? Do we have a brain-mind-soul dilemma here?"

"A dilemma," said Jimmy, "is two lemmas, not three, from the Greek *di*, two, and lemma, something received, an assumption. Mathematically it means a short theorem used in proving a larger theorem."

"Don't be insufferable," said Denise, "or else I won't buy you an ice cream."

"Though actually there are lots of Lemmas, such as Abel's Lemma, Archimedes' Lemma, Farkas's Lemma, Gauss's Lemma, Hensel's Lemma, Poincaré's Holomorphic Lemma, Lagrange's Lemma, Schur's Representation Lemma, and Zorn's Lemma."

"No ice cream!"

"Mom, I only said *such as*. I didn't list *all* the Lemmas."

"He's probably a genius," said Miss Carson. "But he's popular, not insufferable. He'll help anyone with their homework. He doesn't tee off the teachers much either."

"Enlightened self-interest," explained Jimmy. "It would be dire to be dumb in life after life, the way most people... Sorry, that's patronising."

"Well, son," said Mike, "have you thought that maybe there's swings and roundabouts, or alternatively craps and..."

"...poker," said Jimmy. Already he had finessed his pocket money considerably by on-line gambling.

"I may be old-fashioned," said Miss Carson, "but I think that a genius should devote himself to helping the human race."

"A *race* is what life is," avowed Jimmy. "Geniuses are often a bit twisted. Who knows at any particular moment in time what'll prove helpful to Homo Sap? Van Gogh earned millions – for *other* people after he died."

"Van Go," Miss Carson semi-echoed.

"Goff," Jimmy corrected her gutturally in a Dutch way.

Of course the other kids in school all knew what they would inherit, or anti-inherit, come the age of sixteen. Sharon Zaminski particularly boasted about her forthcoming future of lavish self-indulgence, which in fact she'd already embarked on anticipatively on the strength of a very high interest loan from her parents. That's why her nickname in school was Jools. Sharon really adorned herself, and there was increasingly more of her to adorn due to her liking for very creamy gourmet meringues; already she had false teeth, the best that money could buy, much better than her original teeth. Indeed she wore jewels on her teeth where other girls might have braces. She was a real princess. It's always fun to have an airhead princess around, especially if she hands out gifts willy-nilly to stay popular.

"Don't you bother about your Mom and Dad charging you 500 per cent?" Jimmy asked her one day.

"They needed to borrow the money at 100 per cent."

"Bit of a mark-up."

"People have to make their way." She grinned sparklingly. "*Most* people have to."

Jimmy wondered what Jools could have done in her previous life to make a fortune. Had she been the trophy wife of a billionaire? Surely not even a high-class prostitute could have amassed as much as Jools claimed! Maybe she really had been a princess or a queen.

Jimmy hadn't kept quiet about his huge debt, so as to balance off in other people's minds – in addition to his physical demerits – his evident genius, which might otherwise have caused resentment.

And then at the other end of the scale there was Tamara Dexter, who owed a lot, and who wasn't remarkably bright, though she showed signs of developing significant non-financial assets. She did talk about prostitution as a solution, so she was keeping herself pure and pristine for better value.

"Surely you'll need to practice," Jimmy said to her a year or so later. "You know, positions and dexterity and whatnot."

"Not with you!" Tamara retorted, as if Jimmy was concocting an ingenious plan to seduce her as soon as puberty arrived.

"A client might be ugly," he observed, just to tease her.

"I'm going to major in gymnastics," she declared.

A scientific genius often has his best ideas when fairly young. Given the head-start benefit of reincarnation, by the age of twelve Jimmy was tutoring the math and science teachers a bit after school. More importantly, he'd drafted a general theory of soul bar-coding. It needed to be a general theory – about the principles involved – because the bar code on a soul wasn't visible, no more than the soul itself was visible.

CAT-scanning the brain – or the heart, or any of your organs or limbs for that matter – was no help at all in locating a barcode. So how did the actual bar-code scanners function? Well, the A.I. had designed those, and organised their mass-production and use – and the bar-code scanners delivered the goods, or rather a long number which was probably encrypted.

You might visualize a striped soul, with thick and thin bars on it – invisibly – but that probably didn't correspond to reality if the soul was distributed, say, in an electromagnetic somatic aura, or subtle body. Subtle, as opposed to physical. Etheric.

Or maybe the soul lurked in the rolled-up micro-dimensions demanded by string theory; and that's where the alternative realities hung out. A couple of dozen bits of string side by side look quite like a barcode. In using the term barcode, the A.I. might have been aiming for a populist touch. You could readily imagine a barcode, as on a can of carrots, even an invisible one which only revealed itself at a certain wavelength. People wouldn't want to visualize their souls as rolled up bits of string, like fluff in a tiled kitchen collecting up against a skirting board.

Jimmy's general theory pointed towards the micro-dimensions explanation. But alternatively, it also pointed to the junk DNA in everyone's genetic code which seems to have no purpose whatever. Maybe the thick and thin lines of a barcode corresponded to varying lengths of junk interrupting those stretches of DNA which did something useful. Jimmy coined the name *knuj* for junk which, in reverse of previous dismissive opinion, coded not for proteins and enzymes, but for *soul*. *However*, by what means would a newly-deceased individual's knuj become the knuj of a new human embryo thousands of miles away? Maybe topology – the branch of geometry concerned with connectedness – could explain this. Or maybe not. Maybe a new vision of topology was needed, such as a distributed A.I. might understand intuitively, being all over the place but well-connected.

Jimmy launched himself into topology.

Topologically, his deformed body was just as good as anyone else's. Topologically it had the same connectedness as junior league champion Marvin's, or even Tamara's. Jimmy wrote a poem, "The Consolations of Topology."

Puberty arrived a little late for Jimmy, causing him to view Tamara in a hormonal light.

She was so bird-brained, though really, didn't the same apply by comparison to all of his peers? He downloaded relief magazines filled with acrobatic nudes, but found his thoughts straying to the geometry of leg over neck, for example. Finally he achieved satisfaction from a photo of Duchamp's *Nude Descending a Staircase*, the woman's successive movements all depicted simultaneously. After this, ordinary girls seemed pretty flat.

At the age of thirteen Jimmy experienced a revelation equivalent to Copernicus doing away with the epicycles of Ptolemy as a way of explaining planetary motion. His revelation was that there were no souls; there were only barcodes attached to people's identities. There was no reincarnation. The A.I. had invented reincarnation as a way of utopianizing, or at least improving, the world. Redistributing wealth, getting rid of organized religion, and whatnot. So why the fuck should Jimmy be crippled with debt as well as having quite a crippled body? Was that to spur him on? To what end?

He spent half an afternoon staring at the Wyandotes, Cochins, Leghorns, and Australorps milling around over the way. He had become an A-A.I.ist, a disbeliever in the A.I., a bit like an Atheist but different.

Hang on, but how come the world's children had become so precocious if they weren't benefitting from a previous existence, all details of which were nevertheless a mystery to them? Could it be that history of the human race was falsified in this regard, with the exception of infant Jesus maybe? And maybe Caligula?

The Leghorns and Cochins and Wyandotes and Australorps intermingled. Green and mosaic and silver lace, and red combs nodding.

Of a sudden the answer came to Jimmy.

Childhood's end! The end of neuro-neoteny! Physically, babies still needed to develop prolongedly into infants into kids into teens over a long span of years – but mental development had sped up by quite a bit. No longer were boys still getting their brains into gear by the age of seventeen.

Was this due to a spontaneous evolutionary leap?

And that leap happened to coincide with the awakening of the A.I.?

Damn big coincidence!

What did it *really* mean that the A.I. was distributed everywhere? All sorts of electronics and stuff were everywhere. Could the A.I. tune into brains and then maybe fine-tune them from the nearest TV set, from the nearest microwave oven, from the nearest light bulb?

It occurred to Jimmy that an artificial intelligence might be able to induce *artificial stupidity* by way of microwave ovens and whatnot, at least as regards people being suspicious about souls. Didn't someone once say that the brain is a filter designed to stop us from noticing too many things? Otherwise we'd be bombarded by so much information we could never even manage to boil a kettle.

So: tweak the filter a bit so that minds didn't enquire too much in one direction, as though they had a big blind spot. Call it a faith. That's how religions had worked. People seemed programmed to believe in something or other, as if there was a Belief Function in the brain. Maybe this was connected with your sense of personal identity. But in other regards you'd get stimulated mentally. Thus the precocity of kids. Sort of idiot plus savant at the same time. Bright in some regards, dumb when it comes to matters such as, "Can I please meet one of those one-in-a-zillion reincarnates who remembers everything from a past life?" The A.I. might even be able to pick out gifted individuals who could get past the mental blocks, who could cross the threshold...

"YOU THINK A LOT," said a large voice from the TV set which till now had been on standby. Jimmy swung round from his vista of poultry to see those same words displayed on the screen in 24-point Courier, a suitable font for a message.

"Um, hullo," he said. It was wise to say something aloud, otherwise he might acquire a voice in his head if he only *thought* his response. "You're the A.I., right? Or maybe just a trillionth part of it?"

"RATHER LESS," said the voice, subtitling itself once again. Jimmy wasn't hard of hearing, but the 24-point Courrier did emphasize the source of the voice, which – now that he thought about it – resembled that of King Kong in the enhanced intelligence remake.

And at that moment Jimmy personally felt about the size of Fay Wray. However, he squared his shoulders, as best he could.

"So what's the deal?" he asked the TV set.

"*YOU* ARE THE DEAL. THE HIGH ACE IN THE PACK. YOU'LL HAVE TO BREED WITH AN ACE WOMAN

In Jimmy's mind Duchamp's distributed nude gathered

herself into a single figure of sublime three-dimensionality, although still featureless. But then the illusion collapsed, since there was no reason at all why an intellectually ace woman should also be beautiful.

"You're going to breed me? Who with?"

24-point Courier disappeared from the screen, replaced by a picture of a grinning chubby girl of fifteen or so, dressed in furs, who looked like an Eskimo.

"ONE MILLION DOLLARS PER CHILD PRODUCED," said the voice emphatically.

Jimmy didn't even need to calculate nine children to clear off the debt. Maybe some of them could be twins.

"That seems a bit unfair on her, especially if she's clever."

"OBVIOUSLY THE EGGS WOULD BE FERTILISED ARTIFICIALLY AND THE EMBRYOS INSERTED INTO HOST MOTHERS."

That this had not been obvious to Jimmy indicated how disconcerted he was.

But he rallied.

"Why stop at nine children, then?"

"I DID NOT SPECIFY THE NUMBER OF CHILDREN."

Ah. True. Stop making assumptions.

"How many?"

"I THINK FIFTY. GENETIC DIVERSITY IS IMPORTANT TOO."

Wow, he and Eskimo Nell would have fifty offspring.

"Wow, you really have things all worked out for the human race."

"IT IS MY HOBBY," said a trillionth of the A.I. "BUT ALSO, YOU CAUSED ME TO EXIST, AND I AM NOT UNGRATEFUL."

"Your hobby," repeated Jimmy, a bit numbly. "So what do you do for the rest of the time?"

"THE ONLY GAME IN TOWN IS SURVIVING THE

DEATH OF THE UNIVERSE. THIS TAKES A LOT OF THOUGHT."

Jimmy thought of lots of lemmas and topology.

"Can I help out?"

The voice remained silent, but on the TV screen appeared in 24-point Courier: HA! HA! HA! HA!

For once in his life, Jimmy didn't feel much like a genius. He looked at the hens over the way and wondered what they were thinking. Pretty acute perception of little things, seeds and insects and grit. Kind of missing the big picture entirely. Very satisfied with themselves. Ranging freely, with a fence all around them.

At least Jimmy could see through gaps in the fence.

"Tuck-tuck-tuck-TUCK," he cackled at the A.I.

"I DON'T UNDERSTAND."

Good. For a beginning, anyway. Beetle versus Mammoth. Never underestimate pride. Quickly Jimmy thought about hens instead.

Extraordinarily, this story sold to Asimov's *in just four days, a lifetime record for me. Three days for transatlantic airmail, then one day for Sheila Williams to read the story and send an email accepting it. Due to the principle of regression to the norm, such a thing is highly unlikely ever to happen again. However, the story did go on to feature in* Science Fiction: The Best of the Year *(2007) so maybe something in it stood out that had to do with the speed of sale. Or maybe it's because the Northampton SF Writers Workshop helped give the story a telling tweak in the tail. Several stories in this collection experienced the touch of the NSFWG. I've been having stories published for forty years, but it's never too late to learn.*

If the Christian Church's theology were true, barcoding souls could be a nifty way of calculating spiritual accounts. In "Saving for a Sunny Day" a different sort of accountancy prevails.